smoldered

rachel blaufeld

the electric tunnel #2

smoldered

rachel blaufeld

the electric tunnel #2

about this book

Asher Peterson is a self-made man, owner of the Electric Tunnel, Sin City's hottest adult entertainment spot. Brazen and formidable in designer T-shirts and motorcycle boots, he seems unflappable whether he's making his rounds through the decadent decor of the Tunnel, or whipping through the desert heat on his bike. But inside he is a shattered man, desperate to understand what unconditional love from a woman feels like.

Hiding the effects of his emotionally stunted youth behind a gritty persona, and keeping his fractured soul buried deep while seeking out his baser instincts, Asher is convinced he is man enough to leave the past in the past. The only clue to his broken soul is his deep-seated need to provide safety and a good life for emotionally damaged women within the glamorous walls of his strip club.

Fooling himself that he deserves little in life, Asher keeps his big heart tightly guarded with everyone but Sienna Flower, his friend, business partner, and headliner. Until, that is, the night he runs into his childhood friend, Natalie Parker. While trolling a rival strip club, perusing their offerings for his own personal pleasure, he collides with his past. Coming face-to-face with a woman he only knew as a girl, he's shaken when he finds the dark-haired beauty in a precarious position. Now all grown up, she's a hardened soul who reminds him of where he came from, and stirs within him the need to protect yet another woman.

Known as Nat to most everyone, Natalie is a single mom to Quinn. But when she's under the bright spotlights in a thong, she's known as Natasha or Nataleigh Dallas. A girl who once had everything going for her, she's now a jaded stripper with only room for her son in her life, and has erected impenetrable barriers around her heart. The strength of those walls is challenged the night a man she has known since childhood steamrolls his way back into her life, flashing those smoky-gray eyes that have always melted her.

A man she has loved from afar since she was a young girl, one who lights fire to her walls, burning deeper, setting everything ablaze--smoldering her.

Asher and Natalie, two people who are equally tormented by their own demons, set out to rescue each other as part-time lovers in a torrid, desperate workplace affair. Thinking they can remain friends while keeping their hearts at a safe distance, they find themselves at odds when their situation morphs into a messy, tangled mess.

Ripping free of each other proves impossible as they learn that the very web that connects them goes much deeper than they ever expected.

dedication

*Like many women of her generation, my grandmother didn't go to
college.*
*Books were her windows and ladders not only to escape, but to see
what was out there and to broaden her mind. Reading books gave
her a better higher education than she could have ever received in a
classroom. For my grandmother, the world was larger—long before the
Internet—because she had a library.*
*She was the first person to take me into the damp and dusty stacks of
books in the children's section of our public library, and we went weekly
after that, long after I graduated from the children's section to the adult.
We enjoyed checking out books and reading them together, or reading
them separately whether we sat next to each other or were far apart
when I was in college. Sharing tales became a way of life for the two of
us from the time I could say "book" until the day she passed.*
*Not only an enlightened, well-read woman, my grandmother loved
to retell stories, especially during car rides or over dinner. I know she
would be proud that I am now weaving my own stories.*
*This book is for her. Gritty or not, she would adore getting to know
the characters, thinking about how their backgrounds and earlier
actions relate to today, feeling for them and their broken lives, finding
similarities in their lives and hers…and then she would spin their story
in her own way and retell it with glee to her friends.*
For Beatrice.
I miss you and your stories every single day.

Prologue

Natalie

I WAS THREE and he was eight the day his mom dropped him at our neighbor's house and never came back. Of course, I was too young at the time to remember that part of the story, but Mom talked about it. A lot.

"Cards were always stacked against that Peterson boy," she'd say. "Daddy gone, nowhere to be found, then his rotten momma up and left that sweet, innocent little boy. Hope he turns out all right, but sure looks like he's gonna have a lot of uphill fighting to do."

Once my childhood memories actually started to stick with me, there wasn't one without the "Peterson boy." Asher and I lived next door to each other from the moment his momma left him, and together we caused a lot of trouble. Well, to be truthful, I'd watched while he'd done most of it. My mother wasn't sure if our spending so much time together was for the best, but what other choice was there? Our little neighborhood was an extended family, all of us kids constantly being thrown together.

Although I'd forever be "the little stinker" in his mind, for me he'd always be "the one." He was the one I'd watched grow into a man while I was still considered a little girl, the guy of my dreams no matter how badly he behaved, the measuring stick against which every other man in my life would be judged.

As a teenager I'd watched him from a distance every chance I got, keeping an eye on what the other girls had done to get his attention. When I tried a few of the moves myself, the stubborn man had just laughed at me.

As a young woman, I settled with having him as just a friend, snug in my memories, until I couldn't do it anymore. To protect my own heart, I stayed away from him, completely dropped off his radar. For the last five years I had left him alone, hadn't kept in touch, even when I'd needed friends the most. Until, that is, when our paths crossed again on one awful, dreadful night.

I'd known Asher Peterson and had loved him from afar nearly my whole life, yet since we'd last seen each other, he'd grown into a man—a beautiful man—with a larger-than-life personality. And I wasn't ashamed to admit, he had me salivating the minute his face was once again in front of mine.

Then he spoke to me, and it was all over.

one

Funny What You Discover in the Back

Asher
Las Vegas, five years ago

BREATHED A sigh of relief. Coming to this strip club was exactly what I needed tonight. All it took was one lap through the Pink Leopard—or the Leop, as it was known—and I felt as if I'd been transported to one of my dirtier fantasies. By dirty, I meant the gritty, baser shit I tended to think about, but didn't act on, at least not too frequently, anyway. I was no angel; had never claimed to be one. I'd had a lot of women, and tonight I really needed to get off. Hard.

I didn't do drugs, not anymore. I cleaned myself up years ago. Instead I indulged in sex, and not the missionary, lovey-dovey, wrap-a-woman-in-my-arms stuff. Not the handcuffs, whips, and chains variety either, but a rough lay with more than one woman was more my speed. A shrink would probably say I was overcompensating for the lack of a mother's love, but who the hell cared. No way I was going to apologize for what got me off.

Making my way around the main bar and heading toward a side stage at the back of the club, I fixed my eyes on where I wanted to land.

The Leop was set up differently from my club. Instead of a main stage there were four small stages, one per corner, each platform

3

featuring a different tantalizing vignette. I couldn't walk fast enough to the back right, knowing what to expect. I licked my lips as my feet ate up the floor, my heart pounding as I neared the tiny platform.

At my club, the Electric Tunnel, we had a single main stage looping around the front of the club where we featured either one main act, like Sienna Flower, or two or three scenes simultaneously on different areas of the stage. Our lap dance business was most likely quadruple what the Leop did, by the looks of it. Here the customers—mostly men, but a few women too—worked their way around the room as they checked out the different stages, which was wasted time, in my opinion.

Not wasting mine right now. That fucking scene playing out is hot, and my dick and I have to get closer.

My club had one main focal point, but there wasn't room for everyone to get close enough, so we brought the act right to their seats with a private lap dance. It was a win/win for everyone. More money for the dancers and me, and a much better view for the customer.

As I neared the end of the bar, the head bartender, Ryan, reached over and grabbed my shoulder. "Look what the cat dragged in! None other than Asher Peterson, the guy remaking the stripper biz on the other side of town."

I laughed and reached over to shake his hand. "You got that right, but no harm in swinging by and checking out the competition. That way I get to catch up with assholes like you."

Ryan chuckled. "I'm kidding, dude. We all know you got your sights set on something bigger and better over at the Electric Tunnel. Just happy to see you can still slum it over at our fine establishment. We know our market, and you're it." He slapped my back good-naturedly and asked what I wanted to drink.

Practically hopping back and forth on my feet, eager to get to the action, I ordered a shot, figuring it would be quick. When Ryan finally set a shot in front of me, I threw a ten on the bar before lifting the little glass, then tossed the burning liquid down my throat and gave the dude a small chin lift in thanks.

"Catch you later, Ryan," I said, then quickly moved away like a leopard on the prowl.

Earlier I told myself I only wanted to check out the competition, so I could convince myself I was doing better than them. But it was really something more. I had my limits, and I was nearing them. I needed to get off. Period.

The Pink Leop had been around for a while, and had a reputation for allowing quite a bit of crazy shit to go down. Word on the street was you could get just about anything you wanted done to you, or for you, in the private rooms. And for the right price, you could take a girl back home with you for the night. That kind of sex trade was exactly what I didn't want for the Tunnel, but it didn't mean I was immune to the lure of it when I walked through these doors, or that I didn't want to partake a little bit. I did. Which was exactly why I was here, pushing a few fat and sweaty men out of my way so I could get closer to the action.

So what if the owners lost money in lap dances? They obviously made up for it in their private rooms. Yeah, some of the shit they allowed wasn't exactly on the up-and-up. "Heavy touching" was probably putting it nicely, but hey, what the hell did I care? I didn't own the place. I was here for a good time like the next guy. If they got into trouble with the law, it wasn't my problem.

Finally, I sank down into a worn-out red suede chair to the side of the scene that had caught my eye. I couldn't be bothered with how grubby the chair was, pushing out all thoughts of what may have touched its gross fabric over the years. *Thank fuck mine are leather at the Tunnel.*

I was fully reclined in the piece-of-crap chair, which was sticky as all get-out, but I ignored it because the two women directly in front of me were *hot*. Smoking hot, and it had absolutely nothing to do with the fake haze whirling all around them from the smoke machine.

I wanted to take both of them home and test out what they were doing onstage with me in the middle, preferably without any clothes in the way. The girls were both naked other than the thongs they wore, one red and the other gold. They stood on either side of a chair set in the middle of the stage, their long hair falling all around soft and demure shoulders as they ground their pussies against either end of the piece of furniture while leaning over and groping each other's tits.

Absolutely rigid, I watched in anticipation of what the two would do next. Christ, the way they twisted each other's nipples, moaning and groaning like it felt better than anything they'd ever experienced, was incredibly hot. The two luscious babes stared deep into each other's eyes as if they were soul mates doing exactly what they would be doing at home, but I knew the truth. They'd much rather be at home on their couch, drinking wine and watching a chick flick.

My line of work let me see behind the curtain, so I knew it was an act, a charade, nothing but pretend, but I couldn't bring myself to care. They were doing what they were paid to do, which was to titillate the audience, and they were doing a mighty fine job of it from where I was sitting. My eyes burned as I focused on the women, even though I could only see their hazy profiles. My dick, eager to be released from my pants, twitched and screamed, "Let me out to play," while my mind ran through an endless stream of fantasies involving the two women and me.

I motioned to one of the Leop's managers on the floor. When he appeared by my side, I asked him how much it would cost to take the pair back to a private room. I made a mental note to feel them out to see if one or both of them would accompany me back to my house. Of course, I was hoping for both, but I'd settle for one. I needed some action. Badly.

The manager set out the deal and I agreed to the terms. I had cash to burn, with a successful business and no family to support. After paying for the first hour in advance, I headed to the back to wait for the women in my private booth. Yeah, I stroked myself over my pants a little while waiting for them. So, sue me.

When the song changed out in the main club, I heard two pairs of heels clicking down the hallway toward the room where I waited. My breathing sped up in time with my heartbeat, and I sat up and waited for the delicious duo to come through the door.

Here they come.

The outer door opened and closed, then two curvy silhouettes entered my little corner and turned around. I blinked. Then blinked again, hard. I tried to clear my eyes, to get them to focus in the dim, red-hued light.

Why the hell is everything in this ugly fucking club red?

I didn't have time to ponder that right now. Instead I stood up and crossed the space in between the couch where I was sitting and the door in two steps and said, "Holy shit! Natalie, what the fuck are you doing here?"

Not stopping to wait for an answer, I opened the door and pushed the other girl out of the room toward the nearest bouncer. "Never mind," I told him. "I changed my mind. I only want one girl. This girl," *my little doll,* I added under my breath as I gestured behind me to Natalie. When I shouted, "Keep the extra money," the other girl glanced back at me, a confused look on her face as she stumbled on her high heels toward the bouncer. Then I slammed the door shut.

One hand on the door, I stared at it for a moment, trying to control myself. Thank fuck there was no one else in the high-backed booth on either side of me, because I feared I was about to lose my shit.

Turning back around slowly, I said, "Natalie, Jesus Christ, it's been years. I can't even think about how long it's been, but what the hell are you doing in a raunchy place like this? The last time we talked you were taking classes, making a life for yourself." When she didn't respond, I said, "I've got to get you the hell out of here."

Natalie shrank away from me, backing up until her shapely calves hit the booth's cushioned seat. She stared in horror at me as I glared at her.

Muttering to myself, I shoved a hand through my hair and paced back and forth like a madman. I had no idea whether I was whispering or yelling, I was so furious.

With her gaze lowered, her long lashes covering her big, beautiful eyes, she walked toward me and shushed me, saying, "Shhh, they know me as Natasha here. I need this gig, Asher. Stop making a scene... please."

Somewhere inside the hard woman in front of me, I could still see the younger Natalie I remembered. I looked past the long brown hair that hung over her shoulders, the thick bangs brushing over eyes heavily decorated with glitter and dark black eyeliner. Underneath all that caked-on shit, my "little doll," the girl who used to play kickball out in the alley and chase after the neighborhood boys, was there.

I threw my hands up in the air. "Nat, I don't want to hear that you need this job. This isn't the fucking place for you, babe. You want to strip, come work for me. My girls are respected. You want to do something else, go do it. What you aren't going to do is work in this shithole, one step away from being a prostitute."

She shuddered. I felt Natalie's whole body shiver under my hand, which had found its way to rest on her hip as she faced off with me. It made me want to wrap her up in my arms and carry her out of whatever mess she'd gotten herself into.

I completely forgot that I was at the Leop to get a little action. Instead, it looked like I was going to have to rescue the girl like a fucking superhero.

Shit.

Natalie was too good to work in this dump. What the fuck was she doing here? She knew I had a classier club. Didn't she?

Slowly, she lifted one hand and gently pried mine off her hip. Standing in front of me with her very hurt, very green eyes piercing mine, she began to talk. Her voice was so quiet, I could barely make out her words.

"I'm not a prostitute, Asher. I don't sell myself or have sex for money. I do my job. I do it well, give it my all, because I have a son who needs to eat, to go to the doctor and the dentist, and is constantly growing out of clothes and shoes. So if you don't mind, I'm going to get back to the only thing I know how to do. And please, let's just forget we ever met up like this."

With her head bowed, she tried to turn and walk away, but my hand flew up of its own volition and caught her shoulder. I knew I couldn't make any more of a scene or the bouncer would intervene, so I forced myself to remain calm. Taking a few deep breaths, I collected my thoughts while my fingers remained loosely on her bare skin.

Wait, did she say she had a kid?

Had it been that long since I'd seen her? Still, I was pretty sure she knew I would have helped her, given her a job, provided a shoulder to cry on, or some shit like that. We went way back together.

I placed a finger under her chin and lifted her face so she could see the truth in what I was about to say. "Nat, I'm sorry. I didn't mean to insult you. It's just, you and me, we used to be tight, and I was shocked to see you here. And when did you have a kid? You should have gotten in touch with me. We were friends, good ones. I could have helped. I can help now, little doll."

Another thought popped in my head, and I didn't think before I spoke. "Wait, what about the dad? Are you with him? Surely he doesn't want you here. How could any man let the mother of his child do this shit? Here at the Leop?"

Hurt flashed across Natalie's face, and she tried to pry herself away from me again.

Not wanting to lose the little bit of contact I had with her skin, I tightened my grip on Natalie's shoulder and waited for her to explain her choice, to say something that might change my opinion. Looking at the young woman in front of me, I was reminded we came from the same stock. Growing up, our situations were so precarious that all it took was one bad decision and we could end up in the gutter.

Fucking A, I'm never supporting the Leop again. This was a wake-up call, if I ever had one.

Natalie, or Natasha, pulled back. And I begrudgingly let her. She took three small steps backward before she was forced to sit on the bench behind her, her gaze dropping to the nasty dark red carpet.

smoldered

"I know you mean well, Ash, but I need to do this on my own. As for the kid thing—it happened a while ago. You and me, we haven't been tight in years. My son, Quinney—I mean, Quinn—he just turned four. So let it go, Ash, and be on your way."

She rested her elbows on her knees and dropped her head in her hands in defeat, keeping her focus trained on the carpet as she spoke softly. "I got knocked up. I knew it was a risk at the time, and now I have a kid. Nothing more and nothing less. His dad is long gone, and this is the job I picked. End of story. This is what I do, so you have to leave now."

At that, the woman I once knew as a young and vibrant girl stood, took one step closer, and placed a chaste peck on my cheek before walking away from me to find a more willing customer. Her tight ass swayed as her long legs took her toward the door, her shiny brown hair brushing from side to side against the body I'd been lusting after.

At the doorway, she turned and simply said, "'Bye, Asher."

L EFT ALONE in the VIP room, I was stunned that I'd been unable to string the right words together to convince a woman I'd known since childhood to get the hell out of the cesspool known as the Pink Leop. Maybe because I'd frequented the joint for years, living out my fantasies while breaking all my own rules.

How had I never seen her there? Was I that self-absorbed?

Releasing a long, deep breath, I left the back room and headed toward the exit, trying to control my emotions. No longer in the mood for anything but a stiff drink and coming up with a plan to rescue a hopeless, defeated girl from my past, I kept my gaze away from the club floor. Except for glancing out of the corner of my eye at where "Natasha" was giving a lap dance to a group of overweight old assholes.

Goddamn it, I needed to get the hell out of there before I scooped her up, threw her over my shoulder, and carried her out. Knowing that move wouldn't get me far, I left, desperate to figure out what would.

two

King Me

Asher

S HOVING THE club's ridiculous leopard-print door open and stepping
into the desert nighttime air, I thanked God my frequent sidekick
Mike hadn't come here with me tonight. My head of security over at
the Tunnel, Mike was obsessed with pointing out my ongoing rescue
fantasy when it came to young women in distress, and he'd have a field
day with the situation with Natalie.

Sienna was his main case in point.

When I walked out of the Tunnel earlier, I'd pointed my finger at
him, tilted my head toward the exit, and mouthed, "You coming?" The
cocky kid just shook his head and pretended to drive a steering wheel,
signaling he was heading home. He thought he had it all at home with
the sweet college coed he'd been shacked up with in his spacious condo
for the last few years.

Mike had gone to fancy schools where he'd taken a few psych
courses, and even though he was younger than me, delighted in
pointing out my need to save women. About two years ago, the little
shit was new to the adult entertainment scene, slumming it at my club
while trying to escape his rich-bitch mom and absentee father, when
Lila Dasher turned up on my doorstep looking for a cocktail server job.

It was obvious she was on the run, and I took one look at her and swore to myself I would keep her safe.

Ever since Mike witnessed how I transformed Lila into Sienna Flower, a more confident woman on her way to being a star, he never failed to point out how obsessed I was with her safety, security, and overall happiness.

Flash forward two years and the jackass, complete with his smart mind, broad shoulders, and brazen attitude, had risen from his original position as bouncer to my head of security. He'd also managed to become best friends with Sienna. How come *he* didn't get called on it when he made it his personal business to watch out for her?

Still, Mike often brought up how I got some sick satisfaction out of taking care of a damsel in distress. Well, duh, if someone had taken my mom under their wing, maybe she wouldn't have picked up and left me with the neighbors.

And I don't even need a degree from a fancy school to know that.

Kicking the exit door closed behind me, I left the Leop but knew I'd be back, despite my resolution to the contrary.

I floored it all the way back to my place, thinking I was damn lucky I hadn't brought my bike out. As messed up as my head was tonight, I would have laid that hunk of metal down somewhere long before I turned into my serene suburban neighborhood.

After parking my SUV in my two-car attached garage, I stepped out under the floodlight to make sure Sienna's lamp was on in the corner of her carriage house. It was her signal to me that she was home and safe with the doors locked.

Okay, maybe I did have a bit of a rescue thing going on, but the girl had no one but me. Whatever she'd run from before she met me was so bad that even I only knew bits and pieces, but it had her good and scared.

Sienna had moved from waitressing to dancing over the last six or seven months, and her style was starting to catch on. Thank fuck I moved her behind me in the little carriage house I'd planned to rent when I realized she was living in a fleabag motel.

Back there, behind me, she was protected.

Just how I liked her.

I headed back inside my garage, opened the door to my house, and let the coolness of the air-conditioning cover me. Born and bred in Vegas, it wasn't the desert heat making my blood boil this evening.

A s I turned off my alarm and headed straight to my wet bar, I had new worries bubbling up inside me, burning through my veins and heating my temper.

Natalie. Jesus Christ. I hadn't seen the girl since she was eighteen or nineteen years old. The last time was on her birthday, if I remembered correctly, and she was moving out of our neighborhood where we grew up, getting an apartment, taking some classes at the community college, and working as a hostess at a steak joint in one of the newer, shinier casinos.

She was so freaking happy over the whole thing. Her own pad, making something of herself, a good job where the waiters were tipping her out at the end of the night, and getting the hell away from the old Las Vegas 'hood. And I was happy for her.

The whole gang was together that night. All the kids who went to our school…we were all mostly cutups scraping by, doing what we could, and looking for a leg up. A gang of ghetto rats from an early planned development on the verge of adulthood, we were trying to break free from the lives our parents had lived. I was one of the older ones and unfortunate proof we only knew one thing. Vegas nightlife.

It was in our blood, seeping out into everything we did, making it impossible to be or do anything else. We may have fooled ourselves into thinking we were doing better than our folks because the Strip had been classed up, but at the end of the day, we were the next generation of Vegas clubbies through and through.

The night of that party, there was more than Vegas nightlife running through our veins. It was a great night. We all got rip-roaring drunk, lit up on whatever drugs anyone had handy, and toasted to the past, present, and future.

Sadly, the past, present, and future were all the same. But I didn't want to ruin the fun that evening and share my thoughts with everyone, so I made the most of the good time at my disposal.

All the others, the younger ones, had to do was take a long, hard look at me, and they could figure it out themselves. I may have been starting to make money, and lots of it, but I was still working in nightlife. It was all I knew.

Even in my drunken, drugged-out stupor, I was pretty sure I might have envied Natalie that night as her face lit up when she told us about enrolling in classes. I remember thinking to myself: *Nat's gonna be the one to get the hell out.*

The next day, hungover and strung-out like hell, I realized I'd hit

smoldered

an all-time low, so I decided to clean up my act. Determined to push the envelope of the adult entertainment business, I made myself a resolution to make it better, classy, top-notch.

Now seated at my expensive bar in the middle of my luxurious house—I may not have been a well-educated CEO, but I sure as fuck lived like one—I poured myself a highball tumbler half-full of scotch and tossed it back. A bit dramatic, the fiery burn only made me rage harder, not doing its job of settling me down. I was consumed with my thoughts, both caught up in my memories and wondering what the hell I should do now.

What the fuck had happened to Nat to reduce her to working in a hellhole, serving herself up on a platter for cheap jerks to touch any way they pleased?

I should know, I'm one of them. Except for the cheap part.

I held nothing against the adult entertainment business. Shit, I worked, lived, and breathed it. But, Christ, there was a right way and a wrong way, and I was one of the good guys. And kid or no kid, there was no good reason why Natalie should be on the bad side of the biz when she had me as a friend.

three

Cheating Life

Natalie
Las Vegas, present day

I worked into the wee hours of the morning, milking each and every last bachelor party and pleasing every man wanting a lap dance. It was a good night for me at the Tunnel, like it had been for the last five years, and my purse was filled with cash. Tonight I'd been able to do my own thing, slipping off the radar a bit while Asher and Mike freaked out over Sienna visiting some guy's table. She didn't work the floor on weekends, let alone visit one-on-one with customers, so the guys were going ape-shit over their precious headliner's safety. Not to mention her sanity.

As I was saying good-bye to my bouncer, Petey, and a few of the cocktail waitresses, tipping them out for taking good care of my parties, I saw Asher coming down the staircase from his office on the second floor. I wasn't stupid. The man knew it was Friday, the night when Quinn always stayed with my mom, and he wanted a piece of me.

I was weak, more than a little horny, and wanted a piece of him too. We'd been playing this game for years.

Asher was nothing less than mouthwatering as he prowled toward me across the mostly empty floor of the club. I'd changed out of my evening's costume and was wearing worn-in skinny jeans with a hole in the knee and a nondescript black halter covered with a gray wraparound sweater, so I felt underdressed compared to the elegant man coming my way.

My boss was still wearing the dark black slacks he'd worn for work, his dress shirt unbuttoned halfway down his chest, revealing a light smattering of blond chest hair and the very edge of his tattoo, a navy blue bolt of electricity inked over his chest for his one and only baby, the Electric Tunnel. But it was a sight to see, and I did enjoy licking it from top to bottom.

In the privacy of his office, that is.

His hair and goatee were equally mussed from his running his hands through them. Sadly, it was a habit of his I knew all too well, and there was nothing I wanted to do more than dive in and make it even messier.

As usual, Asher was wearing motorcycle boots with his suit pants. He was a hot mess of a man—there was no one else remotely like him. Despite the layer of expensive designer clothing, he was pure bad boy underneath. He'd never ditch his boots, they were as ingrained in him as his past, which was why I should have been hightailing it right out of the place. Instead, I stood planted like a palm tree blowing in the wind, waiting for the storm to arrive, stuck in the ground as if there were nothing I could do to stop the blustery weather heading my way, threatening to topple me over.

The guy was a god, and I was nothing more than a stripper who was smitten with him.

As I ran my hands through my own long hair, my fingers sifted through the big waves running through it. I'd set it in hot rollers on my break for a bachelor party I ran earlier, yet now it didn't seem like enough for Asher. He should get more than the leftovers of my evening at work. He deserved fresh curls and nice clothing, and perfume not mixed with another man's cologne.

I wanted to be more in his eyes. Hadn't I always?

In my dreams, I was the prettiest, sexiest, and most darling of his girls. The one he would keep in the end, but I knew that to be a fantasy, which was why I kept firm boundaries when it came to him. Most of the time, at least. This evening was not one of these occasions.

Asher approached with his usual control and command, wrapped his arm around my neck, and pulled me tight against him. Running his nose along my collar, he breathed in my scent and whispered, "Fuck,

15

Nat, you smell real good, and you look so damn beautiful. I want you. Never can get enough."

"Okay," I said softly, closing my eyes as I allowed myself a second to enjoy the feel of his face against mine.

I didn't try to wriggle out from his grasp, instead I stayed firmly planted next to him for all to see. Who would be looking? The whole club knew we were sleeping together. They also knew it didn't mean a damn thing.

Did it? But it didn't really matter, because what Asher and I had together could never amount to anything more.

Still holding me in his muscular arms, he leaned in close again and said, "I don't want to be with you here, Natalie. I want to take my time with you in a bed, do it right for a change. If you don't want to go to my place, let's go to yours. Your boy is with your mom, right?"

I stiffened, then disentangled myself from his warmth and shook my head. How could we be so close, yet he didn't understand me at all? My club life needed to stay at the Tunnel, and anything related to Quinn remained firmly at home. Apart. Separate. I hated the idea of the personal and professional sides of my life intersecting, and insisted they never merge.

The stubborn man pulled me close again. "Sorry, little doll. I thought you had the rest of the night, morning, whatever it is, to yourself."

"No, I do. But my place is off-limits, Ash. You know that."

I tried to put some space between us, but Asher was having none of that. "All right. I don't get it, but okay." He lifted his hands in the air in a mock gesture of surrender before wrapping his arms around me again. "Let's go to my house. Please. I don't want to stay in my office tonight." He curled a lock of my hair around his finger as he said this, then ran a line of light kisses along my neck.

Another okay was all I could manage, and just like that I was being led by Asher out the back door.

We hit the fresh air with a vengeance. Asher was a man on a mission as he insisted we leave my car. "Come on, I have my bike and it's a gorgeous night. I'll bring you back in the morning for your car."

Apparently unable to say anything other than "okay," I simply followed him to his parking spot, annoyed that I was beginning to sound like a dumb tramp.

Wasn't that what I was?

After I put on a helmet, I climbed on behind the same man I rode behind years ago, and was instantly reminded how much I liked it. His hard back, the ridges and lines of his abdomen that my fingers trailed along as my arms weaved around his middle, his unique scent blowing back toward me in the wind. I loved it all despite knowing this was a stupid, stupid move. This being my getting on the back of Asher's bike.

But I went and enjoyed every minute.

My jean-clad legs pressed against his slacks as I gripped him with my thighs. Who wore slacks on a bike? Only Asher.

As his white dress shirt billowed in the wind, his heart beat fast in his chest—I could feel it straight through his back. My nipples hardened, not only from the cool night air, but also from the damp and sweaty scent floating around me that was uniquely Asher, enveloping me like dew on a cool spring night.

The only other time I had been at Asher's home was for a quick bit of afternoon delight. It had been the single most lighthearted time in our history, a few short weeks where we had a lot of fun exploring each other's bodies, laughing, smiling, and having sex constantly. A brief period where I was having trouble maintaining boundaries—like now—and I agreed on a whim to go home with him on a Thursday while my son was at school.

Now it was early morning, dawn just a few hours away as we pulled into his garage, and a microburst of expectations enveloped us. The air was thick with promises neither of us could keep, obscuring my well-thought-out plans with a thick haze.

The moment he pulled me off the bike and kissed me, a giant cloud of passion burst all over me. It was a welcome storm in a dry desert, washing away any second or third thoughts I may have been having. A heavy rainfall of lust poured down on our bodies, us to find shelter in each other.

Our tongues and lips only separated for Asher to turn off his house alarm before we found each other again. Desperate in his need for me, he led me to his room, and I went willingly. Eagerly. At the doorway leading to his space, he stopped and slipped his tongue deeper in my mouth and twisted it with mine, fusing us together as one before he lifted me swiftly and carried me to the massive bed.

I felt myself being laid out on the decadent down comforter, my hair fanning out around me on the pillow as Asher stretched out next to me and ran his hand along my face, staring deep into my eyes as a low rumble came from deep in his throat. It was a primal sound made by a man who'd been forced to wait too long. As much as it was scary and disconcerting, I found some twisted pleasure in how much he wanted me.

Asher's growl and my unbridled need for him combined to ensure that the rest of the night was not going to be a slow, careful coupling, but more like two starving wild animals set loose on each other. Asher had his hand up my shirt and down my pants within seconds, quickly removing each piece of clothing. I continued to lie there in my black lace bra and matching boy shorts while he made quick work of his own clothes. His slacks and dress shirt quickly joined my tiny pile on the floor.

Like a panther, the man slid in bed next to me practically unnoticed until he ran his tongue down my neck, across my clavicle, traveling lower along my side cleavage peeking out from my bra, past my navel, finally settling at the seam of my panties, teasing and taunting. I closed my eyes, wanting to savor the moment, narrowing my senses to only one as I reveled in his touch.

His finger drifted along the edge of the lace bordering on my skin, drawing it down, farther and farther, until he lost control and ripped the panties right down the middle. It was swift and quick, and then his tongue met my hot center.

We may have not had a lot of experience in a bed together like normal couples, but the man knew how to pleasure me, where to go soft and feather-like and where I didn't need tenderness but pressure. My orgasm built, pushing at the barrier of my skin, barreling through my nerve endings, dying to come out, making me tremble with fear I was going to completely burst into pieces, and then it hit.

It hit again and again, rolling over me like the hot air blowing sand in the desert, decimating the tiny granules, moving them to new places, creating different plateaus and planes with the tiny specks. As I lay there coming down, now with my eyes open, I watched Asher reach over my body, grab a condom, then begin to slide in and out of me at a slow, leisurely pace. At that point, I wasn't the same woman I'd been moments before when we entered the bedroom.

I, too, had been recreated, reorganized into a new being with a new landscape, nothing put back in exactly the same place after Asher and his orgasm blew me to bits. My hardened shell was in pieces, torn to smithereens, and somehow I knew I wouldn't be able to rebuild my well-constructed emotional walls.

Which was exactly why I never wanted to come back to this place, to Asher's home with its warm and inviting bed, an unrivaled refuge.

smoldered

Because it was only a mirage, one where I wanted to lay down roots, to dig deep and never leave.

But it wasn't real. At least, not for me.

four

Charades

Mike

I HEADED OUT the back door of the Tunnel a little early, which was cool because Petey was there. As Asher's right-hand man, I made my own rules, and tonight I felt like getting the hell out.

Asher and I had been together a long time. He got me, and I certainly got him.

It was Friday night, and I knew who he wanted in his office—or his bed, if he got his way. Natalie. The man was unbelievable. He'd been tapping her for years with no real commitment. And she liked it that way. At least, that was what she led us to believe. She knew damn well what he did when she wasn't around the club, and it wasn't work. He remained noncommittal and she pretended to be indifferent.

Sometimes I felt like either slapping the jerk or confronting the woman to try to shake some sense into her, but who was I to judge? I had my own shit storm at home.

Regardless of Asher's feelings for the stripper, Nataleigh Dallas, he was staying at the club until closing time so he could snag Natalie, the woman, for the rest of the evening. I was also privy to the fact that our headliner, Sienna, was finally into a man. He was a customer, which gave us all pause at first, but he was a warm-blooded male who kept her happy. And that was the important thing.

All this meant I was free to cut out of the place, my usual responsibilities all covered.

I took a deep breath as I jumped into the club's extra-large black-on-black SUV with darkened windows and the club's telltale glowing purple license plate frames. It was my work vehicle, but all the locals in Vegas knew damn well it was me behind the wheel. *Big Mike from the Tunnel, and he's not to be messed with—now or ever.*

Before I pulled out of the parking lot, I gave the fuzzy neon-green dice hanging on the rearview a little tap, smirking at their swishing from side to side, unable to stop comparing their movement to the balancing act of my life.

Christ, I deserved a few hours to let loose by myself.

The club was all consuming, and I liked it that way, but at the moment my personal life was imploding. No one at the Tunnel had any clue I'd kicked Rochelle to the curb. We'd been living together since I was twenty. I thought I loved her, and had believed it was mutual until I caught her banging my dad. Now she was out of my place, and I was a liberated man. Free as a bird. To do what, exactly, I had no clue.

Been shacked up so long, I wasn't sure I even knew how to be a free agent on the dating scene. At nineteen, I left my mom's mansion, the one she got in the messy divorce, and took some of my trust fund to buy a condo with a view of the Strip. It was primo real estate, and I was proud to move Rochelle in because she believed in me.

Took stock in me, even though I didn't want to be *the man.* Obviously, she wanted more than just *the man.* Bitch wanted an *older man,* as in my semi-estranged, blue-pill dependent father.

I brought my hand to the touch screen in the car and pumped the music, felt the bass in the rap song blaring through the woofers carry me away from my troubles at home. My fingers beat against the steering wheel as the wind from the sunroof blew through my close buzz, cooling my scalp and growing temper. If I was honest, the work shit wasn't stressful. None of it, not even Sienna's protection.

I lived for my Tunnel gang. Would lie down for them.

Thought I'd do the same for Rochelle. Guess I was wrong.

Asher deserved to know about the breakup. After all, he gave me my first break and had been letting me slum it with him ever since. He never called attention to my lack of drive when it came to my parents' ambitions for me. The strip club owner with the rough exterior supported me unconditionally. Corny, but he did.

I'm going to tell him after this weekend. After I give myself some space and room to breathe.

Not to mention, my buddy Clay from school was in town and throwing a private party in the penthouse of the Palace Hotel, the newest joint to go up on the Strip. I typically stayed away from those prep school idiots, but I liked Clay. We stayed in touch over the years, and he popped into the Tunnel every time he was in town. He was the only one who respected my decision not to go white collar.

I smoothed my hand along the leather steering wheel as I turned onto Las Vegas Boulevard. Even if I wanted to back out, my foot on the gas pedal had a mind of its own and was pushing on toward a guaranteed party. Tonight was about me. I had put my small pistol in the safe at the club, winked at Natalie when Asher wasn't looking, and waved good-bye to my boss before heading out to my SUV. I wasn't packing heat or protecting anyone this evening, or morning if I actually took the time into account. I was just one of the guys heading out for a good time.

As I pulled up to the valet at the Palace, I checked my reflection in the mirror. My hair was recently cropped close to my scalp; I touched my hand to the top of my head, feeling the unfamiliar soft bristle of the buzz cut. I ran the same hand over my face, satisfied with the length of stubble along my jaw. Glancing down at my standard uniform—basketball warm-up jacket, jeans, and high-end hoop shoes—I nodded. This was as good as it got for me. No suits for this man.

I lifted my chin at the valet. They all knew me.

"Keep it up front, 'kay?" I yelled to the young buck as I tossed him the keys.

"No problem, Mike," he said as he caught the keys in the air.

I walked straight to the VIP elevator bank when I entered the hotel. I knew those guys too. The ones manning the elevators and keeping out the riffraff and the low-end hookers. Another chin nod, one more fist bump, and I headed upstairs to party.

The penthouse covered half of the top floor, and I could hear the party raging as soon as the elevator doors opened. Knowing Clay, he had a DJ spinning tunes. Dude was swimming in dough. His dad had tons; gave it freely without strings attached. It didn't even matter that my only friend left from my Saint's One Academy days was practically printing the shit himself, he was a pretty decent guy. Usually.

His behavior tonight might be an exception.

I walked to the door and gave a fist pound to my man, Billy, who was moonlighting, doing a little private detail at the hotel suite.

"Yo, man. All good here? Everyone just having a fun time? No trouble?" I asked my employee. I'd referred him to Clay for the after-hours duty, so it was all cool.

"Nah, nothing. It's all tits and ass and good times in there," he answered, then slipped his key card in the slot and swung the door open for me.

As soon as I set foot in the luxury suite, I was wrapped in the pulsing beat, pulled into the vibe, and immediately felt lighter. I loved good music, and the blaring mash-up filling the air was just my type of antidote to a bad mood. My feet no longer dragging, they ate up the hardwood floor leading to the bar Clay had set up.

Speak of the devil, he was entertaining two bottle blondes with shots from an ice luge and was too busy to even notice me crossing the room.

I smacked him on the back and he jumped. Unable to keep from laughing, I asked him, "What's up, my man, other than your dick?"

Clay tore his gaze away from double trouble and pulled me in for a bro hug. "And to think I was actually excited to see you, Mike."

I stepped out of the guy's embrace before it became uncomfortable. "I can feel your excitement, bro, but this—it isn't my type of thing," I said while lifting my eyes to the ready, willing, and able duo. "But whatever floats your boat. As long as you're not abusive and it's consensual."

He waved a hand at the mess of tall, curvy, and stacked figures still licking vodka off the ice sculpture. "Come on, Mike. Don't be a buzzkill. You know I'm harmless, just a good guy having a fun time. You're just jealous you weren't here earlier to snag yourself a pair of these bombshells."

He was right. I knew he was decent, and this was Vegas. Finding oneself with two women at the same time was practically tame, and I also knew he was one of the good guys.

"You forget where I work, Clay?" I said with a wink. He knew I could get a piece of ass anytime I wanted, whenever I damn well pleased. It also irked him that I never took advantage of that. There was always Rochelle, but regardless, I didn't shit where I ate, and the Tunnel girls were like sisters to me.

"Definitely not, my man. In fact, I'm on the VIP list for tomorrow. I plan to have another spectacular night, courtesy of Asher. Any chance Sienna will do a private for me?"

I punched him in the arm. "Shut the fuck up, Clay. Been telling you for years, Sie doesn't do that shit. She's eye candy. That's it. No lap dances or back rooms for her. Period."

My friend rubbed his arm where I made contact. Yeah, it was a little harder than I should have hit him, but the jerk was always bugging me about Sienna. She had boundaries, a lot of them, and it was my personal duty to protect them. I loved that woman; we all did. And no one would diminish or hurt her. Which was why I was keeping a close eye on that dude who slipped her a note at the club. My girl hadn't dated once in the last seven years, so I wasn't about to let her take off with this customer, Carson, without having my eye on her.

Clay waved his hand in front of my face, dragging me out of my thoughts as he said, "Well, fine. No Sienna, but you find me another gorgeous and willing lady. In the meantime, get a drink and go have some fun, Mikey. Take a load off." He waved his hand around the noisy hotel suite full of partiers before he went back to his babes and vodka.

Motioning to the bartender, I ordered a shot of tequila and tossed it back, feeling the burn all the way down to my stomach while I lifted my hand for another.

I could always get a room for the night. No one to rush home to.

With alcohol surging through my veins, my limbs felt looser and my body hummed with excitement as the tension eased from my overworked muscles. My pulse quickened as I made my way around the room, stopping in the corner to take it all in. It was a good-looking group, people with money who could afford whatever they wanted— top-of-the-line booze, women, cars, penthouses, pills, plastic surgery— you name it, they could buy it. The kind of assholes I'd known all my life. Malcontent pricks and self-serving bitches.

My focus zeroed in on the most striking woman I'd ever seen, and I'd seen a lot of fucking women. With skin the color of coffee with cream, legs that didn't seem to end, firm and perky natural breasts only hidden by a tiny pink bikini top, and long cornrow braids, their tips brushing the top of her ass where she wore low-slung jeans, she was stunning and I couldn't stop staring. Which I happened to be doing, taking my time devouring the little dimples where her lower back met her curvy backside, when I noticed the man she was standing with grip her tiny wrist, trying to pull her closer.

It was obvious she was trying to maintain some type of distance or maybe break free without causing a scene. My feet couldn't help themselves but to close the distance between the two of us and before I knew it, I was at her side. It was my nature to protect and help women,

24

to make sure they didn't end up in trouble, or zoned out on pills like my mom. That was a waste of life whether you were privileged or not.

I positioned myself between the man and woman, forcing him to let go of her small wrist, and I looked the asshole right in the face. "Excuse me, but I've been looking for this lady all evening. There's been an emergency that she needs to attend to. Sorry, man," I said, using my old prep school lingo.

With that, I didn't even wait for an answer, just swung my arm around the girl and walked her down the hall toward the door to the balcony.

When we were a few steps away, I whispered in her ear, "Play along. I could tell you wanted out of there."

She nodded slightly and picked up her pace.

O NCE WE were through the French doors to the balcony, I rushed us to a corner out of the sightline of anyone inside the suite. It was quieter outside, the fountain on the Strip currently sleeping, the dark night sky enveloping us. Chilly desert air washed over me, cooling my surging temper, but I could see my damsel in distress was both cold and confused. I turned her to face me and ran my hands up and down her arms, warming her skin, ignoring the sparks igniting my own hands.

"Sorry, I didn't mean to rush you like that, take you away from that dude, but it seemed like you needed an out. I'm Mike, by the way."

She cocked her head to the side, looking deep into my eyes as if she could see the secrets of the world there, and breathed out a soft thank-you before dropping her head.

I was still running my large hands along the length of her arms, but I stilled myself and reached out to tilt her chin up so we were eye level.

"What's your name?" I asked.

"Lincoln. But really it's Lynx...I just don't want to tell everyone my real name." She stiffened slightly and I wanted to wrap her up in my arms, protect her not only from the greasy slimeball in the party, but every fear, scary notion, or asshole lurking in her past, present, or future.

What the fuck?

"Shit, that's a gorgeous name. Perfect."

She scrunched up her brow, probably trying to figure out what I meant. Clearly, I was a bit rusty at picking up women.

"Sorry, I didn't mean to offend you. I just think it's a really cool name."

"Thanks again. Honestly, I'm so thankful for your rescue, and your compliments, but I got to get back to work or whatever they want me to do here."

"Um, you're working? What the fuck? Who hired you?"

Another scrunch of her face, this time accompanied by her dark eyes almost spilling over with tears. "Yeah, sorry to disappoint you, but I'm just the hired help, a girl trying to make it through school without loans. I'm an escort. I didn't come with the guy throwing the party, but one of his buddies called up and ordered a few of us for the evening." She shook her head and turned to walk away. "I gotta get back."

"Wait." I grabbed her shoulder and pulled her back to look at me. "No worries. I'm a guest and you're here to make sure we're happy, so why don't you spend some time with me? Just talking?"

All of a sudden, I couldn't imagine sharing this woman with the room full of loud, obnoxious wealthy people on the other side of the balcony doors.

She shrugged. "I guess that works."

"Great. Listen, I have an idea. Wait here for a minute and I'll be right back. Okay?" I held up my finger signaling one sec while searching her face for a response.

When Lynx nodded, I asked, "Are you sure? You're gonna be here when I get back?"

She nodded again, so I ran inside and grabbed a comforter from one of the king-sized beds, a bottle of wine, and two glasses.

We stayed out on the balcony, wrapped up together in the warmth of the comforter, drinking wine, talking, laughing, and joking until the sun came up above the Vegas skyline.

It was the most fun I'd had in years.

Then she got a text and the spell was broken.

five

Three's Company

Natalie

ONE WOULD have thought my boss would have wanted to sleep all day after being up most of the night. But this morning he was a thoughtful, golden, soft Asher, all wrapped up in a tough exterior. Which drew me to him like a parched person to a tall glass of lemonade on a scorching-hot summer day.

At the same time, my brain was at war with my steadily climbing desire for the man. My mind cautioned me to pull away from his sweetness, throwing up red flags all over the place that I didn't deserve this soft side of him. After all, there was no way he could honestly be sprinkling me with what I wanted most.

I would rather he have been more of a dick than doling out a decent dose of kindness. Then I could walk away without regrets or cares, head to wherever I wanted, ditch the desert for the beach, never looking behind me, and be the woman I'd always dreamed of being, or at least a piece of her. Because I still had to dance and entertain men. I still had to make a living.

But no, Asher couldn't be an ass. He was all kind and caring, worrying about what time my boy would get home from my mom's place, and saying, "Hope you can stay to eat," while still buried and twisted in the covers, wrapped in each other's limbs.

I couldn't say no to the gentleman version of Asher when he rolled over and said in a raspy whisper, "This is so decadent, Nat. Always wanted to wake up like this. I don't want to rush it."

So I texted my neighbors to see if one of them could go over and wait for Quinn, and perhaps watch him for an hour or two until I got back. Lucky for me, one of them responded quickly; she was up and could go over to my place.

With Quinn handled, I turned my full attention to the man who both gloriously consumed and scarily haunted my thoughts. At the moment, he happened to be snaking his way down my body with his tongue, pausing at the dip in my belly, licking and blowing, then sweeping his mouth gently down a path marked by him, making his way to the screaming, burning heat between my legs.

"Ash, I thought you mentioned coffee and breakfast," I said with a halfhearted tug on his hair.

He looked up at me with those eyes. Neither shiny silver nor smoky gray, but somewhere in the middle, they were a quiet inferno, smoldering when he said, "First, I'm going to have some in-room dining, and then we'll have a proper breakfast with coffee, doll."

He winked and then went back to what he had been doing before I interrupted him. With one solid stroke, he landed the tip of his tongue on my most sensitive spot, and he didn't let up until I was twisting in the silky seven-hundred-thread-count sheets, yelling his name, pulling his hair without any regard, and scratching and clawing at his back without knowing if I wanted him to let up or keep going, giving me more.

As he made his way back up my body, his mouth landing on mine, I reached down and gripped him, squeezing his length the way he liked it. Asher may have been acting all doting moments earlier, but in the bedroom—or his private office—I knew he needed it rough and raw.

It wasn't like I was complaining. I enjoyed a little roughness in the bedroom, always had. But with my hand wrapped around Asher's wide heat, his mouth nipping at my neck, his teeth grazing along my collarbone, this was no time to dwell on the past. I needed to focus on what I wanted at the moment. Actually, *needed* was more like it. I had no idea how much longer I would have this, and my body craved as much connection as possible with the man who secretly owned my heart.

I had to stock up.

smoldered

Without moving the hand sliding up and down Asher's dick, I reached my other hand into the nightstand, grabbed a condom, and ripped it open with my teeth. This action alone brought another one of his sexy growls from deep within his throat. Without a word, I slid it on him and he slipped deep inside me, nearly reaching the depths of my soul. As he burrowed his length in my heated core, filling me, pulling in and out at a fast pace and hitting every nerve, he nearly made me believe in a happy ending for myself. Until I came, so very hard, and immediately remembered my predicament when I came down from my Asher-induced high.

Pushing my thoughts to a less heavy place as Asher pulsed inside me, giving me every last drop of his energy, the condom thankfully catching the gallon of cum rushing out of him, I attempted to savor the moment as he pulled me close and held me tightly.

When he finally spoke, it dawned on me that we'd been quiet, except for all the hushed moans. Apparently, we'd allowed our bodies to do the communicating during bedroom sex, completely different from the dirty, very verbal trysts we'd enjoyed in his office.

Now we were facing each other, Asher's thigh casually thrown over mine, his hands cradling my cheeks as he planted a long kiss on my lips. "Good morning. I'm so glad you slept over. Isn't this fucking great waking up like this?" he said, his voice gravelly in my ear, his breath soft on my cheek.

"It's nice," I said carefully, not wanting to give away too much.

He held my face a tad tighter, stared me down, and said, "Better than nice."

Averting my gaze to avoid the intensity of his, I said softly, "I know."

"Don't worry, Nat. You don't have to admit how sensational this really fucking is. I know you're lying and protecting yourself, I can feel it. But I *will* convince you to see it differently, to see it my way."

He lightly slapped my ass, then said, "Don't even bother to deny it. I know what I know, girl."

With that, he rolled off me and headed to the bathroom, from where he yelled, "Let's go, doll. It's breakfast time."

'D JUST sat up in bed with the sheet wrapped around me when the frustrating man strutted back into the room, picked me up—still draped in the sheet and nothing else—then carried me down to his kitchen and plopped me down on top of his granite countertop. The cool stone felt good on my ass, doing little to chill my desire.

29

Damn. Caveman-crazy Asher is even sexier than the gentleman version.

"What do you want to eat, Nat? I got it all. You name it, I'll make it." Asher moved confidently around the kitchen, pulling out a griddle pan and ingredients to make pancakes and omelets when his phone rang. He took a quick peek at the cell phone sitting on the charger and mumbled, "Shit."

"Take it," I said. "It's no biggie."

Asher gave me a sideways glance. "You sure? I hate to, but it's Mike. It's probably important if he's calling this early."

"Yeah," I said with a tiny nod.

He walked toward his office, phone cradled to his ear as he said, "What's up, Mike? Tell me something good this morning."

I stayed on the counter surveying the kitchen, taking in the calming, subdued color of the tile, the warmth of neutral hues taking me away, filling me with weird hope. For what, I had no clue.

My thoughts drifting to happily-ever-after with Asher, I didn't hear the back door click open. Next thing I knew, Sienna was standing in the doorway of the kitchen with her mouth hanging open while I sat buck naked on Asher's granite counter, barely covered by a sheet.

This is why I don't do sleepovers.

We both mumbled our surprise as we stared at the floor, anywhere but at each other. Sienna then apologized profusely while attempting to make her way back to the door. But before she could, Asher came back down the hallway, shouting something about being sorry for taking the call, until he stepped into the kitchen and realized we weren't alone. At the sight of Sienna, he turned into yet another version of Asher—the strong, brotherly, protective one.

The man he was for only one woman. Sienna.

She needs it. Not me.

Of course, he asked her to stay. She said no, and was out of there faster than I could hop off the counter. It wasn't as if we didn't like each other. Sienna kept to herself and the gang of brooding men protecting her, and I didn't mix work and pleasure except when it came to Asher, which was quickly becoming a huge mistake.

As he prepped and cooked us a gourmet breakfast, he said, "This couldn't get any better, Nat, having you here. I never get to really enjoy this space, really live in it. And your ass on my countertop—that's living."

Trying not to squirm, I said, "Yes, it's nice, but you know, Ash, my

30

life doesn't really lend itself to this all that much."

"Bull! You know I would welcome your kid here." He eyed me up and down with a smirk and added, "I know you couldn't be naked like that, but you don't have to keep everything so compartmentalized. It would be an honor for me to know your son." He turned and gave me a full-on smile before focusing back at the cooktop.

I lifted my long hair off my neck, suddenly feeling hot from the direction the conversation was taking. "It's not that, Ash. Not you. It's me, really. I don't think I want him to be a part of all this. Our lives."

Asher turned around and pinned me with an intense stare. "I call bullshit on that too."

"Why?" I shot back, and crossed my arms over my chest. "You were the one who always said I could do better, break out of where we came from."

Pressing his lips together, he was silent for a moment as he flipped pancakes with steady hands. When he looked up at me, his eyes were blazing.

"For starters, we did break away. We're rewriting the way shit is done in Vegas, and you've done nothing but earn an honest living since working for me." He strode over and placed a hand on either side of my thighs, caging me in and staring me down as he waited for a response.

"I know, but I just like to keep Quinn to myself. Period."

Asher leaned closer, the smell of old cologne and sex filling my nose as he said, "More bullshit. You've been doing this alone forever, little doll. I don't get it. You could have a whole extended family helping you if you would just let us in."

six

Protective to Psycho in Three Seconds Flat

Natalie

PULLED INTO the back lot of the Tunnel the Tuesday after my stupid and weak moment at Asher's, and braced myself for the night ahead as I got out of my car.

Who knew how Asher would act today? I certainly didn't.

Stepping out into the bright afternoon sunlight, I brushed back my long hair that drifted loose across my neck in the chilly winter breeze. With big eyeglasses firmly planted on my face, my usual skinny jeans and wraparound sweater covering my soon-to-be naked body, I kicked my car door shut while balancing two take-out cups of coffee and made my way to the back door of the Tunnel.

God, Asher was a loose cannon, day and night, never letting up, and it wasn't just driving me insane. I could tell he was making everyone bat-shit crazy.

I yanked open the back door of the Tunnel, and right away Petey was breathing down my neck. I loved the bouncer to pieces, but Asher had him on such a tight leash these days—even more so since his promotion to head bouncer—the poor dude was one hair shy of being as crazy as our mutual employer.

It was just bad luck a few weeks ago when a tiny little incident involving me went down under Petey's watch, and now after our sleepover, Asher was on even higher alert.

So I desperately tried to ignore their recent overly obsessive behavior, which had escalated over the weekend, and go on with my life as usual, letting Petey do his job. Especially today as I rushed into the club for my shift; I just wanted to get to work.

It didn't help that Petey reminded me so much of Asher back in the day, the somewhat softer version I knew as a young girl, with his wavy blond locks, scruffy beard, tight T-shirts, and leather pants. Except his deep hazelnut-brown eyes radiated warmth unlike Asher's silver orbs, which were either a burning inferno of desire or a raging storm of fury at any given moment.

As I made my way into the club, Petey plastered a bright smile on his face. His fake grin totally contradicted his tough-guy persona, and made me giggle out loud.

"Hi, Nat," he said with too much enthusiasm. "How you doing today? Oh, look at that, you brought me a coffee. Thanks, baby doll." Then he reached for the second cup of joe I was juggling.

Stifling my laughter, I said, "Here," and shoved the cup at him, causing a little dribble to splat up on his black tee. *Good.*

Petey reached up to brush the coffee off his shirt before taking a big gulp. "No need to be so gruff, Nat, I'm just doing my job. I know you're mad, but what do you want me to do?" He shrugged. "Ash is gonna fire my ass if there's another incident like a few weeks ago. I'm making the best of crappy circumstances. Plus, you know I adore you." He feigned doe eyes, fluttering his eyelashes.

I stopped dead in my tracks, it becoming painfully clear I wasn't going to make it to my dressing room I shared with Petal without first dealing with an overly anxious, insanely protective bouncer.

Staring him straight in the face, I said, "Petey, I've been working in strip clubs for what feels like my whole life. I've been in and out of VIP rooms for the better part of the last ten years, and doing a damn good job of it. In fact, the rooms I used to work at the Leop make the ones here seem like a cakewalk. So back off, okay?"

He didn't. The stubborn man just stood there, holding his ground, staring me down. "No can do, Nat. The boss man laid down the law again on Saturday night. He said keep two eyes glued on you at all times, extra pat-downs and more detailed negotiations for every man or woman entering the VIP room with you. And if we can, keep you out on the open floor."

I resisted stomping my foot in a full-blown tantrum like a teenager, but this whole mess was becoming infuriating. I glared at him, maybe even pointed my finger in his face. "Listen to me, you. I have this. No married couple getting their rocks off in the back with me rubbing all over them is going to slow me down. I *need* the money I make back there. So, *just stop.*"

Petey rolled his eyes at me. "They tried to push Ecstasy into your mouth, Nat. On. My. Watch. So no, I can't *just stop.*" With that, he ended our little conversation, placed one hand on my waist while he held his coffee in the other, and escorted me to my dressing room.

He stopped at the door, knocked, making sure Petal was decent if she was in there, and when no reply came from the other side, he opened it, nudged me in, and said, "I'll be right here. See you when you're ready to hit the floor."

Forget getting the last word, I didn't get to say anything more. At. All. Those two assholes had me on a tight leash, and they were screwing with my plan.

YOUNG AND bubbly and perky as hell, Petal was off somewhere, leaving me alone with my thoughts. To think I actually craved her constant squealing and peppy attitude was something new. My stream of consciousness seemed to find its way to the forefront when I was alone, and I didn't want to go there.

Years ago, when I agreed to come work for Asher, I knew he was a bit overprotective. But this? This was something altogether different. He had me on complete and total lockdown.

And now, Sienna finally crushing on some dude had pushed him way over the edge.

Although Asher's protective nature had only increased over the last five years, this was outrageous, especially when it came to me. We were sleeping together, but that was all it was—sex.

Neither of us was looking for some type of forever—definitely not Asher, no matter what he said—so there was no reason we couldn't be mature adults and have a mutually good time. Something else I told myself, tried to talk my thick head into believing. Particularly after Friday night.

Regardless of our time on the casting couch, I had to work, and Asher had no right to step on my toes when it came to earning money.

I started getting ready like I did six nights a week. With tweezers in hand, I inspected my legs, underarms, and bikini area for any stray hairs, smoothed baby oil over my skin, combed my hair before curling it in waves. While waiting for the hot iron to warm up, I stared long and hard in the mirror. I didn't look too bad for being almost twenty-nine and having a kid. A big kid. Not a toddler, but a boy on the verge of becoming a young man.

Quinn.

If I didn't have Quinn to think about, I would get the hell out of here—fast. Maybe try to do something other than stripping, but really? What else did I know? Nothing. So I was staying for a while longer, putting my money away, and those idiotic men had better let me work. I had an exit strategy, and I would have to do it soon.

Moving the hot wand through my long dark brown hair, creating cascading waves, highlighting its fullness and golden-red highlights, I turned on my Nataleigh Dallas smile. When I left the Leop, I left my Natasha persona behind. Probably because I wanted to shed myself of everything remotely related to that place.

Spelling my stage name slightly more seductively seemed like enough at that point. After all, I was a stripper for better or worse, and I was in fact, Natalie. There was nothing to hide, except for my last name. I had Quinn to consider, who I gave my surname, Parker, when he was born. His dad had never been in the picture; I couldn't exactly attach his name to the birth certificate. My son would come to terms in his own time about my profession. He had a good life, and I hoped he would break free from the Vegas nightlife world, the only life I've ever known. Vegas nightlife. In the meantime, I was doing my very best to keep the two separate.

Nataleigh Dallas stared back at me in the mirror with my very own sea-green eyes, but her gaze was hard, as I'd created her to be, complete with quite the nasty, sordid reputation. Her persona was the reason I was being wooed to Florida.

I'm certainly not Sienna. I could never pull off that whole "innocent" stripper act.

I was who I was. A little bit dirty, a whole lot naughty, and one hell of an entertainer in the back rooms for couples, parties, or whatever kind of kinky combination made their way back there.

Call it jaded, I didn't care. I looked at it as being smart.

With my hair finished and down for the evening, I started on my makeup, running my glitter blush softly along my cheekbones, painting my eyelids a smoky taupe, and lining my whole eye in navy kohl pencil. There was nothing innocent about my look. Absolutely zilch.

It was a totally different sexed-up look than my Leop days, where I tried to completely disguise myself under layers of makeup, and flat-ironed my hair to fall around my face. Working at the Tunnel, I was proud of what I did, no matter what. I didn't need to hide, and I was getting noticed.

In Florida, they needed top-shelf female dancers who knew the ropes, who could put on a smutty act without a second thought, and mostly, who could train others how to work the floor and suck a man dry, financially speaking, for the evening. Miami was hot to trot right now with real high-class places popping up that catered to the older spring break crowds, bachelor parties, foreigners, and business travel.

I needed a few more months to make sure I had enough saved, and we were off. Making sure I had a cushion, a little to fall back on, was my first priority, which was why Asher and Petey had to lay the hell off me.

After the money, the other most important decision was where we lived. Picking an apartment in a good neighborhood, even if it was small, was the smart choice. My son would be able to go to a good school, make nice friends, and I could find a reliable, trustworthy sitter. One who could work nights and sleep over until I got home.

My mom, who had watched my tiny guy for most of his life while I worked, couldn't leave. She wouldn't leave her dad, my grampa, who was in a local nursing home. I understood. *Sort of.* With Quinn's dad never in the picture and my own dad's fatal heart attack right before his grandson was born, my mom and I had raised my son together. We'd been close, and I didn't understand her recent bout of indifference toward me.

I stared hard at my reflection, concentrating on my face, willing the tears in my eyes to evaporate.

My mom loved her own daddy, but didn't she want what was best for her grandson?

Another reason why I needed to get out of Dodge. It was time I called all the shots, made my own decisions when it came to my life, my kid, and my relationships, without relying on anyone else.

Sighing, I sifted through my clothes in the small closet of my dressing room. I pulled out a black mini dress completely cut out across the midriff, baring my tanned skin from a tiny tease of boob cleavage toward no-man's land down below. Way downtown.

The back ran open the same length from the slope of my neck to the top of my ass crack. Underneath, all I had on was a tiny iridescent thong. As I slipped slinky red patent strappy sandals on six-inch platforms on my feet, Petal bounced in, sweaty from working out.

Mentally, I rolled my eyes. *Another of Asher's insane projects to protect the girls.* The stubborn mule recently built an addition to the club with a full gym inside it, so the girls could work out in peace and safety. He didn't want any of us being harassed at the local gyms. *Nut case.*

My work roommate, Petal, was the opposite of me with her constant upbeat attitude, but I still liked the young girl—most of the time. Following suit with Asher's knight-in-shining-armor act, Sienna rescued the young girl and took her under her wing. For better or worse, Asher stuck the two of us together when my old dressing room partner, Chey, got married and quit. *Lucky her.*

Now the happy-go-lucky stripper from the Midwest was drinking water and stretching her quads against the wall. "Hey, Nat. You look hot! Wow! Love that dress. Good thing Asher is out of town for the night. He would bust a gut about you working the floor in that number." She bent over to take her off tiny workout shorts and stripped completely naked.

I realized that with all my arguing with Petey and getting lost in my own thoughts, I'd forgotten that Asher had left for an overnight at Red Rock with Sienna, just seventy-two hours after I slept at his house. Surely, he was trying to figure out what was up with her and her mystery customer, treating her with kid gloves due to her recent brush with a crazy stalker. And knowing Sienna and her maternal nature, she was probably doing her best to fix whatever was going on with Asher and me.

Well, it's not fixable.

I pulled myself out of my Asher-induced haze, waved my hand carelessly through the air, and said, "Please, Petal! Asher has no say whatsoever over what I wear. I actually forgot he was gone, so thanks for reminding me. He's been a jerk lately, but with him away, the cat can play."

Pretending to claw the air with hooked fingers, I let out a little *meow* before walking toward the door.

Petal stood there butt naked, showing off all her tight young attributes as her silky black hair cascaded over her shoulders, and yelled, "Behave, Nat! No one wants to deal with Asher being mad over you. You hear me? He was a bear over the weekend. We don't need this shit!"

WAS OUT the door and walking swiftly toward the club before Petal could say anything else.

Even though no one could see, I rolled my eyes for the second time that evening, this time over Petey being hot on my fire-engine-red heels. Good thing I could move pretty fast in them. I knew I couldn't lose him, but I certainly was in no mood to talk any more with him—or anyone else for that matter—about Asher.

I sashayed my tight ass all the way out the stage entrance, where my shadow of a bouncer parked himself at stage right while I started to flirt and work the club. With dollar signs, palm trees, and a happy Quinn in my mind, I quickly jumped onstage, whipping myself up the pole for my solo number.

With Sienna out for the night, I didn't have to share the spotlight. In fact, for music I used one of the personalized mash-ups that had been made just for her. Shaking my ass to the hard rock beat that was sharing the air with rap, I felt my dress riding up my thighs, exposing my tanned skin as I slid down the pole. I headed to the front of the platform and sank into a squat, spreading my knees, giving the front row a tiny peek of my undies and their glowing iridescence shining in the black light.

I threw my head forward and shook it from side to side, feeling my hair flow through the air and cloak my face, giving me a moment's privacy and allowing me a second with my emotions, which was an occupational hazard in stripping.

Quickly tossing my locks back and standing tall, I took a few steps forward and pulled my dress off in one swoop, discarding it to stage right. *Finally, Petey has something to do—pick up my dress.* Standing before the packed house wearing only my miniscule thong and the shiny white star pasties covering my nipples, I began to gyrate, tease, and taunt from the stage, eyeing up a few prospects for when I was finished.

With one glance, I engaged a group of whales with bellies as fat as their wallets, like a missile homing in on its target. They were an easy sell.

seven

Issues with a Side of Massage
Asher

IT HAD only been a few days since I'd had Natalie all to myself at my house, and she was already back to being a bitch, icing over and freezing me out. I couldn't deal with it at the moment, so I put Petey under strict orders to be her full-time shadow.

I had other problems. Big ones.

Sienna and I were at a resort in the Red Rock Desert, stretched out in the couples' massage room awaiting our "therapists." Christ, I needed more than a massage therapist, I needed my whole head examined, but I didn't have time for that crap. Thank fuck, the woman next to me was finally quiet. I was soaking up every second of silence. The silly girl had been crawling up my ass about Natalie for the last twenty-four hours.

As difficult as it was, I tried not to get annoyed with Sienna's constant harping. After all, she only cared about me, which was why she wouldn't shut up for one second about me deserving happiness.

But it was enough already. Enough. Period.

That whole interrogation was probably instigated by her recent discovery of Natalie with her fine-looking ass sitting naked in my kitchen. Go figure, on the second time in five very long years that I got the stubborn girl to come back with me to my place, Sienna had to walk in unannounced. Now she wouldn't take her foot off the gas when it came to me "making a life."

When I couldn't take any fucking more, right before our spa appointments I finally gave in to Sie's nagging and explained a bit of the history between Nat and me. Then I promised that when I had it resolved, I would fill her in on the whole story.

Except that day might never come.

The good part was that our situation was too complicated for even Sienna to sort out, so she let it go. At least for the freaking moment, so I could pretend to enjoy my massage.

The real problem was I had to get Sienna's crazy mess straightened out first, and it was weighing on me like a five-ton elephant.

Which was why I was currently getting a couple's massage while also sharing a suite at one of the area's luxury resorts with my top-billed stripper and best friend. Sienna needed a break, a respite from the stress in her life so she could get some perspective.

As for me, I required a lot more.

Lulled by the serenity of the massage room, the sound of a rambling brook drifting from the hidden speakers, my mind drifted back to when I took Lila in—now Sienna—when she was on the run, trying to escape an abusive relationship. Hard to believe what a freaking star she'd become since those dark days.

Sienna had done good, had made a life for herself in Vegas, and seemed happy. For seven years she'd shown zero interest in meeting someone of the opposite sex. Now she suddenly had a lunatic fan charging the stage while she performed, and she'd been breaking all her own rules, visiting with a male customer in the audience on Fridays.

Sienna and I had a rule about that, one of many we'd agreed to together when her star began to rise and she stopped performing lap dances. First of all, no walking the club floor on weekends, or I couldn't protect her from the throngs of fans wanting a touch, a taste, or just to snap a fucking picture with Vegas's Adult Entertainer of the Year, two years running. Sienna Flower was too fucking popular for her own good, so nowadays she enticed the crowd only from the stage. No lap dances, no photos, no private rooms. Nothing.

My eyes squeezed shut as I lay flat on my back, waiting, thinking about Sienna and her rules. Imagine my surprise when I saw Ms. Hands-Off gracing the table of a big fucking dude last Friday. No wonder I was so pumped to blow off some steam with Natalie, and pushed so hard for her to come back to my place.

Damn, I had to resolve this little situation with Sienna so I could sort out my own stuff, and do it all quick.

I breathed out a sigh of relief when I heard the two massage girls come into the room. Sensing the lights dimming through slits between my eyelids, I immediately relaxed.

Warm hands coated in oil slid up and down my sore hamstrings and forearms. They were everywhere and I had to resist moaning out loud, not sure if it was the heavy pressure on my body or in my head.

It didn't matter how hard the tiny woman rubbed me or dug into my tired muscles, my thoughts couldn't break free from my own issues. And I really couldn't pinpoint what my issues were, other than they all started and ended with Natalie.

What the hell was up with that woman? Natalie had been driving me crazy for the last five years. She had my balls in her giant tote bag, and she didn't even realize it. Lately, she'd been all testy, up in my face about needing to make good money for her boy, and telling me to stay out of her way.

Well, Nat, no can do, because I own the club where someone tried to shove Ecstasy down your throat. And by the way, I'm fucking you. Did you forget?

Maybe even making love to you.

Nah.

What the hell was her angle these days? I'd known her longer than five years; she was probably the person I'd known the longest at this point in my life. We grew up on the wrong side of the tracks together, which was part of the problem.

The girl had acted weird from time to time since I'd dragged her out of the Leop, but lately, she had a whole new brand of strange going on in her head.

Attempting to put this line of thinking away, I tried to salvage what time I had left to relax as the masseuse ran her strong hands along my neck, making her way over to my pecs. I was wound tight, and not even a whole day of massage would help me unwind. My mind raced as I sifted through all the events of the last several years with Natalie, so I could understand what might be going on with her.

As I rolled onto my stomach for the second half of my massage, my body barely shielded by a thin sheet, my mind shifted back to five years ago, when I got Natalie out of that dump and back in my life...

O<small>N THAT</small> particular Monday five years ago, the day after I'd first run into Natalie at the Leop, I'd been nursing an enormous hangover. I had stopped by the Tunnel to sign payroll for the week, and to make sure the usually light daytime crowd was behaving. There hadn't been a ton of paperwork to do at the club because it was mostly a cash business, but I had to make sure everything was legit.

Then, despite giving myself a stiff talking-to over Natalie and how I didn't need to save her, I'd jumped on my bike and headed over to the Leop. I had leaned into the curves that day, taking the corners with a bit too much speed, rushing to what, I had no idea.

Mondays were the day most strip clubs took inventory and planned to restock after what they hoped was an extremely busy weekend. My bar backs and hostesses over at the Tunnel would be making note of everything we were out of and prepping for another stellar week, and I had hoped Ryan was doing the same over at the Leop. He was my best chance for getting the lowdown on Natalie, or Natasha.

Walking into the dark club, squinting and adjusting from riding outside in the hot sun on my beloved baby, I immediately clocked Ryan at a side bar. I took off toward him, ignoring a chump getting a sultry lap dance from an Asian girl in a purple thong.

Okay, I looked a little, but I just wanted to see what type of girls they had working during the day shift.

"What's up, man?" I called to Ryan from a few feet away, giving him a chin lift.

"You that hard up, Ash? Coming back the next day for a little more? Not too many girls floating around here," he replied with a smirk.

"Nah, I'm good, but I got a few questions for you." I leaned up against the bar while he pulled a draft beer at the tap.

"The girl, Natasha, you know her?" I asked, not wasting any time.

He stopped what he was doing and turned to me, his expression serious. "Yeah. We all do. Love her. She's a good girl, Asher, not one you should mess with. I know your tastes, so just don't go there with Nat."

I pinned him with a no-bullshit stare. "Cut the tough-guy act, Ryan. I know her. Grew up with her, but haven't seen her in a few years. I need to talk with her, finish a conversation we started last night."

Then he stared daggers back at me and opened his mouth to answer, but was interrupted by a tall, slinky figure sneaking up on him, her hair floating all around her face.

The girl jumped on Ryan's back, wrapping her arms around his neck while her legs made their way around his waist, before she'd swung over his shoulder and landed a kiss on his cheek. The little cock tease had been wrapped in her own dark mane of hair and still hadn't seen me standing to the side of the bar, the one on the other side of Ryan, the side she hadn't been kissing.

"Hey, Ry! You have a good night? I stopped in to clean up my dressing room and thought we could grab some lunch. My mom is taking Quinney for fast food, so we could get something decent. Want to?" she said as she settled herself higher on his hip.

In an effort to be seen, I cleared my throat, and Ryan started to look painfully uncomfortable.

Is she sleeping with the guy? Can that little runt be the father of her child? Nah.

At least Natalie looked way better without her nasty stripper face painted on. She looked stunning, all natural and shit.

When she saw me she jumped down, flipping her hair out of her face as she stared straight at me with a confused look and said, "Asher, what are you doing here?"

I moved around the front of the bar and positioned myself directly in front of Ryan, blocking his view of Natalie. Then I leaned in and answered in a low voice. "Oh, just catching up with old friends like you. Glad to hear you're hungry. Let's go, Nat. I'm buying, you're eating."

Ryan didn't say a damn word. At least the little prick knew better than to take me on. I had a reputation, and Ryan certainly wasn't going to mess with me physically.

She hooked her hands on her hips. "Asher, I told you. I have a life here at the Leop. I'm eating with Ryan, but thanks for asking." Then she leaned around me and raised an eyebrow at Ryan, obviously expecting the dude to back her up.

Instead he glanced away and said, "You know what, Nat? I got a lot to do here today. Go get something to eat with Asher, and catch up. You and me, we'll see each other later. Yeah?" He motioned to the door before turning back to his bar duties.

Natalie didn't look happy at his response. In fact, she looked to be on the verge of crying, but she put on a tough face when she said, "Okay. See you later, Ry."

I tilted my head to the exit while holding my hand out for Natalie to take, and wasn't surprised when she rushed by me saying, "I'll go eat with you, Asher, but don't read anything into it. I'm starving and I have a few free hours, so let's roll. It's lunch—nothing more, nothing less. Not today or any other day." She strutted all the way to the door, pushed it open, and walked out into the sunshine, shoving her sunglasses on her face.

I stopped short when I made it through the doorway. "Shit," I mumbled to myself. Looking up at Natalie, I tried to explain, "I have my bike."

"So? I've been on a motorcycle before, Asher. Let's go." She marched right over to my shiny black baby and threw her leg over.

I handed her my helmet and hopped on in front of her, feeling her wrap her arms around my middle. It felt way better than seeing her limbs wrapped around Ryan.

Before I gunned the engine, I asked, "Where to?"

"Feralina's on the Strip."

I guessed she decided to go big because I was buying, and she was obviously put out and all that, but I didn't care. She wanted fancy Italian, she'd have it, and by the end of lunch—if I had my way—she wouldn't be working at the Leop anymore.

We had sped off toward the glitz and glamour of the Strip with her snuggled tight against my back, her tits pressing into my leather jacket, her thighs clenched around mine, and I'd gotten exactly what I wanted that day.

Natalie came to work for me.

UNFORTUNATELY, BEFORE I could think any more about that day and everything that had happened since then, or come up with a solution to my own personal problems and Sienna's looming issues, a little bottle of lavender oil was waved under my nose, alerting me to the end of the massage and snapping me back to reality.

I stood up with my back to my naked friend on the other table and slipped my robe on, leaving the room so she could have some privacy. Outside the treatment room, the facial tech down the hall was giving me *the look*, the one that said, *What room are you staying in? And can I come by later?*

I thought back to the last time I slept with someone other than Natalie. Too long, but sadly, I didn't want the young tech. I craved Natalie, and she was being a royal bitch. We were never exclusive, at her insistence. In the beginning I enjoyed the novelty of the friends-with-benefits thing, but it was getting old.

Natalie doesn't want anything more with me, and I need to get that through my thick skull and move on. I should cut ties altogether, but not before I get her what she needs—child support.

smoldered

Just as I was having second thoughts about the technician, Sienna walked out of the massage room, rosy-cheeked with imprint lines on her face from the headrest. She appeared to be calmer than when we arrived, and I hoped she was ready to talk about her stalker and whatever was going on with that customer she'd been chatting with.

That was wishful thinking because Sienna was only interested in curling up in her robe in our suite and ordering room service.

eight

Lap Dances to Building Forts

Natalie

IT WAS after three o'clock in the morning, and I'd just wrapped up with some guys from Dallas. After a round of drinks on the main floor of the club, we took the party to the back, where the guys were subjected to Petey's pat downs and extra-hard questioning before striking a deal to keep me for the rest of the evening. Just me. The club was busy, and with Petey occupied, I would have a little wiggle room with the rules. And fewer rules meant more profit for me.

I went lenient with the no-touching policy, allowing the well-dressed men to savor their time with me. Their hands roamed over my ass, along my side cleavage, and down my thighs.

A blond-haired, blue-eyed businessman in a dark suit held a rum and coke in one hand while his other stroked my inner thigh as I straddled him. I trained my eyes on his, pretending he rocked my world while I leaned forward and brushed my chest lightly against him. My nipples, now hardened little buds, rubbed along the silk of his shirt. I bent forward a little more, resting some of my weight on his thick thighs—certain he worked out with a trainer his wife arranged for him—and let my hot breath linger on his ear, darting my tongue out ever so slightly, perhaps accidentally grazing the lobe. He moaned and rocked his hips up toward my heat.

I simply shook my head and waggled my finger at him, teasingly calling him a bad boy, and continued to rub up against him like a cat in heat without him moving another inch.

When I finished, he stuffed a hundred-dollar bill in my thong. And the other sheep followed right behind him.

I knew either Mike, Billy, or another of Asher's army was watching on the video feed, and I may have intentionally laid it on a little heavy because of that. I was my own woman, and no one could stop me from earning a living. I could handle myself in the back rooms, even after an altercation with one horny married man who wanted to make his long-gone college-days fantasies come true.

When the private party came to a close, I headed straight to my dressing room to count my tips. Of course, Petey followed to hand over my cut from the suits, chasing me down as fast as he could, wanting to check in on my feelings. It had been a good night, and all I wanted to do was change, count my share, and go home. If I hurried, I could get two or three hours of sleep and take Quinn to school.

"See, Petey, all ends well. You happy? Now you can text Asher and report that I behaved like a good girl and you took care of me, or whatever bull you want to feed him. Good night," I said as I dismissed him.

He didn't follow me for once. The little prick yelled after me as I hightailed it away from him, "Don't blame me, Nat! It's not fair. You need to take a good long look at the whole picture."

I shrugged and kept moving. *Whatever.* I forced myself not to care. Yeah, Asher and I had a lot of good times under our belt. And I probably cared for him more than I should, but I needed to put that aside.

As I hit the back door freshly changed into street clothes, Simon, the club's town car driver, offered to drive me home and come back to get me the next day for work. He usually only did this for Sienna, but she was away and he was allowed to do as he wished. I used to be a little envious of the gorgeous blonde everyone seemed to instantly fall in love with, but then I realized Sienna was just like the rest of us. Hiding from someone or something. If she needed that type of attention and TLC, so be it. I didn't.

Asher had a borderline sick obsession with her, but anything that took the pressure off me was a welcome diversion in my mind. At least, that was what I told myself daily.

Not to mention, the faux vixen with the virgin eyes brought a lot of lap dances and private room invites my way. Who cared if she was a little spoiled when it came to being chauffeured around and saving herself for only the stage.

She made me money.

Smiling at Simon, I simply said, "No thanks," and headed over to my little cherry-red coupe. It was one of my first purchases after Asher had convinced me to switch from the Leop to the Electric Tunnel. It was safe and sleek but also reliable, and with my pay increase, I could afford it.

I realized on that day long ago over lunch at Feralina's, Asher was never going to give up if I didn't agree to leave the Leop. The stubborn prick even threatened to call the authorities on his competition. I didn't put it past him to make up lies; Asher could be ruthless when he wanted something.

So I ended up begging, "Don't do that, Ash. My friends will be out of work, and no one at the Leop can afford that. I'll come over to the Tunnel and dance for you. Okay? Please don't make trouble."

That was it. That was all it took. One idle threat and I was Nataleigh Dallas, the new girl at the Electric Tunnel.

Looking back, going to work for Asher was the easy part. It was everything that came after that was hard. Or rather, harder.

I turned the key in the ignition, shifted into gear, and pulled out of my spot, my thoughts racing back to the day when it all became so much more difficult.

I'd been dancing at the Tunnel for six months. I was reluctant to admit it, but I liked it. A lot. I made great cash tips, the bouncers took good care of their girls, there was nothing remotely sketchy happening in any of the VIP rooms, and I was never asked to go home with a customer.

Pressing hard on the clutch, I down-shifted, taking the ride home slowly as I decompressed, losing myself in my mind and sifting through old memories.

Bittersweet ones.

Like the day when everything changed for the worse…

A HUGE BACHELOR party had just finished. I'd made a ton of cold, hard cash, and I'd been both amped and aggravated beyond control. It was Friday, and my mom had been set to keep an almost five-year-old Quinn for their weekly sleepover so I could get a little rest in the morning. Except I had known there was no way I would be going to sleep when I got home, because I'd been fuming mad.

I had almost a grand in cash in my pocket, and I'd known right away Asher hadn't taken his usual cut. Why he was torturing me like that, I hadn't a clue. A grand! Asher was the owner of the place; he should just take his share and stop treating me differently from the other girls. After sitting at the bar and downing a shot, I'd stomped up the spiral stairs to his newly built, spacious second-floor office.

When I knocked, he yelled, "It better be important."

Not caring that he wanted to be left alone, I shoved the door open, walked in, and slammed it shut. "I don't care that you don't want to be bothered but, Ash, you can't give me a grand! I know what the tally was for the party tonight, and with your cut, my take should be closer to five or six hundred. What are you doing?"

The smug idiot just looked up and smiled at me. "Hey, Nat. You're a welcome surprise. Never a disruption. But I have to say, I got no clue what you're talking about. Pretty sure Mike dealt with the money tonight, and I guarantee what he gave you was correct, little doll."

At this, I slammed my hand onto his desk for effect. "Will you stop patronizing me, and while you're at it, stop calling me 'little doll.'"

Asher stood up from his desk while I was talking and made his way over to me. Reminding me of our confrontation in the back room of the Leop, he tucked his finger gently under my chin and lifted my gaze to meet his.

"Natalie, I've called you 'little doll' since you were eight or so and came over with ice and bandages when I fell off that old motorbike. I wasn't supposed to be tearing through the 'hood, and I remember you watching in horror and screaming for me to stop. But I never was a good listener and I rode on, laying that piece of shit down, banging my arm up, and burning my leg on the pipe. I was thirteen and stubborn as hell back then, refused to admit anything hurt. So, no, I will not stop calling you 'little doll,' and I will definitely not be questioned over my payment terms at my own club." He chuckled. "I'm even more stubborn as a grown man than when I was a teenager."

I had no answer, distracted by the fact the air grew unbelievably electrically charged around us, or maybe that was just me? Sparks fizzled and popped in my body, my skin prickled just looking at him, and my heart started to burn up in flames from his possessive, authoritative tone.

The smart choice would be to leave, go home, take a cold shower, and go to bed. Instead I threw gas on an already burning fire.

With my hand on my hip, my head cocked to the side, I said in my most sultry voice, "Well, Asher, if you haven't noticed, I'm not 'little' anymore and I'm pretty sure that 'doll' is the last word most men would use to describe me."

With my seductive words out in the open, Asher's eyes sparked and flashed.

With need? Want? Desire? Worst-case scenario, anger? I had no clue.

They smoldered like two iridescent silver clouds of smoke billowing up from a five-alarm fire, and they were directed right at me, pulling me in when they should have been signaling to get out.

After all, no one runs into a burning building.

I couldn't see the flame, but I sure as hell felt it. I should have extinguished it. Instead, like a fool, I fanned it.

The man, now definitely not the boy I knew way back when, closed every inch of space between us and spoke firmly. "Nat, believe me, it doesn't go unnoticed that you're no longer a young girl, nor are you a 'doll' in the usual sense of the word, but you will always be my 'little doll.' Now, if we're done discussing my cute-as-fuck nickname for you, I'm going to respond to the challenge I believe you laid out in front of me. Are you offering yourself up to me? Do you want me, beautiful?"

He moved even closer, which I didn't think was possible, but I felt his readiness to the challenge against my stomach when he leaned in and ran his hand down the length of my hair. A ripple of excitement shot through me. I hadn't been that charged since…ever, and I wanted to savor the moment. It was one thing to pretend to be someone's sexual fantasy for a night, a week, or whatever, but quite another to conjure up my own wants.

And Asher all soft and loving was something I had wanted for a very long time. Like forever.

"I do," I breathed out.

Asher's mouth landed on mine as he took my lips in a rough, heady kiss with absolutely no mercy. He pulled my long hair back to gain access to my neck and ran his teeth and tongue up and down my collarbone before he made his way back up to my mouth. He kissed and toyed with my mouth, making way for his tongue to enter and do the most delicious things as it tangled with mine.

I had to stop it all for a moment and clear up one item up before we completely lost ourselves in each other. So even though I didn't want to, I pulled away and added, "But with no strings attached. This is purely physical, Ash."

The last thing I felt before being transported to pure and absolute bliss was the tiny charm of my necklace fluttering against my chest, softly moving with my heartbeat, reminding me of my reason for breathing. Quinn. My choice was solidified. No. Strings. Attached.

The problem was that when this man ran his hand through his thick, unruly blond waves falling in his face, pushing them out of the way to clear the view for his silver eyes, I had always wanted to melt into him. I'd wanted to bury myself, my whole being, into his soul, swirl us together, become one and never, ever separate.

But we had a history, and mixing the past and present would be a very bad idea. Knowing this, I'd settled for a workplace affair. It would be a lawsuit waiting to happen in any other industry, but this was Vegas.

I was a stripper, he was my boss, and no one had cared.

D RAWN BACK to the present as I traveled home, I wondered whether Asher had heard me correctly back then, because after we did it on the couch in his office that one fateful night, we'd been fucking ever since. On the desk, chair, floor, every inch of the couch, and all over the luxury bathroom in the corner of his office.

With Asher now swearing off anything illegal, we were each other's drug of choice. Inhaling, touching, and pleasuring each other every time I would allow it for the last few years.

Sometimes I would intentionally hold out for long periods of time—more for my sake than anything else. I knew Asher enjoyed other women during those times, but despite the separation and knowing this, my self-imposed boundaries always pulled him closer to me rather than pushing him further away.

Soon enough, when I ending up moving to another state, physical distance would serve as the ultimate, much-needed, and permanent separation.

I continued to drive, listening to the soft vibe of some alternative station on the radio, tracing the quiet, dark roads to the small suburban neighborhood where Quinn and I lived in a tiny fourplex. As I parked my car, taking in my place in the stillness of the early hours of the morning, I looked toward the two top units, one of which I rented. As luck would have it, two college students rented the one next door.

The band singing was running from someone or somebody after them, running as fast as they could. Like I needed to run.

Go-go-go-go.

When I did leave town, I would miss my neighbors. What had started as them helping me wean off my mom's help had become so much more. I paid Trish and Lynx to take turns spending the night when I worked. They made good money and could study, hang out on social media, or sleep after Quinn went to bed at nine p.m. It was an easy gig.

We were our own little family with our own routine. *Sort of.*

As I stood in my designated parking spot, grabbed my bag, and prepared to head upstairs and relieve Trish, I couldn't help but feel a bit sad. I was in a good routine, surrounded by decent people, but I just had to make the move. I wasn't completely innocent in the choices I'd made years ago, and unfortunately I felt it all coming to a head.

I climbed the open-air staircase in the cool night air to my rental. It wasn't much, but it was mine. I provided this for Quinn all on my own, and I was proud. It was a perfect safe haven for my boy. I had my reasons for separation of work and family, and had held firm on those. Which was exactly how Asher got me to finally agree to go to his place—even though I swore I wouldn't—after several years of screwing around in his private office.

I'd now been there twice in total, and I couldn't help but fantasize about never leaving. I should have stuck to my guns about not going home with him, but I didn't. And now I had the memory of long sand-colored granite counters in a gourmet kitchen, marble bathrooms, and plush, sumptuous carpet under my toes etched in my mind.

What would it be like if it were ours?

I pulled myself out of my ridiculous daydreaming and opened my door to find a sleeping Trish on the couch and Quinn out cold in a fort in the middle of the living space. I tiptoed over and pulled a blanket over my sitter, then covered my little baby, who was quickly becoming a tween. There was no sense in waking either of them.

I threw my purse in the corner by the tiny dining table and undressed as I walked toward my room, dropping my clothes in the hamper before pulling an old T-shirt over my head and falling into bed.

It didn't take long for me to drift off thinking about *him.*

My hand made its way inside my panties. I ran one finger along my wet core, smoothing down the bare folds, stopping to push inside before drawing back out, bringing my own moisture to my most sensitive spot. It pulsed and throbbed, angry and wanting more, not one bit satisfied with my own fingers down there.

My body ached for his rough touch and large hands, calloused and hardened from years of riding and working hard. My manicured ones, soft from rubbing baby oil on my legs nightly, were no replacement for Asher's coarse ones.

I added a second finger, but my vagina was a traitor, screaming for a sensation only one man could leave in his wake.

In desperation for some release—or punishment, depending on how one looked at it—I reached into my nightstand and pulled out my vibrator. It was a tiny, powerful little thing, humming in the dark night. I kept the covers up over me, buffering the steady hum from the two bodies sleeping outside in the living area, and ran the vibrating tip over my clit, pressing it down, creating a little pain and friction. When I closed my eyes, images of Asher—both then and now—ran through my mind. Memories of his mouth on me while I was laid out in his office on the sofa mixed with wishful fantasies for the future on a continuous loop until I reached the peak.

Using my fingers and sadly, my battery-operated replacement, I moaned quietly to myself, turning my face to the side, biting down on my pillow as I came. Right away, I felt the tears form. Small droplets, but tears nonetheless.

My leaving would be harder than anything Asher and I had endured so far. I tried not to think about it a lot, but the fact remained: Whether we were exclusive or not, he and I were so entwined with each other, making a clean break would crush us.

It was for the best. Especially after his latest interrogation last week when I visited his house for the second and very last time.

Tossing and turning in the bittersweet memory, eventually the aftershocks of my climax and the cleansing of emotion from my body rocked me to sleep.

nine

A Tangled Web

Asher

BY THE time Sienna and I arrived back from our getaway, she was all business and back to work as usual. My headliner danced, lit the club on fire with her moves, and went home all alone. There was nothing I could do about *that* at the moment.

On the other hand, I decided to do something about my Natalie slump, and it didn't involve being alone or attempting to spend time with the temperamental brunette causing me angst. As I walked the club that evening, it was clear that Natalie had frozen me out. She was probably pissed that I'd had Petey keep an extra-sharp eye on her while I was away, but what could she expect?

And I'd had a few revelations while she was gracing my presence last week. Actually, more than gracing. I would say she'd inhabited my soul and took over my body, heart, and home if I were a pussy, but I'm not. Besides, to her it was more like she threw the old dog a bone, judging by the freeze-out she'd been giving me since I confronted her.

The girl would thaw and until then, I had alternate plans. Except for the first time ever, it didn't exactly feel right. Like wearing leather pants when it was hot and they were a bit uncomfortable and restrictive, my chest tightened at what I was about to do.

smoldered

Still, I hit speed dial for my friend, Penelope, who owned the Cat's Meow waxing studio, and told her to come on over. "It's gonna be a late night, Penny, so make sure you're ready for me," I instructed her as soon as she picked up the phone. "And while you're at it, bring your friend Larken, sweetheart."

Penelope and I went way back, and we felt the same way about relationships. They sucked. *At least, I thought they did.*

The only issue was Penelope was good friends with all the girls who worked for me at the Tunnel, especially Sienna, so she was the only person I didn't entertain in my office. When I called Penny, she knew to meet me at my house. We were discreet when we hooked up; she didn't want the dancers she called girlfriends to know, and she was the one hookup I kept hidden from Natalie.

As the boss, I approved all schedules, so I knew Nataleigh Dallas would be on tonight until in the wee hours of the morning, so I jetted from my club. This being Wednesday night meant "Natalie the mother" was on duty the following day. Thursday was always her day off, and the Tunnel gang saw neither hide nor hair of the brown-haired beauty when she fell off the grid with her son.

The kid didn't know it, but he was one lucky little son of a bitch to have his mom all to himself for a whole day. I wouldn't really know firsthand if he got this or not because his mother kept him hidden from the club family. I understood, though. She was trying to break the cycle, give him a life we didn't have, so she erected a brick wall between her boy and us—definitely with me. But I was going to fix that for her now whether she wanted me to or not. I was going to find the kid's father, make him own up or at least pay up, even though she said I shouldn't.

Screw her. I jumped on my bike, speeding home without my helmet, allowing the wind to blow through my unruly hair as I tried to cool my thoughts. But all the while, I was jealous of a little boy because he got what I wanted: time with Natalie with no interruptions.

And how did I come to even want all that? A single woman? Did that mean I was interested in commitment? Please, *that* wasn't me. Or was it?

I pressed on faster, whipping my bike in and out of lanes, passing the few cars on the road as I rushed home to where a little piece of heaven—or at the very least, a little relief—waited for me.

I hit the garage opener as I came gunning down the block. Screw Natalie and her putting me on the back burner. I was raging in more places than my mind, and I hoped to hell those women were ready for me, because I planned to go at it for hours.

I SETTLED IN with a drink while I waited, staring at my tumbler, tapping my boot to the hard rock music piping through my speakers. Unfortunately, the cool beverage did little to temper the heat radiating from my skin.

Penny let herself in before she and Larken made their way over to my wet bar where I waited, sipping a scotch on the rocks. Both wore tiny hot pants, showing off long legs, barely hiding the smooth skin I knew resided where each of their long limbs met in the middle. No way they weren't bare under the shorts, and I had to contain myself from using a hand on each one to rip the little scraps of material off in a hurry.

"Ladies." The word came out rumbling, my voice hoarse with carnal need, but lacking any affection. This wasn't about emotion.

"Asher." My name felt heavy in the air from each woman's mouth.

Lust hung like a cloud of humidity in the room. There was no need for introductions or small talk. The only thoughts being broadcast were smut-filled and infused with raw sexuality, filling the air, getting ready to rain down on our threesome.

Larken was the newest and latest girl Penny occasionally slept with. She was fucking gorgeous with long chestnut-brown hair, deep green eyes, and dark tanned skin. I owned a strip club, so naturally I noticed stuff other men didn't. The young girl had an exotic Mediterranean look to her. Too bad she had a pretty profitable job twisting in a cage, hanging overhead in one of the hippest nightclubs on the Strip. Otherwise, I might have been able to convince her to come and dance for me.

I liked Larken a lot, better than anyone else Penny had ever brought into the mix. She was smoking in the sheets and dirty as all get-out. She also never asked to see me outside the arrangements Penelope set up.

She was down with the plan, if there really was one. At least, she appeared to be down. I hoped to hell Penny set her straight, but now wasn't the time to think about that shit.

Unable to think straight any more, I watched the decadent scene in front of me.

The women slowly stripped off their tight tanks, revealing transparent lacy bras and hard nipples. All the soft, supple pink flesh chased me right out of my brain, leaving only my cock to do the thinking. I stood up and closed the distance between the bar stool where I was sitting and the sofa the ladies were leaning against.

I lifted Larken, smoothing her hair around her neck to free her ear where I whispered, "You ready, baby?" She didn't say anything, only pulled her legs up and wrapped them around my ass as I started kissing her hard. There was zero gentleness in my actions, and the duo couldn't have cared less. Without any words, Penny slithered behind me and rubbed herself up and down my hard muscles like a cat, licking my neck, letting her finger roam along the back seam of my jeans, teasing my ass crack.

My tongue was deep inside the brunette's throat, fucking every corner of her wet little mouth, letting her know exactly what I was going to do down below, when the ginger behind me slipped her hands around front and unbuckled my belt, unbuttoned my jeans, and pushed them down over my waist. I was commando, and it took mere seconds before she repositioned Larken's legs down on the floor, slithered around front of me, and wedged herself between my own feet and the other woman's so she could greedily take me in her mouth.

I moaned as she swallowed all of me, my tip hitting the back of her throat. I pushed Larken onto the back edge of the couch, no longer wanting her mouth. Penny didn't miss a beat as I shifted forward, bracing my arms on either side of Larken's toned and tanned legs. The redheaded inferno just contorted herself smaller under me, never letting up on my dick with her rough lips.

I didn't need to pull off my target's hot pants because the girl had shoved them down in the one second it took to reposition myself. All I had to do was open my mouth and let myself have a taste.

I licked all along the edge of her inner thigh until I made my way to where it met her heat, finally landing at the center of her core, nipping at the bud. She moaned, squirmed, and gripped my shoulders, clawing at my skin while Penny picked up her pace, meeting my thrusts.

"Good? Yeah?" I murmured to the woman spread in front of me, dropping my hand, caressing Penny's mess of curls, pushing her deeper onto my dick.

Larken nodded while biting her lip. Little thing wanted me to stop teasing her and finish. Well, I had no problem with that.

My tongue was lost in Larken's tangy flavor when I felt my own release coming. I moved my free hand around the exotic beauty's ass, my finger grazing the crack, making way for me to trace her little hole. She was hanging off the edge of the couch, grinding in my face, screaming my name while I fingered her ass.

It was all I could take before I shot off in Penny's mouth.

After that we moved to the bedroom and took turns pleasuring one another with lips and tongues in every combination, position, and arrangement thinkable. It was a good night.

I WOKE UP in a mess of legs, arms, and a tangled web of red hair. Penelope was butt naked and spread-eagled over me, her waves covering my face, making breathing almost difficult. Larken's feet were in my face, somewhat tangled in the same fiery hair that was almost choking me, her soft cheek resting on my calf, and her own chocolate-colored tresses running down her back, landing on her perfectly round ass.

Penny and I went way back. The curvy little redhead was just getting started in her waxing biz when I was running a nightclub down on the Strip. That was over a decade ago, and the Strip was really starting to boom; big luxury hotels were going up all the way down Las Vegas Boulevard, and the place was swimming in cash. The infamous waxer to the stars, high-priced escorts, and desperate housewives would come in for a drink in my club a few nights a week.

After a few weeks of eyeing each other up, we decided to chat, discovered we had similar preferences, and we'd been scratching a mutual itch ever since. Penny had been firm when she said over a cocktail in the early days, "No commitments ever, Asher. Not for me. I like to explore, taste, savor whatever the evening's buffet may spread out in front of me, but that's it." She had stared me straight in the eye when she said this, and I knew she meant it.

Unlike Natalie, when she had told me "no strings attached."

Penelope was a woman of her own mind and body, and I doubted she'd ever settle down, which was fine with me. I reaped the benefits of it.

Christ, I'm an asshole.

I rubbed my hand over my face, moving the sea of red out of the way. At least I was honest. Penny knew about my off-and-on affair with Natalie. As for the other way around, Nat definitely knew I messed around when she cut me off. *Just not the details.* And I didn't want her to know about this side of me. Yeah, I had a lot of dark desires and a tendency to push the boundaries when it came to sex, but if I was honest with myself, when I was with Natalie, she was enough.

Before I could let my thoughts become any more strangled by my

smoldered

childhood friend turned part-time lover, I looked down. Both women were still asleep, but it was close to ten o'clock and I had to roll. Plus, I didn't do morning-afters other than the two times *she* had stayed over. I didn't know what I felt for Natalie, but I would never kick her out or make her feel unwelcome, whether we were sleeping together or not. We had too much history, and yeah, she was another one of my girls that I was protective over.

She didn't need the same amount of tender care Sienna needed, but I still watched out for the woman. I got a kick out of how tough Natalie acted, but knew she loved my doting.

This wasn't the time to get mushy. I slapped Penelope on the ass, waking her up, before I ran a finger up Larken's foot.

"Ladies, it was fun as always, but I got a club to run. Make yourselves at home, use the bathroom, eat, do whatever the fuck else you want to do. Just lock up behind you. Penny, you know the code?" She nodded. "Yeah? Lark, you good?" When the brunette gave me a sleepy smile, I stood up and headed to the shower.

ten

Lady Luck Has Left the Building

Natalie

THURSDAYS WERE my day off, and I tried to get all my household chores done while Quinn was at school so we could have dinner together, then spend some quality time doing whatever he wanted. It was during this one day a week that I felt normal, like a regular mom as I wore yoga pants and a big sweatshirt when I picked up my boy at school. I was pretty sure a few of the other moms knew what I did for a living but they weren't mean about it, mostly because my son was a great kid and a good friend to all the boys in his class.

Except today as I raced from the bus stop to the grocery store, I didn't feel normal or right. I worried for my son because Asher was going on a witch hunt.

I just *had to* make a second trip to his gorgeous home and revel in the decadent feel of the whole place, lay on the cool granite and let him lick my body, my skin radiating heat from his touch, and afterward eat breakfast from a single shared plate and fork.

Why?

At the end of the day, I might be a dirty stripper who had seen it all, but I was also a love-struck, round-eyed female, letting my emotions get the best of me. And now I just knew Asher was sniffing around where he didn't belong.

Standing in the checkout lane, completely lost in thought about my lack of self-control when it came to a certain blond-haired, silver-eyed bad boy and what it would be like to sink back into his bed and never leave, I reached for my neck to touch my charm, a nervous habit I'd developed over the years.

My hamsa. When the mysterious gift showed up on my bedside at the hospital after I delivered Quinn, the deep midnight-blue open-fingered hand made from blown glass mesmerized me from the moment I saw it. I assumed it was a gift from the nun who had surprised me with a visit, a gesture made by a secret angel to keep my son and me safe, protected from life's injustices. So I put it on that day, and usually only took it off when I danced.

As I stood in the store with my groceries on the checkout belt, I started to panic when I realized the necklace holding the charm was no longer around my neck. Where was it? How did I not know where it was? How long had it been gone?

Shit, I felt like my luck just ran out. Like the sands dripping through an hourglass, my time was up. The last tiny speck of sand had finally drifted to the bottom of the glass, leaving the top empty, barren, and alone, like me.

Where was my hamsa? *Think, Nat.*

When was the last time I remembered wearing it?

And then with a rush, it came to me…

I HAD STARTED playing with the small charm on my neck while sitting on Asher's counter. He had just turned my most romantic morning ever into a full-blown nightmare with his suggestion that both Quinn and I would be welcome to spend time at his home. He'd said something about my feeding him more bullshit and not accepting help from others. I had begun to fully twist the tiny hand now, as though squeezing extra superpowers from it would help me get out of this awkward moment.

Asher had raked his hand through his hair, not giving me a chance to reply. "Fuck, I've been thinking for years, you should consider finding the boy's dad. Guy owes you something. Money, at the very least, Nat. Lord knows, he's never been there and it doesn't seem like you want him to be, but still. You work so hard, seems like he shouldn't get off so easy."

When his hands moved to cradle my face, all I did was lose myself in the silver depths of his eyes, barely finding the strength to say, "It's not that. I just know he wouldn't want that. Wouldn't want him. Quinn."

"How. Are. You. So. Sure? You know this dude? More than just a one-night thing?" He trained his gaze on me, not wavering in the least.

"I just do," I said vaguely, but Asher pushed for more.

"Stop it, Nat. This is stupid. Do you know the guy or what? I'm starting to think it was one of the guys from where we grew up since you're protecting him so hard."

I wasn't able to stop the tiny shiver that ripped through me. Asher obviously felt it because his hand was firmly holding my shoulders steady, keeping us eye to eye.

"Yeah? That's it? One of the jerks we grew up with is responsible for knocking you up, and you don't want his help? I get wanting a different life for Quinn and all, but the dude should pay up. Who are you really protecting?" He leaned into me, his interrogation becoming a full-court press.

I shook my head. "Ash, please. It's not that."

"No. Some guy gets you pregnant and you raise the baby alone, making him into a decent young man all on your own? He owes you."

I leaned back a little, trying to put some space between us. I desperately needed some air, as this was exactly the reason why I didn't want Asher fishing for answers.

When I opened my mouth to speak, he started up again. "You know what? I know who it was. Yep, that weasel Beck. He was always sniffing around you, making eyes and moves, and you liked it. You loved the attention. Would've done anything for that loser."

A lone tear escaped my eye at the mention of Beck Hadley and the sad memories his name evoked. I tried and failed to sweep the salty drop away before Asher noticed.

"I knew it! I'm right. You don't even need to say anything, little doll. I'm going to make this right. What a shit—Beck."

Smoothing my features, attempting to look neutral, I tried to gain control of the situation and said, "I don't need you to make this right, Ash."

Asher had already closed the subject, though, and moved back from me, freeing me to stumble over the thoughts that rolled like tumbleweeds inside my head.

"I've had enough of this conversation. It's over, and now I know what I gotta do. Let's eat." Asher then turned and grabbed a plate.

And just like that, the infuriating man put the conversation to bed.

I had to find a way to divert him, except at the moment, he had hopped up on the counter next to me and set a huge plate overflowing with food he made between us and handed me a fork.

"Dig in, Nat. Maybe you'll like it so much, you'll want to come back." And just like that, he had flashed me a big grin, his eyes lit up like big silver Christmas ornaments.

As we shared an intimate breakfast, eating from a single plate, every other care in the world had flitted off into space. My hamsa had dangled from my neck as it always did—until I went to take a shower before going home.

KNOCKED BACK into the present, I gritted my teeth as I muttered, "The bathroom," to myself. Damn, my thinking had gone on a long-term vacation that day. Before I took a quick shower, I had taken the necklace off and never put it back on, all because I was too smitten and distracted.

I hurried the hell up, slamming the rest of my groceries on the conveyer belt, paid, and got the hell out of the store. After I rushed home and tossed the cold stuff in my fridge, I dashed to Asher's place.

eleven

Go Directly Home

Asher

Aᴀ̲ꜰᴛᴇʀ ᴄʟᴇᴀɴɪɴɢ up and dressing in jeans, combat boots, and a black shirt, I walked back into my bedroom to find the luscious pair in my bed wrapped around each other, asleep once again.

Oh well. I headed to my garage, then backed out the driveway in my SUV. I'd grab coffee on the way to meet Big Mike. Now in charge of all my security, both inside the club and out, he had investigated Sienna's stalker and was going to debrief me.

Then I had a new assignment for him.

What the hell was making Natalie so cagey? I'd had Petey on her at the Tunnel, but she was giving him lip, and he didn't like the conflict. The guy might resemble me physically, but emotionally he was a cream puff. Pete hid it when it came to the girls and customers, but when it came to me, he couldn't. I knew his feelings were getting the best of him, and he wasn't going to be able to find out shit when it came to Natalie. He felt too guilty over her almost getting hurt on his shift.

I steered my monster of a truck into the parking lot of the local coffee joint, grabbed a large cup to go, and headed straight to my club. The Electric Tunnel was the center of my universe. I loved the fucking place, the large purple lightning bolt on the roof, my constant beacon,

64

welcoming me home day in and day out.

The club now known as the Electric Tunnel had started out years before as a shithole known as the Tunnel-O. I'd won it in a bet, back when I was still wet behind the ears but thought I knew everything. Marv, the original owner, threw the joint in the pot during a late-night poker game in the back room of the last club I managed. Hell, he was dumb.

Once the club was mine, I'd renamed it as the Electric Tunnel. It had been open for seven or eight months when Lila walked through the door, looking for a job. I had a good number of girls working the joint at the time, even during the remodel, but once I'd transformed Lila into Sienna—shit, she was different. She started out waiting tables, and then became a freaking star. Lit up the stage, electrified the whole crowd, had men panting in their seats for time with her. Eventually I had to keep her onstage and off the floor for her own safety, and let all my other gals reap the rewards of how sexually charged she got the audience.

By the time I wandered into the Leop that day five years ago and discovered Natalie, my place was stacked with talent and decorated like a fricking jewel. It was top-of-the-line, plush, VIP all the way. I was also making big coin and had no debt because I'd won the club as well as the building it was in free and clear, and had bankrolled the renovations with money I'd saved from my years as a manager.

Strolling through the Leop years ago, I was just under thirty and rich. Richer than I ever imagined. Now I was even richer, and I was determined to figure shit out with Natalie.

Pushing a tiny pang of guilt over last night's ménage to the back of my mind, I unlocked the back door to the Tunnel. But the internal debate waged on.

She didn't want any strings.

Well, I have needs.

Coffee in hand, my feet up on my desk, I pretended to stare at my boots while I went over last night's tryst in my mind. I listened with half an ear as Mike filled me in on the ass-wipe who was stalking Sienna. The jerk actually had the nerve to watch her from across our driveway before we left on our overnight in Red Rock, and the audacity to leap onto my stage. *Her freaking stage.* Besides being my headliner, Sienna was also my partner, so she owned the club's stage both literally and figuratively. Now she had a psychopath stalking her, and another man pursuing her romantically. My head ached just thinking about it.

Mike interrupted my thoughts when he said, "Listen, boss. I got this. This yokel stalking Sienna is a nobody. He wants to put her in dirty porn films, as if she'd ever agree. I'm not gonna let him get that close."

I nodded my head. The man sitting across from me had been with me since he was just a kid. Mike was loyal and devoted, earning my trust long ago. He had a ton of friends thanks to his dad's deep pockets, and even though he and his dad were estranged, Mike didn't see any reason why he shouldn't use those connections when he needed to.

It was as easy as pulling a lever on a slot machine for him to get background information on the jerk bothering Sienna. Absently, I wondered if we should do the same for the guy who was pursuing her romantically. With Mr. Adult Moviemaker out of the way, I sat up and leaned across the desk, taking a more serious tone. "What about the guy she likes? Sienna thinks she's being all covert, and I'm letting her have that play, but are you keeping an eye on her, making sure she's protected?"

My right-hand man stared me down as though I just asked him if he had a dick. "Yeah, I am. Don't insult me."

All he got in response to his back-talk was a chin nod. We were two swinging dicks in my office, seeing who had the bigger cock.

Mike stood up and said, "That all, Ash?"

He seemed a little off, but I didn't have time to worry about it. I had other shit on my mind. I made a mental note to check in with him personally when this week settled down.

"Nah. Sit back down. I got something else to ask you. This goes no further than this office. You got me?"

"What the hell you going off on?" Mike said, practically snarling at me as he dropped back into his chair. "You know I always got your back, keep your shit to myself."

Leaning a little closer, I dropped my voice and told him, "I know who Natalie's baby daddy is, and I'm gonna find the prick. Make it right for her."

At this, the two hundred pounds of muscle in front of me stiffened, then started to squirm. "Um, you sure you should be wading around in that, Ash?"

"Yeah. It's no secret we've been sleeping with each other for years, and I want to do something right for the girl. Crap, I've known Natalie my whole life, and she's never really had anyone looking out for her. No one. So I'm gonna do just that."

Mike shifted again in his seat, but stayed mum. So I demanded he spit it out, and he sighed.

"Look, boss, I don't think Nat wants us to make anything right. I think she likes the way things are."

"Nope, I'm going to find this jerk. His name is Beck. Beck Hadley. Actually, *you* are going to find him and I'm gonna get him to pay up."

Placing his fist on my desk and leaning in, Mike said forcefully, "I don't like the idea, Ash. Not one bit. Nat doesn't like us interfering in her personal life, and this is gonna set her off. She can be a mean bitch when she doesn't like something, and she isn't gonna like this, rightfully so. You gave her a good job, security, help when she needed it back when she left the Leop. Let. It. Go. Asher."

I slammed my hand down. "I'm not listening to one of your lectures now, Mike. Find the ass. Beck Hadley, grew up in my old 'hood. Don't start telling me about my rescue fantasies or shit like that. Find him and let me know when you do. Now, get out."

Mike left without any further argument, but I wasn't stupid. He didn't like the idea and would try to talk me out of it.

Too late. As sure as my club smelled like stale alcohol, lingering secondhand smoke, and sex from last night, I was going to get Natalie what she was owed.

Why? I didn't know. I couldn't really want more than the occasional sleepover—I wasn't built for more. But maybe with some extra cash, she would have more time for me. Just a little more time and attention, that was all I wanted.

Right?

All of a sudden, tremendous guilt washed over me about my recent three-way. Leaning back in my chair, I ran my hands through my hair, wondering if it was too early for a shot.

But I knew what I really needed.

A reality check. A stiff one.

WITH MIKE out doing some research and hopefully dropping his strange and ornery mood, I decided to take a spin through my old neighborhood. I had some shit to do for the club, so I figured while I was out, it was no biggie to ride down through my old stomping grounds. It had been a while since I'd been back, and I had no idea who was still left behind or what had become of most of the punks I knew back then.

I started up my SUV, letting the windows down and running the

AC at the same time. It might have been winter in the desert but it was still warm, and I was hot. My internal temperature was rising not just from the air, but from my hot-blooded temper boiling up inside me. Pulling out of my parking lot into traffic on my block, I thought I had everything I ever wanted. I had money, a nice house, car, bike, and of course, pussy, so why was I suddenly wanting more? And feeling so shitty about the threesome from the night before?

My car pointed toward life as I used to know it: a crowded, run-down subdivision housing bartenders, performers, cocktail waitresses, blackjack dealers, waiters, and strippers. Those were our parents. No one worked banker's hours and everyone had to pay the bills, so they had looked out for each other, watching each other's kids, running errands. We were all lumped together for dinners or sleepovers at the home of whoever was in charge for the evening. A whole gang of us grew up in a heap, knowing how to push one another's buttons, covering for each other when we were teens, hanging with the only type of people we ever knew, and making the best of it.

With one hand on the wheel, the other hanging out the window, I slowed down and peered at the tiny place I lived as a kid. The place I called home after my mom dumped me with the neighbors. It was too much for her—working nights as a "dancer" and taking care of me during the day. She ran as fast as she could to God only knew where. I didn't care. I'd never even tried looking for her.

Natalie had been doing the same shit as my mom endured, for too long. She deserved some financial help, and when I found that jerk, Beck, he was going to pay up.

As for me, I couldn't even think about making Natalie long-term promises, not that she wanted that. Or did she? Could I do it? Did I want it?

What I could do was help her get what was coming to her, a favor from one childhood friend to another, not from a lover to his woman. Beck was always wild for the girl, and Natalie used to flirt like heck with him. I laughed to myself as I thought back to her nonstop flirting with the boy. It used to bother me a little when we were young and somewhat more naive that she was so gaga for a guy with so few prospects, but who was I to talk. I spent a good number of my adolescent days exploring the landscape of teenage girls in our neighborhood.

I came to a stop in front of where Beck grew up. The place was run-down, almost dilapidated. I wondered where the prick was, what he was doing. Did he get out like me?

smoldered

I got out, right?

Well, whatever he was doing, he had a kid, and he needed to do right by him. Let Natalie make a little better of a life for herself. Even better than the Tunnel, maybe help her go back to her old dreams of doing something else, with someone who deserved her greatness by his side.

As sentimental as I was over the woman who had only been to my home twice, I couldn't be that dude for her. No matter how guilty I felt, I liked threesomes, anal sex, and sixty-nine too much; I was a voyeur and wasn't giving that shit up. If I did, I had a feeling I would only end up straying later on—wouldn't I?

Natalie wasn't totally vanilla. She asked for it hard, took me rough in her grip or mouth, and gave back as good as she got. But still, was that enough? Monogamy was such a foreign concept to me, but there I was thinking of Natalie, and Nat alone.

I sped away. I'd done enough wallowing in both my past and ridiculous guilt over my ménage with Penny and Larken for one day.

Leaving the old place filled with my best and worst memories behind, I set my eyes on the road ahead. It would be better for everyone if I focused on the life I'd built for myself, my future, and my liquor vendor where I needed to stop and check out new wine selections.

69

twelve

It Was Two Women and a Russian in the Bedroom

Natalie

ALL I could think about was my hamsa. Why I wanted it so badly, I didn't know, but for some reason it meant the world to me, even though I had no idea who had left it for me. It felt silly, placing so much stock in a silly superstition, but Quinn and I needed as much luck as we could get, and for some reason that necklace gave me comfort.

As I pushed my gas pedal like I was in a drag race, my mind spun. I needed my charm. There was nothing rational flitting through my brain, simply a pure unadulterated drive to get my freaking hamsa. Just like I made fun of the women who hurried to yoga, getting themselves all harried to go relax, I was a lunatic rushing to my supposed peace.

I didn't even recognize myself as I parked along the sidewalk in front of Asher's McMansion. I'd only been there twice, and here I was showing up unannounced. Ringing the bell once, twice, and then hurrying to the back when no one answered, I found the cleaning lady locking up Sienna's carriage house in the back of the property.

"Hey, excuse me, I'm Natalie. I left something behind at Asher's place last week. Can you let me in?"

She stared at me hard. "No. Mr. P. says no visitors," she said in a broken Russian accent.

smoldered

"Yeah, I know. It's awkward and I'm sure he said that, but I only have to get my necklace," I said while pointing to my neck like an absolute idiot. She might have been rough around the edges, but the woman spoke English.

Immune to my pleas, she just shook her head from side to side.

Shit.

Finally, I had an idea. Cocking my head toward the carriage house, I asked, "Is Sienna there? She knows me, saw me here last week. Ask her. She'll say it's okay."

Not waiting for the Russki to answer, I ran to Sienna's door and banged on it with my fist, desperate for the blonde bombshell inside to vouch for me in my psycho state.

When Sienna asked from behind the door, "Who's there?" I yelled, "It's me, Nat! Open up, I just need you real quick."

A few seconds later, Sienna cracked open the door and told me she was getting dressed to go.

"No problem," I said, "I only need you a sec. I left something at Asher's last week when you popped over. Can you tell her it's okay for me to go in?" I pointed at the cleaning woman impatiently waiting behind me.

Sienna looked out from a tiny opening in the door, hiding her bathrobe, and yelled, "Gloria, it's fine. Let Natalie in there to get her stuff." She waved the two of us off, and the cleaning lady turned around, huffed and puffed over to the side door, and let us in.

I motioned that I needed to go upstairs and said, "My necklace is in the bathroom, okay?"

Gloria nodded but crossed her arms, making it clear she was going to stand at the bottom of the staircase until I came back down. So I quickly jetted up the steep stairs, holding on to the railing, and turned toward Asher's master suite.

The door was closed and I rushed it like a maniac, shoving the door open with more force than I meant to. When it banged into the wall behind it, two women inside Asher's bedroom began screaming. I chimed right in with them, and within seconds a very out-of-breath Gloria was muttering in Russian as she witnessed two extremely naked women grasping for blankets and me yelling, "What the fuck? Penny? What the hell is going on here?"

Wrapped in the same big blanket I'd slept in less than a week ago, Penelope finally said, "Shit."

That was all she could come up with, but I still stood there with my arms crossed over my chest, my lungs heaving, waiting for an explanation. I didn't own Asher. I knew he messed around, but with Penelope? She was my friend; she was friends with all of us at the club and we loved her. She must have known about the on-again off-again thing Asher and I had.

And what the fuck? Who was the brunette?

I pinned my eyes on the disheveled redhead I used to call occasionally to meet me for a cocktail or coffee, and tapped my foot. "Move your lips, Penny. What the hell is this?" I shrieked, waving my arms around desperately.

She stood tall despite wearing nothing but a thin sheet falling loosely around her thin frame, and asked, "Nat, honey, what in God's green earth are you doing here?"

Me? She was asking *me* that?

"Not that I need to explain, but I slept here last Friday and left something important behind. Clearly Asher didn't wait long to miss me or fill his bed again."

Penny shook her head. "Sweetie, it's not like that. We were just having fun. I didn't realize things were at a different stage with you and Ash. Honestly, I wouldn't be here if I did, but I thought…I thought you guys were only friends with benefits?"

The Russian maid was now fully enjoying our soap opera with her head pinging back and forth between the standoff taking place right in front of her eyes.

I shook my head, took a deep breath, and said, "Don't placate me, Penny. Just don't. We *are* friends, right? Friends don't mess around with the same man their friend is screwing, even if it's not serious. Where did you ever come up with this being okay? It's not. And obviously Asher knew it because he kept it well hidden, which isn't what he did with his other little pieces of meat he was enjoying. And you…"

Then I turned to take in the brown-haired girl who, although younger than me, appeared anything but sweet. "I don't know who you are and I don't care. So don't even think for one minute that you being here has any impact on me other than furthering my disgust for Asher and his need to engage with two women at once."

I barely came up for air before I stormed past them to the bathroom and poked around in the corner by the mirror, found my hamsa behind the toothbrush holder, and hurried back out.

Penny and the mysterious girl didn't say a word.

As I was leaving, I turned back around and said, "You're just an ego trip for a man who was brutally bruised by his mother leaving him on a stranger's doorstep. He's spent his whole life chasing any female's attention. But don't think for a minute you represent anything more than a stroke to his delicate ego, making him feel worthwhile. He uses women like you to reassure himself that someone loves, needs, and wants him."

I let out a little snort as they stared at me wide-eyed. "Why the hell do you think I never committed? I didn't want to be that woman, the one who spends a lifetime proving she would never stop loving him. Even though I *am* that woman. Now I'm just fucking glad I don't have to worry about that anymore. Asher made his choice when he picked you two to take to bed. Now he's your problem. Not mine."

Not waiting for a reply, I patted Gloria on the arm and said, "Thanks, dear."

thirteen

Beware of Falling Boulders

Asher

As I walked to my car slightly buzzed after leaving my liquor vendor, I picked up my vibrating phone without looking at who was calling. Mindlessly swiping my finger across the screen, I had no idea that small action would mark the precise moment my carefully crafted world would start to crumble.

When I answered, the female on the line spoke in a hushed voice. "Ash, don't be mad, but I think we have a little problem."

"Who is this?" I moved the phone away from my ear to look at the screen. It read Little Red Riding Hood, my contact name for Penny.

Shit. What now?

She must have answered my question while I was staring at the phone because when I put the phone back to my ear, she was saying, "Ash, you there? Did you hear me? It's Penny."

"What, Penelope? What could possibly warrant all the dramatics?"

I copped a bit of an attitude with her, but Jesus Christ, the women in my life were making me bonkers. Sienna with the stalker and the suitor, Natalie not chasing after Beck for money, and now Penny with God only knew what.

"I don't know how to tell you this, Asher, so I'm just gonna say it. Lark and I went back to sleep like you said we should, and all of a sudden the door to the bedroom burst open—"

I ran my hand through my hair and didn't let her finish before I said, "Oh shit. Gloria was coming to clean. That's no biggie, Pen."

I started to zone out from the silly redhead and her crazy problem.

"Not Gloria. Well, yes, Gloria…and Natalie."

"What did you just say?" I snapped back into reality and yelled into the phone.

Horrified, I launched into full-on pacing the parking lot, moving back and forth like a teenage girl who'd just been dumped. All the alcohol in my system evaporated, and I broke out in a cold sweat.

"Fucking talk," I screamed into the tiny piece-of-shit phone again.

"Natalie. She said she left some necklace at your place last week, and Sienna gave Gloria the go-ahead to let her in, and the rest is history. There we were—Lark and I—stark naked in your bed, tangled in the sheets just as you left us."

I couldn't breathe, a wrecking ball beating against my chest, my true feelings only just becoming clear. Fuck, what had I done? "Well, don't just sit there, Penny. What the hell did you do?" I yelled, blindly kicking my boot into the gravel as I wished I could strangle someone right about now.

She went on to tell me the rest, how Natalie had freaked the hell out about the two of them being friends, and me being a needy son of a bitch, and then had stormed out before they could reason with her. And that was it.

I disconnected without a good-bye.

God, I was such a fucker to be blaming Penelope, but if not her, who the hell else?

Me. That's right.

Nothing more sobering than a phone call from one of the two women you'd banged the night before, letting you know the woman you recently realized you might love had discovered the other two still warm and naked in your bed.

Clusterfuck of all clusterfucks.

Now stone-cold sober, I drove straight to my office and threw a flaming baton on an already burning inferno. I threatened to go to Natalie's place, where I'd never gone before. In a text.

fourteen

Ready, Set, Go

Natalie

I'D LOST track of all time. The seconds, minutes, hours, or days that had passed since I left Asher's house were a blurry mess of tears and apologies.

With Asher's mansion looming in the rearview, I'd cried my first round of tears before picking up Quinn and taking some solace in my gorgeous little boy. I smoothed his wavy hair behind his ear as he told me about his day, then kissed his forehead at bedtime, losing myself in his innocent and heart-stopping eyes. But that comfort was short-lived.

After he went to sleep, a second wave of tears swept me away, pulling me under, making it almost impossible to push through and breathe, fight to live. In the end, I only had myself to blame. I was the one who pushed Asher to make a move that one night in his office, fooling myself that we could play with no strings attached for myself. Obviously, it was hard for me, but pretty damned easy for him.

My cell phone rang and rang endlessly. I should have turned it off, but it could have been my mom. It wasn't. The same number over and over. His number twenty-five times. Then the texting began.

One, two, fifteen messages dinged until finally, the last one dropped the big bomb:

> *Asher: I'm coming over if you don't pick up. I don't want to do something you've asked me not to, but I don't have a choice. Answer your phone NOW.*

The phone rang and I cleared my throat, trying to sound strong before I answered. I had no idea whether I was successful because I could barely hear myself over the ringing in my ears, the blood roaring through my body, and the pounding in my head.

"Hello."

"Natalie, let me explain."

"No. No explanations needed. I knew my place in your life. Christ, I'm the one that made it that way. I only answered the phone to say I'm now going to shut it off. If you dare to show up, I'll call the police. Stay away from me."

"Nat, babe. Please?"

"No. I'll see you at work, Asher, and you better not drag this out there. I may have been fine with everyone knowing we were fuck-buddies, but I can't handle being embarrassed like this."

"Nat?"

"Good-bye."

I swiped my finger across the End Call button, powered down the phone, and finally breathed. Not sure if I even took in any oxygen during the entire conversation, I gasped for air, clutched my chest, and doubled over in bed. After years of hiding my feelings below the surface of my hard exterior, playing the role of the jaded stripper, I was a brokenhearted stupid woman.

Precisely the type of woman I never wanted to be.

ARMED IN my tough exterior and an outfit leaving absolutely nothing to the imagination, I stuffed my take from Friday night deep in my purse, changed my clothes, and hurried the hell out of the club, leaving no time for anyone to interact with me. *Assholes.* All of them.

It worked to my advantage that there was yet another Sienna crisis with all the tweets about her being spotted on her *adorbs* sweet little date with her new perfect hunk of a man, Carson. The two of them ended up having to be rescued from a stalker by none other than Asher and Petey.

Couldn't have worked out better for me. Asher was distracted and the whole club was a little off. I worked, slithered all over a suit, feeling his erection as I rubbed my ass up and down his chest, my hands massaging his thighs, giving him the lap dance of his life. That was what I was good at, and I was getting the hell out of here to do precisely that. I needed to be anywhere other than here *STAT*.

I rushed to my car, barely acknowledging anyone on the way out, and hit the road.

Stopped at a light, I grabbed my phone and texted Lynx, who was with Quinn at my place. My mom didn't take him today for one reason or another. She was being all secretive about her plans, and I didn't have time for her personal problems.

I had my own shit fest.

> *Me: Hey, L. On my way home. If you're awake, go home. I'll be there in 10. No need to stay.*

I wanted her the heck out of there so I could start packing. As soon as I could get a flight, I was leaving, heading to Miami. I didn't want to overreact, but Asher had slept with a friend of mine and that other little young thing at the same time. I mean, really? I was pretty sure that having a ménage with a mutual friend and someone way younger and prettier than me definitely violated the friends-with-benefits contract.

Coming to another light, I acknowledged the beep from my phone.

> *Lynx: Are you sure? Just text me when you're home, OK?*

> *Me: OK. Will do.*

Two more lights, and I was walking up the stairs to my place. As I unlocked the door, I noticed the light was on over at the girls' apartment next door, and for a second, I wanted to go over and explain. But it was too messy. I had needed to move on for a while, and discovering Penny and that other girl in Asher's bed just forced the issue.

An unwanted tear escaped and trickled down my cheek. I thought I was all cried out, but obviously not. Crying wasn't usually my thing, yet over the last day, I couldn't stop. Swiping the salty wetness across my cheek and nose, I unlocked my door with blurry eyes, made a pot of coffee, looked up airline flights, and started packing up my belongings.

Within a day or two, I'd be gone.

I had to tell my mom and someone from the club. The someone

from the club was the tricky part. Who? Petey made the most sense. He was the one I could manipulate; I could force him to wait to say anything to Asher until I was long gone.

My mom would be easy. She'd been acting like a real bitch lately and wanted me to go, she said, if I was going to keep up with my "bullshit." Me? She was the one acting all different and distancing herself. I didn't know what made her change her attitude, but screw her. If she wanted to throw Quinn and me out, let her.

With a newfound resolve slapped on like a suit of armor, I pulled my luggage from under my bed and started tossing clothes inside. Luckily, all we had was our personal items and clothing. My apartment was furnished and everything in it could be left in Vegas, along with my shattered heart.

Shoving sweatshirts, yoga pants, and the remainder of my "mom" clothes into a duffel, my hardened shell cracked like the facade it was. Tears freely fell onto the soft fabrics, darkening their bright colors, marking them in front of me, reminding me of how my own soul both changed and was forever marked when I found out I was pregnant.

I was so naive to think I could do it all on my own, survive eighteen years of parenting without a partner other than my mom. And now as sure as my eyes were puffy and swollen from releasing the pain, there was living proof that I wasn't good enough.

Obviously I wasn't smart enough to have a career other than stripping, nowhere near tough enough to be a single parent without running scared from my issues, and it was painfully obvious I would never be enough, let alone be *the one,* for Asher.

Ha. The one.

As if there was *a one* for that man. He was a man whore. Always had been and always would be a male slut.

Moving to my dresser, I balled up my panties, stuffed my bras with socks, and filled another duffel. I ran my hand along the bureau, taking in the photos of Quinn and me—his baby pics from the day I brought him home from the hospital, a number of class photos, and one of just the two of us riding the roller coaster on the Strip. No sign of the man who gave him life and half of his DNA. I'd secured that destiny for my son because I was too stupid and scared to admit I wanted more than just a baby daddy.

I believed I could be enough, both mom and dad to my beautiful boy, just like I convinced myself getting involved with Asher with no ties would be fulfilling. I'd been freaking in love with him my whole life. What did I think would happen?

Wetness was raining, pouring down onto my bureau from my own face, my nose dripping like a faucet. I wiped my tear-stained face across my sleeve as I stared into the mirror at what a failure I'd become. Of course Asher wanted Penny and that girl, sweet little Larken, all bright-eyed and bushy-tailed with a tight vagina, not one stretched by having a baby. Not a woman who stripped and was rumored to do extra stuff in the back room of the Leop.

No, I was disposable. Like I'd always been when it came to Asher.

Thank God I hadn't totally fallen for his charms and given him my heart on a silver platter since my last visit to his house. I had guarded my feelings, keeping them under wraps, and now I was so freaking thankful for that one saving grace.

I finished shoving all my shit in duffels and suitcases, only leaving out enough for a day or two before getting in the shower. I let the scalding hot water fall over me, washing away the old tears and mixing with the new ones, while I leaned against the wall and ran my hand across my chest in a halfhearted attempt to fuse my broken heart. One that had no business being broken.

At nineteen, I gave up the right to a breakable heart when I did what I did, knowing I could get pregnant while doing it, and let it happen anyway. My heart had to remain intact and impermeable for the young boy who was about to wake up excited about two days out of school.

After my shower, I pulled on a robe and opened my laptop. Five minutes later I hit Purchase for two tickets on Monday, ensuring this would be my final weekend in Las Vegas.

Too bad it had to be this Saturday and not the one from the week before that I remembered as my last.

fifteen

Off to the Races

Asher

FRIDAY FELT both slow and fast. Life continually landing more bullets to my heart, I was unable to do anything other than sit in my office like the wounded chump I was.

Before nightfall, I was forced to get the hell out of my own damn head and deal with Sienna, who'd been spotted by the press on the Strip with her new man, having coffee and dessert at the Palace, of all places. Her stalker had been there as well, and I spent the better part of my day running security detail on her.

I didn't know what to deal with first: my own life, Sienna's changing persona, or the security breach at the club. Mostly because they were all connected, and I was getting tied up in the branches of the very own family tree I had built.

All the chaos allowed Natalie to storm into work, then lock herself in her dressing room. When she came out, she was in the most revealing outfit I'd ever seen her wear—a fire-engine-red thong and matching see-through bustier, her nipples on display for anyone who wanted to look, and there were plenty who did.

Naturally, she found herself a very wealthy, willing, and able man to keep her occupied in the back. On the video feed, I watched her shove an already distraught Petey out of the way as she headed toward the back, ignoring his attempts to keep an eye on her. At the end of the night, she grabbed her take without a word on her way out the door.

Everyone knew something was up, but I couldn't say shit. That would make everything worse. She'd asked me not to, and I wasn't poking the bear any more than I already had. So I was forced to watch her work, then take a customer into the back room—where she knew I hated for her to work—and there wasn't a damn thing I could do about it.

I was helpless and a wreck. And distracted with Sienna. *Shit.*

I was disgusted with myself, acting like a college-aged girl when I'd never even taken one credit in college. Glancing down at my crotch, I reassured myself I still had a dick.

A N AWFUL Friday bled into an even worse Saturday. I was running interference with Sienna and her continuing problems, trying to get close to her boyfriend, Carson, in order to keep an eye on their little budding romance, and my life was shit.

I called Big Mike into my office in the afternoon, and that prick only added to the mix.

I thought he was my friend.

With my boots placed solidly on the floor in front of me, my arms laid across the desk as I stared down the target in front of me, I asked him, "What the fuck, man? You got something on this Beck guy? Natalie is more pissed at me than ever, and I gotta do something to help her, get her back in my good graces. Come on, man."

He didn't sit. Pacing the floor in my office, sucking down a bottle of water, Mike said, "Nah, man. Got nada for you. Been all tied up with watching Sie, and now her man is poking around with his own investigation on the stalker dude. My plate is kinda full making sure nothing happens to our headliner, who happens to be the girl you say is like a sister to you."

I leaned back in my chair, never taking my gaze off him. "Come on, Mike. What's really eating at you? You've never told me your plate is full before."

He finally stopped pacing and stared back at me. "Rochelle is gone. Caught that bitch in bed with my dad."

I jumped up and walked around to the front of my desk before saying, "No shit! What a whore."

He put his hand out to stop me from saying anything further while shaking his head from side to side. "Don't. Just don't go there, Ash. No name-calling. She's out. That's it. End of."

Yeah, right. Not for me.

"Fine, have it your way, but if I see her out and about, I'm calling her a whore to her face." I leaned back against the edge of the desk, kicking my feet out in front of me.

"This is exactly why I didn't tell you."

"Well, no shit. I would have told you to get a fucking backbone and kick that bitch to the curb."

He stepped close, too close. "Be careful what you say, Asher. I know what went down in your little suburban compound this week. Remember, no one keeps secrets from me, and I'm friendly with Penny too. Do you blame Nat for turning her back on your slimy ass? Come on, really? It's one thing to not be committed, but to sleep with her friend? In a three-way, no less. It says asshole all over it."

I stood up straight and stared down my bouncer and long-time friend, but he was right. I was an idiot. More than an idiot.

Not knowing how to admit defeat, I said, "Look, I know it was wrong, that's why I need to locate Beck. Call in a favor for me, okay? If I get her some back child support or some shit, maybe she'll at least forgive me."

Mike stepped up to me, puffing out his chest, showing off the couple of inches he had on me, and said, "If Nat wanted this Beck jerk in her life, she'd have come to me herself. She didn't. I think you're making a mistake. You're opening up a can of worms that should stay closed, Ash."

I sat back on the desk and rubbed my forehead. "Listen, I'm not in the mood to be told what to do. I want to get this Beck dude. If you won't help, I'll do it myself."

Mike sighed and shook his head. "Then you're on your own, buddy. I'm not messing with these girls' lives, especially Natalie. She's a good mom, and she made her choices because that's her right. Remember that, Asher."

He didn't wait for an answer. Just walked out the door.

sixteen

Don't Stay Out After Dusk

Asher

Dusk turned into dawn, except my nightmare didn't come to an end with sunrise and the dawn of a new day. Sunday.

While roaming the club, Carson, of all people, wanted to have a heart-to-heart with me. He'd seen me pining for Natalie and wanted to lend his help. Dude probably had ulterior motives for getting in good with me, but I couldn't put him off.

He'd also let me in on a little secret he'd heard from Petey. Natalie was skipping town the next day.

Carson and I stood huddled together against the bar in the corner, whispering to each other like lovers, but it was the only way I could get any information.

I leaned against the ledge, needing the bar to hold my weight, my eyes squeezed shut as Carson explained. "I didn't want to be the one to tell you—shit—you hardly know me, but I think I know how you feel. I would want to know if my girl was getting ready to skip town."

I blew out a sigh. "Why are you helping me, man? I haven't always been in your corner, you know?"

Then Carson told me a little about his life, how his mom ran out on him when he was a kid. He'd been chasing tail for years, never wanted to settle down, and thought he didn't deserve a forever with anyone. It rang a bell. In fact, he sounded pretty much like a carbon copy of me.

I DIDN'T WANT to think too much on the concept of forever—I was a man, after all. Yet I didn't want to lose Natalie, so when the night came to an end, I went to her place. This time I didn't threaten I was coming or give her a clue of what my plan was because I didn't know myself. Instead I acted on pure instinct and hopped on my bike after Sienna left after work with Carson.

The cool air pushed back at me as I headed toward a place I'd never been welcome. A shiver ran through me. Not sure whether it was the nighttime desert air chilling me or the thought of Natalie rejecting me, I talked myself through the ride.

I'm doing the smart thing.

She'll listen to me.

I didn't know what other choice I had. It had been become painfully clear I cared for the woman more than a childhood friend, deeper than just a lover, harder than anyone else in my life. Even Sienna. And I needed to put it all on the line. Fast.

Needing more speed, I cranked the throttle and the bike lurched forward. I felt a sense of urgency I'd never experienced before.

Of course, I knew Natalie's address—I was her boss—but this was the first time I'd seen her neighborhood. It was a far cry from the ridiculously ostentatious tree-lined street in the middle of the fucking dry desert where I lived, but it wasn't ghetto. It was a safe and secure little development of fourplexes with small coupes parked around the lot. Probably students and mostly singles lived inside the medium-sized buildings.

I slowed as I went over a speed bump before spotting Natalie's little red car. Christ, I'd been in the lot at the club the day she drove up in it for the first time, so proud of her purchase, beaming that she'd bought something safe for her son. Obviously, she was making better coin at my joint than the Leop, and had finally been able to get herself a nice ride.

I remembered clear as day thinking to myself that she'd never leave the Tunnel now after a taste of what she could make.

Now as my bike idled behind her car, I kicked down the stand and cut the engine, then looked up at the small structure in front of me, scoping out which one was 4B where Natalie lived.

The chills came back, and I knew without a doubt why. It was because she was leaving, running away from the Tunnel—and me.

It didn't come as a surprise when I knocked on the door that Natalie slipped out into the cool night wearing leggings and a tank, wrapped in a sweater, surprised as shit to see me. She walked outside and shut the door behind her all the way but for an inch and stood directly in front of it, clearly guarding what was behind it. I wanted to go inside and talk, hold her, run my hand up and down her back, be together at her place. But she'd never allow it.

Her lips pressed tightly together, she said just above a whisper, "Asher, what are you doing here? I told you this is not a good idea. Go!"

"Natalie, I can't go. I know you're leaving, and I don't understand why. Can't we just talk?" I asked as I stood there like a class-A idiot.

"No. No talking. It's too painful, and you hurt me. But worst of all, I allowed it to happen." Crossing her arms over her chest, she didn't back down from her post at the door, but she also didn't move to go back inside. I knew I had to be quick and do something fast to convince her not to retreat.

My throat was closing at the thought of her shutting me out for good. I couldn't let her go back through that little crack in the door because I would never get her back out. Once that door was shut, I knew it would be locked, and she might as well throw away the key. Yet all I could muster up was, "Please."

"Please what, Asher? Please let's talk? Please don't be upset that you slept with Penny, along with another girl in the same bed we just slept in a week ago? Please, you didn't mean to beg me to sleep at your place last week and pretend it meant something?"

Natalie was still only speaking slightly above a whisper, but it felt like she was shouting directly in my ear. My whole head throbbed, and my chest was tight with nerves and some weird form of anxiety I'd never experienced before.

After a brief pause, she lowered her voice a little more to deliver the final blow. "How about, please get the hell away from me!"

This was my last chance, and it was slipping away from me like the heat in the desert on a winter's night. If I didn't do something quick, Natalie would be gone just like my mom, except she wouldn't leave her kid behind. The beautiful brunette with crystal-green eyes would slip away, taking her son with her, and I would never see her again. Like my mom never wanted to be found, Natalie would do the same, and where would that leave me?

I reached out and touched her hand, trying to wrap it in my own, but she pulled away. I leaned in close and whispered, "Let me come in, Natalie. I'll be quiet, and we can talk. I want to apologize. I know it's not gonna be easy, but I want to make this all up to you."

"You're not coming in," she spat out. "Not now, not ever. I told you—I don't want anyone near my boy. He's got a big life in front of him, and I'm not going to let anything pull him down."

I was smart enough not to argue with her. This had been a rule of hers since day one, and now wasn't the time to break it. I'd hoped she would eventually lift the ban on me meeting her son. I had only seen him once, when out of curiosity I'd tailed Natalie to school pickup. There had been a rare rainstorm in Vegas that day, and the kid was all rain-slickered up as Natalie hurried him into her car. I didn't get to see much of the kid, and had found myself strangely disappointed.

Sighing, I gave in and asked, "I understand. How about we just go sit over there on the step and talk things over? I won't make any trouble, I promise. I just have to say my piece."

I don't know why, but she acquiesced, and we moved toward the small staircase and settled in on the top step, our thighs grazing as we sat next to each other. Natalie wrapped herself tight in her sweater and placed a neutral expression on her face, even though I knew she was anything but.

With the palm of my hand, I turned her cheek to face me, the pale moonlight shining down on us, dawn only a few hours away like a clock ticking loudly in the background, rushing me to make amends fast.

"Nat, I'm sorry. I know I fucked up, but you said long ago no strings. Yes, this isn't what you bargained for, but still…you didn't want all of me. I don't know—shit—it was wrong, okay? Wrong. There are no excuses. Penny was a bad idea, but she shares some preferences with me, and I guess by now you know that one of those is I'm partial to groups. I always have been."

The woman in front of me looked deflated and defeated with her head tilted down, her shoulders slumped, cradling herself in her own sweater.

She didn't reply, so I went on. "I guess you may think there's something wrong with me. Probably is. But other than being with you, I find it impossible to get charged up unless it's a threesome. Did you hear me? You *alone* are enough for me. Enough in my office, more than enough in my bedroom, with you I only need one woman. When I'm with you, rough or slow, all I need is to see your beautiful smile, and

I'm fucking hard. It's never been like that with anyone else, little doll."

At the sound of my old nickname for her, she lifted her eyes, now glassy with tears, and shook her head, signaling she couldn't take any more. I paid it no mind.

"I'd give it all up in a heartbeat, Nat. I see that now. I don't want to lose the one woman in my life who is enough for me—even though I could never be man enough for you. I want you. All of you with me. Tell me what to do." I leaned closer and ran my nose along her cheekbone, breathing in her pure scent, filling my soul with her, infusing my blood with something better than oxygen.

She remained silent. So did I.

Finally, the one person I'd come to realize meant everything to me—although a day, or maybe fifty days too late—broke the spell. "I don't know what to tell you, Asher. It's pretty much all my fault. Yeah, I said no strings, but what I should have said was simply no. No to anything between us beyond you being my boss. I never did a good job at keeping my emotional boundaries up with the whole no-strings thing, and now our relationship damaged beyond repair. There's nothing you can do. I knew you slept around. I was hip to your proclivities. I'm not stupid, even though I'm only a stripper."

At that, I interrupted her. "Stop. Don't ever say that. You're way more than just a stripper. Shit, that sounds so cliché, but please stop," I begged.

We sat there talking, going around and around in circles. She was enough, she wasn't just a stripper, and I was an ass. We beat the same topics into the ground until they were dust and there was nothing left to say.

She stopped me with her hand on my leg. I looked down at her small palm resting flat on my thigh, and I got a fucking boner. Yes, the man who liked to surround himself with multiple women, who got off on several mouths and sets of hands in bed with him, had a full-fledged erection from one woman's hand resting on his leg.

I shifted a little to somewhat attempt to hide what was happening, and sadly, Natalie took it as a hint to stop touching me.

No, I wanted to scream. Instead I pulled her in for a hug, and she again misinterpreted my actions as meaning good-bye.

She stood. At this point, the moon was waning, the sun about to burst over the horizon, and I began to dread what I would look like in the orange glow of daylight. Not really how I *looked*, but I feared in the light of day I'd be seen for the traitorous asshole I was.

smoldered

I wanted to hide in the shadows of the night, to make amends wrapped in the warm glow of the moon and stars against a background of mystery and suspense. Forgiveness seemed so much more attainable in the shadows, and now brightness was chasing me away, bringing me back to reality where I was meant to live a life without the unconditional love of a woman.

Wasn't that what my mom taught me?

I was in a mental fight with the sun when I heard Natalie speak.

"This is it, Ash. I'm leaving. I know you came here to try and stop me, but you can't. You can't always be my protector, boss, friend, and sometimes lover. It's all too much. Together—separate—it doesn't matter. It's too consuming. You're both my salve and my kryptonite, and I have to get out on my own."

I wanted to roar, but remembered the sleeping kid behind her slightly ajar door. Bracing myself against the railing and the rising pain in my chest, I felt my heart clenching. I squeezed my eyes shut in an attempt to block the tidal wave of emotion from flooding out, and then I remembered my pride.

So I stood up, kissed her on the cheek, and walked away. The sun was coming, and I wouldn't be exposed in the light of day. I'd laid my heart on the line. And I'd be damned before I stood with the hot desert rays beaming, burning down on me, and begged.

Only looking back once or twice, watching the woman I so desperately wanted slip back into her apartment, I jumped on my bike and sped the fuck out of there.

I DROVE FOR an hour or two or three; I didn't really know. Leaving Natalie had left me numb, unable to take responsibility for the role I had played in walking away. Did I just make that choice? It was what she wanted. Right?

Tearing down my street on my bike, I dismissed the unnerving feeling running down my spine. Basically dismissing Natalie's feelings and mine, I had run away. Sped away from it all because it was too much to face. I couldn't admit to myself or anyone else what I had ruined, decimated, and destroyed. Basically I had just walked away from the only woman I'd ever cared about other than Sienna. I had grown up thinking of one like a sister, with my feelings later growing into much more than just friends, and the other had truly become my sister.

Now I needed to get my head right. Desperately.

I couldn't go to Mike. He was being a class-A jerk, and I didn't want to bother Sienna on her day off. She always took Monday to rest and enjoy some alone time. I knew she often dwelled on the past and reconciled her new life as being the best choice, and she needed that weekly affirmation.

But today I needed the only family I knew, my sister, someone who would make sense of all that I had turned to shit.

I pulled down the drive and didn't bother to put the bike in the garage, instead leaving it sitting outside. Normally I was more protective of my bike, but nothing seemed to matter at the moment. Walking over to Sienna's door, fighting the urge to have a drink, I saw it was open a bit. Sighing, feeling a brief lightness at the thought that help was on the other side of that door, I realized the woman who I needed to comfort me must have heard me come roaring down the driveway and was ready—

Except as I made my way to the door and gave a soft knock, pushing it open, my fucking heart dropped out of my chest and what was left of it fully cracked. The place was a mess. There was a broken vase and a used syringe on the floor. Sienna's Adult Entertainer of the Year award lay in the corner on the floor, out of place, and it was eerily quiet.

I screamed, "Sienna! Lila! Sienna?" to no one. Someone took my family, my business partner, my freaking headliner at the club, the closest person I had to a blood relative. *My Sie.*

I screamed again before running out the door, winding my way to my backyard and roaring the entire way, knowing no one was going to answer.

Flipping open my phone, I first called Mike, then left a half-hysterical, half-accusatory message for Carson. Then I stood in my kitchen, wanting nothing more than to break everything in sight, frustrated over the opposite directions I was being pulled in.

Finally, I came to the difficult decision that I had to concentrate on finding Sienna rather than chase Natalie. After all, I'd already pushed her away, and it seemed to be what she wanted.

seventeen

The Game of Life

Natalie
Miami, three months later

I WAS WHIPPING through the grocery store, tossing cereal and other junk in my cart while my mind oddly kept returning to Sienna. I didn't really miss her, we were never that close, but I did hope she was okay and safe. Maybe it was because I had first learned about her being kidnapped and taken all the way across the country by a crazy stalker while in the checkout line when I first moved. There had been a little article on it in one of the trashy rags I liked to flip through while waiting for them to ring up my groceries.

The article had been vague about the details other than some guy who ran a porn studio, mostly filled with underage actors, stole Sienna to be his star. I didn't know anything more than she had been rescued, and I was too stubborn to reach out to any of the old gang to ask.

I didn't care that much. Did I?

So I'd gone about my new life in Miami, trying not to dwell on the past, Sienna, my old friends, my mom, and definitely not Asher. My life was basically the same as before—I worked Sunday through Wednesday, taking Thursday off before going back for the big money on Friday and Saturday. Quinn went to school, had made a few friends,

91

and seemed happy.

I had no one. Nobody.

I'd pretty much resolved myself to a life of loneliness when a divorced dad asked me out last Thursday at the park. He was a good-looking, clean-cut, all-American type, and it was clear he was well-off. George being a full-time single dad to a boy a few years younger than mine meant we had a lot in common. He didn't know what I did for a living, and I didn't feel pressured to tell him. I brushed off the question, saying I was my own boss. *Ha.*

When he asked me out, I simply told him Thursdays were the only day that worked.

Today was the day of the dinner date, and I was hurrying through my usual day-off errands during school hours, and freaking out about going out with a man. Ironic, wasn't it, that I made my living giving men what they thought they wanted, but outside a strip club's four walls, I had zero idea what to do with a strange man, aside from taking my clothes off for him.

Sighing, I lifted the bags into the back of my car—a used two-door hatchback, the only thing I could afford after using the proceeds of selling my old coupe for moving expenses and my first month's rent. As I went about my errands, I desperately tried to keep my mind on George, my date, and not on Asher. Not on holding him tightly while riding his bike, definitely not on the glorious night I spent at his place, and far away from the memory of him walking away at daybreak.

I pushed Asher to go when I didn't accept his apology, but it was my only play. My heart was getting too entwined with him, and soon I wouldn't be able to tear away. Plus, he was playing with fire with the whole Beck Hadley search-and-rescue bit. And there was the little threesome thing. Yeah, I'd known for a long time how he liked groups, but with Penny? I couldn't accept that from either of them.

But when he told me that I was enough for him, that he didn't need anyone else when he was with me, I couldn't stop myself from wavering on the inside.

I was so close to folding, grabbing the man I'd been in love with since I was three years old, wrapping my arms tightly around him while pushing my tongue inside his hot mouth, and taking everything he was offering me. But years of telling myself it would be a mistake stopped me. That damn little angel had reappeared, the one who'd sat on my shoulder for over a decade, whispering in my ear to stay away from Asher, and it was about time I listened.

smoldered

Which left me grinding the clutch on a ten-year-old piece-of-shit car, heading home with only a few grocery bags for my lonely life with Quinn, helping some sleazy asshole build his strip club, and getting ready to go on a date with a guy named George.

George!

My life was a mess, and I had no one to blame but yours truly.

With that in mind, I parked, carried in the groceries, and tried to get myself excited for dinner—and whatever might come with that.

I hadn't a clue.

eighteen

Get Your Game Face On

Mike
Las Vegas

I WALKED INTO the club with a smile on my face. Rochelle was long forgotten. Sienna, who we now all called Lila in private, was back safe and sound, and falling deeper and deeper for a good dude. My job was the bomb, and I was into my new lady. A lot.

As I strolled to the back bar to chat with a few of the girls and hear the scoop on the bachelor parties hitting up the Tunnel that night, I caught Asher stomping up the stairs to his office. He wasn't that moody every day, but close. He put on a happy face for the dancers and bartenders, but when it came to Petey, Sienna, and especially me, his mood came in varying shades of pissy.

Petey had lied. Sienna was his scapegoat, even though it wasn't her fault that she was kidnapped and had diverted Asher. And me? Well, I refused to find Beck Hadley. I had my reasons, and the fact that I wouldn't share them aggravated the boss man even more. So the fuck what. Like I said, I had my reasons. I could handle Asher. We were like an old married couple: we had differences, ups and downs, but in the end, it turned out all good.

Looking over to the stage, I caught Sadie dancing. She was quickly becoming a star, following in Sienna and Petal's footsteps. She would probably be taking over for our very own Sienna in no time. There was no way Carson was going to wait much longer for his woman to give up the stage. I got it. Was struggling with a bit of a similar issue in my latest relationship.

Completely lost in thought, I absently followed Sadie's legs wrapped around the pole and her eyes trained on the crowd, glimmering of sex and lust, tantalizing everyone present. I watched carefully to see who she was setting her gaze on for the evening—to take their money. I was so preoccupied, I didn't notice Asher had come up behind me and was standing right next to me.

"Hey. What's up?"

I noticed he had his club face on, masking the frustration I knew all too well was barely underneath the surface. He might look tough in boots and ratty jeans with a designer dress shirt, but the stubborn jerk was falling apart.

"Not much. Keeping an eye on Sadie. Crowd's been eating her up lately, and I don't want her to get in a situation."

At this, Asher perked up and turned toward me. When it came to his club, he ran a tight ship. "Is that so? What do you think?"

"I got it. She's just attracting a lot of attention, drawing a huge crowd, lots of jerk-offs asking for her. I'm thinking of putting Billy on her exclusively. He's new, but after a few mix-ups, he's got a handle on this job. Kid doesn't drink, smoke, or really do anything. Pretty sure he'd do a pretty decent job of being her eyes and ears."

Asher nodded. "I see. Yeah, that sounds good. Petey still taking good care of Lila and Petal? He okay handling both of them?"

I saw him give a tiny flinch. He was holding back; I knew damn well he wanted to say something about Petey letting a few things slide with Natalie, but he bit his tongue.

"Pete's good," I told him. "Carson trusts him with Lila. And Petal is practically her sister and shadow, so it makes sense."

Glancing back to the stage, doing another check on Sadie, I traced her sightline to a small group of overdressed suits in the back corner, sitting along the navy velour banquette. *Shit.* I decided it was time to send Billy to sniff out the wolves.

Getting ready to part ways with Asher, I turned and he caught my shoulder.

"We're not done," he said.

I lifted an eyebrow. "Okay, what else, Ash? I'm all ears. You know it."

"I found him. Beck. Beck Hadley, the fucking prick who knocked *her* up."

He rarely said her name out loud. *Her* being Natalie.

I steadied my tone, tried to make it sound casual when I said, "Oh, yeah?"

"Yep. Fucker lives right next door to Chey and her husband. Remember Chey?"

"Of course. Natalie's old dressing room partner. Married the lawyer from Reno."

"The one and only. Well, her hubby set up shop here. Got some big contract with that online shoe gig in town, so they bought a joint in the high-rise on the opposite side of the Strip than you. I ran into them a few days ago and when they invited me over for a drink, guess who was coming out of the place next door as I was leaving? *Bingo.* Beck Hadley."

"That's pretty fucking lucky for you." I had no idea what else to say. Again, I had my reasons.

Asher grinned, practically bouncing on his toes as he went on. "I played it all cool. Acted like I couldn't have been fucking happier to see the dude. We're gonna have drinks tomorrow."

"Is that so? What's your plan?"

"Oh, I'm gonna get real close with him, old friends and shit. I'll draw the sucker in and then, boom, turn him over to the she-wolf."

All of a sudden, I felt guilty. I might have had my reasons for keeping my mouth shut, but Asher was my man. We weren't blood, but that didn't matter. I needed to protect him from some ugly shit.

I said carefully, "Listen, don't do anything rash. Keep me in the loop, and maybe I'll meet up with you two sometime. I got your back."

"Oh, now you do?" He raised an eyebrow.

"Yeah. Of course I do, bro." I slapped him on the back and ran off to task Billy with his new assignment.

I needed to call my girl, Lynx. She was just as concerned over this Beck Hadley deal as I was, and we'd forged a behind-the-scenes bond to protect Natalie.

Unfortunately, in order to do that, I would end up betraying someone else.

Fuck.

nineteen

Stop Playing in That Cage

Asher

A s I turned my bike onto the Strip, I felt like King fucking Kong
beating his chest on top of the Empire State Building.

I'd never felt such a natural high as I did when I discovered Beck
Hadley right under my very own nose, living the life in a big rich-
boy's condo. It might have felt better than a few lines of coke when I
accidentally stumbled on his sorry ass.

On top of the world.

Despite the darkness, I wore my Aviators to block the wind and
conceal the pain in my eyes. I didn't talk to anyone about how I was
pining for Natalie, but sadly, it was all I did. My insides were constantly
churning with anger, regret at lost chances, and an overwhelming
sense of powerlessness.

Now a golden ticket was in my hands, giving me something to lure
Natalie back.

That was for later because at the moment, I was driving faster than
I should be to the Strip, as fast as I could to Larken and her little cage-
dancing gig. Even I could recognize the irony, agonizing over one girl
while on my way to fuck another, but there was only so much I could
beat off. I needed some pleasure and pain all rolled up into one—or

two.

There was also the little fact that nowadays I could only get it up by myself to thoughts of Natalie. I could run through my entire mental Rolodex of threesomes, and it wasn't until I gave my mind free rein to think of her that wood actually happened.

And I really hated thinking about her. I wasn't some spineless prick who would walk away from a woman who was hurting, who would allow a girl to intentionally push me to leave, or who would sleep with a friend of the girl I was fucking.

Oh wait; I was all of those. Which was why I hated dwelling on Natalie. It made me feel small.

But now I was going to have Beck and his luxury condo by the balls, and that would make me insignificant no more.

The lights of the Strip lit my way, shining down on my bike, reflecting off the metal, and marking the road to release. Short-lived, but relief nonetheless. I fooled myself into thinking it was okay. Natalie was off in Florida; I knew this much. She was living in a decent apartment, worked for a shit club, and was making good money building some asshole's business.

What I didn't know was how much she could be making if she was in a different club, and what the fuck she was doing in the back rooms. Carson had a PI buddy look into the basics, but he wouldn't let me send someone in the back room of the Peppermint Kitty, so the thought of whatever Natalie might or might not be doing back there was eating me alive.

Slowing my speed, I turned into the valet for Papyrus, the hot night club of the moment on the Strip, kicked the stand down, and threw my keys at my regular guy. I made my way to the front of the line, where the bouncer let me in to the sounds of many moans and complaints from others patiently waiting their turn.

Too bad. I was Asher Peterson, and the bouncers all ended up at my club at the end of the night. Mostly because at my club, the girls took their shirts off, rubbed themselves all over the horndogs, and that was way fucking better than a little risqué dancing in a cage.

Heading right for my usual bar, I grabbed a stool as I nodded toward Chico, my regular bartender who knew my drink. With a frown, I looked up at the ridiculously dumb palm tree hanging upside down from the ceiling over the cage that housed a scantily-clad Larken, and realized just how regular this had become.

This being me seeking out Larken and Jewel—not Penny—for a

few hours of pressure release. Penny and I weren't really speaking, each of us playing the blame game. It didn't really matter.

So now I was pummeling Larken with regularity, and she had introduced this other little ginger, Jewel, to the mix. The tiny little redhead with crystal-blue eyes like gemstones was about as wide-eyed and bushy-tailed as they came. New to Vegas, fresh out of school, she wanted a taste of the wild life, and I was happy to give it to her.

I was the absolute worst kind of prick, but I had no other way of dealing with the stress. Pussy was the best stress reliever I knew, and I needed to be balls deep in it to let the pain slide out of me.

Larken looked down from the cage and winked while giving me a salacious smile. I didn't even get a chubby, just turned to Chico and said thanks before tipping back my scotch on the rocks. It burned, chasing away my remorse, making me numb, taking my mind away from Miami. Briefly, anyway.

I signaled for another before asking Chico how business had been.

"Been steady, but rumor has it there's another big hotel casino going up with more shit to do, if that's possible. They plan to have an 'epic club' with waterfalls and pools and shit like that," he answered, using air quotes.

"Well, for me," I said, "the more hotels, the more people there are to come to my place. Nine out of ten suckers end up pulling one after being at my joint." I let myself laugh.

Chico started to ramble on about the theme of the new hotel, and I thought to myself I might even like chatting with the snarky bartender better than watching Larken. I really was reaching a new all-time low.

Sipping my second scotch, still not willing to abandon my plans for later in the evening, I turned my thoughts to the girl in the cage. She was getting a bit attached to me. I'd always been straight up with Larken, and even with being there the day all the shit went down with Natalie, she seemed to be set on catching me on the rebound.

I was trying to keep the boundaries, leave some space, but at the end of the day, I was a hard-up male desperate for the attention of a few females because two of the only three I'd ever cared about had up and left me. First my mom, and now Natalie. Go figure. Thank fuck I still had Lila.

Jamming myself out of my therapeutic bullshit, which I picked up thanks to Mike, I looked at my watch. One o'clock in the morning, and it was time for my evening's snack to come down from her post. Thank fuck.

I fist-bumped Chico before leaving a big tip and roamed to the back of Papyrus to meet Larken. I hoped like hell she didn't want to stay for a drink.

She did.

And I was a sucker for what we were hopefully about to go do, so I gave in. I gulped down a bottle of water while watching Larken sit pretty in painted-on electric-blue leather pants and a tight white halter that left nothing to the imagination. In no hurry, she sipped her Cosmo, obviously delaying my gratification on purpose. We made small talk until the bitch cut to the chase.

Twisting her little toothpick stuffed with fruit around her glass, she said, "Ash, I don't know if I want to ask Jewel to meet us tonight."

"Why the fuck not?" I ground out.

"Because."

"Don't act like a schoolgirl, Lark. Speak up."

Stilling her toothpick, she looked straight at me. "Because I think I like you. Like-like you more than what we currently have. That's why."

I murmured, "Shit," to myself before taking her hand, leaning in toward her face, and whispering in her ear, "I can't do that, sweetheart." My lips grazed her earlobe, stopping briefly to suck on it, enticing her to give up her current pursuit of more with me, and just go back home to bed with Jewel and me.

She shook her head. "No. I deserve more. I've been with you since that crazy bitch raced through your house, calling me names and pointing out your faults."

I was done with trying to convince Larken to come back with me. It wasn't worth it. "Don't go there. And don't ever call Natalie a crazy bitch. That was all me. It's still all me, acting stupid, when I know she deserves better. I guess you're off the hook. You don't have to go home with me and Jewel tonight or any night because you and me—we're done."

She sat there with a look of surprise on her face, her lips forming an *O*, her brow crinkled. "But…?"

"No buts, Lark. This is good-bye. Be good, darling," I said before I patted her on the back and left the Papyrus for good.

I was getting too old for this shit.

twenty

It's Like Riding a Bike

Natalie
Miami

I LAY IN bed, thinking about my date the night before. It was early morning, and I was enjoying some peace and quiet before Quinn got up for school. Trying not to think about being tired later when I had to go to work and stay until twenty hours from now, I reflected on my first time ever going out on a date like a normal woman. It wasn't like I didn't think I was normal, I just had never spent much time with anyone other than nightclub, strip club, or casino people, the kind of people I was raised by. It was incredibly hard to break away, but I did it.

Even if I still worked in the industry, I was now a normal woman after the night before. I was moving on. I lay back on my pillow, sank back into my double mattress, pulled my soft quilt up to my chin, and closed my eyes...

GEORGE HAD rung the bell at precisely seven p.m. like he'd promised. My new sitter, Violet, had already situated Quinn with a game and some cookies, so all I had to do was give him a quick peck on the forehead, grab my jacket, and head right out the door. The truth was I'd done that intentionally. There had been no reason to let George see a slice of my real life yet.

As we'd walked to the car—not a bike or a monster SUV—I'd sneaked a long look at the man taking me out. He'd looked calm and confident in designer jeans, a white button-down with the cuffs rolled up to his elbows, and loafers. Loafers.

I'd never been out with such a clean-cut man before. Sure, I'd danced for thousands of them, but typically they were imagining they were not so honorable or good when I grazed their lap with my ass or ran my tits along their face. With me, they could be the bad boy they'd always imagined being.

And there, right before my eyes, was George opening the car door for me, smiling and saying nice things like, "I'm so glad to be going out."

No leather, ripped denim, tattoos, or boots in sight. I had no idea how to handle myself, but I pulled it together, smiled back, and tried to act as though I did stuff like this all the time.

We went to a cute little Italian joint in South Beach. We were seated on the patio, ordered drinks, and settled in our seats before the conversation really turned intimate. And by intimate, I meant when George said, "So, what do you do?

I'd already heard about his investment firm and how he'd grown it into something big from his father's small business. So in that moment, I made up my mind to be myself, not pretend I was someone I wasn't.

"I dance at the Peppermint Kitty." I had no reason to make excuses. It was what I'd always done, and I had raised my son alone for a decade doing it.

To my surprise, George merely cocked one eyebrow and said, "Really?"

"Yep. I've been a single mom since the beginning. My parents were old-school Vegas night club workers, and I had no idea what else to do to support my baby and me. The rest is history. The Kitty brought me here to help them rebuild, and that's what I'm doing."

He took a long sip of his drink before responding. "Wow. You may be the most interesting woman I've ever been out with. Including my ex."

Not being at all experienced with regular dating, I had no choice other than to take that as a compliment, so I sheepishly responded with, "Thanks."

He leaned in at this point but his eyes remained focused on my face, not wandering once to my cleavage. He'd been a perfect gentleman so far, his whiskey-colored eyes trained softly on me, hanging on every word I said, not passing judgment. And yet my stupid fucking brain kept thinking of scotch when I looked into his eyes.

Every time I looked into George's eyes, I was forced to lower my gaze and push thoughts of Asher out of my mind.

The man had walked away. Yes, I'd forced him, but he still went willingly, and that had been it. Good-bye and good luck.

Eventually my thoughts stopped wandering and my date and I drifted to a safer topic. Our kids. We laughed and joked about various stages of development and the sometimes awkward moments of being a single parent.

Then George told me, "My wife just didn't want a family. She got pregnant by accident and shortly after Nathan was born, she wanted more fun than diapers and evenings in with takeout. She signed over custody for a lump sum, then took off. Where to, I don't know. I knew I was picking the harder route by demanding to keep Nate, but honestly, I couldn't stomach her attitude."

I sat there with my hand over my mouth, trying to disguise my disgust. I'd only been able to mutter, "Oh my," when George interrupted.

He narrowed the space between us even more and said, "Nah, don't feel bad. It's all worked out for the best, and I have the resources to give my son a good life. And look at where I am now—out with the most beautiful woman, who understands what I've been through."

With my mouth wide open, I wasn't able to digest his story or his compliments any further. It was all too much. There was no way I could form a response, but I didn't need to. My gentlemanly date slipped his hand across the table and gave mine a squeeze before closing the subject for the evening.

"Enough of that. Our food will be coming soon, so let's not ruin a great night with bad tales."

Or thoughts of a man so opposite of you.

Eating, drinking, taking our time over dessert, I forced myself to relax in the moment, take in the rest of my first normal date, and not linger too long on what Asher might or might not be doing without me.

At the end of the evening, of course George walked me to the door. He wrapped his arm around my waist and drew me close, landing a closed-mouth kiss on my lips.

Desperate to feel something, I'd tried to lose myself in it. Pushing myself a tad closer into his warmth, searching for something so absolutely unknown to me, I might as well have been sitting in a college classroom or preparing for an accounting exam.

I hadn't been able to feel much, but I had no intention of giving up.

QUINN YELLING good morning from the bathroom pulled me out of my fog.

As I slid out of bed and my feet hit the floor, I dug my toes into the little plush rug on the side of my bed, promising myself I would do the same with George. I was going to dig in and plant myself firmly in a normal relationship with a good man. I came here to make a new life, and I was too proud not to do it.

With that, I slipped on some yoga pants and a tank, then helped Quinn get off to school like a normal mom. All before I went to get a Brazilian bikini wax, so I could shake my smooth ass in some stranger's face.

twenty-one

Truth or Dare

Asher
Las Vegas

I SLAMMED MY hand against my kitchen counter and yelled in pain. Fuck, that granite was hard. Fairly certain I'd bruised my wrist, I flung open my giant built-in freezer for ice, kicked it shut, and thought about how stupid it was to have this big house just for me.

What the hell happened to me? I went from being on top of my very own world to moping around the house I once thought was a castle.

And I'd basically just walked away from Larken at the Papyrus, giving up my chance to get off. I was full of pent-up anger and wanted to continue to slam my hand into the counter until it was shattered like me.

Except I was standing in my freaking kitchen, acting like a New Age idiot, taking deep breaths trying to calm myself. All part of trying to be a better man. Like leaving Larken. I didn't want her and her overzealous demands for intimacy.

I shouldn't want just sex with her—and one other person—either.

Filled with self-loathing, I walked toward my home office, holding ice on my left hand. In the hallway, I paused to mouth *shithead*, *cocksucker, motherfucker* at myself in the mirror. It did little to make me feel better.

Once in my office, I sat down in my butter-soft leather chair and swiveled toward the cabinet, using the key to unlock my latest dirty secret. This was a bit worse than my intended escapade with the Papyrus girls. But I needed this.

I pulled the disks from the top shelf and laid them across my work surface.

How many would I need to watch? Would one be enough, or would it take all of them to start to take the edge off?

If anyone knew what I'd been doing the last few months, they would not only laugh themselves silly, they'd probably be tempted to turn me in to the law. I was pretty sure it wasn't exactly legal, but I couldn't give a flying fuck. I needed those disks like I needed air to breathe and scotch to ease my pain.

I slipped one into my computer and leaned back in the chair, its back reclining slightly, and eagerly watched as the screen came to life. The image was clear as day, and a shit-eating grin spread across my face, knowing I had top-of-the-line video surveillance at my club.

Which made it possible for me to beat off to old video of Natalie dancing, stripping, baring herself to everyone but me.

It was sick, as most of the shit I liked was, but it was all I had.

There Natalie was in all her glory, spread across the lap of a married woman seated in a deep purple club chair, her firm thighs capturing the woman's as she lightly rubbed against her. The husband watched from the navy bench in the corner as Natalie leaned over the woman. I could tell she was blowing in the woman's ear, making a humming vibration. It was a signature move of Nat's, and one I knew made married women in particular go nuts. After all, I used to be her boss; I knew these things.

I dipped my right hand—the non-injured one—into my pants and immediately made contact with my dick. I was commando, so it didn't take long to take hold of my engorged and ramrod cock. Squeezing its length, pulling and tugging on it, roughing the sucker up, the combination of pain and pleasure forcing a little pre-cum to drip out, I moved my focus back to my giant computer monitor.

The woman on the screen was squirming and squeezing her legs, obviously trying to maintain some decency or increase friction. Who cared? I wasn't watching that woman. My eyes were homed in on the brunette with fire-engine-red streaks running through her hair. Those flames of red were fitting. Fucking woman set me ablaze every time I saw her. Those freaking locks that used to brush over me on my office couch were now grazing some Mrs. Happy Homemaker, and I was jealous. Seething mad. Why couldn't I just feel her hair graze my cheek one more time?

My hand now pumped faster, up and down, working my own shaft, chasing a brand of relief that I knew would never fully come.

Natalie's head turned a bit to the side and I caught her profile on the tape. Long lashes, high cheekbones, gorgeous shoulder— Oh God, I was going to blow. Like that, I made a mess in my pants.

I was no better than a teen sneaking off to watch porn on their dad's laptop, whacking off into a bunch of tissues, and yet I wasn't done. My new routine had become all too familiar. I would stay and watch the films, rising to the occasion again and again.

To SAY I didn't get much sleep would be an understatement, but I didn't give a rat's ass. Tonight was the night I was meeting up with Beck to finally set my plan in place. It was a simple plan; I didn't even need to be a genius to come up with it. Make friends with Beck again, reminisce about old times, insert myself into his life, take mental notes on his spending and lifestyle, drop hints about Natalie during one of our upcoming walk-down-memory-lane sessions, take his temperature on where he stood, and eventually turn him over like a prize fish to my girl.

Natalie would get her cash, I would get all the credit, she would come back to Vegas, and we could try again.

My mood improved just thinking about it as I begrudgingly got out of bed and drove over to the Tunnel. As I pulled into the parking lot I checked my phone, finding a text from the man of the hour himself.

> Beck: *Hey dude, drinks at 7? How's the bar by the fountain? Across from my place.*
>
> Me: *Sure. Good. I may be a little late. Gotta make sure the Tunnel is set to run for a few hours without me.*
>
> Beck: *OK.*

I knew I'd be late; the jerk could wait for me. I would show up when I was damn good and ready.

Walking into my own little empire—well, mine and Lila's—I ran straight into the woman herself. Lila had been my business partner and closest friend for years, but that friendship had been a little rocky since she was kidnapped. I had no idea at the time that my decision to go after Lila rather than chase after Natalie would eat at me like it had, and as a result I'd been snippy with her since she got back from the Bahamas with her man, Carson. The big ex-FBI guy was giving me shit for it, and I knew I needed to back down. Christ, I loved that girl, would do anything for her, and I needed her voice of reason, not her anger directed at me.

I must have zoned out because when I ran into Lila, the next thing I knew she was poking my shoulder and saying, "Ash, you okay?"

I waved her off. "Yeah, all good."

"Listen, can we talk up in the office for a bit?" She tilted her head toward the stairs up to my private office. Lila was an equal partner, but the office space remained mine as she preferred her dressing room or home office.

My jeans felt tight all of a sudden, a drop of sweat trickled uncomfortably down my spine under my black shirt, and I might have started shaking in my boots. Lila was probably going to confront me about how I'd been treating her lately, and I was about to lose another person from my life. *Shit.*

"Sure," I said and led her toward the stairs, already grieving over yet another lost "family" member and beating myself up because it was all my own fault.

Feeling like a kid in the principal's office, I leaned into the edge of my desk, my boots kicked out in front of me, as she shut the door.

Lila turned around and said carefully, "Ash, this is hard and you're not going to be happy, but just be open-minded."

Terrified about what she was about to say, I couldn't form words. They were all stuck in my throat, my vocal cords twisted like a traffic jam and unable to make a coherent sound, so I just nodded.

"I'm going to stop dancing."

"What?" I yelled.

She frowned, probably mistaking my raised voice for anger when it was actually relief and excitement.

"Really?" I asked, lowering my voice. "That's what you wanted to talk about?"

"Yes. That's it. I don't want you to be disappointed in me, but I think it's for the best. Carson won't say anything directly, but I know he wants me all for himself. Watching me on the stage isn't easy for him. I see it on his face every night that he's here, and I know he rakes poor Petey over the coals when he's not here. And you and I both know Petey has been through enough."

"Lila, babe, I got you. No need to explain. If you were my girl—in that way—I'd want you all to myself too. And, hey, you're your own boss, so you make your own rules." I ran my fingers through my hair, running the sweat through its waves, making note of how I'd let my looks slump a bit with you-know-who gone.

"Well, I was thinking I'd dance for another month, keep building the excitement over Petal and Sydney before my act, and slide Sadie in after me. She's caught on like fire, and we can give her my slot when I leave."

Lila stepped forward and wrapped her arms around me in a hug, not allowing me to respond. "Ash, I know you're in pain. I love you, and I don't care if you need me to be your scapegoat. I can take it because you saved me from a life that almost destroyed me, a husband who was brutally beating me in the name of God. You took me in, no questions asked, and gave me a job. On top of that, you showed me what *real* family does for one another, so believe me when I say that I will take your attitude with no questions asked. If that's what you need, I'm going to give it to you."

Before I could respond, Lila leaned back in my arms and gave me a sad smile. "But you're a good man, Asher Peterson, underneath all the leather, black shirts, and those ridiculous combat boots. You're a sweet man, and you deserve happiness more than anyone. There's no need to suffer. You need to make things right."

I shook my head. "Lila, babe, I know you love me, but I screwed everything up royally. I had no right to take it out on you, and I'm really sorry. The truth is, I need to figure this out on my own. 'Kay, babe?"

After giving Lila a tight hug, I let her go and looked straight into the depths of her blue eyes, which were really colored contacts, but I was one of the few who knew her little secret. "And I think it's great you're going to set Sadie up to take over for you. The club will definitely feel a little financial strain from you retiring, but we'll rebound. Hey," I said as I smoothed her hair behind her ear. "Maybe you can start taking over some management?"

She nodded. "I have some ideas, Ash. Good ones, I hope, but I'm thinking a few business courses may be good for me. Then maybe I can roll out some of my plans for you."

I stared at my girl, taking all of her in, thinking about the scared runaway she had been and the confident woman she'd become. I'd always known that bringing Lila on board was smart, and now I was even more convinced.

"Of course. I'm behind you. Now, get," I said, taking her by the shoulders and turning her toward the door. "Go figure out how we're going to bring in several million bucks without you headlining." Then I gave her a light slap on the butt to lighten the mood.

Lila paused at the door and turned, her blond hair framing that beautiful face, and said, "Don't worry, Ash. I'm going to make it all right here. You just worry about finding your happiness."

I gave her a tight smile. When she shut the door behind her, I turned and walked back to my desk and dropped with a sigh into my chair.

Happiness, right. Like that'll ever fucking happen.

twenty-two

It's All Smoke and Mirrors

Mike
Las Vegas, three weeks later

I LEANED OVER in bed, glancing at the clock before rolling back, settling my hands behind my neck, and shutting my eyes. I had five or ten more minutes before I had to get up and shower. The clock might have said six p.m., but I didn't keep regular hours, and who was I to turn down a little afternoon delight?

I would have liked a repeat performance in the shower, but Lynx was on the phone with Natalie, and I knew for certain that Lynx hadn't told her we were *a thing*. In fact, no one really knew we were doing whatever it was we were doing. There was a lot that needed to go down for us to be official, like Lynx quitting her job with that escort service that she thought she so desperately needed to survive.

I should give her an ultimatum, but I couldn't bring myself to do it. So I was stuck sneaking around, wrapping my dick up tight in rubbers, and hoping Lynx would quit that shit soon.

She was also the only tie left to Natalie, and I felt responsible to keep up with whatever was going on with her. Especially with where I was about to go later tonight.

I heard Lynx laughing on the phone, the sound echoing through my condo from the great room, and I smiled to myself. No doubt, she was probably listening to some goofy story about Quinn. She adored that little boy and wanted only good to come his way.

So did I, which was why I was about to head out for drinks with Beck Hadley for the second time in two weeks. Christ, if I heard that name one more time come out of Asher's mouth, I was going to go postal. Hearing it was like swallowing poison, a burn like no other slipping from my ears, down my throat, making my belly burn with rage.

My boss was flat-out hell-bent on revenge with this guy, and I couldn't interfere. My only option was to helplessly keep an eye on the situation. Eventually it was going to explode and I would have to watch the train wreck, but until that moment, I needed to know where Asher was and what he was planning.

I knew a few things he didn't, and I wanted to make sure I was around when he figured it all out.

I definitely wasn't looking forward to it. Neither was Lynx, which was why she helped me keep tabs on Natalie. Lynx felt the same responsibility to her old neighbor as I did to the man who employed me.

Startled, I was knocked out of my thoughts when my girl jumped on top of me and started kissing me—all over.

Maybe I was going to get a repeat after all?

FRESHLY SHOWERED, I was reaching into my beverage fridge to grab a water before heading out when Lynx wrapped her arms around me from behind and kissed my neck. When I turned around to face her, she stopped me from planting one on her full lips by saying, "She's dating someone."

I knew who she meant. *Goddamn it.*

"Well, it was bound to happen, baby. She deserves a life, yeah?" My words might have sounded calm, yet I was anything but that. Asher would shit a duck if he knew, and the reality of Natalie moving on made my mission to protect her harder.

"Of course she does," Lynx said. "I *want* her to move on, but that's not my choice. You know better than anyone why I can't stand Asher. But this guy she's dating, it sounds like she's forcing it. I don't think she wants to move on. Mostly, I think she has no one down there, and she's grasping for something so she doesn't feel so all alone." She leaned her head against my chest, nestling it where my heart was beating, her breath warm through my lightweight T-shirt.

"Fuck, Lynx. I don't think there's much we can do. She doesn't know about you and me, so I can't get involved, and Natalie wants zip to do with anyone at the Tunnel. And you know I can't tell Asher. He'll hire a plane and drag her right out of Florida, probably chain her up inside his mansion until she swears to give up the dude. I think we have to let her live her life." I smoothed my palm down the braids that hung over her back, and she snuggled closer.

"I know," she murmured against my chest. "I know it's all true. We have to figure out what we are and let Natalie do the same. But still, I don't want Quinney to get hurt. We know he's about to get the wind knocked out of him as it is." She looked up to me, leaning her head back, her golden eyes meeting mine.

I nodded my head in agreement, wanting to talk more about us, but now wasn't the time. I was already late for my rendezvous with Hadley.

"L, I know it's tough, but we'll work it all out. I gotta go. You never know when Ash is going to lose it and drop the bomb."

Lynx stood on tiptoes and planted a kiss on my cheek. Grabbing my track jacket off the back of the chair, I turned to say good-bye and caught her worrying her bottom lip. "L, look at me. It's all going to work out. I care about you, and it's all going to be fine."

She didn't respond. I took one last look at the gorgeous woman leaning on my kitchen counter, her hair still wet from the shower, her tiny frame swimming in one of my T-shirts, and my heart swelled. But knowing where she was going and where I was headed made my head feel like it was going to explode.

Who had time for that?

No one, so I pressed forward.

twenty-three

Caught with My Pants Down

Natalie
Miami

THURSDAY HAD come and gone four times since our first date, and I'd tried to convince myself that what I felt with George was passion or heat, when I knew it was anything but. The gentleman had wined and dined me on my night off each week, and on the weekends we'd had brunch together with Quinn and his son. George had played tag with the boys at the playground, and once had sneaked into the club to see me.

Although he kept to the back, hid in the shadows, and only stayed for a half hour.

Thursday was here again, and as I walked the grocery store aisles searching for corn-syrup-free snacks for Quinn, I repeated my recent mantra to myself: *George is good for you. George is great for Quinn. Florida is better than Vegas.*

At the end of the day, it was bullshit. Life with George in Florida was nothing but normal, predictable, and painfully fucking boring. I barely recognized myself when I sat at brunch like a desperate housewife in skinny jeans, a big bulky taupe-colored sweater, and ankle boots. Often I found myself looking around the restaurants at the perfectly manicured, carefully plucked, and well-dressed women there doing the same as me, and my heart ached. I missed Petal jumping around our old dressing room with her tits bouncing, and I missed my mom and her stories of the good old days. My body screamed for Asher and his gruff words, the way he would pull my hair to the side and kiss my neck. My body had never felt as empty as it did with this perfectly respectable, well-to-do man and our two children between us.

Sneaking a look at the *Gentleman's Quarterly* in the checkout, I swore the guy on the cover was modeling the same type of shit George wore to the club.

Ugh.

If this was truly a full life—here in Florida with my investment banker—I now understood why so many men sought escape in strip clubs. It appalled me the way all these people sat around at brunch, pretending to smile while hiding their true desires. My mind would wander during these meals, and I couldn't help but wonder what those people *really* wanted to do. What would happen if they caught sight of my bare pussy, just a glimpse as I slid up and down the pole in nothing but a thong, my breasts swaying to the music, my recent nipple piercings catching the glint of the strobe light?

Would they get turned on? Or would they suppress it?

I giggled to myself, thinking of a way to test my theories as I threw my items on the checkout belt, and the clerk gave me a wary glance before shaking her head.

As I loaded my bags into the car, I decided that tonight I was going to conduct an experiment. Violet, who had become the only person I considered family in Miami, was taking Quinn to the movies and keeping him for a sleepover. George was making reservations for the perfect evening out, and had arranged for his boy to spend the night with his grandparents.

I had other plans, which I carefully crafted on my drive home from the store.

As soon as Quinn was out the door, Plan B went into play. I'd kitted myself out in a brand new emerald-green thong and matching lace bra, five-inch black-patent stiletto Mary Janes, a magenta kimono-style dress covering all the goodies up, and my hair curled in light waves. Just as I was putting the finishing touches on my makeup, the doorbell rang.

When I opened the door George was on the other side, looking dapper in professionally hemmed designer jeans, a white oxford tucked in, and his standard Italian leather loafers. I grabbed hold of his collar, wrinkling his shirt, and pulled him inside the door, my plan firmly taking root. The poor guy looked a little confused with my come-on. We'd been taking it slow.

Of course we had. Between the kids and the formal brunches, who had time for any sexual urges?

George is good for you. George is great for Quinn. Florida is better than Vegas. My mantra playing on repeat in my head, I added one more message: *You are hot for George.*

I ran my hand down his arm seductively, turning him to me and initiating a kiss. George rose to the occasion, literally and figuratively. Our bodies touched and we stilled, kissing a bit more. There was no grinding, he didn't push himself against me, and I didn't press my somewhat less than hot and bothered body against his.

George pulled away, breaking the moment by asking, "I thought we were doing this right with a fancy dinner and all tonight?"

"Well, I was thinking we could stay in and enjoy some quiet. And each other. Maybe some Chinese takeout?" I said while continuing to run my fingers up and down his arm.

He swallowed. Pretty certain I'd caught him by surprise—he'd probably never been with an assertive woman—I let him take his time.

"Sure. Sounds good."

Somewhat awkwardly, he wrapped his arm around me and pulled me in, tucking my head under his chin, then kissed me on top of my head.

I wanted to tell him to grab me roughly, bite my neck, mark me, get a little possessive, but I didn't.

Instead, I repeated my mantra. *George is good for you. George is great for Quinn. Florida is better than Vegas. You are hot for George.*

Caught up inside my head, I didn't notice George on the phone canceling our reservation until he stood, lightly took my wrist, and led me over to the couch.

"Now what?" he asked.

Now what?

"We could have a drink," I suggested. "Relax, order some food? I could dance for you."

His brow furrowed. "Dance just for me?"

I nodded.

"Where would we do that?" He looked around the room. I didn't know whether he thought he was being punked or just trying to understand *where* we would actually do that.

"Anywhere. I can improvise. The dining room. My bedroom."

George is good for you. George is great for Quinn. Florida is better than Vegas. You are hot for George.

This really wasn't working. This being my attempt at making something out of nothing.

The silence in the room was killing me, so I stood, walked over to the side table, and picked up the remote to my iPod dock, looking for something sensual. Not as obviously screaming sex as Buckcherry, but a little toned down. I found my hips moving to the soft beat of Enigma, the chords pulsing through the room, growing deeper, setting a more adult tone to the moment.

I swayed toward George. He stood and walked toward me, his feet eating up the floor between where he'd been sitting and where I was making a fool of myself. His eyes were hooded and he appeared to be affected by me, but he didn't move beyond the halfway mark. I slithered a little closer, my heels clicking on the hardwood, announcing my arrival.

George swallowed hard, his Adam's apple sliding in his throat, but he didn't say a word. He was entranced by my seduction, and I'd barely done anything yet.

I reached for my neck and started popping the buttons on my dress, releasing them one by one until my cleavage was on display, the edge of my green bra peeking through. Licking my finger, I ran it down my breast bone straight into the valley between my breasts. It was there I paused and lifted my finger, crooking it, motioning for my prey to advance.

Christ, I've never had to put this much work into a man. No wonder those housewives bitch all the time.

Needing a small sign that the man actually wanted me, I held my ground. George moved closer until there was nothing but an inch or two between our bodies. A combination of need and apprehension spilled from his; mine vibrated with nothing but anxiety. There was no pulsing between my thighs, no wetness dripping from my core, and my nipples were only hard from my own fucking finger.

What the fuck?

George lifted his hand and gently slipped it around my back as though he couldn't believe this was happening to him. It was as if he was witnessing this moment as though he were someone else.

I can't do this. The thought hit me like a freight train racing through the night, spreading a fine layer of sweat over my skin and making panic rise in my throat. I didn't want to go through with this, but how was I going to stop what I had started?

That was when a horrible pounding started at the door. Someone was banging on it incessantly, and it sounded as though they were ramming their shoulder into the door. Because this was an apartment, the door wasn't very thick. At any moment, the only protection between us and whoever was on the other side was going to come flying off the hinges.

George froze, his mouth hanging open as his gaze pinged between me and the door. My tits were hanging out and my fingers were shaking so badly, I couldn't close my dress. Damn those fucking little buttons.

Seconds ticked by, and still the man didn't move. I knew I should never trust a guy in loafers.

George is good for you. George is great for Quinn. Florida is better than Vegas. You are hot for George.

My resolve hardened as I forbid myself from repeating that ridiculous mantra anymore. I couldn't talk myself into anything with George; the man was barely equipped to confront who was banging down my door.

Shaking my head as I cleared my thoughts, I thought I heard my cell phone chime.

What is this? Armageddon?

Feeling faint, I took a deep breath and inhaled as much oxygen as I could before I walked over to the door, ignoring the ringing phone and trying to react despite the commotion. Mentally thanking God that Quinn wasn't home, I leaned as close as I could to the door and yelled, "Who is it? Stop banging or I'm calling the police."

The knocking came to a halt. Then the phone started chiming again as I heard, "Nat, it's me, little doll. Let me in. Please."

twenty-four

Let Me Color You a Picture

Asher
Las Vegas, the night before

Back at another bar where I was quickly becoming a regular, I was watching the jumping water across the way and thinking about what a freaking crock it was to have an enormous fountain smack in the middle of the desert, when I spied Beck heading toward me. God, he looked like a first-class jerk in his preppy getup. I knew where the dude grew up, and he certainly didn't wear polo shirts back there.

I lifted my glass and tilted the twelve-year-old single malt down my throat, then signaled for another. I was not on a good path—in fact I was traveling a rather rocky, precarious journey to hell—and I couldn't give a damn.

Three weeks of hanging out with Beck, and I had nothing. The guy was a goddamn sap, boring as all get-out, and nearly pissed himself with excitement every time we got together. The loser almost creamed his pants the one time he came to the Tunnel, and he was one giant question-seeking asshole about the girls there. *Will she do me in the back with her shoes on?* What an absolute idiot. I couldn't believe this was the father of Natalie's son.

Honest to God, he acted like a virgin. If I didn't know Beck had

119

fathered a child, I would never believe he'd ever been laid.

No wonder Natalie didn't want him in the picture.

Here he came, waving and gesturing to me as if he had to take a crap rather than meet another dude for a drink. As he sat down next to me, the bartender—Louie—brought my second scotch. *Thank fucking whoever is up in the sky.*

"Hey, Asher. Isn't this great? You, me, getting together all the time? Never would have thought back in the day that you and me would be buds." The freak plopped on the seat next to me.

I gave a small, barely perceptible nod and tipped my drink back, sending fire racing down my throat, spreading through my belly, warming my insides, making me yearn for a female's touch. A certain female. My mind wandered to Natalie's ass while Beck placed a complicated drink order.

Pulling my head out of the gutter, I felt a hand on my shoulder and turned to see Mike had arrived. *Thank fucking whoever* for the second time in five minutes.

"Hey, man," Mike said to me and lifted his chin toward Beck, sitting pretty in his jeans and a polo, looking like he was a banker. I knew my right-hand man didn't exactly like the dude, and I couldn't blame him. Beck was about a zero on a scale of one to ten, but Mike was taking one for the team.

More than anything, I needed the jerk in order to redeem myself with Natalie. I just hoped to Christ she took his money and didn't get too close to the man himself; I didn't know if I could stand the idiot for too much longer. And I planned on sliding into the picture after I served Beck Hadley up to the woman I wanted to claim.

Mike yelled, "Heineken" across the bar to Louie as Beck sipped on some orange-colored drink served in a martini glass. *What a pussy.* We were a funny-looking group for sure, but I was on a mission, and tonight that shit was getting done.

Screw the small talk. I launched right in with, "Speaking of the old days, Beck, do you remember Natalie? Small world, she was working for me for a while." Then I threw my hand up in the air, motioning to Louie because I needed a fresh scotch, pronto.

Beck brightened and said, "Yeah, of course I remember Natalie. Haven't seen her in years. Not since I left the old 'hood, my man." Something crossed his face, a fleeting look of adoration, compassion, or some other girly emotion before he schooled it.

I tried to hide a cringe. God, I hated when he called me "my man."

smoldered

"Is that so? I forget, when did you get out of the neighborhood?" I asked as I reached across the bar and took my drink from Louie.

"Probably right after Natalie. You know what? It was right after that going-away party for her. The one where everything got so out of control on her birthday, and I decided I needed to do something with my life after seeing all that shit go down. Enrolled in community college two weeks later, got a job bartending, and made my way out. Now, look at me." He waved his hand up and down his scrawny chest like a game-show host, sporting a smirk.

I can't take much more of this loser.

Mike got up and mumbled something under his breath about not being able to listen to the ass, then he headed over to talk to one of his bouncer buddies.

I brought my attention back to Beck. "Hmm. I vaguely remember that night. I think I got pretty faded…I was still hitting the powder back then pretty hard. Had to clean up my act because the Tunnel was just starting to get real, and I needed to be running on all cylinders. Natalie was off to break out of the life too, back then. Shit, we all thought we could escape our destiny. No fucking way. We were Vegas through and through. Look at us. Still here."

I leaned back in my bar stool and closed my eyes for a moment, trying to picture young Natalie. She was curvy in all the right places, so young and vibrant with lush brown hair, long lashes…and not jaded. She had her eyes set on something better.

"…too bad you don't remember."

Deep in my memories, only hearing a part of what he said, I sat up and said, "What? What did you just say?"

Beck leaned in real close, too close, raising his voice a tiny bit, making sure I could hear him. "I said, that night was fucking insane. You, Natalie, and Shayla were high as kites—at least you and Shay were—and you all disappeared in the back room for two hours. The party raged on without you guys, but seriously, *you* weren't quiet, and we all got a good idea of what was happening. That's why I said it's too bad you don't remember. Must have been one hell of a good time."

I just stared at the man, unable to take my eyes off him, bearing down on him with my evil gaze, begging him to tell the truth—not some bullshit story. *Because that did not happen.*

I started running my hand through my hair, over and over, and said, "Dude, seriously, don't make shit up about me. I don't particularly like it. Fucking hate it."

The guy was a flat-out liar.

Beck held up his hand like he was taking an oath. "I swear, my man, I'm not. I almost blew a wad in my pants listening to you guys. Afterward you came out with just Shay—danced for a while, grinding all up on her, tossing back some more booze before Lee drove you home."

"You're bullshitting me. I was not with Natalie back then. She was just a kid. I fucking knew her my whole life, and she was practically a baby at that party. I think it was *you*, and you're feeling guilty."

There. Now I was finally getting to the point of why I was hanging out with the prick. How dare he try to place blame on me when it was all his doing? I didn't care that I was already buzzed, I flicked my hand in the air, grabbing Louie's attention.

Beck shook his head emphatically. "Nope. No way it was me. I wouldn't have the balls to be with one of those girls, let alone both at the same time. Plus, Natalie never came back out of the bedroom, so when you left, I headed back there and found her curled in the corner crying. At first I was pissed off, worried she might have been forced to do something, but she quickly set me straight. After insisting that the whole thing was consensual, all she did was rock back and forth, crying, holding her stomach until she fell asleep on the floor in my arms. When I woke up in the morning, she was gone." He shook his head again, frowning regretfully. "That was the last time I ever saw Natalie. She turned nineteen that night, and I got to hold her in my arms. Too bad she was a sobbing mess."

When he crossed his arms over his puny chest, I wanted to break the fucker in half. Why was he getting pissy with me? This was the first I'd heard about this obvious crock of shit. The first time I slept with Natalie was in my office on the couch. Not in the back room of some party with that skank Shayla and a bunch of voyeurs listening in. No fucking way.

"That's crap, Beck. You sure you never slept with Natalie? You know she has a kid?" Pissed off and determined to get Beck to admit the truth, I barely noticed that Mike had sidled up, apparently ready to rejoin our little group.

Beck's eyes grew huge. "A kid? You're shitting me? When?"

I pointed my finger at the little prick. "I thought it was you, but you're saying you never slept with the girl? You always liked her, followed her around."

"Well, yeah, I liked her, but she never returned the feelings. In fact, the closest I ever got to her was the night she cried in my lap after sleeping with you…and Shayla. Who's the asshole now?"

Itching for a fight, I rose from my seat, ready to pounce on Beck. I jumped, surprised when Mike put one of his huge hands on my shoulder and forced me back down.

I shrugged Mike's hand off and leaned forward, pinning Beck with a glare that should have scared the shit out of him. Slowly, I gritted out, "What. Are. You. Saying?"

Beck narrowed his eyes. "I'm saying you screwed both Natalie and Shay while the whole party listened in on your coked-out, drunk ass pounding the two of them. Then you left Nat a crying mess." Then he stood and turned to leave with the upper hand in his back pocket. "I'm out of here. You were always a jackass, Asher. I thought maybe you'd changed, but you haven't."

I didn't respond. Cradling my head into my hands as I leaned on the bar, I tried to think through my scotch-induced haze. Mike's hand landed on my shoulder again, and I looked up. "What the fuck, Mike? Did you hear what that jerk just accused me of?"

"Yeah, I did." He took the seat Beck had vacated and said, "I think you gotta let it go. He doesn't know shit and you need to move on. This is a crazy wild-goose chase, Ash, and Natalie is gone. Move on. You can't dwell on shit that happened a decade ago." He held up two fingers to Louie, signaling for two more of what I was having.

"Move on?" I shouted, not giving a shit that we were in public. I ground my teeth, leaning into his face as I spat out, "Did. You. Hear. What. He. Said? Beck Hadley didn't have sex with Natalie. I did. Ten years ago, I had a threesome with Natalie and a skank we grew up with. And I was apparently too coked up to remember."

Mike suddenly became fascinated with his phone on the bar, spinning it around, not daring to make eye contact. So I ignored him, knocking back another single-malt scotch before throwing a wad of cash on the bar to cover the tab.

Standing up, I said, "Mike, get me back to the Tunnel. Set up a limo to the airport, and get me a flight to Miami *now*."

Lifting my phone to my ear as I walked out of the club, I said, "Hey, Carson. Sorry, man, but I need you to get a hold of your detective friend right away. I'm on my way to Miami. I know who the father of Natalie's baby is…"

twenty-five

I'll Take What's Behind Door #3

Natalie
Miami

WHEN I heard Asher's voice addressing me by that stupid pet name, I laid my palm flat against the wooden door, the burning connection between us running up my arm and coursing its way through my body. And I hadn't even opened the door.

Breathing had completely ceased for me as I tried to figure out what to do with the dumbstruck man standing behind me—and the obviously irate one on the other side of the door. Was there a third option?

Words bubbled up in my throat, but I was having trouble putting them together into something understandable. George approached me and the door, which quickly snapped me back to reality. As he was about to speak, I held up my hand and shook my head while mouthing *no*. Hearing a man on the other side of the door would only inflame Asher more.

Gathering myself, I closed my eyes, leaned against the cool wood, and said, "Shhh. Asher, step back. I'm coming out."

Opening the door a crack, I slipped out into the muggy Florida night and took in a disheveled Asher slumped down next to my door, sitting on the concrete with his head between his legs.

"Ash? What are you doing here?" I whispered, closing the door behind me.

He held his head up, and I expected him to shine his silver eyes on me. But tonight they were a deep smoky-gray rather than the silver orbs that normally smoldered for me. Dark and full of animosity, they were like storm clouds threatening an angry, ominous rain. And they were narrowly focused on me.

I watched his Adam's apple bob as he swallowed. "Isn't this familiar?" he said. "You sneaking out in the middle of the night to sit with me outside? Keeping me away from what's mine."

I slid down the door and crouched on the damp concrete floor next to him, the hem of my dress riding up, making it impossible for me to sit comfortably unless I straightened my legs out in front of me. My hand reached out of its own volition and stroked his shoulder until he flinched and moved away. Deciding to play dumb, I said, "I don't know what you mean."

How did he know about the man on the other side?

Asher combed through his ratty hair, reeking of the booze that seeped from his pores, making it clear that it had been some time since he showered, but not since he drank. He reached into his pocket and pulled out a pack of cigarettes, something I hadn't seen him do in over a decade. My mind flashed back to a brooding Asher as a teen, sitting on the steps to his house having a smoke, and I smiled.

"What's so fucking funny, Natalie? Why are we sitting on the damn concrete when we could be inside your place? You don't want me to come in and see…who?"

He inhaled as he lit his cigarette, the ember crackling and burning brightly as he drew air through it. Impatient, he flicked at the cigarette with a finger, prematurely trying to dislodge ash that hadn't formed yet, a nervous tic of his I'd forgotten. When I didn't respond right away, he glanced at me, the cigarette's glow reflecting in his tortured eyes.

Looking away, I sighed. "I'm on a date, Ash."

He didn't say a word, just continued to puff away. Why this information didn't set him off, I had no clue.

I ran a hand down my thigh, smoothing my dress. "Nothing's funny. I was actually thinking back to the last time I saw you smoke. God, we were kids. You always broke all the rules."

He stubbed out the cigarette and turned toward me so fast, I thought he might get whiplash. His scotch-flavored breath hit me as he opened his mouth to yell, "ME? I broke all the rules? What about the night you had a threesome with me and Shayla? How many rules did you break that night?"

My mouth dropped open. *Shit. He found Beck.*

Asher glared at me, then stood and paced the small hallway balcony outside my apartment like a panther stalking its prey. I was unable to move despite the fact I was the prey being hunted.

"That's right, Nat. I just learned you never slept with Beck fucking Hadley. In fact, he claims to have consoled you after a drug-induced orgy between you, me, and Shayla at your birthday party ten years ago. A threesome I don't remember, which clearly you must have figured out by now, but you certainly have the evidence that it did actually happen. So, yeah, I want to know who or what you're hiding on the other side of that door. And I couldn't care less if you're on a date. I'm not talking about him. I'm talking about *our* son."

"Asher. That's not exactly what happened." I stood up and walked toward the half-crazed man.

"Oh yeah? Stop, Natalie. Where's the kid? Let me have a look at him. You've certainly done a bang-up job of keeping him from me. I've never even laid eyes on him, and he's mine." Asher stood tall, towering over me, a huge hunk of muscle, his eyes smoking clouds of fury, but I wasn't scared.

Fear wasn't driving me as I shouted, "Enough!" Warm, salty tears ran down my face, a complete contradiction to the fury that shook me.

At the sound of my raised voice, George decided to make an appearance. I didn't know whether I loathed him for waiting this long or hated him for coming outside at all, but it didn't matter because at the sight of him, Asher yelled, "Get the hell out of here! You have no business here, and unless you want me to physically remove you from the property, I'd move pretty fucking fast." He whipped his arm toward the stairwell, and that was exactly what George did. He moved as fast as his loafers would let him.

Now that my date was gone, leaving the door fully open in his haste, Asher rushed past me and into the apartment. Following behind him, I breathed in, taking in the unpleasant aroma that accompanied Asher. Even with him reeking to high heaven of alcohol, cigarettes, and sweat, I wanted him.

Now isn't the time for dirty thoughts like that.

He didn't know it, but I wasn't arguing with his current trek, heading down the short hallway toward the other rooms, because

Quinn wasn't there. When Asher got to the first room, he flung the door open, nearly throwing it off the frame. Noting it was not the one he was looking for, but rather mine, Asher seemed to stop and take stock of the time of night. He stood tall, looked at his watch, and sighed, obviously realizing a young kid would be sleeping at this time of night, before gently opening the second bedroom door and peeking inside.

Turning on his heel, he yelled, "What the fuck? Where's the kid, Nat?"

"Not here," I whispered.

"What did you do with him? Where the hell is Quinn? This is not freaking funny. Don't be playing me, Nat. Did Mike and Lynx warn you I was coming? Let me see *my fucking son*." He raged at me, his veins bulging.

Mike? Lynx? I didn't have time to think on how those two were even connected to all this. Asher was about to erupt like a volcano, bubbling over with words spewing from his mouth I knew he would regret later.

"He's sleeping at my sitter's house. I was on a date, that's it. I'm not playing you." I turned and walked to the kitchen.

Time to surrender.

Asher followed, hot on my heels, just as I expected.

I walked straight to the fridge and pulled off the single picture laminated to a magnet. As I turned around, I ran smack into a hard, sweat-soaked chest and looked up to see a face of pure agony. The wavy blond hair I loved so much fell limp and lifeless in his eyes, much like I felt.

Limp. Defeated.

I handed Asher the picture and was surprised to see a single tear roll down his cheek.

Fully knowing why, I watched in silence. Stepping back, I leaned against the coolness of the fridge and looked on as the man in front of me took in a pair of silver-gray eyes identical to his—staring back at him from the photo. Those eyes, a constant reminder of that naive and reckless night a decade ago, were set in olive skin and framed by thick blond waves. Quinn had been begging for a buzz cut in the Florida heat, but I couldn't bring myself to allow him to shave off the golden waves. They were one of the last threads linking me to the man I'd loved for nearly my whole life.

Asher ran a finger lightly over the boy in the picture, tracing his profile with his finger, not looking up for a long time. How long, I wasn't exactly sure; I couldn't mark time or think about the future. It was difficult enough just to breathe as my emotions overwhelmed me, wrapping tightly around my chest and preventing me from drawing air.

When the man, the one who was my *one*, finally did look up, he set the picture reverently down on the counter and said nothing. Closing the distance between us, he lifted his hands and in one sharp tug ripped my kimono dress straight down the middle. As the silk fluttered to the floor, I was left in nothing but the emerald-green lingerie I'd bought for George.

George who?

Asher, now a stinking holy mess, lifted me, and instinctively my legs wrapped around his middle, my thighs gripping him for dear life. His mouth came down on mine, hard, rough, frenzied. Feeling his tongue dip inside my mouth and catch mine, I couldn't stop myself from pushing my heated core toward his erection, looking for the right amount of friction.

He ripped his mouth away and said, "Natalie. I have a son. We made a baby, and he's gorgeous. And, Christ, I'm so mad at you. How could you keep this from me? But I can't even think straight now that I got you in my arms. Fuck, I need to be inside you. Deep inside, punishing you--it's been a long time. But oh God, its gonna be fucking amazing 'cause you're the mother of my son."

There was no need to answer; the wetness seeping from my panties and soaking his jeans spoke volumes.

Unable to respond, I felt my body being lifted and carried toward the bedroom. Now, like earlier with George, I was the one watching from the outside as my life played out in front of me. I sank into the mattress in the darkness, the only illumination a bit of moonlight that streamed through the open window, framing Asher's gorgeous silhouette. I reached up and grabbed his neck, drawing him to me. After rubbing my face like a cat along his rough goatee, I ran my tongue along his lips.

He only allowed me a few seconds of control before he took over again, pulling my breasts out of my bra, ripping the straps in order to free them completely. Sucking one nipple while pinching the other, he explored my new piercings. "Doll, these are new. Jesus, I thought your tits were perfect before, but now they're fucking heaven," Asher said while dragging in a breath, his voice coming out raspy.

smoldered

All words having escaped me, I moaned.

Our movements were rushed and urgent, a fine mixture of agony, pain, suffering, and unadulterated joy lay beneath both our actions. It wasn't time to analyze, though, as Asher made his way down my body, his tongue setting it afire before dipping into my folds. I felt his finger glide inside me, dipping deep and then pulling back, finding my spot, the nerve, tweaking it hard, making my body reach for the stars.

His tongue flicked my tiny bundle of nerves, swept across it lightly, and with just a few passes, I was sailing through the sky, screaming Asher's name before riding the aftershocks of the first orgasm I'd had in months that hadn't been self-induced.

Raising my leg, bending my knee, I used my foot to snag the top of his jeans, signaling I wanted them off—fast. He quickly stood and pushed them down, his dick immediately springing forward. Commando. Asher was not a man of many layers, at least when it came to clothing.

I didn't have to tell Asher to open the nightstand drawer. He did, and pulled out a condom. Within a matter of seconds, he was inside me, fully stretching me, gliding in and out at a slow, leisurely pace. My body heated again and I could feel myself clenching around his length. I was going to go off like a rocket in no time.

Picking up the pace, he started to punish me as he'd promised with his cock. He took over my body, his hands coming under my ass and lifting my hips so he could go deeper, harder, faster. Sweat dripped from his brow into my cleavage and ran down my stomach, pooling in my belly button. It should have been gross, but it was so pure and natural, I couldn't help but be turned on even more.

I reached my hand down, touching our connection, coating his dick in my moisture, rubbing my clit, and within moments, I shattered. As I came, I let my hands go around and squeeze Asher's ass, my head falling backward into the pillow as I let out one more hoarse cry.

He flipped me over, dragged me up onto all fours, and continued to drive into me with no mercy, passion filling each slap of our bodies, marking what he believed to be his in the most primitive way.

After he pulsed inside me, plunging as deep as he could, leaving nothing for later, he fell down on top of me, bracing some of his weight on one elbow.

He turned me over once again, this time gentler, less hurried. We met face to face, skin to skin, our gazes wholly focused on each other. There were no words, just looks and expressions, weighted and heavy with meaning.

Asher kissed me lightly before getting up and disposing of the condom.

By the time he came back, I realized what a mistake I'd made. "You have to go now. I'll contact you when I think we should proceed with telling Quinn." I stood up, wrapped myself in the robe lying on the chair next to the bed, and walked toward the door. Steeling myself, I said nothing more, keeping my emotions at bay.

"You're kidding me?" Asher barked from behind me, but I kept walking.

Once at the door, I opened it and slowly turned back. "No, I'm not. Good-bye, Asher."

He made his way toward me wearing only his jeans and boots, his shirt shoved into his jeans pocket, pulling down the waistband just the right amount to off his perfectly shaped *V* leading to the promised land.

Dragging my gaze from it, I prayed I didn't go back on my words as I stood motionless at the open front door, waiting for him to leave.

If I thought Asher's face was furious earlier, that was before I saw his current expression. "I'm leaving," he said through clenched teeth. "I'll play this shit your way. But I hope you know, I'm not leaving Florida without my son or my woman."

And then he was gone into the night.

I slammed the door shut without a clue how he got to my place or how he would leave, and told myself I shouldn't care.

twenty-six

This Is No Game of Beer Pong

Mike
Las Vegas

I PACED THE perimeter of my condo, the lights of the Las Vegas Strip flickering in the background, an almost empty bottle of Jack in hand, my cell phone on rapid redial in the other. Taking the last swig of whiskey from the bottle, I threw it across the room, the glass making contact with the stainless steel fridge and shattering all over my kitchen floor. There was a sound, someone shouting an evil-sounding nervous laugh. It sounded a lot like me.

It is me.

Thankfully, I was home alone and no one was around to bear witness to how fucking ridiculous I was acting. I should have never allowed Asher to get on that flight to Miami. I should have gone with him, but I couldn't get my head out of my ass with Lynx refusing to leave the party she was working in order to help me.

Stubborn woman. Dumber man.

How was it that I was emotionally involved with an escort? I was a sorry excuse and a pathetic piece of shit who refused to let his girlfriend do her job, which was screwing other men, while my only true friend in life boarded a plane to royally screw his life up.

131

The whole damn episode could have been avoided if I would have just confronted Natalie that day after I met Quinn for the first time. I could have set the record straight, helped the situation rather than destroying everything and everyone around me.

My luck was shit.

I stomped over to my liquor cabinet, my feet still laced in my high-tops, although at some point I had ripped my shirt off my body. When? I couldn't recall.

I was a raving lunatic in jeans, basketball shoes, and no shirt, in hot pursuit of more booze to drown out my memory of the day I ruined everything for Natalie…and Asher…and me…and Lynx.

That one night when I went out to have a good time, ended up meeting a girl I actually liked, and crossed too many lines to count. Leaning over to peruse the selection of booze in front of me, it all came back to me…

HADN'T HAD such a good time in…ever. Holy crap, I'd been missing out big-time while shacked up with Rochelle. While I was curled up on the balcony of Clay's hotel suite with Lynx, I'd pushed the knowledge of her being an escort to the far recesses of my mind. She'd been the best company I'd ever had, and I hadn't wanted it to end.

But it had to when her phone chirped with a text. A single fucking text. At that moment I hadn't known that little message would rock my world; as far as I knew it just marked the end of my time with the girl in front of me, and I hadn't wanted that.

"Oh, it's my neighbor," Lynx said. "I help her take care of her son, and she needs me to meet him at home." She looked closer at her phone, squinting at the time. "Shoot, it's the morning already." We'd been so caught up in each other, we barely noticed the sunrise.

I racked my brain, trying to come up with some excuse to stall her, to not let this girl slip away into the early morning light. "Can I drive you home?" I asked, hoping she hadn't brought her own car. Parking was pretty pricey at the fancy hotels.

She flipped her long braids behind her back and said, "Really? That would actually be awesome. I gotta get back quickly. My neighbor thinks I'm at home—she doesn't know about this job. If you could run me back, then I'll be there on time to meet her little boy. He's coming with his grandma."

"Yeah, no problem." I stood up and held a hand out to help her up. She held up one finger and said, "One sec. Let me confirm I can do it." After sending a quick text, Lynx stood up and straightened her clothes, tossing on a sweater before readying to go. The girl looked radiant even after pulling an all-nighter on a balcony, sitting on a crumpled blanket, sipping wine.

Walking through a suite full of hungover pricks sleeping it off, we quietly made our way to the door. Down the elevator, through the casino where the clanging never stopped, without a single word to each other, we held hands, our tightly woven fingers saying it all. Once outside, the valet threw me my keys and we sped off into the sunrise like two young lovers with happily-ever-after spread out in front of them.

Brushing off any feelings I had about being a stupid romantic, I asked her for her address and off we went. It sounded somewhat familiar, but I wasn't able to place it until we pulled up in front. Just my fucking luck, Lynx lived right smack next to Natalie, and I quickly gathered it was her son we were heading home to meet. I had only driven by the complex a few times, checking that it appeared to be safe and well maintained—for Asher.

And there he was, the mysterious boy I'd never met. Natalie had always kept him far from the club, and as I parked and Lynx jumped out to meet an older woman with a young kid in tow, I quickly understood why.

I watched in horror as the woman I'd become smitten with ran over to a mini-version of Asher. My boss and closest friend, Natalie's boss and part-time lover, the man who rescued women from awful situations and took care of them—that Asher.

Only one thought ran through my mind. *Holy. Fucking. Shit. Asher has a kid.*

Natalie had kept the boy away from us because one look at the kid and you'd know. He was the spitting image of Asher. Wavy blond hair curled around his face, and as he came a bit closer, I saw them. Silver eyes.

Not having a clue how I'd control my expression, not to mention my emotions, I kicked my own shin with my heavy shoe to distract myself.

Lynx was in the middle of a little intro. "Hey there, Quinn-man, what's happening? This is my friend, Mike." She pointed my way.

I nodded, not trusting what might come out of my mouth if I opened it.

"Hey, Lynx," the older woman said. "Thanks a bunch. I have to get over to the nursing home to see my dad, and Natalie is tied up."

Yep, she was Natalie's mom, all right. She had the same green eyes and tone of voice.

"No worries, Mrs. P. And this is Mike."

Too choked up to speak, I managed another nod.

"Hi, Mike. Nice to meet you." Mrs. Parker turned on her heel and called over her shoulder, "Take good care of my boy, Lynxie. And make sure Natalie pays you time and a half. You got school bills to pay, make something of yourself."

Longingly, I wished it was me walking away, wishing this whole little meet-and-greet had never happened. I turned to face Lynx to find her crouched close to the ground, smoothing the little man's blond curls behind his ear and giving him a kiss on the cheek.

"Where's Mom?" the little kid asked.

"You know what? I don't know, buddy. She just needed me and here I am, because no one I'd rather be with than you, Quinn. No offense to you, Mike," she said with her gaze pinging back and forth between me and Asher's mini-me like she was at a tennis match.

"None taken." They were the first words I'd spoken since I got out of the car, and they came out tense and sounding like I had a frog in my throat.

Lynx took a moment to shoot me a questioning glance. "Well, okay, I think I'll take Quinn up to my place now. Thanks for the ride," she said carefully, obviously trying to wrap up an awkward moment.

"Um, sure," I said before leaning in and saying in a more hushed tone, "I'd like to see you again."

"I'd like that," she whispered back while being pulled in the opposite direction by the kid I was sure would end up destroying my life.

My head spinning, I had to have just a few more answers before I left. Finally finding my voice, I said, "Hey, Quinn, want to check out my SUV? The tires are huge. I need to say a proper good-bye to Lynx, here."

That made the little kid stop pulling my target away from me and run over to my truck. I opened the back hatch and let him climb through the interior. Knowing he'd be busy for at least five minutes, I grabbed Lynx and pulled her behind the car, where we were blocked from his sight.

"Mike, I can't make out with you here!" Apparently she thought I wanted to kiss her good-bye, or more.

I only wish.

"No, I don't want to make out," I said, and when she lifted an eyebrow at me, I raised a hand to clarify. "Wait. That came out wrong, I do, but I got to ask you a question. How much do you know about Quinn over there? And his mom."

"Why? I watch Quinn for his mom, Natalie. She's a good person. Single mom. Takes good care of her kid and keeps an eye out for my roommate, Trish, and me." Her head tilted to the side as she studied me.

"Natalie works for me."

"Wait," she said, her voice rising. "You work at the Tunnel? You said you were a bouncer, but didn't mention where."

"Shhh. I am a bouncer, well, head of overall security. At the Tunnel. My boss, Asher, is my closest buddy. Nat works for us. We take care of her, but she's kept her personal life—and kid—from us. Doesn't like to mix the two, and now I know why—" I couldn't finish because Lynx interrupted.

"Oh crap." Lynx stomped her foot dramatically and pretended to smack her head. "She's gonna be pissed that you were here then. We can't say anything to Natalie. That woman is crazy protective of her son...and shit! Shit! Shit! She doesn't know about my side job."

That little comment gave me a light-bulb moment. "Well, I'm not going to be the one to tell her. And you're not going to tell her about me. Listen, that kid," I said, flicking my chin to the inside of the SUV where Quinn was pushing every button in sight, "is Asher's kid. There's no denying it when you take one look at him. Natalie is hiding the boy for a reason, and you and me got to watch out for both the kid and her. Deal?"

"Quinn's dad? She's never talked about him. Holy shit—you got a deal." She leaned up on tiptoe and kissed my cheek. "You'd better go. I don't know when Nat will be back or what she's doing. This is strange, but nonetheless, go. We don't want to get caught."

WELL, WE'D been caught, all right, which was why I was roaming my apartment like a wild animal desperate for a meal. But I wasn't hungry, I was desperate for something to drink to help me forget my problems.

Ransacking my wet bar, shoving bottles to the side, I continued to look for more of my booze of choice. When I found another bottle of Jack, I triumphantly snagged it, then set about trying to dial Natalie over and over again, but my phone didn't work. It was fried.

Taking my liquid courage, I moved into my office and grabbed the landline. I needed to warn her what was coming her way. Explain myself. Protect Lynx. Not only would this whole little scenario reveal Natalie's secret, but Lynx's too. Her involvement in this would be blown wide open, and now I was at fault for not protecting two women, a small child, and a grown-ass man.

There was nothing I could do to stop the man. Once we left Beck at the bar, Asher had rushed back to the club, opened his safe in a rage, then held a fucking gun on me and waved it around in the air, threatening to use it if I didn't get his ass on a private flight to Miami. He insisted I get Natalie's address from Carson, and arrange for a driver because he was packing a bottle of scotch or two or three for the flight. He kept screaming, "You knew about this fucking shit, Mike? You let me walk right into this! You're nothing but a cocksucker."

Brandishing the gun in my face, he yelled, "Move quick and do what I want, or I'm gonna blow your balls off."

Foolishly, I had thought he'd eventually give up on the whole search for Natalie's baby daddy. Natalie was gone already, after all, and I figured he would get bored with Beck. That dude was about as straight-edged as they got.

Who knew Beck, the loser, would drop that bomb about the threesome? It was bad enough to think that the two of them—a young Natalie and a much younger Asher—had got together the regular way back then, fucked, and she got knocked up. But this?

I'd known about Asher's coke problem back in the day and his penchant for ménages, but this news was like a fucking bomb being set off in the middle of Las Vegas Boulevard.

And stupid me thought it would all just go away, like I dreamed Lynx would stop being a high-priced call girl, and my dad would stop screwing girls younger than me.

Furious, I tossed back some more whiskey, and as fast as it went down my throat, it raced back up. I ran to the bathroom and threw up in the sink, emptying my stomach in the porcelain bowl before smashing the bottle into the counter. The heavy glass shattered, but it wasn't enough. I kept slamming it into the marble until it was nothing but a bunch of cracked pieces of dust.

With my hand bleeding, I slid down onto the tile floor. My head swirled like a tornado, the funnel of questions closing in and pouring down over me.

Wrapping my hand in a towel, I lay all the way down on the chilled floor, becoming one with the lines of grout, studying the way they connected in a pattern, thinking my life was nothing like that. Instead, the intricacies of my screwed-up existence were as tangled and twisted as a spiderweb, and I was stuck in the middle with no way to get the hell out.

Where is Lynx? Fucking some asshole?

Where is Natalie? Fucking some other asshole?

Where is Asher? Fucking up his life?

Where am I? Helping nobody, that's where. And I'm just fucked.

twenty-seven

Wet 'n' Wild

Natalie
Miami, one month later

On that awful night a month ago, all I'd wanted to do was lie down on the hard floor and cry. As I lay there, sobbing my heart out, a tiny puddle of salty tears had formed on the floor by my face.

I had shed tears for the young me, the one who foolishly thought she could make a man high on coke fall for her while having a three-way with a slut.

I'd cried for Quinn and how his world would be shattered, blown to bits like one of the buildings in the action movies he loved to watch. All because I'd once been a stupid nineteen-year-old who couldn't face the truth.

Then I cried for the present-day me, the one who'd been busting her butt in Florida, making a new life, only to have it unravel in a matter of minutes.

Why the hell did I ever bare my heart to Beck Hadley that night all those years ago? Why didn't I have an abortion? And the sixty-million-dollar question for the jackpot—why the hell did I ever start up with Asher again?

It was obvious. Asher made me do crazy things like play with fire, or emotions, or people I cared about.

Since the night I threw my one-and-only out into the dark and muggy Florida night, I'd been minding my own business and doing my usual thing—working, taking care of Quinn, and zero socializing.

Except now I was doing it all with Lynx living with me, and Asher renting a mega-house in a much fancier part of Miami.

How I ended up with my old neighbor sleeping on my couch was still mostly a mystery. Apparently, Lynx had met Big Mike at a party, and had introduced him to Quinn sometime after that. When I called Mike in a fury, wanting to know how the hell this happened, he kept stressing that he didn't know Lynx was my neighbor when he first met her. Well, duh, I knew that.

As soon as Mike saw my son, he knew who his father was. And knowing that, it wasn't a large leap to realize why I'd actually kept Quinn away from the club. At least, he'd been right in thinking I wanted my son kept a secret, but those two idiots had concocted some plan to hide the whole meeting from me, thinking they could keep a lid on it. Hoping and praying that Asher would never be the wiser.

The man we were all hiding from had gone out and befriended Beck. All the while, Bonnie and Clyde—I mean, Mike and Lynx—had convinced themselves that whole friendship would not end the way it did. Like a fucking train wreck, carnage all over the tracks, bloody and messy.

I was pretty sure they knew the situation with Asher and Beck would blow up, but didn't see a way out. Lying to themselves was a better way to go. Now Lynx felt tremendous guilt over it all, so she moved to Miami and here she was. Living with me.

I also learned that the two of them—my old babysitter and my old bouncer—liked each other, but were in some sort of stalling pattern or never-ending fight. Over what, I didn't know, and I didn't have the time or energy to worry about it.

What I did know was school was out for both Lynx and Quinn for the summer, and now my old neighbor/sitter was making amends by living with me, rent-free, and babysitting Quinn for nothing.

Asher was a much different story. Shortly after the night he showed up banging on my door, I learned he was renting a monstrosity of a house near South Beach with marble pillars and gorgeous grounds. I knew because I drove by a few times. He kept his distance, didn't beg to meet Quinn, biding his time wisely. Yet he spent every fucking night at the Peppermint Kitty, watching from afar, looming in the back, glaring at me and my clients. After my shift was done, he walked behind me to my car without a word, then followed me home and watched from a distance, peeling off when I walked inside my apartment. Every single night.

I hated him. Wanted him gone. I kept thinking I should call Sienna and beg her to make up a reason to drag him back to Vegas. She was the only person who rated higher in his eyes than me, but I really had no desire to drag her into my current situation.

The truth was I still held on to hope that Asher would give up and go home, that the whole Tunnel gang didn't know about the nasty three-way we'd participated in, and the worst part, that Asher had fathered a child during it. So I put on blinders and kept plugging ahead with my new life. It was easier than confronting the mess my existence had become.

It was a joke, I knew it, but sticking my head in the sand was the only way to preserve any self-pride.

Here it was Thursday, my day off once again, and Lynx was being absolutely belligerent to me about taking a few hours for myself. She planned on taking Quinn to some park with a water spray thing, and they were all gung-ho. Deviously, she'd gotten Quinn in on the act, having him give me a gift card for a massage because she knew I couldn't say no to my boy.

Which was why I was reluctantly sitting in a eucalyptus steam room after a massage at one of Miami's hottest day spas, wet steam camouflaging the tears running down my face. I spent the whole massage remembering what I'd spent the last decade trying to forget. As a result I felt ripped open, raw, and exposed, angry that Lynx had spent her hard-earned money on me, upset at such a waste of money, but even more distraught over the memories I had kept buried for longer than I cared to remember.

Thank God I was the only one in the steam room. My face was puffy, salty tears burning their way into my open pores, sweat dripping down my cleavage. I leaned back against the hotter-than-hell tiles, tilted my head back, and closed my eyes, the faint scents of pine and eucalyptus transporting me to a more sensual place.

My heart beat to its own rhythm, fast and furious, pulsing as it took in the snapshots of what had happened that night. The evening I thought I would finally snag the man of my dreams, but instead conceived the boy I never imagined having.

I tried so hard not to remember that long-ago night, but when I did, the memories were crisp and clear, as if it had happened yesterday…

THE LATE hours of the evening had bled into the early hours of the morning, the sky not quite black anymore, a tiny sliver of gray appearing as dawn approached. We'd been at it for hours, partying, celebrating my birthday and my enrolling in community college. We'd been drinking, dancing, high-fiving, sniffing blow—well, Asher and a few others had, but not me. My friends were notorious for raging. To all of us, partying was a way of life, one we'd always known.

We were the kids of the real Las Vegas, the one that pumped and thrived three hundred sixty-five days and nights a year, the city that awoke when the lights dimmed on the fake tourist version. We grew up behind the scenes, watching our parents host parties, bounce at clubs, or deal cards, then party with their friends when their night or day shift had ended. They'd throw us all together with one parent to babysit, whoever had drawn the short straw, then would party all night long.

Our generation was the first to witness the burst in growth on the Strip, the overdone, ostentatious hotels fueled by unbelievable wealth, and we liked it too much. There were better jobs for the taking, and we'd done just that, loving the tips, accepting the perks, learning of better booze, high-end drugs, and top-of-the-line pussy for the men. We couldn't shake our partying ways if we wanted to, and we had no intention of letting go of the lifestyle.

That was exactly what we were doing when I decided it was my time to finally get Asher. Even if I had to share him with Shayla this once, it would be a step in the direction of making the man totally mine. Asher had been all I ever wanted. Ever. And I'd grown sick of my flirting not working.

People were seriously lit up on the coke that night. It was the good stuff, probably laced with something else like synthetic Ecstasy, judging by the sexual heat filling the room. That was one of the fringe benefits of the bigger and better Strip. X. My friends fell in love with that shit right away, and judging by how good everyone was feeling, I couldn't blame them.

I preferred pot; that was it for me when it came to the illicit stuff. But this dose of X and coke was obviously some kind of crazy high because people were flying, half of them taking their clothes off, their eyes sparkling with something I'd never seen before.

When I slipped next to Asher on the dance floor, he wrapped his big arms around me and started moving to the beat. A rush of heat went straight to my belly with a direct line to a little farther down, all from this little bit of drug-induced affection. Wanting Asher had become a religion to me, and I was seriously devout.

I'd been drinking pretty steadily, and downed the last of my cocktail so I could wind my arms around the man of my dreams. Asher moved pretty quickly to grinding up on me. I wasn't a virgin—I'd spent the better part of the prior two years trying to educate myself for the man whose erection was rubbing against me as we burned up the small dance space. We didn't say much, only moved like lovers well acquainted with each other.

When Asher finally spoke, his words were heated. "Little doll, you got it going on tonight. Christ, can't take my eyes off you. Where you been hiding all those goods?"

I looked down at myself, taking in what he saw. A gold halter, skintight jeans, and platform heels. I couldn't stop myself from smiling at the tiny compliment.

In the far corners of my mind, I knew it was the drugs talking; I wasn't really winning the prize I so desperately wanted. But I'd loved Asher from afar for so many years, I wasn't able to make myself care.

It was ridiculous to care for him as much as I did because he was seriously flawed, troubled, desperate for attention from women as long as I'd known him, but I was unable to stop myself. I knew the boy inside the shell of a man moving his fiery gaze and steamy body against mine, and I wanted to save him, fix it all, make it better.

Taking a moment to form a response, I finally said, "I've been here all the time, Ash. Watching and wanting from the other side of the room for all these years." The alcohol had clearly dulled my inhibitions, or maybe it was simply watching all the horny people in the room.

So when the man of my dreams started to lead me to the back with Shayla in tow, I went. Willingly.

The night wasn't the loving culmination I'd dreamed of in my head, but rather a scene out of a raunchy porno movie. The only saving grace of the time back in the bedroom was that Asher relegated Shayla to "oral only." She sucked and licked him while he kissed me. Then he used his hand to get her off fast before he told her to stick her nipples in his face while he screwed me doggy style.

It wasn't making love. That would have been impossible; I was wise enough to know Asher was too emotionally messed up for that. We'd been good friends forever—our whole lives—and we were nothing more than two buddies who screwed to get our rocks off that evening.

At least, Asher did.

As he pounded into me from behind, chasing his release, he moved his hand around to my clit, stroking it perfectly. The best I'd ever had, but I couldn't get off because the moment was so absolutely dirtied by Shayla's boobs in his mouth. How dumb I'd been to think I could change the man ramming into me. So I played along, tinkering on the verge of orgasm, thinking I liked it rough, but this whole scene had been royally fucked up from the beginning.

There was also the little fact that we didn't use protection. When Asher first plunged into me bareback, the realization of just how far gone he was hit me. Years of emotions burst like a hemorrhage in my brain; this wasn't at all what I had wanted. My feelings crashed through my heart, causing a big gaping hole as they seeped out through my body, consuming me with regret. All hope bled out of me like a deflating balloon. This meant nothing to Asher, and I was nothing more than a silly, love-sick fool who had asked for it.

When I turned around to look into his stunning silver eyes, I found them mostly black, his pupils huge from the drugs. As sweat ran off his face and dripped on my back, I realized then and there that this night had no purpose. Other than for the man behind me to get his rocks off, which he did half in me, the rest dripping over my ass from his half-assed attempt to pull out in time.

Shayla chirped, "Let's go get a drink and another hit of blow," as soon as Asher finished. He yanked his pants back on after he using his shirt to wipe the cum off my back.

Asher had dropped a ridiculous kiss on the top of my head, as I had frozen in place in disbelief, not even moving from being on all fours. He said, "You gonna come have a drink, little doll?" before he'd followed Shayla out the door like a dog in heat, and I had been left to cry on Beck Hadley's lap.

S TEPPING OUT of the tiny room moist with heat, I forced my brain to close the steel door on my past mistakes and childish thinking.

Based on my foggy head and pruned fingertips, I had overstayed my welcome in the steam room, my body feeling as wrung out as my thoughts. When I stepped into a cool shower to rinse off, my thoughts moved from having been left to cry with Beck alone, but also to parent—and pay for—Quinn. Alone.

It was time I allowed Asher to meet his son. To help, or whatever he wanted to do. I deserved that. I was never going to make a life here in Miami if I didn't let the guy meet his kid, pay for some shit, and hope that he got the hell out of my space.

I doubted he wanted anything more than to feel he'd paid up. He certainly couldn't want to take any more responsibility for his son than that.

Asher had cleaned himself up; this I knew already. His drug use was a long time ago. As for his sexual tastes, those hadn't changed, judging by my finding Penny and the other girl in his bed. Either way, that didn't affect his ability to be a dad, and I needed the help.

This time, I had no false illusions of him falling in love with me. Just his son.

And Quinn would like that big house.

twenty-eight

Go, Speed Racer

Asher

IT HAD taken me awhile, but I wore Lynx down. Mike had helped as much as he could. He wanted his girl back, and I promised him I would help if he got his girl to get me in front of Natalie. The plan was simple: Use my money to purchase a gift card for a day at the spa, have Quinn give it to her, allow her to relax, then surprise her with dinner when she walked out.

I stood there in the blazing Miami heat, leaning against my car. I had leased a fucking Audi A8 sedan. It might have had a V8 engine and sick rims, but it also sported a whole slew of safety features like air bags and shit like that. It was for Quinn—when I was allowed to meet my son. Even I knew you couldn't put a kid on the back of a bike. Lynx told me that Natalie thought the car was part of an act. The stupid woman had no idea how serious I was about my son and her, but she was about to find out.

Parked directly outside the spa, I let the heat warm my bare arms and run through my veins, heating my already boiling body. I looked down at my black T-shirt and ripped jeans, thinking I didn't make much of a dad, but I was trying. I had rented a big house with the option to buy, but I was fully planning on taking my woman and kid

145

back to Vegas. No reason to say anything about that now as I watched Natalie walk out the door in front of me.

She was looking at her phone, busy typing a message on the touch screen and not watching where she was walking. I approached with caution. She didn't know I was coming, and I'd been keeping my distance even in my ever-present state in her life. Now wasn't the time to scare the shit out of her.

Approaching slowly, I watched as her head popped up as soon as I was in range. "Hey there. How was your afternoon? Relaxing?" I said as I stopped a few steps from her long, lush, massaged body.

"Asher? What are you doing here?" Smacking her head, she let out a loud, "Gah." Then she took a step backward. "Geez, I'm so stupid. You guys set me up."

I stepped closer. "Not set up, indulged. You deserved a break."

Shaking her head, she tried to walk swiftly around me, but I stopped her with a gentle hand on her arm.

Natalie stilled and looked away. "I should have known you were behind this little day out for me." We stood shoulder-to-shoulder, yet she refused to turn and look at me.

I stepped in front of her and held my hands up. "Guilty as charged. I only wanted you to enjoy yourself. You work so hard."

She pivoted to fully face me. "You, of all people, should know how hard I work, you follow me everywhere. I should report you to the police for stalking. In fact, Greg at work suggested it."

Squinting, I glared at the stubborn woman. "What the hell? I leave you alone, Natalie. I'm making sure the mother of my son is safe. I don't trust the security guys at that dump. They're not like Mike or Petey, or even Billy."

"They're fine." She moved her hands to her hips, accentuating the small dip in her waist before it met the luscious curves I wished my hands were resting on.

"Okay. Let's not argue about bouncers. I came to take you to dinner." I nodded my head toward my car.

Narrowing her eyes, she said, "You know what, I was just thinking about giving you a chance to meet Quinn, and in a matter of three minutes, you've managed to change that."

"Come on, Nat." I tilted my head to the side, giving her my most charming smile.

She leaned in a little closer, her breath vibrating on my ear, making my dick rise to attention at the thought of her making a move. Instead she whispered, "I may have been a foregone conclusion ten years ago, let you have your way with me any way you wanted to on one stupid drunken night. I may have even fallen back into your bed—or couch—in the last few years, but that was then. This is now, Asher, and *now* is on my terms."

"Please, Natalie. Please. Just give me a chance." I didn't dare move. I was a prisoner to her whims.

I waited silently, my heartbeat pulsing in my ears. All I heard and felt was my desire for the woman in front of me, taunting and challenging me to be someone I wasn't.

Suddenly she tapped me on the shoulder. "Aren't you going to get that?"

"What?" A heavy layer of lust—like a thick fog—had taken up residence in my head.

"Your phone. It's ringing. Been ringing. Earth to Asher," she said as she poked me with a finger.

Reaching down, I absently patted my pocket where something was vibrating and making unwelcome noise.

twenty-nine

Remember the game, Telephone?

Natalie

GOD, THE nerve of him. To think Asher had infiltrated my life enough to orchestrate this day with Lynx was sending chills up and down my spine. I felt a fine layer of nervous sweat rising on my skin. I was so mad, I was ready to punch him all the way back to Vegas. Here I thought he was letting me control the situation, waiting for me to be ready to introduce him to Quinn.

Boy, was I wrong. As usual, he was pulling my strings, and I had been a nice little puppet, letting him do what he wanted, giving him carte blanche when it came to my life.

When was I going to learn? Falling for Asher Peterson had brought me nothing good. Except for my son.

I looked at Asher, standing as still as a statue, waiting for me to say yes to his dinner invite, and felt myself starting to take pity. *He's all alone.* Always had been, and it looked like he always would be. My mom said it best when I was a young girl: Asher was fighting an uphill battle, and sadly he was losing.

That was when his phone began to ring. The immobile man in front of me was in such a fog, the sound didn't even register with him.

Tapping him, I asked, "Aren't you going to get that?"

148

"What?" He looked over at me, utterly confused.

"Your phone. It's ringing. Been ringing. Earth to Asher," I said, trying to rouse him out of his funk.

He reached down and pulled his phone out of his pocket, sliding his finger over the screen.

"Yeah?" He paused to listen. "What the fuck? That doesn't make sense. How the hell did he have the nerve to come back?"

Only able to hear half the conversation, I looked away as if I weren't listening.

"Goddamn it," he growled. "No, you did the right thing. It's me, I have no right being away for so long. Everyone else okay? Lila?" Another pause. "Uh-huh. Well, what did they say? What kind of time are we looking at?"

From Asher's tone, something big was going down. Giving up the pretense, I stared at him and listened. My blood chilled when I saw the color drain from his face.

"Wait, what did you just say?" Asher paused as he listened, his knuckles white as he clutched his phone. "Well, I'll be damned. I do. On my way. It's the least I can fucking do."

Forgetting my earlier stance to let Asher go, free my head of him, I was beyond caving at this point when I saw the pained expression in Asher's eyes as he slid the phone back into this pants and looked at me with hollow eyes, the sparkle all but gone.

Although, I didn't have a chance.

He looked up at me and said, "I'm sorry, Natalie, but I need to get back to Vegas. It's clear this isn't really working anyway between us. I wanted to try and everything. I was trying, but sometimes life has a way of showing a man when it's time to give up. I surrender."

Asher started to walk away, shoulders slumped, wearing desperation on his sleeve.

"Wait!" I chased after him until we were in front of his car. *Stupid ostentatious thing.*

He shook his head. "Listen, Nat. I can't do this. Not now."

"Okay." I bowed my head, hiding the fresh crop of tears coming on that clouded my vision, making the man I would always love a hazy mirage.

He lifted my chin and said, "One last thing. Quinn is mine and I'll never forget that, even if you don't want me to know him. I mean, I'll provide for him. I'll talk to the bank and my lawyer and send you back child support, make arrangements for you to get some type of monthly payments from now on."

Asher opened his car door and slipped in. Stunned, I stepped back, walking backward, and watched him pull away. Just like that, he was gone. His stupid, expensive, ridiculous statement of a sedan quietly sped down the road, leaving nothing in its wake but a little dust, like the man himself had done to my life. He sped in and out, leaving only my hollow shell behind to take care of his son.

Now with financial support.

thirty

That Was Some Matchbox Car

Mike
Las Vegas

Pissed off, I pulled onto the side of the tarmac at the charter aviation company and killed the engine of my SUV, then rolled down the windows as I watched the piece of shit's plane land. How was I to know he was going to ditch Natalie when I called to tell him about Petey? I hadn't been regularly talking to Lynx, and yeah, I knew she and Asher were cooking up a plan to get him together with Natalie, but how was I to know it was going down at the exact moment I needed him?

I rubbed my hand over my face and flinched when I saw my reflection in the side mirror. My hair had grown out a bit; since Lynx moved to Miami, I no longer had a reason to keep it buzzed and clean. Greasy strands fell across my forehead, drawing attention away from my eyes, bleary and bloodshot from too much whiskey. That was good. Looking down, I noted my clothes were clean. I still had to work, run the Tunnel, especially with Asher down in Florida trying to make up for his mistakes.

The asshole was definitely not fixing anything. In fact, he was only adding to the pile, screwing shit up even more than it already was. Now I had added to his problems for the second time in only a few short months with my fuckup.

The plane taxied in, coming to a stop, and I leaned my forehead against the cool steering wheel. The car's air-conditioning blew in my face, cooling my temper that was mostly directed at myself as I fought through the memories of the last twenty-four hours…

HAD BEEN fucking up a little bit, heading into work with a drink or two in me, but I had a lot going on. Asher had never been one to monitor drinking on the job; in fact, he was known to knock back a shot or two himself in his own club. Still, I had the security of the girls first on my plate, so drinking should have not been happening at all. I needed to be ready to chase a bad egg or nasty perv at a moment's notice.

It's just my life had been in the shitter. I'd only just been a part of making sure Sienna, now in private going by her original name, Lila, was safe and in love. Before that, I found my live-in girlfriend shacked up with my dad. Now, I had jacked up my closest friend's life, and as a result he and the high-priced escort I cared for had hightailed it to Florida, leaving me to run the club—and my life—into the ground.

Lila had been picking up a lot of slack at the club, taking over the business shit now that she had plans to get off the stage. The Tunnel's reputation spoke for itself, so crowds were still pouring in, money flowing freely to the girls' pockets and Asher's.

Then there was Petey. He'd been working furiously to keep everything status quo, not saying a word, minding his own business, and filling in wherever needed. My man, my number two, had pushed everything aside to help me run the place, probably doing more than he should have been.

Last night, I had only rolled into work an hour or so before, having spent the afternoon down on the Strip dealing with a few casino hosts who were sending some people our way. They'd asked me to stop and have a drink with them, and who was I to argue? The couple of cold ones I had at home before heading their way added to the mix, and when I realized I had a decent buzz going on as I exited the casino, I called for the Tunnel's limo.

After coming in through the back entrance, I made my way to the front of the floor, checking on the girls onstage and the ones doing lap dances. Everything looked normal, and I had just sighed a breath of relief when Petey ran up to me.

"Mike, fuck, my man. That dude, the one from the Ecstasy incident back a while ago with Nat? He's outside, demanding to get in," he said as he gave me a fist bump.

"Shit, let me go out there and get rid of him." I started moving toward the door.

Petey was hot on my tail. "You okay, Mike? No offense, but you kinda reek. Want me to handle it? It's no big deal."

"I got it, man," I said with a wave of my hand, dismissing him, but he still followed.

I blew through the main door, coming up behind Billy, who had been keeping the peace outside. Wouldn't you know that asshole who had been thrown out just months earlier was making a royal stink.

"I'm a fucking lawyer," the dude yelled at our youngest bouncer, "and you got no right to keep me from a good time."

I put my arm around the lawyer and started walking him away from the crowd. "Listen, man, we don't want any problems. Let's you and me just talk about this, maybe come up with a different place for you to have a good time—not jail, where I'm going to send you if you keep harassing my guys."

The guy had the nerve to push me, or at least he tried to, but made little headway.

I might have had a little bit too much to drink, but that fucker was lit up. He reached into his pocket and pulled out a Swiss Army knife, then started to wave it in my face. Petey who had been watching from afar, was now up on the guy, gently suggesting he leave quickly.

But the jerk didn't want to listen and kept waving that stupid little knife in our faces.

Petey went for the phone in his pocket to call the cops. I'd wanted to avoid that, but this guy was a class-A douche.

The sight of the phone lit a fire under the dude's ass and he started to run. I didn't know why, we should have let him roll, but Petey ran after him. He yelled back at me as he sped off, "I'm gonna get that fucker arrested. After what he's done, he's gonna spend the night getting an ass-rape in jail."

And then he took off like lightning, running after the waste of life. Petey was looking down, trying to shove his phone back into the pocket of his stupid tight leather pants, when a goddamn bright green Porsche convertible, music blaring, came speeding out of nowhere on two wheels. It hit the curb and flew right past Petey, clipping his leg hard as it flipped over the curb and went like a tumbleweed across the sidewalk, finally coming to a grinding, ear-shattering halt a hundred yards away.

Pretty sure I almost pissed myself as my whole body broke out into a sweat. I was standing above myself, watching as I ran to my friend, my coworker, the guy who had just stood up for my drunk ass. Vaguely, I heard Billy take control of the club, keeping everyone who was already inside there, while at the same time letting in all the people who had been waiting outside so they were far away from the scene. As he radioed to the inside guys, I had one mission. Petey.

I dialed 911 as I raced toward where Petey lay crumpled on the concrete. His face was contorted with pain and his eyes were wide, his breath coming fast and jerky as I yelled at him not to move, then tried to talk to the emergency dispatcher. His leg—oh God, his leg. I couldn't even look at it.

The first responders came fast, too fast; they had reason to lurk near the club waiting for crime. The convertible was a mangled mess of steel, and I didn't care about what happened to the driver, but the paramedics apparently had to check.

After they determined the driver was beyond their help, they focused their efforts on Petey. Horrified, I stepped back and watched as they stabilized his crushed leg, strapped him on a gurney with a neck brace, then shoved an oxygen mask over his face while they shouted questions at him, asking if he knew his blood type. Apparently in shock, he wasn't able to answer, his body convulsing as blood seeped through the bandages they placed over his severely damaged leg.

Unable to breathe, I leaned over and placed my hands on my knees, bracing myself against fainting, taking large gulps and feeling like I'd just run a marathon.

No patience for the police when they tried to question me, I'd told them, "Catch me later, I gotta get to the hospital," as the ambulance raced down the street. *Fuck 'em.* Where had they been when the car was speeding on two wheels?

I'd slammed through the emergency room doors just as they were pushing Petey into surgery. The last thing the nurse had said to me was, "Sir, your friend is O-negative and needs a lot of blood. Do you know if he has any close relatives?"

Now I sat in my SUV, stone-cold sober, weeks of Jack still seeping out of my pores. Watching my boss run toward my car, also no doubt dry as a bone, I was jerked back to reality. Asher had no family, at least he didn't think so until a month ago when he found out he had a kid. Now he had picked up and left his son to help his club family.

I would have thought Asher had the Tunnel running through his veins, but it was actually O-negative, and he felt obligated to come and donate some of his obviously ice-cold shit to Petey.

thirty-one

My Ship Sinks Yours

Asher

HOPPED IN Mike's big truck, not bothering to buckle up, just grabbed hold of the bar above the window and said, "Let's go," while smacking my other hand on the dash. He nodded and turned on the ignition, pulling away from the tarmac with the windows down, the dry air floating through the car. My lungs questioned their sudden locale change; they had only just adjusted to the moisture hanging in the air in Florida.

It was early morning and the sun was breaking over the horizon. I had gone straight to the airport after deserting Natalie, flown all night back to my hometown, the time difference working in my favor. I arrived in Vegas in time for Mike to get me to the hospital for the doctors' morning rounds, which was good, because I had a lot of questions for them.

Sucking on a water bottle as Mike pushed the car ahead, I finally found my words. "So, tell me again what happened. And don't leave anything out."

Mike went on to explain the guy who had tried to slip Natalie an Ecstasy had come back, trying to push his way back into the club. The dude had shoved Mike and the other guys around, then pulled a knife

156

and had taken off running when Petey threatened to call the cops. Mike gripped the steering wheel with white knuckles as he described the car careening in on two wheels and Petey not seeing it.

When Mike hung his head and admitted to being drunk, I said, "I don't give a shit about that. This wasn't your fault. Probably mine. I was an asshole the way I just picked up and left. I thought I could drag Nat and my son back here if I waited long enough, but I was wrong. I was an idiot to leave my club and my club family behind."

He waved me off, still assuming the blame. "Nah, this is on me, Asher."

His skin pale, Mike described what they had to do to Petey's leg. There were tiny pins and big broken bones and future skin grafts and physical therapy, so much shit my head was swimming with details, unable to process it all. My buddy had had two transfusions already, and probably needed another one.

"Shit," I said as I shook my head. "It's really something, me and him having the same blood type. So rare, but I'm glad as fuck. Did you set me up to donate as soon as I get there? I need to do something after deserting all you guys. God, I'm a fucking shit, leaving my club and the only family I got for something that's never going to happen."

"Yeah, I got you registered to get in and give blood."

"Well, I'm gonna give it and check on my man, Petey. Then I gotta go to the office, straighten this out with the cops before I go home and check on my house."

Mike turned to look at me. "What? Why home? Aren't you going back to Florida?"

I shook my head before lowering it in shame. "Nope, that was a pipe dream. Nat and me and Quinn, being a family? She doesn't want me, and I finally get it."

Mike turned his eyes back on the road, but he stayed silent, urging me on.

"My family is here with the Tunnel—Lila, you, Pete. Christ," I said as I ran my hand through my dirty hair. "Damn it, I knocked Natalie up during a threesome I don't even remember. She had my baby, provided for him, was both his mom and dad because how could she come and tell me what happened that night? It makes me sick just thinking about it. Imagine how she felt. So, nope, I'm not going back. I told Nat I'll send money, make back payments, let her get on with her life. I'm nothing but a piece of shit, anyway. Quinn doesn't need that."

We pulled up to the hospital, and when I moved to get out of the car, Mike grabbed my arm. "Don't let yourself be consumed with self-hatred, Ash. Look what you just did for a friend."

I gave him a chin lift and got out; I'd already made up my mind on the flight from Florida to Vegas. For five hours, all I thought about was how I had no business having a son. I might have money, fancy cars, and bikes, I might live in a big house, but I was nothing but a deadbeat, like my own father. And I'd never even met the man.

History had a funny way of repeating itself.

M Y BOOTS beat heavily on the shiny linoleum floor as I held up my arm to inspect where I had just given blood. Mike walked next to me in his high-top tennis shoes, both of us in our standard club clothes—T-shirts and ripped jeans. On our way to check on our friend in his hospital room, we were about as out of place as a couple of kids in a casino.

Petey lay asleep in the hospital bed with monitors beeping, IV tubing running in and out, and his leg supported by a huge air pillow. Mike and I settled our large frames in the flimsy piece-of-crap hospital chairs, taking in the raw sight in front of us. Together we breathed the antiseptic-tinged air, witnessing firsthand how precious life can be. Neither of us were the type to get emotional and sappy over a cup of tea, so we didn't speak, just took in the feelings swimming in the room, drowning us in reality, a testament to how fucked-up shit could get. Those emotions pushed down our testosterone and drew our feminine side to the surface.

Tears pricked at my eyes. I'd built the Tunnel from a shitty nothing club to a major player in the adult entertainment business. I was a celebrity in Vegas, my strippers were stars, and men acted like decent people at *my* club. Now Petey was down for the count, could have been dead, all because I ran off after Natalie and left my baby to fall apart.

I smoothed my hand over my hair and down to my neck, then let it fall back into the cradle of my palm in my lap and breathed. In and out, in and out. This wasn't Mike's fault. I had put him in a terrible position when I went to Miami, but how was I supposed to know he knew about Quinn? If I would have let him explain, even go with me, it would have been better. But he couldn't reason with me that night. I was a raving lunatic when I found out from Beck about the threesome, and put two and two together.

I had pulled a gun on my friend, all because I was rocked with the knowledge that I had a son. Now my relationship with Mike was on the rocks because he took my side and let me fly off the handle, and his girl, Lynx, took Natalie's side. If only I had let Mike talk some sense into me; he could have told me a lot sooner why Natalie didn't tell me about Quinn.

I have no business being a father.

In general, I was a lousy person, no matter how many women I rescued and provided with a safe haven.

I sat up straight, wanting to wake Petey and let him know I was here now. A little too late, but I donated blood, O-negative, which he needed. But I let the man sleep, more for my sake than his.

Standing up to leave, I motioned to Mike I was heading out. He gave Petey one more hard look, willing him to be okay. I knew what the desperate look meant because I was doing the same. We stumbled into the hallway, two strong, normally confident men, barely able to walk a straight line. Not because we were drunk or high, but because reality had hit us like a monsoon wiping out a small village. We were human, not invincible, and reeling with the knowledge that we could be crushed, devastated, washed away like flotsam, and in the end all we had was one another.

Passing the nurses' station, I looked up, trying to figure out who could tell Petey for us that we'd been there and would be back. I barreled up to another pretty big old dude waiting by the desk; we stood shoulder to shoulder and waited for someone to help us.

When a woman in scrubs walked out of a nearby room, he piped up first. "Hey, excuse me...I was called for Pete Clark. I'm his emergency contact."

Seeing as how he was yelling this to the nurse in charge, I wasn't really eavesdropping. Turning toward him, I tapped him on the shoulder. I suddenly had a few questions.

Who the hell was he? Here for our Petey? We'd only ever heard about Petey's mom, who died of breast cancer a while back.

His emergency contact? *Bullshit. I'm his emergency contact.*

Not so patiently, I waited for the man to turn, and when he did, I was met with the only set of silver-gray eyes I'd ever seen, other than my own.

The man who looked like an older version of me took one look at me and said, "Oh fuck."

Yeah.

thirty-two

Quit Before It's Too Late

Natalie
Miami

Stunned, I stood there in the middle of the sidewalk as more tears dripped down my face, chills making their way up and down my spine as my heart splintered. He'd walked away. Once again, Asher had gone without even glancing back. Just up and left me on the street corner to raise Quinn all by myself.

Wasn't that what I wanted? To raise my son without his father knowing?

And who the hell is Lila?

Why was Asher always racing toward some other woman? Any feelings that still remained for him, I needed to purge.

I pulled my hair back behind my neck and gripped it like a lifeline, closing my eyes as I let out a long moan, then released it as I took stock of my surroundings. This was ridiculous; I was standing outside the day spa talking to myself. I had to get a hold of my emotions.

Stomping back to my car, the serenity of the massage and the steam room a distant memory, I ducked into the driver's seat, determined to forget this whole day. It was time I went back to my original plan to make a new life in Miami, and raise Quinn on my own as had always been the case.

Asher can go home to Lila, for all I care.

FRIDAY MORNING came too quickly. I had eaten dinner with Lynx and my son the night before, giving him extra hugs, even though he had no idea why. My meddling sitter/houseguest tried to pry at bedtime, curious as to why I was home for dinner and not out with Asher as the two of them had originally conspired, but I'd held up my hand and shooed Lynx away. I didn't have it in me to even mention his name without breaking down and crying, and I was sick to death of tears.

Now I had to drop Quinn at his camp program, get a quick eyebrow wax, pick up some clothes for my job at the Kitty, and get to work. With a big party on my agenda, I didn't allow myself a moment to dwell on the man who ran away from me—over and over again.

I had a bachelor party coming in that had requested me. Lots of men who were running toward me rather than away from me, wanted me to share my body with them, had money and wanted to spend it on letting their hands linger on me. It wasn't much, but I would take it.

It was all I had.

Even though I wasn't speaking to her, Lynx was doing camp pickup and dinner with Quinn. I drove to work with the music turned up, trying to pump myself up for the night, forcing myself to think of dollar bills and men in suits. But all I saw was ripped jeans, boots, and a lightning-bolt tattoo.

Entering my latest place of employment, I took in the garish purple-draped walls, the ridiculous sparkling Christmas lights strung along the ceiling, and the cheap furniture made of faux pine covered with vinyl. I hated it. As I stared at the long fake white marble staircase that led upstairs to the VIP areas, I actually craved the run-down Leop with its no-frills approach to stripping. The Tunnel was something different altogether. It was five-star, class all the way, navy leather and dark brown mahogany, the Ritz of strip clubs, the Leop being a motel and the Peppermint Kitty nothing but a foolish imposter.

I didn't have time to dwell on the decor. I needed to make money, so I headed back to the large communal dressing room. Another difference between the Tunnel and this hellhole.

Oh God, I really hope I don't do this comparison thing all night.

Not having time to do much more than touch up my makeup and get changed, I was out on the floor within forty-five minutes of arriving. In no time I had already snagged someone to entertain before the party, a looker who smelled like money.

The tall, strong man in a custom suit was already five lap dances in when he suggested we head to the "champagne rooms," which was just another way of saying a room where we could bend the rules a little.

The guy actually wasn't half bad looking, but he was bubbling over with excitement like the suds spilling from the complimentary champagne the club doled out upstairs. There was no mystery as to why he was so charged up; it was clear he didn't get much action outside the club.

What the hell was wrong with him?

I didn't have to ponder this for very long. As soon as we were situated on the lilac banquette in the back corner of the champagne room, a new song came on—"Everything Zen" by Bush—which was funny because nothing was Zen about what happened. I was climbing his body, my knees braced on his, my high heels jutting behind me. Leaning in, I ran my chest along his as my tongue peeked out, running around the edge of my glossy, red-painted lips. He reached forward as though he was going to touch my hair or my neck, and I let him proceed.

Instead he dropped something out of his sleeve and before I knew it, he'd clicked some collar contraption around my neck before hooking his finger through it and pulling me closer so he could bite down on my neck. Immediately, I tumbled over, my body filling with anger and rage, then I righted myself and full-on slapped the dude, my bracelet catching his cheek and drawing blood.

Good. Motherfucker.

Within a moment, Brad, the upstairs bouncer, had restrained the asshole and was walking him out, demanding the key to the collar.

He didn't have it. The police were called, the guy was searched, and he was telling the truth. He really didn't have it.

I ended up in the emergency room where they had to cut the thing off, so I missed the big bachelor party and my chance to make big bucks.

I was starting to hate Florida.

162

thirty-three

Home is Where the Heart Is

Asher
Las Vegas

"WANT ME to come in?" Mike asked as he pulled up in front of my Vegas house. The reality that I owned a home in the desert and rented a mansion on the Florida coast suddenly seemed hysterical. Laughter bubbled up my throat as I said, "Hell no."

"You sure you're okay, man?" Mike brought the big SUV to a stop and turned to face me. I must have looked like a freak—smirking, giggling, and cursing all at once.

"Yup," I said as I jumped out of the truck, slamming the door behind me.

Choosing the front door over the back one, not wanting Lila to know I was home, I planned on self-destructing. I didn't want Mike or my fair-headed neighbor seeing me like that, now or ever.

After pushing the door open, I immediately kicked it closed behind me. I disabled my alarm before I grabbed my phone in one hand, dialing both the solution and the cause to my problems.

"Hey, Pen." I paced my large hallway, waiting for her to respond.

"Asher? What's up? What's wrong, babe?"

"Oh, not much. I'm back." My boots fell heavy on the marble floor.

"Oh."

"Yeah, 'oh' sounds about right. So, I guess you know it all. I got a bastard kid with Natalie. Did you also know I knocked her up during a threesome I don't remember?"

"Ash—"

I sat down on the bottom step and stretched my legs out in front of me. "Yep, I did. Drunk, high on coke and God knows what else, I screwed Natalie over a decade ago and we made a baby. A boy. Looks just like me. At least from the picture I saw. I've been living down in Florida, hoping she would let me meet him. She didn't. I don't deserve to."

"Aw, sweetie, don't say that."

"Nah, it's the truth. I'm a big-time fuckup. Look at what happened to my club and my guys when I up and left. Fucking Petey is laying in a hospital bed with tubes sticking everywhere. Did you hear that too? He could have died. Mike is a goddamn mess, and what do I have to show for it? Nothing." I punched my hand into the nearby wall, cracking the paint and plaster. Blood burst from my knuckles, marking the ivory-colored paint like the scarlet letter I left on Natalie.

"Do you want me to come over? Asher?"

As I walked into the kitchen, thinking of the morning Natalie sat naked on my counter, I barely heard Penelope asking if she could come over. I was a desperate, broken man with nothing to give or offer my own son. And I just accidentally met my own father for the first time in thirty-plus years. My self-pity knew no bounds. My pride was so far gone, I wasn't sure it would ever be resurrected.

"Sure. Come on over. Bring an eight-ball, Pen. Don't come without it," I ordered, then hit End Call.

I couldn't ask her to bring another girl. The act of being with two women would forever be tainted; it was inevitably what broke Natalie and me apart. It would also be unrivaled, because the same type of proclivity ultimately gave life to my son. There was no way I could straddle those two opposite ends of a continuum with a mediocre excuse for a ménage anymore.

I was giving that shit up and getting acquainted with my old friend: Mr. Blow. As in white lines, not getting my dick sucked.

Roaming the house, waiting for Penelope, I decided to put the hunk of junk on the market. It held too many bad memories, and it was an empty, void shell. Like me.

I hadn't even been there when Natalie found Penny and Larken in my bed, but the thought of it was enough. The place was haunted with bad karma. I talked to Beck Hadley here, made plans to meet up so I could learn about my son from that sack of shit. The woman I loved was destroyed within these four walls.

The mini-mansion was meant for a family but served as a vapid space with unfilled bedrooms, ones my son could have slept and played in if I wasn't such a waste of a man. Just like the man I came face-to-face with only an hour ago, the big, strapping, sorry excuse of a father of mine. Unfortunately I was just like him, and I needed to blow that theory wide open. With an eight-ball of coke.

I pumped the music up high, blasted the air-conditioning, and got started on a special bottle of single-malt scotch while waiting for Little Red Riding Hood to arrive with the Big Bad Wolf's treat.

THINGS WITH Penny didn't go as planned after Lila interrupted and insisted I kick the bitch out. Too caught up in all my own drama, I didn't think the girls would turn on Penelope, but they did. The waxer had just started to tell me she lost all the business of the Tunnel girls, carefully planning her own pity party, when my neighbor burst in unannounced through the side door.

After a minor mishap with the coke—none of it ending up my nose and all of it landing on the floor—Lila showed the redhead the door, kicking it closed on her ass. Then I spent the night curled up in a ball with my head on Lila's lap. Something I had never done, and would never admit happened.

The woman who had been the only constant in my life for the last seven years stroked my back and told me everything would work out. Except she still didn't know about Quinn. I couldn't bring myself to tell her about him, revealing exactly how much of an absolute loser and a fuckup I was.

Lila offered to call Carson over for a drink, but I declined. No way I was letting another bro see me like I was. I was a first-class mess. Afraid to even look at myself, I stayed on the ground where I deserved to be, like a dog.

thirty-four

Knock, knock. Who's there?

Natalie
Miami

I WASN'T *ALLOWED* to work on Saturday. My new boss forbade me to come in, paying me for the weekend up front with tips added in, saying he wanted me to rest, put my feet up, forget about what happened. In other words, he wanted to be sure I wouldn't make a big deal, cause a commotion, or bring bad publicity to his club.

He had nothing to worry about because I wasn't going to do any of that. All I wanted was to work my tush off, forget what happened, move forward and onward. Which was becoming a recurring theme in my life.

Snuggled on the couch with Quinn, both of us in old sweats and T-shirts, watching a movie, trying hard not to be aggravated with... well, with everything, I heard a knock at the door. My skin broke out in goose bumps at the possibility of it being Asher. Could it be? Did he come back?

Although it wasn't the same banging from his first visit, my heart raced, pumping and pounding, fluttering at the small chance it was *him* on the other side of the door. My whole world crawled in slow motion as I felt my hand wander to my neck to clutch my hamsa. My

166

brain turned sluggish as my mind ran through every possible scenario.

Forgetting who was sitting with me until it was too late, I froze to see Quinn rush to the door in anything but slow motion, yelling, "Who's there?"

I jumped physically and mentally out of my fog, and called out forcefully, "No, Quinn. Let me handle this. Go back to your room. Now."

"Mom, come on. I'm a big kid. I can ask who is at the door," he said while standing firm, hands on his hips, staring me down before he turned back to the door.

We both yelled, "Who's there?" in unison.

A quiet voice came back through the door. "Sienna."

I mumbled, "What the fuck?" to myself as I slipped by my son, tucking the stubborn kid behind me so I could answer the door.

"Mom!"

"Sorry, Q. I'm not myself today, but you stay behind me. It's for your own good," I said, rumpling his hair before turning the lock.

Looking like a stunning tourist in dark skinny jeans, a fitted white tank top, and espadrilles high on a wedge, Sienna stood there with her blond hair falling loosely down her back, a perfect shade of pink on her lips.

"Sienna? What are you doing here?" I said without moving, blocking her view of the boy she had never met.

"I needed to see you, talk to you. Nat, I need to explain in person what's been happening back home," she said, never taking her eyes off me.

Suddenly I realized her eyes were green and not blue. Feeling myself sway, I gripped the door frame, my brow furrowing.

"Are you okay, Nat?"

"Yeah, I'm fine. You look different, I can't put my finger on it. Is everyone back in Vegas all right?" A shiver shot down my spine, traveling the whole length of my body. Something was wrong.

"It will be—eventually. Listen, can I come in? So we can talk privately?"

When she inched her way closer, I held up one finger and said, "Give me a sec. Let me get Quinn settled." I shut the door quickly because my son, who had no clue what had been going on, was jumping all around, full of curiosity about who was at the door.

Very quickly, I promised him a trip to the arcade if he went back to my room and finished the movie there. Quinn let out a little whoop of excitement and took off toward my bedroom.

After clearing my throat and wiping the fine sheen of sweat off my forehead, I reopened the door and stepped out into the Florida heat. As if I already didn't feel like I was choking, the humid air took up residence in my throat, clouding my eyes and slowing my thoughts.

I leaned back against the warm wall while taking a calming breath, then said, "I'm so confused, Sienna. Why are you here? And why are your eyes green?" I looked up, focusing my gaze on the pretty blonde.

She moved over to the wall and stood next to me, shoulder to shoulder, not eye to eye anymore. Looking straight ahead, she said, "I'll get to my eyes in a minute. They have nothing to do with why I'm here. Asher needs you, Natalie."

"Ha!" I laughed as the word burst out of my mouth. "I doubt that. I'm sure you know he was here. Ran out of here like a tourist to a free buffet as soon as he got a phone call from home."

She leaned into me, grazing my shoulder with hers. "Seriously, Natalie. He's in a bad way. I know he didn't explain why he left…which is why I'm here. We need to talk. Can we go inside and sit down?"

"I don't think that's a good idea. Just get it out. I really have no idea why you think Asher needs me. We are nothing to each other. Really."

Still not entirely sure how much everyone back in Sin City knew, I didn't want to risk Sienna finding out about Quinn if she didn't know.

Turning her shoulder into the wall, Sienna faced my profile. "Please, Natalie, you know he cares for you more than anyone. Why else would he have been down here in Miami, sweating bullets, other than to get you back, salvage what you two have between you?"

Before I could answer, the door swung open with such force it hit the wall behind it. "Mom, that movie was awesome! There's a second one! Can I rent it? Please, Mom." Of course, Quinn picked the most inopportune time to poke his head out.

Sienna's head whipped around and although she was trying to whisper to herself, when she said, "Now I know why he was down here. Son of a bitch," it came out much louder.

A lethal gaze fell onto me from my former coworker and Asher's closest friend. I wanted to turn away from the death stare, but I couldn't because I was guilty of what she was thinking. I had hid Asher's son from everyone, but more importantly, I'd hid him from his own father.

Without moving, I said, "Sure, baby," to Quinn. He didn't seem to feel the tension. Pleased as punch I was allowing two movie rentals in a day, he ran inside before I changed my mind.

"Oh my God. Oh my God," was all Sienna kept repeating while gripping the wall she now turned to face.

"Listen, Sie, I know what you're thinking, but it's not like that. I'm shocked you didn't know about Quinn—after all, he's what brought Ash down here. Not me. Definitely not me. He's got someone new back home anyway. Lila. I'm sure you know."

The tiny force whipped around, grabbed my arm, and whispered to me in the angriest tone I'd ever heard from her. "No, I don't know, Nat, because I *am* Lila. Me. You see, I came from an abusive background. My husband was beating the shit out of me until I escaped and came to Vegas. Asher took me in and created Sienna, with blond hair and blue eyes. Then when you flew the coop and ran out of town, I was kidnapped—I'm sure you heard that part—by my ex. I was drugged, brutally assaulted, and manhandled across state lines. That's why Asher didn't come to you right away. He and Carson had to find me. Thank God, because I was almost raped."

Her chest was heaving so hard, I could see the outline of her heart beating through her fair skin, racing a mile a minute. Worried she was going to pass out, I said, "Calm down, Sie. I didn't know any of this."

"Well, that's obvious," she replied through heavy breaths.

"Still…Asher didn't sign up to have a kid or anything when he slept with me on a whim, fucking me without a condom during a drug-induced threesome. Did you hear that?"

I had to move, so I started pacing. Turning on my heel, I didn't wait for an answer before I said, "So if you're Lila, and you're here, what the hell is going on back home?" For the first time since moving to Miami, I yearned for home—Vegas.

Sienna took a wary step toward me, steadied her breath, and said simply, "Petey happened."

"I'm not following you."

She put her arm around me and explained. "Petey was in a horrible accident while chasing the guy who tried to force drugs on you. He came back to the club, wanting in, and when they said no, he pulled a knife before running and Petey followed. A car came speeding out of nowhere and tipped onto Petey, his leg got clipped by the bumper or something. He's in the hospital, pretty out of it. Asher blames himself because he was here with you. Mike blames himself because—I don't know why. Not sure what's going on there."

Then they came flowing again. They being the tears that found themselves dripping so easily lately from my eyes.

"Oh God," I muttered.

"That's not all of it, Nat." Sienna let out a long sigh and went on. "Geez, there are so many lies and holes to the story going on here. Your kid, Mike's sudden mood swings and drinking, and then the real kicker. Not knowing Asher was back yet from here, I saw some lights on his house, so I popped over, only to discover him staring at a bunch of lines of coke on his table while Penny tried to—"

I couldn't let her continue. "Penny is a bitch! Don't even tell me anything more about her…and Ash."

"I know you don't like her. You shouldn't, but let me finish. She was trying to talk Ash out of going down that path again. He was shaking, his shirt soaked through with sweat, red rimming his beautiful big silver eyes—"

"That was the coke," I spat out as disappointment in Asher washed over me.

"Actually no. No, it wasn't, Natalie. He hadn't even touched the stuff yet. The shaking was from meeting his father. A man with his silver eyes, claiming to be Petey's emergency contact, showed up in the hospital. It all makes a lot more sense—coming off of discovering he had a son. I never thought Ash would be such a mess over meeting the man who deserted him, but life has a weird way of coming full circle. Can you believe it?" She grabbed her forehead as she finished speaking.

"His dad? Quinn's grandpa? They all have the same eyes?" I was stunned, confused, reeling into a dark abyss of my own thoughts, wondering what this meant for Asher, Quinn, and Petey. How did this all tie in with my good friend and protector, Petey?

Realizing she had been squeezing me tight during the whole exchange, I moved out of Sienna's arms and braced myself against the wall, leaning my head against the cool concrete. "Petey? How is he?"

"Bad. Banged up. Lots of recuperating to do, but alive."

My head felt ready to explode with what I was going to ask next, my consonants and vowels getting jumbled in my windpipe like a bowl of alphabet soup. Not sure it was going to come out right or even make sense, I paused, breathed, paused some more. "And Ash? Who is with him now?"

"Nobody. When he saw me, he took his hand and swiped the cocaine off the table, making an expensive mess on the floor, before throwing Penny out. She wasn't who he wanted."

"Oh, please."

"She's not what he wants. He doesn't know what he wants. Look, he's a man, Natalie. One who's been torn up inside all his life, part tough, the other half gentle and sensitive. He's never had the real love of a woman, you know that. Read into the threesome thing—he was searching and getting more lost—and his avoidance of you right now. He needs you, but is afraid to ask for you. Of course, he would be. I knew this without even knowing you were the mother of his child. Which is why I spent half the night lying on the floor with his head in my lap before coming here to get you with my tail between my legs."

Sienna took a deep breath. "Look, you and I were never close, nor were we enemies. I should have paid more attention to your affair with Ash, talked to him more, encouraged him to do the right thing earlier. I'm really sorry for that, but I'm here now."

I shook my head, new tears coming, merging with old dried-up ones. I couldn't speak anymore. Nothing could come out. Pulling my cell out of my pocket, I texted Lynx. She was at the beach, but I didn't care. Now was her time to pay me back for all the shit she had helped orchestrate.

thirty-five

The Big Bad Wolf

Asher
Las Vegas

THE LANDLINE started ringing but I ignored it. Eventually it stopped, then immediately began to ring again. I sat up from lying on the couch for way too fucking long and took stock of my surroundings. There was a fine layer of coke on the kitchen floor, the air-conditioning was blasting yet I couldn't stop sweating, a table or two were turned over, mail was spread across the bar with half of it fallen on the floor, and I stank like a pig.

I stood to get the phone.

"Yeah?"

"Asher, it's Mike."

"I know. Got caller ID."

"Where's your cell? I've been trying to call you for hours."

"It's here. In a million pieces."

"Well, glad I got you. Petey's up. Dude is awake, tolerating pain, talking to PT right now. He's gonna move to a rehab place in a few days."

"Good. That's good. Tell him I'll see him...there."

Maybe.

172

I walked over to the mirror in the hallway, holding the phone between my neck and my ear while I took in my greasy hair, dark black circles under my tired eyes, and my ratty, sweat-soaked T-shirt. I was a fucking mess. Counting backward in my head, I realized it had been four days since I got back from Miami. Ninety-six hours since I deserted Natalie for Petey, the little shit, and met with my worst enemy yet. Fate was a terrible cunt, a mean son of a bitch.

"You there, Ash?"

"Here."

"You two—you gotta talk, man. Petey knows some shit."

"I gathered as much, Mikey-boy, considering my dad's his emergency contact."

"Why don't you come over here?"

"Nah. Not ready for that. Maybe never."

"I feel you. Petey can wait. Want me to come over? Is Lila there with you?"

"Nope, don't need you or Li. I don't even know where she is, now that you mention it. Saw her a few days ago, and she's been a ghost. Listen, I'm fine. I gotta roll."

"I'm gonna let you go now, Ash, but not forever. I'm gonna be hounding you. Nothing you can do about that."

"Later."

"Sooner than later," he said before disconnecting the call.

I set the phone back in the charger. Okay, slammed it back in before heading to take a shower. It was the least I could do; I couldn't even stand smelling myself.

As I threw my shirt off my back while walking up the stairs, the bell at the side door started to ring. I tore my jeans off on the top landing, leaving me totally nude as I headed straight toward my master bath, and ignored the ongoing bell. No one ever came in through the side door but Lila, and she knew the code. If she needed me, she knew how to get me.

Screw her.

I reached into the shower and turned on the water, knowing it needed a minute or two to heat up. My mouth tasted like a sewer, so I brushed my teeth, looking anywhere but in the mirror.

Hot water rushed from the rain head and I stepped in—letting it pour down on me, baptize my sins, take away all the bad shit I'd ever felt, wash my soul, and cleanse my heart of feelings. Not only was I cleaning my body of the days-old odor, but cleaning my life. The good and the bad, the nasty and the even more evil, everything.

I tilted my head back, allowing the water to cascade down my hair and over my shoulders as I took stock of my life. My hard fucking life with no dad, a mom who up and left, neighbors who took me in and did the best they could, a giant missed opportunity with Natalie, two decades of meaningless sex and threesomes, too much drugs and alcohol, a kid who didn't know me, and the only decent thing to come out of it all was I owned the best strip club west of the Mississippi.

Ha—what a joke.

Despair took me over as I slid down the tiles. When my ass connected with the wet floor, I dropped my head back against the wall. I sat there with my eyes glued shut, desperately trying to erase the last twenty years of my life with scalding hot water.

Pretty sure I was close to falling asleep when my head whipped up and flung back at hearing the shower door slam open.

"What the fuck?"

Standing there in front of me, her eyes wild with fury and desperation, wearing a pair of leggings and a big, old ripped sweatshirt, her hair tied up in a ponytail that flicked from left and right as she took in my predicament, was Natalie.

Throwing her arms in the air, she yelled, "What the fuck to you? I thought you were dead, Asher. I was ringing the doorbell over and over, scared to death at what you had done on the other side of it. Jesus! Sienna let me in—the last she saw you was with an eight-ball spread all over the floor. What the hell was I supposed to do when you didn't answer."

She turned around and slammed her hand into the bathroom counter while taking in her wild appearance in the mirror.

"Nat." I stood up and leaned back into the shower, but didn't have the courage or strength to move and shut the water. Natalie was there, in my bathroom. She'd come for me.

Whipping back around, she came close again and stepped into the shower fully clothed, wrapping her arms around me, rubbing one hand up and down my back as she kissed my cheek. I ran my hand down my thigh and pinched my leg, pretty fucking sure I was hallucinating. *Nope.*

"Asher, baby. You can't do this to yourself. Look at you—you're a mess," she whispered into my cheek, her breath catching my ear.

"I saw my dad," I said, suddenly finding myself a man of few words.

"I know." She reached her hand down and squeezed mine.

"I'm like him. Deadbeat dad. Don't know my kid. When I saw him, I got a good look at what I'll be like in twenty more years. Lonely, missing life, and watching it all go right by me."

Natalie moved our clasped hands up to rest on my heart and looked at me with soft eyes. "No, Asher, you're not. I never told you about Quinn. That's on me. I've loved you since I was a little girl, and I wanted you to love me back my whole life. And I was so stupid, thinking that night after the threesome with Shayla, that maybe you'd love me back. I didn't think things through, and I ended up knocked up and alone."

She edged even closer as she went on. "Then I couldn't make myself part with the only piece of you I had left—Quinn. I spent years avoiding you, and then that one night, when you and I ended up in the private room at the Leop, it was over for me before it started. I realized it didn't matter how many bartenders there were to eat lunch with, none of them would be you. When you took me as your lover, I decided I would take you any way I could have you. I was so afraid telling you about my secret would ruin everything, take away the tiny piece of you I had."

I brushed my lips along the side of her face, breathing in the scent of her, inhaling my life back as I thought about what she'd just said. *"I wanted you to love me back my whole life."*

"You're not a deadbeat," she whispered. "You didn't even know you had a kid, Ash. I'm the bitch in this scenario. I kept him from you, and I know it doesn't make anything right, but I'm here for you now. You don't have to love me back or anything. I'm here as your friend, lover, a shoulder to lean on, whatever you need."

What? Is she nuts?

"Shhh," I said as I turned us so her back was to the wall. Begrudgingly, I unhooked our hands, but used mine to lift her sweatshirt off, tossing the sopping fabric out of the shower before unclasping her bra. I slid my hands up her body, worshipping each curvy inch, taking stock of the beauty in front of me. I stared at her gorgeous nipples for a long while, afraid for our eyes to meet, and then I lifted my gaze. Swimming with tears, her eyes were two tiny shining embers of green, burning strong for me, welcoming me home.

"I love you, Natalie. Probably always have, little doll. Just didn't know it, but I do—now."

My mouth crashed into hers before she could say anything, my tongue diving in, tangling with hers. I couldn't get deep enough. I'd never had the love of a woman in all my life, and now in my shower, here was the best woman I ever knew—telling me she loved me. We had a connection, a son, and I loved him, even though I'd never spoken a word to him. He was mine.

Like the woman I was kissing.

My whole body hummed for the woman in my arms; there was no hiding my hard cock. Pulling back for a second, I reached down and ripped Natalie's soaked leggings off, tearing off her tiny thong. As I brought my lips back down on her mouth, I lifted her ass up, and her legs immediately wrapped around me. I moved us to the center of the shower, allowing the water to fall all around us, now washing away our combined pasts, and making this a fresh start.

She leaned back and looked at me. "Asher, I don't need you just to say it back."

"Shut up, Natalie. Be quiet and keep kissing me." I grabbed her ass even tighter, pulling her into my erection, rubbing my dick along her core, hitting the sensitive spots. God, I needed the woman.

Turning off the water, I walked us out into the bedroom, then pulled the covers back and laid our wet bodies on top of the sheets, hiking Natalie's knees up to my hips. I held my weight on one elbow, but couldn't bring myself to move from being on top of her. Finally, the feel of her wetness on my cock, the smell of her arousal drifting through the air forced me to move down her curves and take a taste.

Settling on the floor in front of her, completely submissive on my knees as I worshipped the woman in front of me, I placed my tongue on her heat and started slowly licking, sucking, and swirling. Her little body bucked in my face, reaching for more, begging without any words for speed and friction, crying for a release, and I gave it to her. Twice I gave it to her, and she screamed my name the whole time. Each time she did, my erection felt like it grew a little larger.

Finally I crawled back up her body, my mouth lingering along her abdomen as it made its way back to her tits, taking each of her taut pink nipples inside it in turn, grabbing like a greedy kid with grubby hands in a candy store, unable to settle myself into reality.

Natalie in my bed, naked, loving me.

We were the only two there in bed, and I was harder than I'd ever been before. No need for anyone else. Ever. Natalie was all I needed. It had always been there in my mind, but I didn't see it. I'd told her that being with her was different, but the intensity of *us* felt greater at that exact moment.

"Nat, doll, you're it for me. Just you." I grabbed her hand and brought it down to feel me and she squeezed tightly, the way I always loved it. I leaned my head back and hissed, "Yes."

Looming over her, I said, "Just you, that's it. Do you understand me?" I was so ready to enter her, but waiting to make sure she got me.

She nodded and with that, I was deep inside her, my length getting lost in her tightness. Christ, I felt her pulsing around me, still riding a few aftershocks, squeezing my dick, making it hard for me not to blow my load.

I moved gently and slowly at first, building friction and heat, but there was only so long I could take the slow pace. Natalie moaned, speaking my name in a raspy voice, and I was a goner. As I began to pound into her, she stretched one leg up to hook over my shoulder as the other one stayed tight around my waist.

"Look at me," I demanded.

She opened her eyes, tossing her head back on the rumpled comforter. I leaned down and ran my tongue along the outline of her lips before giving her a long kiss, letting up on the pace for a minute. She extended her arms, pushing me up, giving me more leverage. My hand went to her hip for purchase, and I began pumping into her.

"Harder, Ash."

She didn't have to ask me twice. I obliged. Sweat ran down my back and I was burning up, as if a fever was running through my body.

Her whole body began to shiver under mine and she came hard, her pussy squeezing my dick like a vice. I followed right behind, yelling, "Love you, Nat," as I came down from the high of Natalie.

We lay there for a long time in silence, tangled up in each other, letting our breathing settle.

Finally, I asked what I needed to know. "Where's my son, Nat? It's time for me to meet him."

thirty-six

Intermission Over

Natalie

"I N Florida. With Lynx," I said. I was snuggled into Asher's neck, legs intertwined, our naked bodies refusing to separate of their own volition when he asked about his son.

"What? Why?" Asher's voice was a bit raised as he sat up on one elbow.

I took my arm, drawing the man who said he loved me down toward the bed, coaxing him closer. "Well, when Sienna—I guess you all call her Lila now—showed up at my door, she said you were in bad shape. I wasn't sure how you would react to me coming back, so I left Quinn with Lynx. They're fine."

I was tracing figure eights on his arm, which was now thrown across my side.

He brought his hand to my cheek and smoothed his palm over it, his eyes now a clear metallic silver, looking right into my soul, setting tiny fires in my heart. "Nat, I can see how you would think that...I didn't mean to walk away from you. It's just that Petey got hurt, and I felt like I was spinning my wheels down in Florida, like I didn't deserve to meet Quinn. I should have never given up, but one thing you can be sure of—I've wanted you to come back since you left, and now that you're here, I'm not letting you go anywhere."

Tears burned behind my eyes as reality settled in my gut. Asher wanted me with him, something I had dreamed about as long as I could dream.

Turning toward him, I planned to say sweet words, a declaration of my adoration, but Asher lightly slapped my butt and jumped up, throwing his jeans on.

"Come on," he said.

"Where? What are you doing?" I sat up, grabbing the blanket and wrapping it around me.

Of course, Asher leaned in and pulled the blanket down, taking a quick second to pinch my nipple and tug on the ring, before saying, "To Florida. I got a son to meet."

I was speechless. There was no reason to stall, Quinn had to meet Asher sooner than later, but I was secretly shaking inside, afraid of how my son would react. Thankfully, Asher had made his way into his walk-in closet, buying me some valuable time to think.

"Um, Asher. Quinn may get really angry with me for keeping this from him. I don't think we should rush," I said as he walked back toward me, throwing on a dark blue T-shirt. *God, his eyes are amazing with that color.*

"Doll, he's not gonna be mad because I'm not gonna let him. This is on me. I didn't give you any reason to think that I wanted to be a dad. You didn't have any other choice than to keep Quinn from me. Now, he's got to know that first and foremost. Straight up. I got to take responsibility for that. Second, he needs to know that now that I know about him, I'm never letting him go. He's my boy."

"Okay," I said slowly, hesitating while looking down at my naked body, worried that Asher grossly misunderstood kids. "I have to get dressed. My bag is by the side door where I dropped it when I rushed in. And you should probably let Sienna, I mean Lila, know you're alive."

"I'll shoot her a text after I get your bag." And then he was gone, rushing down the stairs.

Deciding to take my time getting dressed, I stalled in the bathroom, fixing my hair. As I was making sure my makeup was perfect, I heard Asher on the phone, barking at Mike, making arrangements for the club and our travel, saying we would *all* be back in two to three days.

I stepped out of the master bath and caught the tail end of their conversation.

"Tell Petey I'll get to him when I'm good and ready. And yes, I'll bring Lynx back, you can be sure of that. No, I don't care about that prick right now. I'm more concerned about not becoming like my father than making nice with him."

Asher was sitting on the edge of the bed, hunched over his knees as he spoke on the phone, but he looked up when I came back into the room, his focus bearing down on me as he said the last sentence.

I couldn't hear Mike's response on the other end, but he didn't have time to say much because Ash stood and said, "I gotta go. We're heading to the airport. See you in seventy-two," before disconnecting.

Turning to me he said, "Ready, little doll? Just leave that bag here. We'll be back soon enough, and you have crap down in Florida. Shit— we'll have to get it all packed up and moved back to Vegas."

He was back down the stairs before I could answer.

"Uh, Ash, I have a job in Florida. I can't up and leave. Quinn has made some friends," I said as he started to put the house alarm on.

Not even faltering for one second, he grabbed my hand and walked into the garage, opening the door to the SUV as he said, "If you think you're working one more second in that two-star, sorry excuse for a club, you don't know me, Nat. Don't worry, I'll take care of it."

Oh, I knew he would. I sort of asked for that when I up and left for Florida. Whether I was dating Asher or not, he wasn't going to stand for one of his girls moving on to a shithole like the Peppermint Kitty.

"Well, what about your dad?" I asked as we pulled out of the garage.

"He can wait." Asher flipped on his shades, and off we went for him to meet his family.

thirty-seven

She Did It, He Did It

Mike

"Lynx, PLEASE call me back. Look, I know I've been unreasonable. It wasn't fair, but you have to call me. Please. Natalie is on her way back down with Asher, and there's something else you need to know. Call me. I need to hear your voice. Please, baby."

As I slid into my personal sauna, I was desperate to hear more than her voice mail message, just a few syllables of her voice, a *hello, how are you?* Even a *fuck you*. Anything. My whole body ached with a need to connect with Lynx. Sitting in the small tiled steam room, letting the last few weeks of alcohol sweat out of my pores, I wrung my palms and racked my brain. Physically and emotionally, I was a wet noodle.

Why couldn't I be more like Carson? He knew better than to ask Lila to stop dancing as Sienna, letting her decide on her own, which she did.

Who was I to think I could even begin to understand Lynx's burden to put herself through school? I was a trust fund kid playing dress-up as a Vegas hoodlum. My dad owned half the fucking Strip.

We might have parted ways—my parents and me—but I had more cash than I knew what to do with in the bank. More than I let on to anyone except Asher. And Rochelle, but a lot of good that did me. She decided if I had that much, why not dip into the source, who had even more.

Stepping out of the heat, drops of sweat dripping down my body, littering the floor as I waited for the cold water to fill the shower to cool both my body and temper, I bore a hole in my own face in the mirror. Looking deep into my hardened green eyes, I told myself to get over it. I wasn't meant to be in a relationship. Take my own parents as an example—they were a screwed-up mess. Who would believe I would escape that unscathed.

Yeah, I could send Lynx to a million schools if she wanted, but I wanted her to want me, to make decisions for her and me, like quitting the escort business, before I told her how much I was worth. Leaning back into the chilled marble shower, I realized I was being about as stubborn as she was.

God, I hoped Asher was able to get her to come back with them.

thirty-eight

Ten-Year Reunion

Natalie
Miami

ASHER HELD my hand the whole flight, his lips grazing my neck, sucking on my earlobe, kissing his way up and down, making way for the words he was whispering. "Love you, Nat. Feels so good to fucking say it out loud."

I was somewhat relieved we flew commercial for fear of what the man would have done up in the friendly skies if we weren't surrounded by a bunch of other people.

My nerves were on edge, little shockwaves of fear running up and down my spine like a volcano about to erupt, small sparks of lava flitting up and down its core. Grabbing one of those small airplane bottles of wine from the attendant did little to help, but it was about as much relief as I was going to get.

Asher was the picture of contentment. I felt a giggle bubble up in my throat over how ridiculous this brand of excitement looked on the man sitting next to me in motorcycle boots, frayed jeans, a five-hundred-dollar Dior shirt, his hair a rumpled, sexy bed head of unruly blond curls.

I said, "Shhh. Stop, Ash. My thoughts are going as fast as this airplane. We can't just barge in on Quinn and drop the bomb."

He held his head up and said, "Okay. Don't worry, Nat. It's all gonna work out. How about I go pay a visit to your boss while you have a quick heart-to-heart with Quinn?"

Lifting my fist in the tight quarters of the first-class cabin, I punched him in the brick wall known as his bicep. "Don't you think I should handle both? You could go to your house and relax for a while until I'm ready for you."

Asher ducked in close and whispered in my ear, "Nope. Nat, you're not getting away with that coy shit. I'm taking matters in my own hands, doll. Gonna talk to the idiot who runs the shithole you're working at, and then be back to meet my son."

My stomach dropped at the thought of what he would say to my boss—especially when he heard about the collar incident—but it was the lesser of two evils. I cared about Quinn, not my employer. I placed my hand on top of his and squeezed.

"Ash, I don't know how to say this, but…"

He turned to face me while holding my hand in a death grip, and in a low voice I gave him the short details on the other night.

As expected, it didn't go well, and for the second time during our flight, I was glad to be sequestered on a tight flight with lots of people. Otherwise, I was positive it wouldn't have been pretty.

"Uh, Ash, I can't feel my hand. Loosen up. It's all going to be okay. I'm quitting. You don't need to go nuts, okay?"

He lifted his hands behind his neck, shaking his neck back and forth as he let the tension bleed from him, then settled me in the crook of his shoulder and kissed me on top of my head. "Yeah, yeah. I know, but I'm still going to have a little heart-to-heart with your soon-to-be ex-boss man."

Closing my eyes, I knew there was no sense in responding. He wasn't going to listen, so I tried to get some rest. Unsuccessfully.

B ACK AT my tiny, yet tidy, apartment, Quinn sat on the sofa, his mouth wide open, fist pumping the air. "I have a dad!" he yelled as he jumped up from the couch. Lynx high-fived him. I sat and watched the whole celebration unravel before my eyes like fireworks on the Fourth of July.

The two of them were a kaleidoscope of color as they whirled around the bland beige living area, chanting, cheering, and whooping. I, on the other hand, was stuck to my kitchen stool as though there was superglue between my butt and the vinyl. Part of me ached for Quinn to actually be mad at me for what I did—because it was wrong, and would probably haunt my every waking hour for as long as I lived. But he was such a good kid, he wouldn't.

Now, the boy I had raised from day one all on my own was about to meet his dad, who was apparently the cat's meow without anything to even base it on, and I was jealous of Asher and felt murderous at myself. None of it had to be this way.

I started to dream up a reason to pick a fight with Lynx. After all, what the fuck was she even doing here, taking part in this reunion? I couldn't do that, though; she was just a young girl who had stuck her neck out for me.

"I got a dad, oh yeah! He's gonna be so cool and teach me stuff and do stuff with me!" Quinn kept singing to the girl.

My head bobbed and my foot tapped to his enthusiasm, but my heart kept plummeting through my chest like I was on the death drop at the fair, over and over again.

I hurt my son. For close to a decade.

The bright royal blue of Quinn's T-shirt slid past me as he mimicked a touchdown dance he saw a football player do on TV. A zigzag-printed maxi-dress was not far behind, copying the ridiculous shimmy. Setting my head into my hand, I closed my eyes, keeping the tears from falling. I couldn't help but think about the few days in the hospital when my son was born—and I was alone...

M Y MOM had been with me during the delivery. God, the pain had been unbearable at times. I was still nineteen, just like the night I had gotten knocked up, and I'd been unable to control my emotions. Tears had flowed freely, wetting my hospital gown, soaking it. As my mom held my hand, I had cursed at anyone I could think of, but her. She was there, after all. It was the least I could do.

I thought of my dad, who had been gone for a while, and part of me was relieved because he would have been so disappointed to see me throw it all away on becoming a single mom. The other half of me was sad that he wasn't around to meet his grandchild. He wouldn't have stayed mad forever.

Mom hadn't been thrilled when I told her I was pregnant, but she'd never been a fan of parents abandoning their kids, so she had stuck by me. As she took me to appointments and helped me pick supplies, she had known all along who the father was. She would say, "Nat, you're not fooling me. There's only one guy who could have gotten you pregnant and you would keep the baby. I'm not dumb, and I know exactly who you're protecting."

Her thoughts were confirmed as soon as the nurses cleaned up my little blond-haired baby boy, wrapped him in a blanket, and handed him to me. I had always been a brunette. Mom too.

Dad, also had dark hair. I guess there was a recessive gene somewhere in me, but this blond was so pure, a dead giveaway to the other person who created him—even at one day old.

It had to be the fair-haired bad boy from next door, the one I had always loved, and my mom knew it. I tried to deny it, to fight against it, up until the day my water broke.

When the pain finally stopped and my son was placed on my chest, my momma smoothed her hand along my brow and said, "It's water under the bridge now, Nat, honey. You got a baby boy. A beautiful, healthy one, and now it doesn't matter who planted him inside you. He's yours and yours alone. Keep it that way."

I let the fight go.

Dazed from giving birth, I wasn't sure if she meant I shouldn't tell Asher, or if he didn't deserve to know. I only knew I had a son, and he'd been born out of the most unconventional scenarios—meaning I needed to do what a mom did. Take care of him.

The little fair-headed bundle smelled so good, was so innocent and helpless, and when he finally opened his pale blue eyes—they hadn't turned silver yet—and looked at me, my whole heart jumped and leaped to belong to him.

Because I was just a teen at the time, my doctor pulled a few strings to snag me an extra day in the hospital. Having an additional twenty-four hours for me to rest and the nurses to help show me what to do with an infant was a godsend, because my mom had to get back to work and caring for my grampa.

I didn't know the first thing about babies, so I was eternally grateful for anything and everything extra to help me out.

I was most appreciative of the time to rest, and I used every minute Quinn was in the nursery to stock up on some Zs. If I knew one thing, it was that I wouldn't be getting much of that when I arrived home. It was during my second day in the small hospital room when I finally got around to showering and cleaning up.

Bending over to check my phone, I saw a tiny gift box on my nightstand. Right away, I had opened it and found the most beautiful charm dangling from a chain. It was a four-fingered hand made of glass, blue like the ocean, deep as the night sky, inviting like a warm pool sparkling in the midnight moon. I had no clue what it stood for or who had brought it, but I put it on, figuring it had been from the hospital nun.

And who didn't need good luck?

REACHING FOR my hamsa as I always did these days when stressed, I froze when I realized it wasn't around my neck. Apparently I hadn't put it back on after I went to retrieve it from Asher's that awful day. Shaking my head at the little party going on in my apartment, I decided this was the perfect excuse to take both myself and my rampant thoughts back to my bedroom to look for it.

Just as I found my lucky charm in the bottom of my underwear drawer, I heard the front door open.

I barely made it to the archway where the hallway to the bedrooms met the living space when I heard, "Are you my dad?"

Watching Lynx slip outside, closing the door behind her, I wanted to call to her, pull my friend close, steal her strength. Instead I leaned against the threshold, then watched and listened like a voyeur in a strip club, afraid to move, knowing all too well I wasn't allowed to touch.

"Yeah, I am," Asher answered, standing stiffly in the foyer.

"*Wow*. My dad."

The two stood stock-still taking each other in, digesting the person in front of them.

"You are some little man. I'm already so proud to call you my son," Asher said without moving a centimeter other than nervously tugging at his own unruly hair, the same messy mane as the small child in front of him.

"I didn't think I would ever have a dad."

Quinn hadn't moved a muscle. I couldn't even say for sure if he was blinking.

"Fuck." Asher tugged his hair harder and pulled his head back, exposing his neck and beating pulse. "Oh Christ, I guess I shouldn't have said the F-word, buddy," he said, snapping his head back up.

"It's okay, I know it. Mom says it sometimes too. By accident, she claims. And Christ. She doesn't let me say that either."

The man slid to the floor in front of the boy.

Witnessing Asher bend down on his knees and get close to Quinn brought a lump to my throat, one I couldn't clear. It clogged my windpipe with a vengeance, making it hard to breathe, bringing on a sense of light-headedness. I felt like I was falling into some kind of deep, dark abyss where I witnessed my dream come true before my very eyes.

"Listen, Quinn. I know this is kind of crappy, you and me meeting like this. I'm going to make all kinds of screw-ups, but we are forever now. That's all you have to know. You hear me?"

His hand was visibly twitching, probably because he was unsure whether to reach out and touch his son or not. Finally, he fisted his hands in front of his stomach, wringing his fingers. I'd never seen the confidence knocked out of Asher before, and it was bringing me to my knees. I slumped down to the cool tile.

"What about Mom? I'm staying with her, right?" Quinn finally made some movement, his head turning back, catching sight of my limp body, worry spreading across his small brow.

"Yes. I'm never gonna take you away from your mom. Never. I promise."

My son nodded his head, agreeing.

I saw Asher lean in to say something in a whisper, but he made sure it was loud enough for me to hear. "In fact, buddy, I would like very much for the three of us to be a family, but I know I got to win your mom over first. Maybe you'll help me." He looked up and winked at me.

Quinn turned at the same time and gave me a huge smile.

They might as well have said, "Game over." The man had won my kid over in five sentences, and I couldn't peel myself off the ground.

The two had turned their attention from me and were back to getting to know each other when Asher asked, "Can I get a hug? Would that be okay? I know we're both men, but I missed all those years, and I just want one quick one."

"Uh-huh."

And just like that, father held his son, and I remained lifeless and listless across the room, floating on some imaginary cloud where happily-ever-after happened for the stripper and the boy next door.

thirty-nine

Pimp My Ride

Natalie
Las Vegas, two months later

WE'D BEEN back in Sin City for close to two months now, and I wish it had been all perfectly romantic with Asher and me riding into the sunset with our son in tow. But the reality hadn't even been close. After meeting Quinn in Miami, Asher went into instant protective-father mode and arranged to have all of our belongings moved back to Vegas with five phone calls. He asked Lynx to wait behind until it was all packed and gone before she followed behind with a first-class ticket bought and paid for by who else? Him.

And he sold my car! I knew it was old and not fancy, but it was reliable and worth some money. Even though my new one, which he procured without asking me, was quite fabulous, driving the enormous thing consumed me with an insane fear of losing control over my life.

I was shattered—all because of a damn vehicle.

I'd been in charge of myself for way too long, and now the idea of someone calling the shots led to ice-cold chills shooting up and down my spine, warning me not to give in to someone who had continually let me down.

Which was exactly why I tried not to use the damn car unless I was

189

driving to work, like at the current moment. Work being back at the Electric Tunnel, protected by a bighearted and very controlling boss.

Sighing to myself, tapping the steering wheel to the music, I was lost in thought. Somehow after four weeks of nonstop battling with Asher after arriving back in Vegas, I got my life back as I knew it. Or as close as possible considering my secrets were now exposed and out in the open.

Currently stopped at a five-way intersection, I thought about how furious I was with Asher for making the decision to unload my beat-up car in Miami, but as it unfolded, I quickly took notice that I had bigger problems. Like where Quinn and I were going to live in Las Vegas.

Of course, Asher wanted us to move in to his place right away. He had plans to turn his gorgeous bachelor pad full of leather furniture and grandiose wet bars into a family home, where I would presumably be home cooking dinner every night.

Well, that wasn't how things went down exactly. And knowing me as well as he did, I can't believe he ever expected otherwise.

Fight number one occurred as soon as we boarded the charter plane home. Quinn was ecstatic, running up and down the short aisle, jumping up and down with excitement over the plane and its luxurious interior, oohing and aahing over his newfound luck. Already pissed at the way Asher was spoiling my son, who had lived a decent, but definitely not extravagant life so far, I nearly clobbered the man when he declared we would be moving into *his* house.

"No freaking way, Ash. I'm not ready for that. Not for a long time, and definitely not until I forget about who and what I found in your bedroom," I said into his ear with gritted teeth while our child bounced through the cabin.

"Nat, honey. That's my kid. I want him—and you—with me," he begged softly while kissing my temple.

"No. That is not how this is going to work. I'm moving back so you can get to know Quinn, but you just don't get to have it all, just like that, Ash," I said while settling in my seat. Then I closed my eyes, pretending to catch some shut-eye, eavesdropping on the conversation between father and son, and wishing I could give in to Asher's wants. I'd told him I loved him and wanted to be there for him "as a friend or lover" before we made love, but some nagging voice inside me wouldn't allow me to go all-in with him.

Wasn't being with the bad boy from next door what I had always wanted? Didn't I dream of taming the tiger who was sitting next to me, radiating heat, lust, and passion all for me? For so many years, playing house with Asher and our child was my deepest, darkest fantasy, and it was being served up to me, but I was too stubborn to grab it.

After refusing to talk for the whole flight, I called my old landlord as soon as we landed and got our old apartment back. Then I called a cab, grabbed Quinn's hand, forced him to say good-bye to his father, and hightailed it out of there.

Now, as I parked and ran into my new waxing studio, the Smooth Lips, to get a quickie, a shiver ran through my body, thinking about my first forty-eight hours back in the city where I was born and bred.

Stuck inside for two days without a car, listening to my kid beg to see his dad while my mom babbled on about how she warned me this and that, I was going out of my mind. On the third morning, I woke up to make coffee, and while looking out my small kitchen window, discovered a shiny silver Cadillac SUV parked in my designated spot with a big red bow on the dash.

That was fight number two. I texted the stubborn man right away.

Me: Come and take it back.

Him: Never. You and Quinn need a safe ride. Trish has keys next door. When can I see you guys?

Rather than answer, I just shut my phone down for twenty-four hours.

After another day of being trapped in my apartment, refusing to even retrieve the keys to the monstrosity, I decided I needed to go back to work. Knowing full well he wouldn't say yes to the idea, I called Asher and told him to pick his son up for dinner.

And, of course, he did.

I laughed to myself about how I set him up as I waited in the treatment room for my new waxer, one I didn't know. Any one of those bitches would do. Becoming serious as I sat naked on the table, I allowed my very mixed and tormented emotions about going back to work take up residence in my idle brain.

Asher had taken Quinn out for burgers the night of my return. As soon as they'd pulled out of my apartment's small parking lot, I threw on some confidence and went to the Tunnel, then got dressed to perform as if I'd never left. Just as I was about to hit the floor, my dressing room door flew open and Asher stormed in with Big Mike dutifully at his side. This quickly became fight number three, thanks to Petal ratting me out.

Peppy little bitch.

It was a biggie, but I won. Now freshly waxed, my ass as smooth as a baby's bottom, and back in my ridiculous top-of-the-line SUV and heading to the Tunnel, I couldn't help but mentally pat myself on the back. Asher was so aggravated that night.

Well, he would eventually learn I was my own woman, I thought as I recalled our most heated argument…

WHEN THE door to the dressing room swung open, I had gone into a full-on panic as soon as I'd seen Asher. "Where's Quinn? You didn't bring him here, you stupid jerk?" I had yelled while smacking his chest—hard.

"Nat, no, of course not. I'm stupid, but not that stupid. As soon as Mike called me, I dropped him with Trish. He's all good. As soon as I get you back home, I'm going to grab him again."

I felt weak and pained in a way I couldn't even begin to describe that my impressionable son might have seen me in my work clothes. Falling into the chair at my vanity, I had to remind myself to breathe. Taking in large gulps of air, I turned to look at Asher, who was staring back at me, and Mike, who was already gone, apparently escaping as fast as he came in.

"You're not working here anymore, Nat."

I stood and met him, front to front, death stare to death stare, and said, "Yes, I most certainly am. This was my job for a long time, it is my profession, and I need to make money. You can't take that away from me."

Hands on his hips, Asher shot back, "I got plenty of money. You don't need to work, little doll."

"Yes, I do," I said through clenched teeth.

"Not here, then. We'll find you something else."

Brushing past him, I turned when I made it to the door. "No fucking way, Asher. I'm going to work here, and you're going to like it. If you want any chance of moving forward with me—and Quinn—you can't take all the control away from me. This is my job, like it or not, and you told me years ago that the Tunnel was the best place for me. Want me to go back to the Leop?"

After I'd delivered that low blow, I hadn't waited for him to follow behind me. I just walked straight out onto the floor and did what I had always done.

I'd sold myself.

I DRIFTED BACK to the present while making my way past familiar streets, landmarks, and intersections, and then I made my way to the back lot of the Tunnel to put my body on display for anyone who paid the right amount to see.

Touching was extra.

I wasn't sure when my personal ideas on life became so twisted, but lately, I couldn't make heads or tails of my emotions. I kept insisting that I wanted to be independent, forcing my sometimes insane decisions down Asher's throat, threatening with the only thing I could—Quinn.

For some odd reason, I wouldn't allow myself to get lost in the only man I had ever wanted to lose myself in, despite the fact that he was begging for me to dive in.

When it came to Quinn, I knew I couldn't hold him back. He and his dad were learning all about each other, growing accustomed to each other's ins and outs, going out to eat for every type of junk food known to man, watching movies, and playing video games. Of course, my son was drawn to his dad's bike, dreamed of riding one himself, and talked about it nonstop.

It was everything I didn't want.

It was everything I had ever dreamed of.

There was no gray for me. I couldn't mix the wants of my past with the desires of my present. One was black and the other white, and I couldn't paint the two together.

So I remained distant, stayed a challenge for Asher, a mountain he couldn't just climb, but had to excavate first. Slapping on hard layer after hard layer, I made it nearly impossible for the man I loved to dig his way inside. I had some dark and twisted need for him to peel back my layers, taking the time to understand what made me tick. Which lately, I had no clue myself.

Before entering work, I stood for a long time in the parking lot staring up at the huge sign, the purple lightning bolt with the words Electric Tunnel running vertically inside it. The hot desert sun beat down on my dark hair and sweat trickled down my back, yet I just stood there and stared, hoping the flashing neon sign held the answers I so desperately needed.

It was hard to admit, but I also wanted some grand apology. For Penny. For that other ridiculous young bitch.

Although we had made decadent love that day after the shower of truth, I didn't allow myself to forgive when it came to Asher and his indiscretions. Our threesome was water under the bridge, but the one with Penny was too fresh in my mind.

So I worked, strutted around the club, rubbing my tits and crotch up and down strange men, pocketing tips, while the father of my child, the man who claimed to love me, watched from his private cameras.

Asher walked the floor less and less when I was at the club, often ducking out to spend a few hours with Quinn before letting Trish tuck him in.

Petey was still recuperating, and for some strange reason I didn't understand, Asher was staying away from him. With Petey out of commission, Billy was my newest detail.

Billy was a cream puff and, thankfully, smitten with someone other than me, which helped me in my directionless pursuit of nothingness.

Like at the moment. As I hit the back door of the club, ready to get down and dirty, my little pussycat of a bouncer approached with a simple, "Hey, Nat! How you doing today?" Billy walked me to my dressing room with no arguments, zero pomp and circumstance, and without bossing me around.

I loved that kid, needed him more than anyone else. He was the only soul who gave me any mental reprieve from the war constantly taking place in my head and in my life.

Stopping at my dressing room door, Mr. Goody Two-shoes Billy said, "It's gonna be a great night!" He pushed open the door for me and took his post outside, waiting patiently for me to get my game face on.

Then, like every other shift six nights per week, we made our way out into the club when I was ready, scantily clad and sexed up. He kept one eye on me and one on Sadie. Eventually Billy always moved two eyes to Sadie, as he was doing at the moment, and I was free to loosen my rules, make extra money, all the while throwing a stick of dynamite into an already burning building.

forty

Father, may I?

Mike

LYNX DIDN'T come back as Asher had expected her to do. She apparently didn't mind wasting his one-way ticket back to Vegas. Initially, I'd gone out of my mind with obsessive wondering and nonstop thinking about what she was planning or doing. Afraid for her and sick for myself, the very bottom of a JD bottle lured me in for a few days, until I finally picked up the damn phone and called the woman.

Not sure how I would survive another broken relationship in six months, I located my very own set of balls and took destiny in my own hands. *I will get the girl back*, I chanted in my head as the phone rang.

Should have clued myself the fuck in that my confidence was misguided when I felt the need to *67 my phone number so it came up private.

After all, did Lynx and I even have a relationship? Or was I slipping into bad habits like Asher, rescuing helpless beauties?

As Natalie's first few days back wore on, I told myself, "No, we certainly didn't have anything close to real." Nothing about Lynx and me was pure. We were both living behind a facade.

Neither of us were who we appeared to be, but I couldn't get the woman out of my head. I wanted to save her in the worst way, make her

195

mine, and take care of her.

Which was why I was blown the fuck away when she answered the phone and said, "Mike, I know it's you, and you have to stop. Stop calling me and torturing me with what could be, because it can't. This is good-bye." And then she hung up.

I wanted to grab the bottle, but I didn't. I decided to man up and be who I really was. Yeah, I had money and resources at my disposal, and I was throwing them away on a great big nothing. Fully convinced I didn't have to be the country club boy in golfing whites who ate lunch before starting the back nine anymore, I made a choice to stop pretending. I could use my money and resources but still stay true to myself.

Of course, there was no way I was leaving the Tunnel. Never. No fucking way. Those four walls and the people inside them were the only version of *real* I'd ever known. I was working on something else for the crazy crew who brought life into my vapid existence. It was about time I got around to making bigger plans, ones with them in mind.

Like a dream, my larger vision for success came to me at night, as I was tucked deep in bed after stroking myself.

Which was another thing I stopped doing after I tossed out my generous supply of booze. I was a man and there was no way I was going to sit around and jack off to nudies on the Internet night after night. It had been a long time—practically fucking never—since I'd played around, and that was what I was doing.

Despite a revolving door of women in and out of my bedroom, gorgeous ladies of every shape and size—long, luxurious, curvy, athletic, waif-like, I sampled them all—I still pined for *her* supple café-au-lait curves, long braids, and big smile. But I made up my mind. I needed to be a better man for my friends *and her* before I convinced Lynx that her reasoning was shit.

Which explained why I was having breakfast with my dad at seven o'clock in the morning on a Friday. The two of us were seated in a deep gold banquette in the luxury diner tucked in the back corner of the casino in one of his four casino/hotel monstrosities. Yep, that was the kind of mega-money I came from, and I was on my way to make even more.

Every business journal, major newspaper, and magazine on three or four continents had covered my dad at one point or another. I didn't want that kind of notoriety. I wanted to be a man with my own rules, and in my world, all that cock sucking wasn't necessary. Look at Asher—he played by his own rulebook and he was king of his own empire.

So, my dad and I lowered our swords at each other because being rich was always my destiny, and he would rather I did something with it than nothing. I didn't give a shit if he was fucking Rochelle or not; I needed his knowledge, and he needed me to move the hell on with being an adult.

So after getting sober and draining my dick in a bunch of willing women, I decided to channel my energy on business. My pops was currently giving me an earful on supply and demand while I ate an egg-white omelet and turkey sausage, slot machines clanking in the background. We were discussing the hotel biz specifically and why hotels either set up in remote locations where there was no competition, versus building something strategically bigger and better in an overpopulated, well-visited area like the Strip. Neither was a shoo-in. In no-man's-land, how could you be sure anyone would come? And in terms of the Strip, what if you weren't the best? What if you weren't doing something different from anyone else?

My head was swimming with the information, and I was contemplating how my dad had four very different properties all catering to a different audience, each one definitely being the best in its category, when my phone buzzed.

Jesus Christ, now what? Who else does business this early? I was used to three and four a.m. in the adult entertainment world, but seven a.m. was a quiet time in my current industry.

When I looked at the screen and couldn't believe who was calling, I held up one finger to my dad, signaling I had to take the call.

"Man, what's up?" I stood up to walk out toward the entrance to the casino floor from the diner, far away and out of earshot of my old man.

"I'm fine," Petey said. "Actually, breaking out of this place today and heading home with visiting nurses and PT. Hope they're hot." We hadn't been talking as much because things were tense between us. I felt he blamed me, he insisted he didn't, and Asher wanted no part of the dude right now.

"That's good. Great news, Petey, and I bet you they're all babes." I paced, holding the phone to my ear.

"Yeah, listen. His old man has been here visiting a lot. Said he's done taking no as an answer in talking to him. He's gonna head to the Tunnel today. You gotta help."

"Shit."

"I know. Shit. It's not gonna be pretty, but Asher won't talk to me. I suspect you know why, so it's up to you."

"I got you. I'll head over there early and deal."

"Thanks, Mike. Would love to see you soon."

"Yeah, I'll swing by next week. Definitely." I looked toward the restaurant, catching a glimpse of my dad waiting. He looked like he was aging a little. Crap, life was short. "You know what, I'll swing by tomorrow."

"Cool," Petey said, and we both disconnected.

Walking back to my table, I decided to have another pot of coffee. I would need to be alert today.

forty-one

Throwing in the Towel

Natalie

IT WAS Friday, and I was reveling in a full night's sleep after a relaxing day off when I woke to an incessant banging on my door. Quinn tiptoed into my room, and I felt him tapping my shoulder. "Mom, it's Dad. He's here. I know I'm not supposed to let anyone in, but can I let him in?" he whispered.

This is what my life was turning into. The stubborn man was infiltrating every little corner of my existence, including my sleep. I pulled my shit together for my son and said, "Yeah, baby, go ahead. You two can hang out and have some time together." I had already denied Quinn close to a decade with the man; I was in no position to keep him from his dad.

I had just rolled back over and started to doze when I felt the bed shift and dip on the other side. By the weight of it, I knew it wasn't Quinn long before I heard the sound of boots falling to the floor.

"Good morning," he said in a gravelly voice. Wetness flooded my panties, soaking them at the sound of two words.

"Trying to sleep, Ash," I said without turning over.

"I can see that, doll. Want you to rest. Came to make you breakfast, but then I couldn't resist seeing you all sleepy and natural." He ran his hand down the length of my back, heat burning through the sheet. With his palm firmly settled on my lower back, I became immobilized with want and need for him. For Asher.

Turning slowly, forcing him to move his naughty hand, I found the man who haunted both my private fantasies and everyday life lying comfortably on the other side of the bed, his muscular arms tucked behind his head as he smirked at me. Of course.

"Now you see me," I said with a bit of snark.

He reached his arm down again and lifted the cover, eyeing what was underneath before sliding his hand under and down my thigh.

Swatting at him, I said, "Ash, you do know your son is right out in the living room?"

"Uh-huh. Babe, he's so involved in a video game, he's gonna be there for an hour. I know this shit now that I've been a dad for a month." Bigger smirk for him; huge gush down below for me.

"Well, we're not at this stage right now." I moved his hand. Reluctantly.

"I know, but I want that to change." His eyes turned a light silver, softening both in color and intensity.

I shook my head.

"Come on, Nat. I told you I need you, I love you. I'm trying more than I've ever fucking tried at anything. What else do you want? Because all I want is you. And my son." His eyes darkened a bit, the color starting to smolder and burn right in front of me.

"I can't, Asher. Not yet. There are too many unknowns. Like whether you can survive the next few decades without a threesome? Imagine if Quinn ever walked into a scene like I did? Or what about your dad? You never talk about that. Ever. That's why I rushed back. He's Quinn's grandfather, you were so distressed over the man, and now—nothing. I'm not sensing anything long-term from you. Do you understand what lifelong means?"

I felt my ever-present tears welling up and prickling the back of my eyes as my constant state of anxiety rose and fear pooled in the pit of my belly. I worried I was pushing the man too far, but I couldn't stop. I was my own worst enemy, sabotaging my own hopes and dreams with my big mouth and inability to surrender to what I wanted. It was right there for the taking. The man, the promise of a family, a life I never believed to be within reach was all there for me, and I was pushing it far away.

Asher ducked his head and lowered his blond lashes, his hair falling into his eyes. "I don't know what more long-term you want from me. I'm trying to make a life with you. I wanted you to move in, build a home with the three of us, provide for you and Quinn, but you insisted on living here in this crap apartment. You work night in and night out, going out of your way to shove your assets in other men's faces with me watching, and refusing to give at all. You haven't given one bit. And as far as my dad is concerned, he's a closed subject. End of. Period. He hasn't been in my life, and he's not going to be. I'm doing things differently with Quinn, that's what I learned from that jerk."

"I have given, Ash. I gave you access to Quinn."

He stood, bent over to put his boots on, and said, "I can't take it anymore, Nat. It's all too much. I'm trying and fucking trying, but it's not good enough, and I'm sick of feeling like a failure. *Sick of it.* You know what? I'm not going in to work tonight. I can't take that bullshit tonight either. How about I keep Quinn all day and night so you don't have to pay a stranger while you go shake your ass for someone other than me?"

The dam on my tears broke, and they began flowing like a rushing river. The wetness burned down my cheeks, making its way over my collarbone before pooling in the neckline of my T-shirt. My throat was clogged with something else.

A huge lump of regret and confusion made it impossible for me to respond, growing bigger with every step he took toward the door.

"Is that cool with you?" Asher turned and pinned me with his stare when he was at the threshold to the hall. "I would love to have my son overnight, but I'm a slave to you and your decision making, Nat."

I barely made out a yes before I heard celebrating in the kitchen and Quinn's quick footsteps running to his room so he could pack a bag.

Curling back up in a ball, I only sat up to give my son a kiss and hug good-bye. As soon as the dynamic duo was gone and I heard the door lock shut did I allow the saltiness to drown me, washing over me like a tidal wave. Unable to bat it down, I was forced to ride it out, gasping for air, and treading for my life.

forty-two

Playing House

Asher

Spending time with my son was the only way I quelled the anger stampeding through my veins, threatening to gut me, urging me to do something very stupid. All because Natalie was at work. The girl was downright crazy. She was the one who rushed back to Vegas to save me, held me in the shower when I felt my world crushing down on me, made love to me, took me to meet our son, and allowed me to get to know him.

Then, bada-bing bada-boom, suddenly she was little Ms. Independent, not wanting me to buy her a car or handle anything when it came to her and my son.

And they are mine.

What the fuck?

As for this bullshit with her being back at work, it was getting fucking ridiculous. Yeah, there was nothing wrong with the Tunnel, and I made the place as good as it could be for my girls, but Natalie was my woman. I made millions—why the hell did she need to work? Let alone be rubbing her bits all over some other dickwad, when the only man she should be rubbing against was me.

I wasn't stupid. I knew she was overdoing it with those pricks, making her point that she made up her own mind. She didn't need to let those jack-offs' hands roam what was mine to make her point. Staying out of my bed, refusing to move in, not allowing me to help… everything she did made it crystal clear.

The only way I could keep my head from blowing up was to do something permanent about the other person who was mine. My son. We spent the afternoon buying gear for his new room at my place. I was transforming one of my guest rooms into a preteen's mecca complete with a double bed, locker shelves, a huge freaking TV, DVR player, video game console, and a life-size soda vending machine.

Quinn was pumping his fist into the air at the moment as he watched the furniture delivery guys bring everything in from his haul.

My heart was pumping as fast as his fist at the sight. I had a son, and I was already more of a dad than I'd ever had. The idea of what lay ahead thrilled me.

Except for the fact that his goddamn mother was probably making her way onto the floor at this time to shake her ass for another dude. Why couldn't she be with us? See how serious I was about treating the two of them right?

Fucking hell.

forty-three

Blast from the Past

Natalie

I WAS DEFINITELY in a pissy mood by the time I pulled into the Tunnel. Hauling open the heavy back door while shuffling two coffees—one for me and one for Billy—only reminded me of when I used to do that for Petey. Where the fuck was he? I thought he was doing better, and I was shocked he didn't swing by the club to say hello to everyone. Asher was being crazy weird and removed regarding him, even more so than before.

There were so many holes in the stubborn man's excuses and reasons, I was back to not trusting him. Whether it was unfounded or not was pointless; I had full-on convinced myself that Asher was no good for me.

I didn't have time to think on it much, though, because as soon as the door slammed shut behind me, Billy was there to escort me down the hall to my dressing room. I was back in my same old room with Petal, except she was moving out soon to take over Sienna's palatial space. I only had to stomach a few more weeks with Ms. Perky Pants.

Or Ms. No Pants At All, like at the moment. I walked into our shared space to find my roomie stretching in a thong and sports bra. What was with her? I didn't mind nudity, but Jesus, the girl could at least try to cover up.

"Hey, Nat!"

I hurried and closed the door behind me, so Billy didn't get a glimpse of her ass crack peeking out at me.

"Hi," I muttered. Sitting down at my vanity, I started to put on my makeup, examining my face in the bright lights.

Petal strolled over and placed her hand on my shoulder. "You okay, Nat? You look kind of emotionally spent."

"Is that a nice way of saying I look old, past my prime?" I turned and asked my much younger coworker.

"No," she said slowly as she frowned at me. "Seriously, I just meant you look like you have too much on your plate, and I'm worried about you. I mean, you were always a bit distant and sad, but we loved you despite it. It's just now—you're almost like an island, alone, floating in the ocean. I don't know why you want to be that way."

She knelt on the floor and took my hand, running her thumb back and forth across my knuckles, consoling me for something she didn't know the first thing about. What could someone like her possibly know about heartbreak, misery, never-ending loneliness, and chest pain from a broken heart?

I sighed. "It's not you, Petal, it's me. I've made my life this way on purpose. I know it sounds crazy, but now that you all know Asher is the father of my son, I just want to be left alone. At one time I dreamed of making a life with the man, but it's not a reality for a girl like me. I just have to earn a living and support myself, because now that Quinn has a dad, he'll be taken care of. That's all I can hope for."

I pulled my hand away and stood, pretending to choose my outfit for the night, when I really wanted to curl up in the younger woman's arms and have her tell me what to do. Tell me that it was okay to want to run back to Asher and believe everything he said.

Sliding the clothes along the rack, the hangers screeching on the bar, I might have taken my growing anger out on the poor thing, but I was so confused. My mom was zero help. She had actually distanced herself more since I moved back, telling me it was time I made some big-girl decisions, lecturing me on how she knew for years that Asher deserved to know the truth. Stubbornly she refused to take responsibility for telling me to let the idea of him go in the delivery room. She also stopped babysitting Quinn while I worked, like she was in cahoots with the father of my child, saying she "would spend time doing stuff together, but a real plan, not babysitting."

So it wasn't exactly me who put myself alone on an island. Was it?

I slipped into a bright green bodysuit, mostly cut out. It ended up being a thong connected by one skinny strip of fabric up my abdomen attached to tiny slivers covering my nipples, highlighting the outline of my piercings. Surveying my side cleavage, the front of my boobs, and my mostly flat stomach in the mirror, I tried to tune out the other woman in the room.

I didn't look that bad, did I? Years of dancing had kept me young and toned.

From somewhere behind me, I heard, "I call bullshit, Natalie. You, me, and everyone else who works here knows Asher is ripped up over this. He spent the last two years freaking out every time you went in the back with a man, openly hated you working the VIP areas, and totally lost his shit when you left. Now you're back and you mean even more to the man, if that's even possible. Because you're the mother of his son."

Holding up my palm, I said, "Please stop, Petal. I need to get ready for work."

"No, I won't. If you thought we hated working for Ash after what went down with that Ecstasy guy close to a year ago, you were right. Now with you being back on the floor, it's worse. Ash is a good guy. I never said he wasn't confused, but no one is going to deny he is good. The best. Get your head out of your ass, Nat. And do it soon."

As I leaned over to take off my hamsa and place it in my drawer, Petal stuck her round butt in my face as she bent over to grab a bottle of water from the fridge, and said, "Now, I'll stop."

WALKING ONTO stage right to perform my first dance of the night, I was already fit to be tied. How dare Petal take me on like that? Who did she think she was? We weren't really friends, were we? Except, I didn't think Sienna was my friend either, and look what she did by coming down to Miami to get me.

The platform darkened as I made my way to the pole, and a premade mash-up of that young pop girl and a techno rock group blared from the speakers. I wrapped my legs tightly around the metal, squeezing my leg muscles, gripping hard with my inner thighs. As the purple and blue strobe lights lit up and spread across center stage, I released my grip and spun around the pole with my arms, my hair flying with the motion, my skintight outfit staying in place although the audience probably would have liked it to shift to the side an inch or two.

smoldered

I could have sleepwalked my way through the song, gyrating and pulsing, tweaking my hips, flipping my auburn-highlighted tresses, winking, and spreading my legs just the way the crowd had dreamed about all week.

At least, that was what I kept telling myself. But my stupid brain wouldn't absorb my own arguments, and now I had Petal in my ear about the whole situation too.

I wanted Asher in the worst way, which was why when I moved to the front of the stage to let some of the men stick bills in the side of my panties, I saw Penelope having a drink at the back bar. Immediately, I saw red. And I didn't mean her hair.

Finishing out the song, I immediately jumped down from the large platform and started moving like a lioness on the prowl, my tiny green outfit shimmering in the bright lights, all the way to the back of the club. Catching Billy off guard with my quick and unconventional stage exit, combined with years of experience of dancing on platform heels, I beat him to my destination.

As soon as my feet came to a stop, the red-haired bitch smiled. She was freaking gloating, waiting for me to come over and make a scene. I couldn't fucking believe it. This woman had been our friend forever, and now after showing her true colors, Penny had the nerve to show back up at our club to embarrass me? For fuck's sake, she'd waxed my pussy. She knew damn well I was sleeping with Asher. Everyone did.

Of all nights for Asher not to be at the club, he picked this one. The one where the woman who he was screwing in a three-way when I wasn't available showed up. They could make a TV mini-series about this type of stuff, and this was my reality.

With a smirk, Penny spoke first. "Hey, Nat. Glad to see you back."

I cocked my head to the side and glared. "How did you even get in here?"

"Oh, that was easy, Mike was busy with Petey and some old dude, who looked surprisingly like Asher, and I slipped right in past some new idiot. I guess the person filling in for Petey."

She took a sip of her drink, vodka straight up with a twist of lime. I knew this because we had hung out plenty of times.

"Well, why don't you leave before I have Billy escort you out." My cupcake of a security detail had finally pried himself away from watching Sadie and was standing behind me, watching, so close I could feel his body heat.

Penny smirked. "This isn't your club, Nat. I know you have a bastard child and all with Ash, but I heard you're back living in that tiny dump, begging for any scrap of attention from Asher you can get. How come you're not living the fairy tale like in *Pretty Woman*, playing housewife in Ash's gorgeous house?"

My blood pressure skyrocketed. "I've heard enough. I don't know where you get your information, Penny, but you're wrong. Trying to explain anything to you is a waste of my time."

I turned to walk away and said to Billy, "Take care of this bitch."

Without even turning to see what happened, I went straight to the VIP area to find myself a lucky victim to take my assertive nature out on.

forty-four

Mr. Mom

Asher

My PHONE started blowing up as soon as Quinn and I finished having pizza and tried making his bed. Jesus, I really couldn't take a night off. As I swiped the screen, I also saw I missed a call from Mike. He knew what he was doing; he'd figure it out on his own.

But my whole fucking heart dropped to the ground when I saw Billy's name come up on the incoming call. That sweet-as-all-get-out dude was on Natalie duty, and I was going to kill him if something happened.

"Talk to me," I ground out after accepting the call and walking outside on the back patio, signaling to Quinn I would be one minute.

"Asher, I'm sorry to do this, but I think you got to come in. Here's what happened—"

"Get to the motherfucking point, Billy," I said, interrupting the kid.

"Penelope is here and won't leave. She and Nat got into it, and now Natalie is back in the VIP room...with two sets of eyes on her, don't worry. But Mike is tied up out front with some other scenario—Petey's here apparently too—and I can't get Penny to listen to me. She's saying she'll only deal with you. I don't know what to do."

"Jesus Christ. What the hell happened? I take one night to be with my son and there's more drama than a sorority. Where is that little bitch, Penny?"

"She's at the back bar."

I began pacing the length of the stone patio. "Take her to my office and stay with her there until I can get in. Now, who's watching Nat? Please tell me they're on her like white on rice?"

"Yeah, Theo, the new guy, and Brad are both stationed back in the VIP area."

I blew out a big breath. I wanted one frigging night with my kid, and now I needed to find someone to watch him. God, how did Natalie do this by herself all those years?

"Listen to me, Billy. Do not let Penny out of your sight. Do you hear me? I need to find someone to watch Quinn, and I'll be right there."

I pushed End Call before he could respond, and then walked across the yard to see if Lila was home. She could watch Quinn. Knowing her, she'd love it.

But she wasn't there.

I was definitely not calling Natalie's mom. That woman scared me, resented the air I breathed, and if I showed her how incapable I was, it would become worse.

I had no one else to call other than Trish. Crap, that girl was spending more time with my son than anyone else. Seeing as how her place was the size of a matchbox, I invited the sitter to come to my house, spread out, and have some fun with my boy.

Then came the hard part. Explaining—lying—to Quinn about why I had to run.

A GAINST MY better judgment, I took my bike, wanting to speed over to the Tunnel as fast as I could. It was summer and as I throttled the bike forward, the heat rose from the pavement, circling around me, fueling my own rising temperature. There wasn't even a welcome breeze as I pushed on faster. Arriving at the club in one piece was a small miracle, and I scolded myself for not bringing the SUV, but now I had much bigger problems than my transportation.

After flying around back and leaning the bike up, I walked quickly toward the front where Mike was pacing by the edge of the sidewalk.

"Mike, what the hell are you doing? Penny's in there, harassing Nat," I yelled at him.

He looked up, dazed, confused. "What did you just say?"

"I said, Penelope—you know, red hair, the source of all my recent problems? She's inside the club, starting trouble with Natalie. What the hell are you doing out here?"

He stood still, staring at the ground as he said, "Shit, Ash. I didn't know." He let out a long sigh and kept going, looking up at me to say, "We have another problem on our hands. Petey was here."

"Yeah, I heard that from Billy, who called shitting himself, not knowing what the fuck to do with Penny. I'll have to worry about Pete later, Mike. Natalie's my first priority."

I started to walk toward the back entrance of the club when Mike caught up with me, grabbing my shoulder, stopping me.

"Pete's only got your best interest at heart, Ash. You have to know that. He's a good dude. Your dad was here with him, looking for you. He's sick of waiting. He wants to talk with you about the connection. Petey told him you have a son. I guess he heard from one of the girls, and decided to share that info with your father."

"Christ!" I screamed. "I can't catch a break today. First, I try for the millionth time to do something nice for Nat, only to be fucking rejected. Then I figure I might as well spend the night with my son, which gets interrupted by Penny and her theatrics. And now this shit. You know what? I know the damn connection—Petey's my brother. Half brother, and he obviously had our dad when I didn't, so he can keep him now. I'm trying to make a go of the only relationship with family I may ever get—Quinn."

I pulled past my currently ineffective head of security and stomped toward the back door, trying to salvage what might be left of my relationship with the mother of my son, Mike hot on my tail. Fucker grabbed me again.

"What the hell, Mike? Why do you keep stopping me from getting any shit done?"

He shook his head like he was clearing cobwebs from his brain. "What did you say? You were spending the night with your son? Where the fuck's he now? At the sitter's?"

"Well, I didn't leave him alone, shitface. I may not know a shit ton about parenting, but I didn't just leave my kid and run out. I got Trish to come over and stay with him until I get back. He's sleeping over for the first time, and I want to make this quick so I don't miss the whole night."

"Fuck!" Mike roared. "That's where Petey and your asshole father were heading to find you. I was convinced they'd find an empty house.

Tried to talk them out of it, but your old man's a stubborn one, and I let him go, thinking you were on your way in to work. How was I to know your goddamn kid would be there?"

I smacked my hand into the back door, the sound of my skin hitting the steel reverberating into the night. It was a thunderous, loud crack, like the one silently making its way down the middle of my chest.

"God-fucking-damn it. Come on, let's get rid of Penny and then you have to drive me home. I already almost wrecked my bike once tonight." I gripped my hair tight as I walked through the door, pain reverberating through my scalp, bleeding into the constant hum of anxiety pumping from my heart.

Rushing up the stairs to my office, I did my best to rid myself and the club of Penny before hurrying the hell back out, hopefully with Nat being none the wiser about who her son was probably meeting as I scurried around the Tunnel, fixing the current redheaded mess.

forty-five

What Really Happens in the Back Room

Natalie

MY ASS was in some suit's face in the back room. He was sitting up against the dark blue banquette, trying to remain wrinkle-free in his designer clothes, and I was leaning over, hands on the floor, placing my crack right at eye level, bouncing my goods at his nose. I could smell sex on the guy; he was primed and ready to go. Dude would probably pay me the big bucks to head back to his place and simply tug on his dick. But this wasn't the Leop or the Kitty, and Ash would freak the fuck out if he knew I was even thinking in those terms.

I wouldn't do it, though. There was Quinn to think about, and I had personal limits. So I just continued to dance for him, working him into a full-on lather, hoping he would find a nice, willing, friendly woman when he went back to his hotel. Or maybe he had a wife waiting at home, and he was simply hanging at the Tunnel getting worked up, living out a fantasy.

Every so often, my gaze wandered to the security detail, making sure they did and didn't have eyes on me. One eye would be fine; no need to have two or four or six eyeballs on me. I only needed a tiny bit of protection, but definitely required a wide range of space. Noticing Billy was back, I figured he dealt with Penny, because he knew I certainly

213

wasn't heading back out onto the main floor until she was gone.

Bringing my full attention back to Mr. Designer Duds, I flipped around, front to front, and slithered along his body. It was hard; obviously he worked out, probably at a gym with some fancy trainer, but he had zero character. No laugh lines around his bland eyes, soft hands instead of rough, heavy cologne masking his sweaty smell. He was just too clean and smooth and prissy for me, but he wasn't paying for my opinion.

Just my tits and ass.

And the guy was paying big-time. I was a top biller at the club now that I was back in town, five hundred bucks per half hour in the back to be paid to the club, not including tips, which were slipped directly to me. With the man spread in front of me, my wad of cash was growing and I had mentally gone to where I went when I danced—no-man's-land, a place where my thoughts ceased to exist.

With my mind totally devoid of anything significant other than the beat of the music and dollar bills, I remained mentally distant while my body did not.

Allowing my tongue to come out and lick my lips, I stared down my night's prey, also known as this week's meal ticket. When I lifted my knee and brushed it along his inner thigh, I felt a shiver run through the man in front of me, his erection visible now through his expensive suit. He shifted, adjusted, and I kept slinking around his firm body.

His hand lifted, caressed the side of my breast. That was okay. Then he was quick and moved in to tug on my piercing. I was quicker and lifted my hand, gently removing his, and wagged my finger at him.

He wrestled with my hand a bit, trying to make his way back to my nipple ring. Obviously, the outlines of the piercings were doing it for the guy. I leaned back, brought my feet to the floor, and stood.

"I think we're done for the night." Like I'd been telling everyone for months, I knew how to handle myself in the back room.

"Wait. I'm sorry, Nataleigh. Let's stay and play," he begged.

"Sorry, buddy. Time's up. Time for my break, anyway."

I started moving out, making sure one of the young buck bouncers had stepped in to get payment, before clearing the curtain separating the back of the club from the front.

I should have stayed back with Mr. Nipple Piercing Lover because as soon as I hit the floor, I ran smack into Penny...with Asher hustling right behind her.

"Penny, get the hell over here," I heard him yell.

I couldn't worry about the redheaded slut at the moment because like a lightning bolt in the dark sky, thoughts of Quinn burst through me. Shoving Penny to the side, I said not so quietly, "Asher, where the fuck is my son?"

"He's fine, Natalie. I'm his father, like I keep telling you, I'm not going to do anything to hurt him. Get that through your head already," the asshole said as he put his arm around Penelope and led her to the back door.

The man didn't offer any other explanation of where he was going or what he was doing. Just walked away with his arm and gorgeous bicep slung around my arch enemy. That was it. My night had gone to shit, and it was basically my fault. I knew I was pushing Asher away and eventually, I would get what I deserved. Nothing.

Walking back to my dressing room, I refused to cry, only violent anger rising in my gut over my loss of control when it came to Quinn. He was my son. I had raised him alone for close to a decade and didn't want any of this world for him. Now, not only did I not know where he was or who he was with, but he might even be up in Asher's office.

With vengeance in my heart and a violent pounding in my head, I made my way to the stairs to the second floor. On my way, I held my head up high, shook my ass, and smiled at the clientele. I needed them and couldn't afford to lay my problems on them.

Bursting through the door without knocking, I found Mike alone in the office, standing behind Asher's enormous desk.

"Natalie, what's wrong?" he asked as I made my way through the door, looking wildly in every corner for any small clue or remnant of my son.

"Where's Quinn? I just saw Asher chasing after his fair redheaded lady of the night, and he was supposed to be spending the night with our son."

Mike stood still, hands flat on the desk, and said, "He's fine, Nat. Ash got a sitter…and he wasn't—" when his phone started blaring.

"He wasn't what, Mike?" I asked, but the stubborn jerk held up a finger and answered his phone.

"Li—you home? Get my message?"

He listened quietly to Lila as he turned away from the desk, resting his butt on the edge, his face now toward the back wall, making it impossible for me to read.

"Uh-huh," he said. "Yeah… Right, do that… Yep, I'm coming now. Leaving in five."

After a few rounds of cracking his neck, Mike turned once again and ended the call, saying, "I gotta go, Nat. Wait here. Asher was trying to get rid of Penny, not chase after her. I'll send him up."

As if I was going to do what he said. "No way, Mike. I'm leaving, going to get my boy. I guess Asher dropped him at Trish's after making a big deal of him not wanting him to be with a sitter. God, he's a shit."

"Stop, Natalie. Asher only left because Billy called him to let him know Penny was here bugging you. When are you going to get it through your head that you're his first priority?"

With that, the big, scary bouncer stormed out of the office, and I went down to my dressing room with my tail between my legs.

After cleaning up, removing my makeup, slipping on my street clothes, and placing my hamsa back on my neck, I decided I needed to give Asher the benefit of the doubt. I would lose my son if I didn't stop pushing his father away. Throwing my tiny outfit from the evening in my dry-cleaning hamper, I grabbed my bag and headed toward the back door.

As soon as I opened my dressing room door, Billy was there to hand me my take. I'd been so preoccupied, I forgot about my ever-present shadow and my money.

"Thanks, Billy. And thanks for looking out for me."

I placed a small kiss on his cheek, which kind of shocked the guy, but I was turning over a new leaf. I wasn't going to be the jaded, emotionally stunted stripper anymore.

Kicking the back door open, I was ready to live my life.

forty-six

Monkey in the Middle

Asher

Gᴏᴅ, Pᴇɴɴʏ was really such a queen bitch. It took me forever to get rid of her. She was absolutely belligerent; she kept suggesting that I pay Nat off and shack up with her instead. Whining in my ear about how I didn't need the responsibility of a kid. Hanging on my shoulder, promising to bring Larken back.

As if that were enticing?

All these years I'd known Penelope, I had always thought she was unbreakable. Sadly, I was the one to do exactly that. I broke her. She was shattered, her feelings scattered throughout my club as she laid them out for me. It was all me. I should have seen this coming, she was always too eager to do what I wanted, she inserted herself inside the Tunnel family, she made a point of knowing Natalie's comings and goings. The writing had been on the wall for a long time, but my head was too fragmented to put it all together.

But I didn't have time to think about that shit because now Mike was driving me to my house. The guy wanted to go in without me, handle my problems for me. He said Natalie was inside my office waiting for me, but she would have to continue to wait. Needing to deal with this on my own, I would explain to Natalie when it was over, and make it right if I still could.

Shit, we'd already been to hell and back. If Natalie and I couldn't get over this, then fuck it all to hell.

When the car lurched to a stop in front of my place, I jumped out before Mike put the thing in park and ran up the driveway, which was blocked by a silver sedan. They even had the nerve to park in my driveway.

I walked right in the front door, which was unlocked, and ran toward the noise in the kitchen. Lila was trying to reason with the man who'd played a hand in creating my life. He was irate, yelling in her face, saying she had no right to keep him from his grandson. She continued to quietly remind him that she had no idea who he was.

Trish had set up camp in the corridor between the kitchen and the back hallway. I had to guess Quinn was upstairs. Where the fuck was Petey?

"Ho!" I shouted. "Hold up!"

I faced the man with the same silver eyes as mine and said, "Step back from Lila. She has more right than you to be here, and you have absolutely no right to speak for my son. Now. Do it now."

He did.

I walked forward, approaching the person who claimed to be my father. I didn't need him to tell me he was my long-lost dad that day I bumped into him. Not only were our eyes the same, but I was built just like him. Although his had grayed a little, he also had wild and unruly blond hair. In a lineup, anyone would determine that he, Quinn, and me were three generations of the same family.

As for the man who seemed to be missing at the moment—Petey— it also didn't take me long to deduce he was my brother from another mother. It all started to make sense. How often he was told he looked like a mini-Asher; it had been almost annoying at times. Now, I knew why.

I caught my breath, my lungs burning from all the yelling I was doing between Penny and my father.

With me on the scene, Lila moved to comfort Trish, who was a holy mess, obviously oblivious to all the family politics at play. Lila smoothed her hand down the girl's back, comforting, whispering in her ear what she knew of the situation.

Turning to the older man, I spoke quietly, mindful my son was in the house. "Listen, I don't know what you're doing here, but you don't get to show up here unannounced. It's not right. I don't even know your name," I said while holding my hand extended to the door.

"Nash. It's Nash. Same last name as you. Peterson," he said, but stubbornly didn't make a move to leave.

"Okay, this is crazy. We're not going to sit here and chat, have coffee talk, fucking get to know each other. You're several decades late for that type of shit." Once again, I pointed to the front hallway.

The old man shook his head. "I'm not going. I know I was wrong, fucked in the head, but this whole thing with Pete had me tied in knots. What if that had been you with a crushed leg? Who would be your emergency contact?" he asked as he stepped toward me.

I backed away and put my hand out, motioning for him to stop. "Well, definitely not you."

Regret disguised as frustration sparked across the old man's face.

"Speaking of Petey," I said, "where the hell is he?"

"He's waiting to deal with your son's mother. Talk some sense into her," my father said with confidence, like he was in control of everything.

"What?" I roared into the night, my kitchen vibrating with the power of my voice, glasses clinking inside the cabinets. I felt a wave of violence overcoming me, pulling me under, like I had never experienced before. How dare these fucks take over my life?

We were all cut off by the shrill of Trish's cell phone. With a shaky hand, she pulled the phone from her back pocket and glanced at it, then looked up at me. "It's Natalie."

I shook my head. "You have to get it. Make her understand that I didn't mean for any of this to happen. Tell her Quinn is fine," I instructed her, more for my own well-being. Quinn wasn't just fine. He was up in a bedroom that he only first started calling his own today, and I knew better than anyone how hard it was to claim a new space as a young boy.

"Nat?" Trish said after answering the call.

"Where are you?" I heard my woman yell through the phone.

Unfortunately, before Trish could answer, I caught a glimpse of my son rounding the stairs and pushing his way past Lila. He grabbed the phone and spoke before anyone could stop him.

"Mom, I'm here at Dad's. I got a room and everything set up today, but I want to come home." He stared at me with hurt and distrust in his eyes as he said this.

Okay, maybe I didn't know the first thing about being a father, a man, or a devoted lover. I let out a long, painful breath, my ribs feeling as though they had been cracked by Quinn's expression.

"Okay. Uh-huh. Yeah, I was up in my room, but I know. I heard," he went on, then nodded his head. "Yeah, Mom. I'll wait up there. Here's Trish."

Handing the phone to a stranger, yet one who had more experience with him over me, my son turned, deflated and despondent, and walked upstairs. I swiveled to look toward Lila, silently begging her to fix this for me, but knew this was ultimately up to me. I couldn't be the broken man any more. I had to stand up and take care of what was mine.

Rather than running after my son, Lila stood firm and proceeded to point her finger at my father and finish what I couldn't do.

"Get out! Haven't you done enough by breaking the grown man's heart in front of you? Now, you go and put your nose where it doesn't belong with a little boy?" Now fully in charge of the situation, she said forcefully, "Go! Get the hell out. Asher will deal with you when he is good and ready."

My dad, all two hundred-plus pounds of him, listened. He took his large frame out the front door, pulling his phone out of his pocket, hopefully calling off his other son.

I didn't have time to watch the door hit his ass because Lila had her finger back out and she was pushing into my chest, saying, "Go. You go to your son. Explain to him what you missed growing up and how you want to be better than that. I'll wait for Natalie."

I didn't hesitate, just started moving toward the stairs when Lila called to me again. "And, Ash, don't forget, I told you I would be here for you months ago when we were in Red Rock. I'm here and not going anywhere."

She was the first woman in my life to say that and fucking mean it. Natalie had told me that back when she first came back, but then she kept her distance, creating a wedge between us, and now I knew why. I was a sorry excuse for a man. Natalie had kept harping on me about my dad, pleading with me to show her I understood lifelong commitments. I ignored her, and now my dad—and Petey—had gone and made a mess of the situation because I didn't man up and make the first move.

Well, first I needed to repair what happened with Quinn. I certainly wasn't handling things well with him, and I was pretty sure that Natalie would have nothing to do with me unless I righted my first wrong with our son.

forty-seven

Double Vision

Natalie

STEPPING OUT of my car into the stagnant nighttime air, I saw a shadow sitting on the stairs leading to my apartment. Moving through the heat, I lifted my hair off my neck, tiny beads of sweat forming on my nape. It was summer and the heat was nonstop, all day and all night, keeping all hope of a breeze at bay. But that wasn't why my pulse was racing and heat was rising straight through my core. It was the muscular frame sitting on the step, hunched over, deep in thought, resting his arms on his knees as his hair fell over his profile.

Slowly I moved closer, and with some apprehension. As I made my way up the staircase, the figure lifted his head and I met with dark eyes, almost black with pain and confusion, not the ones of steel I was envisioning.

"Petey? What are you doing here? Are you okay?"

I had just noticed that one of his legs was stretched straight out, bearing a long black brace fitted over his loose pant leg. Without leather or jeans, my old bouncer was an imposter in track pants.

With a frog in his throat, he answered, "Yeah, I'm fine. A little banged up, but I'll be just like new soon. Been working on my guns." He flexed his arms while flashing me a grin, resembling at least part

221

of the old Pete I knew back then. The heavy lifting explained his even closer resemblance to Asher.

And then like a ton of bricks, it hit me. Like a wrecking ball tearing through a dilapidated building, turning bricks into dust, my legs felt weak, like tiny particles tasked to hold up my frame. I swayed, reaching out to grab the railing and missing it. Petey faltered on his own gimpy leg to get to me, but he caught my waist before I went down.

Sinking toward the step, I relied on the man with a handicap to help me find purchase. Pushing air in and out of my lungs, I attempted to find words, maybe even just think of them. I couldn't even remember my native tongue.

Seated behind me, Petey spoke first. "I guess he didn't tell you. We're brothers."

I still had no voice. It was like my vocal cords had been ripped from my throat. I swept my hand to the base of my neck, massaging, palpating, hoping to resuscitate my voice, but I simply couldn't make a sound. For the second time in one evening, I had let Asher down, and my own problems seemed miniscule to me at the moment.

Not long ago, I had stood under the warm spray of a shower and told Asher that I loved him and I wanted to be there for him, but I hadn't followed through. Instead I'd raced away from him when he needed me the most. The man who had no one, not a soul, now not only had a father but a brother. Quinn now had a father, a grandfather, and an uncle, a whole host of fucked-up men to show him how *not* to live his life.

I leaned my head back and tried to make sense of the stars lingering in the night. They made as much sense as the labyrinth of my life and Asher's.

Seated on the cement stair above me in the darkness, Petey gave me this time. He seemed to sense I needed a moment.

Finally, I spoke. "I don't know how none of us ever saw it. I mean, we joked about you two, but wow. We should have picked up on that."

Petey let out a little sigh. "Well, I was kind of hoping no one figured it out, so I certainly didn't help. I was actually working at the club to keep an eye on you. Not Asher. Well, you and Quinn."

I jumped up. "Quinn! Where is he?" In all my years of being a mom, I had never forgotten my boy for a minute. Now, an indeterminate amount of time had passed before I remembered why I rushed home.

"He's at Asher's. Our dad wanted to go meet him, so he went there, and I came here to explain it all to you. We never meant to scare you,

smoldered

Natalie, which is why we kept our distance all those years. He's safe."

"Pete, honey, this is all too much for me to take. You have to stop. STOP! I'm absolutely blindsided, paralyzed by this, but Quinn has to be a million times worse. I have to go to him."

He reached out to touch my arm and turned me toward him. "Natalie, please let me at least explain. It's complicated, but nothing you can't work out."

I wrestled loose and said, "Not now. I just can't," before bolting around him and up the stairs to call Quinn. My brain and heart were split in half, one side sick with worry for my son, the other filled with anguish for the man I loved with my whole heart.

Once I was safe behind the door of my apartment, I called Trish. She must be with Quinn. Who else would Asher leave our son with?

A few seconds later, I was shocked when my son grabbed the phone and told me to come and get him. That was when my entire body fractured down the middle, my heart unable to stay whole.

Apparently, all of us in our crazy threesome had their chests pulverized that evening.

forty-eight

Sorry

Asher

Tossing my boots at the bottom of the stairs, I tiptoed up to the room I just made that day for my son. The ugliness of today's events had bled all over and through any pleasure I got from constructing the tiny mecca of preteen happiness. Now, it felt like I was entering a horror movie. Although the former guest room was still painted navy and furnished with a newly bought bed and gigantic TV, on the bed lay my son curled into a ball, sniffing back tears, which made me see red.

If I thought I was ill-prepared before to be a parent, the scene before me was overwhelming. In all my life, I had never cried until him. Not when I asked where my dad was as a little boy, or later when my mom ditched me, never over a girl, or when Lila was abducted. All the tears I had ever shed were for this boy. I'd cried when I found out about him, come apart when I discovered my dad was alive, but that was more over me not wanting to repeat history with Quinn. And now my son, the one who had grown up way before his time to support his mom, was a teary mess.

Standing at the door frame, looking in, I desperately wanted him to beckon me closer, to fucking call me to him, letting me know he had forgiven me. That didn't happen. Quinn just lay there staring at me,

224

smoldered

blinking back more tears, not speaking a word.

I thought about what Lila said. To tell him. Tell him about me, my dad, and how I never wanted it to be the same.

It couldn't be the same.

"Can I come in?" I finally asked.

He nodded his head.

I entered slowly and sat on the edge of the bed, but he remained still.

"Quinn," I said slowly. "Listen, buddy, I'm new at this, at being a dad, and I'm pretty sure I'm messing the whole thing up. I know today we were supposed to be together all day and night, and I never would have run out unless it was an emergency, and it was. An old friend of mine was not being nice to your mom, actually, and I went to fix that."

He shook his head.

"What?" I asked without moving a muscle.

Quinn fixed his big silver eyes on me and said, "It's okay. That. You needing to go fix something." He paused and let out a sigh. "It's that man downstairs. He says he's my grandpa, but I don't know him. And he knows me. I also heard him yell to that blond lady that he's known me since I was born. How is that possible?"

My son shivered. Fucking shivered with fear right in front of me, and I nearly passed out from the pain I felt because I had caused him to do that. But I had to be strong for my kid.

"I don't know, Quinn. I really don't know. What I do know is this is so hard, you and me just getting to know each other, but I'm gonna make it work. I have loved you, little dude, since the minute I found out you were my son, and that is not going to change. No f-ing way. I can't help but want to keep you by my side for...for forever...and make up for the time I lost."

My tiny almost-swear got a little grin from him. It was worth it.

"As for that man, he is your grandpa, and I don't think he meant to hurt you. He did hurt me. My feelings. I just met him a few weeks ago, like you just met me. I don't ever want to be like him and not know my son. Do you understand?"

Another head nod before he said, "But if you just met me and love me right away, what about him, Dad? He could love you right away too."

With that, I grabbed my son off the bed, pulled him into my arms, and kissed the top of his head because he was so smart. So damn smart. Smarter than anyone I ever knew, but still it was complicated, and he

225

didn't get that my mom had walked out too. Emotional bruises like that don't fade so easily, but I was starting to think with Quinn's help, they would be gone soon.

We hugged in silence until Quinn said, "Oh no! I told Mom to come and get me. She's going to pull me out of here now, and we just made up."

forty-nine

Pole Position

Natalie

I BUSTED MY tail to get over to Asher's house before Petey made it there. He was a little slower because of the leg brace, but I didn't have time for concern or empathy. Needing every little advantage I could use, it would be a lie if I didn't admit I wished he'd broken his driving leg. Speeding down Asher's street, barely coming to a stop, I threw my car in park and sprinted up the narrow cactus-lined path. My heart pumping in my chest, my breath caught in my throat, fear running through my veins, I had no idea what to anticipate.

As soon as I got to the door, I found Sienna—I mean Lila; fuck, was that confusing—sitting on the bottom step in the foyer. With tear-stained cheeks, she looked up at me and motioned for me to be quiet as I barged through the door.

Quiet? Was she kidding me? My kid needed me.

And where was Trish?

I didn't waste time on formalities, although the entryway made of marble and stone begged for it. Instead I asked, "Where's my Quinn?" as soon as I made it over the threshold.

"Shhh. He's upstairs with his dad. Asher is explaining stuff to him, calming him down." Barely audible as she whispered her words, Lila implored me with her eyes to be quiet and allow the father of my son to handle this.

But I wasn't quiet, my voice reverberating in the hollow space around me, bouncing off the walls and rising up to the high ceilings. "Bullshit! We wouldn't be in this mess if it weren't for Asher. You told me to come back to him, Lila. Begged me, and I did, but all he's done since I've been back is make decisions for me and ignore my requests to see what his dad wanted or needed. He failed to see how all this affected Quinn, and now it's coming back to haunt him. I never wanted to see Asher upset, but I definitely made it clear that Quinn was never to be hurt."

Seeing my son in pain was something I could not handle.

Lila shook her head. "That's not true, Natalie. He was so consumed with making you happy, trying to win you over, he ignored his father and what he may or may not have to say for himself. You and Quinn have been his main priority since he came back from Miami," she said, standing and walking toward me.

Asher's voice startled me.

"I can see I was wrong. I should have listened to you, Nat," he said from the top of the stairs.

I looked up to find Asher standing there with a smiling Quinn tucked under his arm.

"Quinn!" I yelled, and my son came barreling down the steps and into my arms. Squeezing him tight, I felt his father approaching, my skin prickling from a tender combination of tension and lust.

When I refused to let go of our child, Asher slid his hand down my back and bent over to whisper in my ear, "I mean it. I was wrong. You wanted me to make amends and I didn't. I should have listened."

I stood up and ran my hand along Asher's cheek, succumbing to the shivers from feeling his stubble. "When I first came back to you Ash, I wanted to make you whole, reunite you with your father, let you know your son, make you into a family man. You're not that, or maybe you are, but just don't know how be. This is partly on me. I should have guided you, helped you, and instead I left you to your own devices."

"I am that…a family man," he said as he slid his arm down mine, grasping my hand. "You're right, I don't know how to be that, but you know who's teaching me? Quinn is. Our boy said something very wise to me upstairs that f-ing shocked me, and he was right. And you know what else? You know where he gets that from? His sense of family and loyalty? From you."

smoldered

Asher's eyes turned a smoky gray, marrying the passion of the deep silver with the dark loneliness underneath. It was apparent that he felt bad, awful in fact, but truly didn't know what to do with his father, and with his own constant sadness.

I couldn't move my gaze from his. With one hand tight around Quinn's and the other wrapped up in Asher's, I had just opened my mouth to reply when the front door burst open with such force the marble floor shook beneath my feet.

fifty

And the Hits Keep Coming

Asher

I WAS LOST in Natalie, holding her hand while consumed with her green eyes. They were digging deep when it all came to an abrupt halt. My front door swung open for the millionth time that evening and on the other side was Petey. And to think I was even concerned about him earlier. Now I wanted to sucker punch the gimp, but I thought that was the type of thing I shouldn't do in front of Quinn.

Without letting go of my woman's now shaking hand, I turned toward the commotion.

"What the fuck, Pete?" I yelled into the air already rife with conflict.

"Ash, Jesus Christ, I flew over here as fast as I could, but it's not so easy getting around with this damn brace. I was at Natalie's to let her know we didn't mean any harm with Quinn, but she ran off. We wanted to explain."

"Well, she doesn't know all about you—yet," I said with fury in my eyes, shooting daggers at the asshole's heart.

"I do," was all I heard from Natalie before I released her hand and barreled toward the man with a leg brace, ignoring the fact that my son was steps behind me.

"It wasn't your information to tell, Pete. Not yours. It's mine, and I hadn't told Nat yet."

I had the guy by the neck of his shirt, holding him close to my face so he could have a front row seat to my tirade.

Just as I heard a muted "Stop," I slumped to the floor. Squatting on my haunches, I dropped my head between my knees and mumbled, "All I wanted was the time to make everything right with Natalie before all this other shit fell from the sky. I wanted to have a solid base with my woman, the mother to my son, but I couldn't bring myself to see she wanted it the other way."

I stayed like that, breathing hard, trying to control my temper, desperately holding my emotions at bay with my head buried.

Then there were arms wrapped around my back, pulling me up. "Asher, stop beating yourself up. I had as much a hand in this as you did. You wanted it your way, and I wanted it mine. It didn't work out for either of us."

"I'm sorry, little doll," I said as I pulled Natalie's slight frame against mine.

We stayed like that for a while, giving everyone a good show, until Lila suggested she take Quinn back to her place for cocoa, so we could all settle and calm down.

With the two of them across the backyard, I made quick work of questioning Pete, not even allowing anyone to move from the hallway.

"Pete, what do you want from me?" With Natalie by my side running her thumb along my hand, I kept my rage in check.

"Nothing. I just want you to know that I'm your brother. It's been a nightmare holding it in all these years." He leaned against the doorframe, giving his bad leg some relief for a moment.

"Yeah, what does that mean? All these years? Quinn said something to me that didn't sit well. He overheard your dad, our father, tell Lila he'd been watching the kid his whole life?"

Pete nodded, pulling his mouth in that way he always did when he was embarrassed. "He has been. When he heard Natalie had a baby, he kept a watch. He knew the boy was a Peterson. He also knew you didn't know, so he made it his business to keep an eye on the kid."

I roared. That didn't even make sense. "How? I didn't even know I had a dad or a kid, and yet he knew all this? Everything? Mike told me you heard about Quinn from one of the Tunnel girls."

"He wanted to protect your son, look over him in a way that he didn't do for you," Petey said, still relying on the wall for support.

I opened my mouth, but I was speechless. Nothing came out. *Look over him?*

Trying to gather my shit, I watched Natalie touch her neck, fingering the charm resting in its small hollow. She shook her head and breathed her thoughts out loud. "No, it couldn't be. This was from your dad?" Her gaze was on Petey, the question directed toward him.

"Yes."

"But how? I was so discreet."

"That's a question for your mom and our dad."

"My mom? That's impossible. She doesn't know anything about this," Natalie said as she slipped down to the marble, her cheeks flush with heat.

"You were why I was at the Tunnel, Natalie. When Asher took you away from the Leop, we lost our eyes on you. Ryan, the head bartender at the Leop, he was a buddy of mine. So I applied for a job with Asher and kept tabs on you and the boy for the last five years. It doesn't excuse me, but it explains why I was so hard on you. When you left for Florida, my dad went nuts. He was climbing the walls with worry for Quinn. Then I got hurt and Dad was scared it could have been Ash, so he freaked the fuck out. Now he wants to come clean. Know you, his son, and grandson."

Petey had moved in closer, standing over Natalie, but he couldn't get down on the floor with her. He stood hovering over her, watching what was mine, the depth of how well he knew her showing all over his face—something he'd been doing for half a decade.

And I both loved and hated the fucker for it.

fifty-one

Rainbow Bright

Natalie

I HEARD ASHER ask Petey to leave, telling him it had been enough for one night, before I felt him lifting me off the floor. He carried me up the stairs and laid me down on his bed. It was only the fifth time I had been in his bedroom, but I was pretty certain I'd experienced every feeling along the continuum in there. From unadulterated bliss to rage and venom, from sheer confusion and madness to despair, Asher's bedroom had seen a myriad of my emotions. Like a rainbow on a confused day—sunny but wet—the memory of experiencing each emotion came flooding back in this perplexed moment.

The pillow welcomed the weight of my head as I allowed the soft, billowy puff to take me in and envelop me like a cloud, stealing the weight of my problems. Soft light filled the room as Asher turned the bedside lamp on and lay down by my side. He turned me to the side and spooned me, his warm breath ghosting across my neck. I didn't speak, just felt my curves sink against his hard frame.

"Nat, doll, I know we have a lot to discuss. I'm going to play it your way this time, but first I got to know you're going to stop these games. They're burning me up, killing me. I need you in my life. All the time, full-time, each and every day. And I'm gonna make decisions for you and it's not gonna be easy to stop, because I missed all those years when Quinn was young and innocent and breakable. I need to make up for that somehow. Please get that."

I settled closer against him, if that was possible. My motivation wasn't sex driven or lust induced. It was pure love. I needed to feel him against me.

"I'm done playing, Ash. I'm so sorry for all that I put you through. I just think I've tried for so long to convince myself you didn't want me that I couldn't believe it when you said you did. Now I do. I want you too, every day, full-time, and all that comes with it."

He lifted my hair and kissed the back of my neck, his lips lingering along my skin, leaving a trail of warmth that traveled all the way to my toes.

With Asher at my back, his breath hot on my skin, his fingers digging into my hips holding me tight, I found myself relaxing. I drifted off to sleep, experiencing yet another emotion within the four walls of this bedroom.

Contentment.

fifty-two

Sleepover Party

Asher

NOT WANTING to force Natalie to talk, I allowed her to lie there in silence. Forcing myself to be patient, I relaxed, taking in the sound of her breathing, feeling her pulse beating next to me, keeping her tight against my frame with a firm grip on her hips, and wondering when this would all settle. But I knew better than to steal the woman from her thoughts.

We both must have dozed, so when my cell phone rang, I startled. It was Lila letting me know Quinn wanted to come home. The sound of my son calling my house "home" woke me the hell up. Fast. I kissed Natalie before rushing downstairs to open up for him.

Not bothering to ask Natalie if she wanted to stay over, I made the decision for her. I told her I was going to do that from time to time—or all the time—I couldn't help it. Tonight was supposed to be Quinn's sleepover and it was practically the middle of the night already, so there was no way I was letting my family leave.

As I walked Quinn up the stairs to his new room, he asked the question that everyone was thinking, but no one was brave enough to say out loud. "Dad, did you figure out how that man knows me? I mean, I know he's your dad, but I didn't even know you and you didn't know him, so how does he know me?"

When we reached the top step, I turned to face my son. With my hand on his shoulder, I said, "I didn't yet, Quinn, but I'm going to get to the bottom of it. You don't have to worry about it."

He leaned in for a hug, and I obliged. I would hug the kid forever if he would let me.

Just as I was getting ready to shut the light on the navy bedroom, Natalie appeared in the doorway. Her eyes surveyed the scene, taking in the new-furniture smell and the TV complete with gaming system along the wall, before they started to well up. The tears didn't fall, just filled her eyelids with wetness glistening in the night. I watched her chest rise and fall with emotion, and again, knew better than to steal her moment. I was learning.

I was right. She walked toward the bed and sat down on the edge, running her hand through our son's hair, speaking in quiet tones while I took in the moment from across the room.

"You okay, Quinn, baby?"

"Uh-huh."

Leaning in, she kissed our son's forehead. "I know it's a lot to take in, but I'm going to fix it. In the meantime, you have sweet dreams in this awesome room. I'm sorry I didn't see it earlier."

"'Kay, Mom."

One more kiss to his forehead and Natalie was walking toward me. She flicked the light off, pulled the door partway closed, and walked straight back to my room. Who was I to question that?

WOKE EARLY, which was unusual for me, but there was shit that needed my attention. And I also wanted to be up when Quinn woke up. It would be something I'd never experienced before—my son sleepy and groggy coming down to my kitchen for breakfast.

Making a pot of coffee, I grabbed my phone to contact the two people who had answers. I didn't care that he was recuperating or up late, I texted Pete and told him to get our sorry excuse for a dad over to my place. Then I called Nat's mom, Ellie, and she answered as though she was expecting the call. I instructed her to get the hell over here. Clearly neither of us were in the mood to chat, so we hung up after I curtly gave her directions.

I poured two mugs of coffee, putting milk and sugar in one, and went back upstairs to Natalie. On the way, I looked in Quinn's room, peeking through the tiny crack his mom left in the door. He was still asleep. Good.

When I entered my bedroom, I found the bed empty. Taking a quick look around, I found Natalie in the bathroom, washing her face. She looked up as soon as I appeared.

"Good morning. I brought coffee, doll."

"Hey. Morning." She walked toward me, her body language timid, which wasn't at all like her.

"What? You okay?" I asked, setting the coffees on the sink.

"Yeah, just making sure you still want all this," she said, waving her hand around.

"Every fucking second of it, Natalie," I answered before handing her a mug and bringing her in carefully for half a hug while we held our mugs.

I kissed the top of her head before warning her, "I called your mom. Told her to get her ass over here."

She nodded.

"And my dad. We need some answers."

"Thank you."

"Doll, don't thank me. It's what I should have done when we first got back. Made peace with my dad. Figured shit out."

That was the end of that because Quinn half-knocked, half-entered the room, obviously unsure of what to do with the two of us sharing a room. Something else we would have to deal with—later—because there was breakfast to make at the moment.

fifty-three

Showtime

Natalie

After getting dressed, I came downstairs to find my son sitting on the very same granite counter I sat on months ago while sharing a plate of eggs with Asher. Taking it all in—the man cooking, wearing old jeans and a black T-shirt, comfortably working in the kitchen, making his kid breakfast—I felt like an imposter in a life that up until two months ago wholly belonged to me.

And I didn't mind.

Quinn was eating bacon, chatting mindlessly with father, when the doorbell intruded. Why couldn't I just watch them for a few more moments?

"Hey, Quinn baby, we have to have an adult talk with your grandma. Do you mind playing a video game for a bit? I can grab you when we're done," I asked my son, knowing full well who was on the other side of the door.

"Sure, Mom," he said as he jumped down from the counter, then turned to his dad and asked if he could take his juice upstairs.

"Q, you can do whatever you want here. This is your house as much as it is mine," Asher said, and my heart splintered with all the mistakes I'd made over the last two months. I felt weak, paralyzed with remorse,

238

and sick that I almost threw this whole life away.

God, my kid was such a good kid too, as he made his way up the back staircase while the man of the house went to get the door.

"Hello, Ellie," I heard Asher say at the door. "Nat's in the kitchen."

My mom said nothing in response to Asher's greeting.

She rounded the wall into the kitchen and stopped, frowning at me as she said, "I told you a long time ago, Natalie, this life…being a mom to his kid…would never be easy. You simply wouldn't listen to me, always chasing after him, waiting on the sidelines for whatever sloppy seconds he would toss you. Can't say I didn't warn you about Asher Peterson. That guy gets all his bad shit from his momma."

I refused to let the dreadful tears come. I fisted my hands at my side and willed myself to remain neutral while my whole existence was being shred to pieces by my very own mother, no less.

Before Asher could blow up at her, I said, "Well, there wasn't much you could do about it, was there? We were all lumped together day and night while you and your cronies worked the casino crowd and partied hard whenever you pleased."

My mother flung her hand to the side, her long red nails knifing through the tension in the air. "Pfft. We deserved to blow off some steam. After all, we had to earn a living and raise our daughter, unlike his skank of a mom who whored herself around. It's why Nash up and left while she was still pregnant." As she spoke, my mother jerked her head toward Asher. At least she was smart enough not to get physically close to me or him, remaining glued to the wall separating the kitchen from the hall.

Asher had wound his way around her, maintaining a safe distance, obviously aware of his own feral instincts, to settle by my side.

"Ellie, I think we're the ones with the questions, and you should probably shut the eff up before I throw you the hell out of here," he demanded as he ran his hand over the back of his neck, obviously struggling to control his temper.

At his words, my mother turned her glare on him. "Asher, this can't be easy, but I never wanted your shitty life to rain down on my daughter and that's all it's ever done. She loved you like a sick puppy for her whole youth and the way I see it, the first time you threw the dog a bone, you knocked her up. For reasons that still remain a mystery to me, she protected you, never fessed up to you being the father of her child. At first, I was behind that choice, because who the hell wanted you to be a part of their family. But lately I thought to myself…look at that son of a bitch making bank, watching my daughter get naked for a crowd full of strangers night after night when he should be paying for her to be home with their kid."

"Mom! Stop!" I pleaded. "Why are you doing this? Don't you love Quinn? You're destroying his father and you don't know anything." I stared at the woman who I used to think was pretty and saw nothing but weathered skin full of wrinkles and lies.

Asher stood stock-still, apparently shocked into silence.

"I know that a few months ago," my mother went on, "the father of your child found out he had a kid for the first time, and when he finally brings you home, you're stripping again. God, it's like you're just like her—"

"Stop!" Asher yelled as he started pacing the floor, slashing a hand through the air for emphasis as he spoke. "Enough, Ellie. I don't know what you're getting at and I don't owe you any explanations, but I certainly didn't want Nat fucking going back to work. We were working out some shit. But you gotta put an end to comparing her to my mom. I barely knew the woman, but seems like you did—pretty well, in fact. So, start talking about what we asked you to come and talk about. And stop being a bitch or I'm gonna toss you out. Last warning."

She took a step forward and then moved back again to lean on the wall, crossing her arms over her chest before she spoke. "Your mom, Celia, was my best friend growing up. She was stunning, gorgeous, and every boy wanted her. Except for Nash Peterson. He was the neighborhood bad boy and your mom's biggest conquest. He was older by a few years and she pursued him with a vengeance."

My mom ran her hand through her poorly-dyed hair, the gray peeking through the brown, and pulled her head back a little before she continued. "God, she would put on these skimpy little outfits and spend all her time chasing after Nash. He finally gave in and started seeing Celia. He wasn't serious at first, had a whole stable of girls. A Monday night girl, Tuesday night one, and so on. But Celia was determined and she got him hook, line, and sinker when she started fooling around with another guy, pretending to do it behind his back, but knowing full well he got a whiff of it. Nash got insanely jealous and gave up all his other girls for her. I should know," she said as she pinned her gaze on Asher. "I was always the Friday night one."

Asher had stopped pacing and was in a standstill next to me, gripping my shoulder, giving me all his weight. I feared he might collapse.

"Oh, poor you, so this is all about you, Ellie? You didn't get the bad boy and my mom did? That's why you messed with all our lives? What happened next, do fucking enlighten me," he demanded, his voice hoarse with pain.

"She got your dad, but couldn't give up the other men. It's like a switch flipped in her. Nash always thought maybe mental illness or something, she craved the constant attention of men, almost needed it to survive. The two of them were living together when she got knocked up, and your dad couldn't stand the idea of the baby not being his, so he left. After you were born, we all knew he was the father. The hair, the eyes, you were pure Nash. And of course, she named you Asher, a constant reminder to all that she was the one who beat down the man everyone said couldn't be conquered."

"Oh my God." I gasped, covering my mouth.

Asher bore down more on my shoulder.

"Babe, you're hurting me," I had to whisper in his ear.

He stared at me with red-rimmed eyes. "I'm so sorry, Nat." He picked me up, turned me around, and held me to him, crying in my neck, whimpering like a little boy who'd lost his mother. Something he probably should have done years ago.

"Didn't you tell Nash, Mom? Call him and explain about Asher being his son?" I asked, not understanding how this secret could have lasted over three decades.

My mom looked away, unable to meet our eyes. "I did. He couldn't come back, though. Celia was turning tricks at this point, which is why all of us began looking after Asher, including him in our gang, and Nash couldn't bring himself to live with his woman hooking on the side. It was a sorry excuse, we all knew, but he wanted nothing to do with Celia...and Asher, I'm sad to say, was an extension of that. And because of that crazy, insane woman and her inability to stop parading around, I couldn't see Nash. Not seeing him every day, but caring for his bastard kid instead. It was like a knife slicing through me."

My mom didn't get to finish because the door opened and in walked Nash, Petey by his side. Asher ran by me so fast, I saw stars. He ran toward his father and sucker punched the old man, whipped him straight into the wall behind him. Petey broke the old man's fall, bad leg and all.

"You fucking deserted me," Asher choked out. His heart was cracking so loud, we could practically hear it, the pain visible on his face, his gorgeous features shredded.

Nash fell to his knees and sobbed. "I know. I know I did. But Celia—never mind, there are no excuses. But when Ellie called me that day and told me Natalie had a baby and it was yours, I tried to find a way to redeem myself. I didn't get why, but for some reason Ellie said you weren't to know about the boy. So I looked out for him, made sure Natalie was well-compensated at the Leop, placed Ryan there as a bartender to watch after her until you came back on the scene. I've been hoping for five years that you'd find out you had a son."

Asher went wild with fury and punched a wall, causing blood to ooze from his hands. I whispered to him, "Ash, Quinn is upstairs." He shook his head, somewhat tempering himself, then grabbed fistfuls of his own hair, pacing like a lion at feeding time.

"I'm sorry, son."

"Don't you call me that! That's your son," Asher said, pointing directly at Petey.

Nash shook his head. "Don't blame him. Pete's been begging me for years to come clean. Think about how hard this was for him. I put him in an awful position, making him watch Natalie and Quinn from a distance while he fell in love with all of you as though you were family—when you actually were his blood family—and he couldn't say it."

"Sounds like a fucking piece of cake to me," Asher threw back at them.

"You're right," Pete said quietly.

"So, you up and left my mom—the whore—to raise me alone until she decided to ditch me, to do what exactly? Make a new life? Why didn't you come back then? When my mother dumped me? Sounds like Ellie, here, kept you in the fucking know."

Asher had moved back and found his way by my side once again. Being more careful this time, he leaned gently into me, his anger transferring from his frame into mine.

My mom stood in the background, taking it all in, obviously afraid to wade in, blatantly pining for Nash from afar. *God, she is a sorry excuse for a woman.*

"Not quite. I met Pete's mom on a blind date, liked her, started to see her regularly. I may have even loved her but, Christ. We started a relationship that resulted in Pete, but couldn't ever go further because I was too caught up in leaving *you* all those years before. The only good thing was Pete's mom was open to me staying close, having a part in his life."

Asher turned away, his jaw rigid, his body taut as he shook with anger. Whipping back around, he ground out, "I've fucking heard enough for one day. I need you all to clear out and leave me to contact you when I'm ready, which may be never."

It felt like a gunshot to my heart. Did he mean me too?

When I started walking toward the stairs to collect my son, he said, "Not you, Nat. Them," then cocked his head toward the others. I felt like a sledgehammer had been removed from my chest.

Nash approached me and asked, "One more thing, if I may?" while looking at his son.

I looked to Asher too. This was his life being ripped open, I had no business making a decision like that. I didn't owe Nash a damn thing; this was all Asher's call. He nodded his head and said, "Make it quick."

"This was from me," he said reaching out to touch my hamsa, telling me something I'd already deduced on my own. "I came to see you when Quinn was born. Looking at his tiny blond head in the nursery and watching you sleep peacefully were some of the happiest moments of my life. I wanted to stay and tell you who I was, but I thought that was selfish of me, just popping up out of the blue, taking your attention. So I left the necklace on your nightstand and ran."

Then they fell. The tears.

"I was so happy when Pete saw you wearing the charm when he first came to work at the Tunnel. I hope it protected you and my grandson for the last few years like it was meant to do."

I didn't answer. I wasn't sure if it had.

Nash and Petey turned to leave, but my mom lingered. I said, "You too," to her, pointing at the door.

Right before she walked out, I added one more thing. "Mom, it's up to Asher whether he forgives his father or Pete, but as for you and me, we're on a long break. A very long one. You played a hand in ruining a young boy's life. The boy who grew up to be the man I fell in love with, and you still continued to destroy him after you knew he and I created a life. You could have told Asher all this years ago, come clean. You didn't."

I stopped to take a breath, but I had no intention of that being all I said despite the look of horror on my mother's aging face.

She opened her mouth to speak and I held up my hand, before I said, "You threw me with him as a kid, then told me not to be with him when I was a woman and had his baby, and finally, asked me to tell him the truth years later, which means you played with mine and Quinn's life…and for what? To stay in touch with Nash, gossip here and there, play this card and that card with him. Tell him our secrets and then think a reunion would solve all your woes. You need time to think about that, and I don't know if I will get over this. Plus, I think it's about high time you got the hell over Nash. Geez, Mom, the dude isn't into you, and what about Dad? Is this how you disgrace him?"

With that, I was done and apparently so was my mom. Biting her lip, she crossed her arms over her chest and walked away.

When the three of them were through the door, Asher locked it, armed the house with the alarm, and came to find me on a stool in the kitchen. His arms wrapped me tight, and he said, "I guess we have our god-awful fucking answers."

"Yeah," I said while trying to stop crying.

"You know what? None of it matters, Nat. None of it except you, me, and Quinn moving forward. I can't be held responsible for my mom, or that man who says he's my dad, but I can take matters into my own hands when it comes to you and my kid."

"Thank you." I buried my face in his T-shirt.

"For what?" he whispered against my hair as he held my face tight to his hard chest.

"For loving Quinn right away, for letting me get away with shit, for waiting."

"Doll, I love you."

I didn't answer, just stayed tucked tightly in the arms of the one man I always wanted to hold me.

fifty-four

Moving on Up

Natalie
One month later

THERE WAS no way of avoiding it—I never left Asher's house after that day we found out the difficult truth about his parents, and the even crazier connection my mom held with it all. The stubborn man picked up his phone, like he had in Miami, and within a handful of phone calls, had made arrangements for all my stuff to be packed and moved over to his house, my apartment to be sublet, and that was that.

Of course, it annoyed me a little, or to no end, but he said he was going to do it, and who was I to judge? Watching Asher's heart wrenched from him by my own mother, witnessing him fall to his knees with hurt and suffering, was enough to convince me to give him some leeway.

Which was why I hadn't pushed anything with Nash. I was allowing Asher his own play with his father, although I secretly hoped they would bury the hatchet—at least for our son. Now that my mom was out of the picture, he deserved to have one grandparent, and the man seemed like he genuinely wanted a relationship with our child.

After all, he gave me my hamsa, even bought me a new chain for it recently.

As for my bitch of a mother, she called a few days after the big blowup and asked if she could explain a bit more.

Thinking back to the conversation, I should have never even answered her call…

M Y PHONE had rung twice, both times from my mom's number. After I had hit Ignore two times, I picked up on the third call.

"Hello."

"Natalie, it's Mom. Please let me say my piece."

"Mom, is that necessary?"

"Yeah. I mean, I helped you all those years with Quinn, I think I at least deserve that chance."

I sighed into the phone and said, "Fine. Go."

"I'm sorry, Nat. How was I to know you would actually end up with Asher? He was a childhood crush of yours, and he was always up to no good. When you had that baby, I was torn. I didn't want you to end up like his mother, abandoned, and who knew what Asher would do when he heard the news, so I agreed with you to cover it up."

"But you liked having an excuse to contact Nash?" I put her right on the spot, called her on the carpet with her bullshit.

"Well, yes, and he deserved to know. There were so many lies. Lies from when he was with Celia, untruths about him and me, and I didn't want him to live not knowing he had a grandson."

"If that makes you feel better, than tell yourself that, Mom, but the whole thing was devised for your own personal gain. My secret allowed you to talk regularly with Nash, and encouraging me to hide Quinn gave you a reason to touch base with your old flame."

A pause, then, "I'm not going to argue, Natalie."

"Because you know I'm right. I bet you didn't come to Miami because of Nash, not because of Grampa. I'm starting not to believe anything you have ever told me, and I'm still on a long break from you."

"If that's what you want, there's nothing I can do."

A ND THAT was the end of my facade of a relationship with my mom; she let go that easily. She only wanted to stay close in case we repaired the relationship with Nash.

Stupid, I wasn't.

Pete was a different story. Asher wanted that relationship, and I wanted him to go after it. And he would. When he was ready.

Now waiting for Quinn to finish his first week of school, I stood out in the blistering dry heat, waiting for the bus to come in our new neighborhood wearing my mom clothes—capri yoga leggings and a tank with flip-flops on my feet. It was what I wore most of the time, now that I no longer danced. I didn't go back to the stage after that fateful day of truth either.

I still went into the club, some nights filling in at the bar or just spending time in the back, helping with makeup or clothes. It was a part of me I couldn't just let go of, couldn't stay away, and I finally realized that was okay. I loved the club, and I owed it everything.

I never realized it while I was working there, but those people were my family, the life force that pumped blood through my veins, and I was done with shunning them or what we all did for a living.

That was an easy choice.

Likewise, sitting down with Quinn and explaining our new living arrangements, that he would have a mom and a dad under the same roof and we would be sharing a bed, hadn't been too bad. With him being a few years away from puberty, some of it went over his head, and I was thankful for that.

With it being the end of summer, we explained he would be able to start the school year fresh at a new school, where he'd already made a ton of friends. With me being home more, he brought them around and took to living in the big house like he had lived in one his whole life.

Like at the moment, he came barreling off the bus with a friend in tow, ready to go home and play video games or head out in the yard with his buddy. Asher truly meant that his home was Quinn's and the kid could do whatever he wanted…even eat candy and popcorn in the living room or run through the house soaking wet from water guns.

His dad just wanted the boy to have what he didn't.

Walking up the driveway, Quinn asked, "Hey, Mom. Can Benny stay over at Trish's tonight with me? Pleeease?"

Yep, Trish was now living in the carriage house behind Asher's. A couple of weeks ago, Lila and Carson moved out of the carriage house and bought a house around the corner so they could be close yet still have privacy. Carson had moved to Vegas to be with Lila, but he still traveled for work, so having us nearby was nice for her. And with it being empty, Asher moved Trish right into the carriage house, telling her not to worry about rent, just school. She could watch Quinn when we needed to cover her board. He still "tipped" her every time she stayed with our son, like tonight they were having a sleepover because my man was taking me away for the night. To the Strip.

"We have to ask his mom, baby, but I'm sure Trish will be fine with it. But remember who's in charge."

"Yeah, I know. Trish is."

The two kids ran off into the garage, climbing all around Asher's bike and my outrageous Cadillac, looking for super soakers.

I ducked into the house to get ready for my date night.

fifty-five

Date Night

Natalie

WE TOOK the bike. With the wind whipping against my back, my hands wrapped tightly against his abdomen, the scenery slipping by, I thought back to when Asher drove me away from the Leop and to our lunch date at Feralina's. Both of us were guarded, keeping our true feelings under wraps, sealed up extra tight with duct tape, staples, and safety pins.

Not wanting to make a commitment to seek out the truth, both of us were happy to stick our heads in the sand, to live our lives in a constant state of denial, unable to see a future. Especially together. Eventually all those lies came unraveled, leaving both of us with new fears. Could we make it? Shove all the shit off to the side and move forward?

Quinn being a boy about to turn ten years old didn't allow us to hold on to those fears for long. He was the new glue that bound us together. Well, a third of it. The other two-thirds was all Ash, me, and our mutual commitment to not wallow in our past, or to repeat the mistakes of those who came before us. That was the superglue—our vow not to become our parents or their friends.

Maybe it didn't matter that we worked in adult entertainment, if we could find a way to have a solid base? Starting with a family uninterrupted. At least, not anymore.

After all, we were good people. Asher was golden, even though he liked to think of himself as a bad boy. *So did I*. He was my bad boy, the one I'd loved since I was three years old.

As we roared onto the Strip, Asher slowed his speed. I gripped him tighter as I took in the lights of Las Vegas Boulevard, lit up for the whole world to see, beckoning anyone and everyone to come and play. Taking in the view, I suddenly knew what I wanted to do for the night.

Most people came to the Strip to live out fantasies for a night or two, to shut the door on their real lives and be someone else when they stepped outside their hotel room. Not me. I was living my very own fairy tale, and had no desire to step outside my life and be someone else.

As we came to a stop at the valet, I whispered naughtily in my man's ear, "Can we just get room service and stay in?"

He turned his head and with only a raised eyebrow, asked me if I was sure. I nodded my head.

"Hell, yeah," he said and tossed the bike's key to the valet. Then he dragged me into reception, rushing the front desk person, practically pulling me to the elevator bank as the slot machines rang in the background. As we hurried through the casino, the air around us swirled with booze and excitement while mobs of people enjoyed unrestricted playtime.

Smiling to myself, I anticipated a little playtime of our own.

While waiting for the elevator, my man swept his finger across his phone and dialed Feralina's, canceling our reservation.

Score one for Natalie.

With our small overnight bag thrown over his shoulder, Asher rushed me in and out of the elevator, his hand roaming my ass as the elevator rose, then marched me quickly toward our suite as soon as we stepped out of the elevator doors. Opening the suite and pushing me inside, he dropped the bag on the floor and suggested with his body where he wanted me to go.

And by *suggested*, I mean he slammed me into the wall, his mouth crushing down on mine, not leaving any room for interpretation.

Tangling our tongues, my bad boy fucked my mouth, giving me a little preview of what he wanted to do with other parts, other places. I answered him back with my hips pressing forward, searching for his erection, some friction, anything. Moaning down his throat, I made sure the man knew I wanted him.

Bad.

Asher broke free from my mouth for a minute to pull off his long-sleeved tee, and I couldn't help but let out a sigh at the sight of his hard chest. I moved right in, running my tongue along his tattoo, the lightning bolt that had taunted and teased me for years in his office. I moved on to his flat nipple, leaving a path of damp heat from my tongue, followed by the cool blowing whisper of my exhale. He grabbed my ass hard and lifted me, my legs winding their way around him as he walked toward the huge bed.

After laying me down before him, Asher dipped down and ripped my shirt off. I kicked off my boots and he shimmied my jeans down with little to no patience, until I was spread before him in a white lace bra and boy shorts. Lifting my elbow up, placing my head in my hand, I watched as Asher unbuttoned his jeans and stepped out of them, showing off all that was him—commando, of course.

I didn't have long to admire because the man was between my thighs in an instant, leisurely running his tongue over me. I wanted more, faster and harder, so I picked up my feet and placed them on his shoulders, digging in, urging him on. "Rougher," I murmured.

"Nat," he growled. "You'll get it when I say you're gonna get it, doll. Stop pushing me, I'm enjoying," he said with a wink.

I leaned up on my elbow again to take in the sight of him between my thighs, and it was forcing my hormones to go wild. But I couldn't take my eyes off of him. The wink, his gorgeous silver eyes smoldering hot and bright for me, his muscles moving beneath his skin, and his new tattoo along his shoulder blade. It read Little Doll with a hamsa underneath in a deep black, all the fingers of the hand pointing down, warding off evil.

When he got it, he'd told me, "You, little doll, are my hamsa, and now I got you right on my back, watching out for me, forcing evil away. Right where you belong."

And I had cried.

Now I couldn't linger on the sights, though, because the man down there had decided to do what I wanted and picked up his pace with his tongue exactly where I wanted it, his fingers pressed deep inside me, my wetness coating them.

I exploded hard, grinding into his face the whole time, screaming his name, my feet pressing down harder into his back. Thank God this was Vegas and the rooms were soundproof.

When he crawled back up my body, I playfully shoved him down to his knees, catching him off guard. As I slithered down his body, he gave a little tug on my nipple rings. I kept them in. Turned out Asher was a huge fan, and so was I, when it was *him* who was pulling them.

Leaning over, I took all of the man in my mouth, deepening my pull, dragging my mouth back up his length and adding my hand, sucking on the tip hard and fast while squeezing him. Our time in bed was a little grittier, edgier than most—at least I thought so—but it was us and only us, and I was absolutely fine with that.

I tasted a little pre-cum and kept my grip, using my tongue to lick the salty substance, begging for more.

"Oh fuck, Nat, you're so good to me," Asher said, his head thrown back, the cords of his neck popping out.

In the end, I was all he needed. We never saw that redheaded bitch after that night at the club. I was pretty sure Mike had a little private conversation with her that resulted in her leaving town. Buh-bye.

With my mouth on Asher, I didn't waste any more time thinking of Penelope. Instead I lost myself in the moment, hearing his voice call my name, feeling him shoot down the back of my throat, tasting all of him, drinking him in, finally knowing the man both inside and out. I reveled in the feeling of him pulling me close after we both came, and him whispering how much he loved me.

We lay front to front, naked, each of us stroking the other's back as we came down. Asher and I were eye to eye when I realized he was ready to go again. This was not uncommon. Neither was the way he made slow, leisurely love to me that night.

Even when making love, he was still my one and only bad boy.

Epilogue

Asher
Four years later

I DIDN'T EVEN fucking laugh at myself kicking off my boots in the garage, tiptoeing in the house a little after three o'clock in the morning, trying my best to be quiet.

Tiptoeing was serious business these days.

As I stepped into the kitchen and quietly set my keys down, letting my eyes adjust to the dim light—the one left on just for me—I did smile.

Fucking smiled at no one or nobody or nothing. Full-on grinned at absolutely zilch, other than the mass chaos spread through the house.

As I surveyed the mess around me, taking in the pictures taped to the expensive-as-hell stainless fridge, righting a candy jar half-spilled on the counter, and out of the corner of my eye, catching a long line of forts and tunnels made from various quilts and blankets in front of the fireplace, I headed to my first stop. Feeling my way along the small village of tents, trying not to trip, I walked toward the small bar in the far corner of the great room and poured myself a scotch.

Gently putting back the bottle, digesting my life spread all around me, I wouldn't even dream of slamming the fucker back down on the counter.

My freaking great life with a great room, where I act all docile and

253

behaved. Ha.

Even I couldn't believe how perfect my world was turning out—perfectly fucking messy and crazy. And the messier it got, the better it felt.

It wasn't the lonely, isolated, negative, messy shit I knew growing up, but living large, ingesting each moment fully, breathing every second in, and taking big gulps each and every single time. Surrounded by people who loved me, who made a pretty huge mess everywhere they went.

Knocking back my drink, I allowed my night at the Tunnel to travel all the way through my body. It washed through me before drifting into space, bringing me completely home. My new home dwarfed my old one, and that place was big as fuck. This joint was enormous, made my former digs look like a shack, and I grew up in a real piece of shit, so I'd know one.

This house was the tits, cost me a pretty penny, and I couldn't have cared less what kind of goopy or crazy disaster went down inside its four walls because my family made that shit. The family I never imagined having.

I couldn't put a price tag or a number on my wife and kids. As long as I had them, I was rich.

But it helped that I was pretty loaded and could give them anything they wanted—materially.

My heart was theirs for the taking. Any day, any time, always. No holds barred.

But they would never know how hard I'd worked to be able to give that to them…and the soulless, open-ended emptiness that surrounded me before I had Nat all to myself.

With Natalie in my life, I could give them my whole fucking heart. They would learn sooner than me that having people care about you meant way more than any money in the bank.

It's a good woman that makes a man complete, not how fat his bank account is.

I stared down at my huge platinum watch, clocking the minutes I was wasting with my fucking grandiose daydreaming, watching the seconds tick down, each one marking a second I wasn't between my wife's legs.

The expensive timepiece, a gift from Natalie, was something I never would have bought myself. Not because I skimped when it came to me; I did have a brand new smoking-hot bike and a shitload of

smoldered

designer motorcycle boots. But I had a family to feed and clothe, so I'd been forced to step up my business, and fucking A, I did.

The Electric Tunnel brand was growing, known every-fucking-where, steadily bringing in more hard-core cash. And I had some other shit in the works. A new biz I hadn't mentioned to my wife yet.

Christ, Natalie was going to kill me when she found out, but I wanted to make sure it was right. No reason to show off anything if it was going to flop.

Finishing my drink, I left my tumbler in the sink and made my way through the hall to the stairs, climbing two at a time to check on my family, eager to get to my wife, wondering what she was wearing in bed. Hoping for nothing, but thinking that wasn't exactly possible.

We did have a teen in the house.

I'd take baggy sweats. Who the hell cared? Not me. I was going to lock the door and rip them straight off her curvy body.

Reaching the top of the stairs, I stopped and enjoyed the wall of photos. There were fancy as all get-out staged portraits as well as candid shots. Everyone was there. Not just the flesh-and-blood family under my roof, but my Tunnel gang, especially Lila. Without her I'd be screwed, and never have my girl back.

Glancing at the phone in my hand as it buzzed and glowed, I saw the e-mail report come in for the night at our Los Angeles club—the Electric Cove.

My Lila was living the good life out in Cali with the man of her dreams, a beautiful son, and a girl on the way. Carson was having daily shit fits over raising a girl. Son of a bitch was going to put a GPS on her before she could even crawl.

I couldn't help but laugh out loud at the thought and tried hard to stifle it, not wanting to wake anyone. I needed to have my wife at least twice before I knocked off for the night.

The Cove was doing well. Along with Lila, Petey was a major stakeholder, and the joint was bankrolling money.

God, Petey. Running my hand over his photo—the one where he was hanging with Quinn—I still couldn't believe I had a fucking brother. Finally the dude was a constant in my world. Took me a while to accept him, but when I did, I realized I couldn't live without him. Guilt rode his ass for the last few years, the stubborn man refusing to acknowledge the bond we had despite him deceiving me, but we fixed that.

I might only make time to see my dad from time to time, a beer or two a few times a year, but I downright refused to lead a life without Pete being a player in it.

At first, the little shit kept turning down my offers for business partnerships. Then Lila got knocked up and needed someone to help in Cali. Who better than my brother?

She convinced him, of course. That girl was forever the peacemaker in my world.

Now absolutely no one could touch the California club on the adult entertainment scene with Pete and Lila co-owning it. Our brand was unstoppable, mostly because we were a class act.

And I'm going to make it even classier.

Peeking inside the room at the top of the stairs, I continued to take in the further destruction of my house. Clothes, toys, little electronics were everywhere. Once again, I grinned for no reason.

Skimming my hand down the wall, I quietly shut the blue bedroom's door--a close match to the one I set up for Quinn at the old house but bigger--and caught a picture of Big Mike and me. Like two crazies, we had our arms slapped around each other's backs with shit-eating grins at the opening of Miami's Electric Wave. He was my main man from day one. We'd been through the ringer together, and he'd seen me at my worst. Fucking hell, I hoped my man was finding his own little slice of happiness, because he'd hit the bottom of the barrel for a while—right along with me.

Our joint, the Wave, was also on its way to being unbeatable down in Florida, the same location where I would reveal the new biz. Yeah, I kept that ridiculous mansion down there. Bought it for the right price and let Mike live there. After all, he was instrumental in blowing the Miami club out of the water, along with my latest plans. Wouldn't have either with anybody else.

And I had a sweet place to stay when I headed east. Took Quinn with me a few times so we could escape the craziness of Vegas, just the two of us for some bonding.

My phone lit up for a second time since I got home, letting me know the closing status at the Tunnel. Mike was back in town for a few days. He just flew into Sin City yesterday, leaving Petal to run the Wave, so he could fill in for me while I took my family on vacation.

I needed it. They deserved it.

I also guessed it was a big test for Petal. I knew she could run that place all by herself, but Mike had to be sure. She would be doing it more and more after we opened what we had started to call the Firefly.

smoldered

We had a trip planned for later today, and I couldn't wait. The five of us were meeting Carson, Lila sporting a baby bump, and their son, Aston—named for yours truly—at the private airstrip in LA after the plane picked us up in Vegas. All of us were off to a huge villa in the Bahamas, the same one where we'd all stayed for Carson and Lila's wedding.

I fiddled with the alarm on my phone, setting it for a few hours later, making sure we didn't miss our flight.

That's right, I did say *the five of us*. Natalie, Quinn, our twins Lillie and Parker, and me. *Twins.* Let's just say, my bad boys were good swimmers, and after a small winter wedding in the Red Rock Desert, I made quick work of knocking Nat up again on the honeymoon. I didn't mean to go for double the trouble, but it was definitely worth it.

Now.

I eased open the door to the pink bedroom—Lillie's private domain. I was probably already as psycho as Carson was going to be, but my little lady was every bit as gorgeous as her mom at almost three years old. With shiny brown hair and silver eyes, she captured my heart with one little look.

And I was never giving it back.

Yep, I'm gonna lock her in her princess room forever.

I couldn't move from the doorway, peering into the room dimly lit by the pink crystal chandelier hanging from the hot pink ceiling. I was a goner when it came to both my girls. A prego Natalie was no one to mess with, especially carrying two babies at the same time and complaining she was as big as a house, but the outcome was so worth it.

My babies were the most amazing creatures, and the whole experience was so fucking mystifying for me because I didn't get to do it with my oldest son.

As for my wife, the damn woman looked even better after giving birth to twins, which drove the women members at Fusion Fitness, the gym I bought for her, downright wild.

After Natalie quit dancing, she began to mope around, wanting to do something other than sit around and wait for me. I got it. Quinn was making a lot of plans with friends at the time, and the woman had always been so independent, so I purchased a small high-end gym in the 'burbs. Natalie ran the place during her pregnancy, but now we have a manager that she oversees. She also teaches several fitness classes—many of them pulling from her dancing days—which I definitely don't

257

mind. *Oh yeah.*

Seeing my wife in tight yoga pants, shaking her ass, was the best part of my day.

Quinn, a boy on the verge of adolescence when the twins were born, surprised us by being pretty much unfazed by the change involved with having two little babies around.

I stopped outside his room and just listened at the door; I didn't dare open it. He was old enough for some space, but shit, I'd missed a lot of the good years with him. I wanted to go in, open up a couple of sodas, and just hang out. I spent every second I could with him, making up for the years I'd lost, and that little fucker was so smart. He was going to make me proud, go to college and all that shit, even though he planned to take over my clubs one day. He knew what I did for a living—he was old enough to get it—and he was damn proud, but still, he was getting out.

That was why I got the Firefly thing going, something legit for him. I might not be a big-time CEO or doctor, but the Tunnel was mine and I did it. I made something bigger and better out of nothing, and I owned that, but still, Quinn was going to do something even grander, and I was going to put down the first bricks for that.

My kid was going to be just fine out in the world, doing what his mom and I couldn't do. That was what Natalie always wanted for him, and she deserved that.

Lingering a few extra seconds outside his room, my body began to heat at the thought of his mom, asleep and all twisted in the sheets, in the room on the opposite end of the hall.

And I knew just how I wanted to wake her.

I did love talking with my son, though. He was mature beyond his years. Part of that was my fault because he had to be, but I spent a lot of time not letting that eat me alive and trying to move forward.

Making my way down the hallway, careful to stay quiet on the hardwood floor, I felt my heart beat with pride. That kid was always coming up with plans and sound arguments. Like when the twins were born, he made his own decision to legally change his last name to mine. I was his dad, after all, and he didn't want his birth certificate to say Quinn Parker anymore. Which was when he suggested the baby, now a little boy tucked in soundly in his blue bedroom, could be Parker Peterson, and he could finally be a real part of the family as Quinn Peterson.

I hadn't been able to hide my pussy tears that day. We went right to

smoldered

the lawyer and got it done. And now there were five Petersons.

Smiling inside now, I quickly turned toward my final destination for the night, practically racing to our bedroom door.

Without the woman sleeping in my bed, none of this would be possible. It took us a long while to find our little slice of heaven, but now we had it and I wasn't ever letting go. Natalie always said she'd been in love with me her whole life, and I think I'd always felt the same—just not able to understand it.

I was just a dumb man. Who was I to deserve being in love with a woman my whole freaking life?

At one point, I thought what I needed for my life to go out with a big fucking bang was multiple women to fuck, money to burn, and booze to drink.

Turned out, it was actually one woman who burned me up, helping my remaining years to smolder slowly.

I took in the delicious sight in front of me of my woman fast asleep. Smiling to myself, I ran my gaze over her long, muscular legs peeking out from under the covers, the soft waves running through her brown hair, her skin all smooth and creamy in the faint light coming from the bedside lamp turned on low. I pulled off my shirt and slipped out of my jeans as I walked over to the bed, letting my clothes fall into a pile on the floor. I thought about taking a shower, but couldn't wait.

Maybe we would do that together after I got my wife all dirty?

I slid onto the bed and gathered Natalie's tiny frame in my arms, pulling her ass in toward my front, laying a kiss on her neck as I smoothed the hair away.

"Mmm," she mumbled.

"Hey, doll," I whispered.

She rolled over and ran her hands down my sides, settling at my hips. Her thumbs grazed over the area, each one running back and forth on its respective side, causing chills to run down my spine. Me, the master of the threesome, the man who needed a three-ring circus to get off, had shivers from a thumb lightly touching me. My dick was instantly hard and at attention, poking its way over to where it wanted to be.

"All good tonight while I was gone?"

"Uh-huh. The twins are so excited to go away, and Quinn's very worried about whether his phone will work in the Bahamas. I think there's a girl, babe. A girl." She pressed her hip bone forward, looking for what she wanted while we made small talk about our kids.

259

It was so freaking domestic, except I owned a strip club empire and Natalie taught pole dancing classes at the gym.

"Well, I'll talk to him."

We didn't need any more words between the two of us. Our bodies took over, my mouth meeting hers, our tongues tangling while I reached my hand down and slipped a finger inside my wife, the only woman to ever fulfill me. Natalie's head dropped back into the pillow as she worked herself on my hand, and another smile spread across my face as I watched my woman get some.

I added another finger and pressed my thumb against the exact spot she needed, causing a shock wave to run through her. It ran like a lightning bolt through her body, traveling to mine.

Using my free hand, I brought Natalie's face back up to meet mine, kissing her, swallowing her moans, and riding her climax before I slipped something much better than my hand deep inside her. I moved slowly at first, taking my time, not rushing what was mine to have—forever.

Sneak Peek
Tinged

Coming Spring/Summer 2015

one

Mike
Miami

PULLING MY convertible out of the Wave's lot at two o'clock in the morning, I turned my metallic-white baby toward the beach as the ocean waves slapped against the dark night. I told myself to go home, but knew I wouldn't listen. Instead I did the same thing I'd done several nights a week for the last year.

I headed for a drive.

As much as I needed to clear my head, unwind, and allow Miami's moist ocean breeze to wash over me, it wasn't that type of drive.

It was a mission. One I shouldn't be on, definitely a self-appointed assignment I should drop. Immediately. I was a renegade on a journey to hell because my assignment would certainly only end in heartbreak and pain.

Oh well. *Fuck it.*

I glided my car along Washington Avenue, my eyes scanning bar crawlers on a crazy Saturday night, party-goers on a mission, and vacationers out for a good time. They weren't who I was here to see.

Narrowing my focus on the locals, I searched for a familiar face. When I saw who I was looking for, I pulled over, shifted into park, and levered out of the small sports car. After patting my little lady's door for good measure, I took short strides down the street, pretending to be out looking for a good time.

"Hey, Chantilly, how you doing, girl?" I said, wrapping my arm around the shoulder of a tall, curvy blonde clad in black leather and lace, walking confidently on mega-heels.

"Hey-a, Mikey baby. How ya doing, tough guy?" she answered, pulling me in for a hug.

There I was, Michael Wind, Big Mike, the prep-school-educated, bad-boy bouncer turned strip club owner to everyone who was close to me, caught in a full-on embrace with a high-end escort in the middle of South Beach. And it was the best I'd felt in months. Fucking months.

Lingering in Chantilly's arms a second or two longer than appropriate, I finally said, "All good, Chan. All good," before releasing the woman from my arms, feeling empty as soon as I did. She was all I had…my only true connection to *her* was a five-foot-nine-inch bottle blonde with a tube of KY and a box of condoms in her small purse.

She hooked her hands on her hips. "Come on, Mikey, don't play games with me. You good? Business booming at your joint?"

I smiled. "Yeah, business is always booming. Got good girls who make even better money. You should come work for me. Got a girl who'll show you the ropes, help you make a decent living."

She laughed. "Nah, baby. I got a good gig. Heading over to the upscale joint on Seventeenth now for a big-money job. Don't you worry about me, honey."

I tilted my head toward the sidewalk and said, "Come on, I'll walk you."

She hooked her arm in mine as we started making our way.

"So, did you have some extra free time and decide to take a walk on the wild side tonight, Mikey, or you here for your regular?" Chantilly asked as we made our way to her destination.

"Regular," was all I said.

The pesky call girl stopped moving and turned to face me. "Michael, honey, I haven't seen her. She's gone. Haven't seen her in thirteen months. Told you she was cagey the last time I laid eyes on her, was up to something she knew I wouldn't like. A gig even I wouldn't be down with, so she clammed up. I'm worried just like you, but there's nothing we can do. This isn't something we can involve the authorities in, honey. We gotta let it go."

Arriving at the entrance to the Fritz Hotel, I lied when I said, "I know," before letting her go do her thing. I might have not approved of what she was about to do, but Chantilly was her own woman. And I knew better than anyone, when a woman was an escort...there was little to nothing anyone could do to change her mind.

I figured it was a mindset so deeply ingrained, a facade any self-respecting girl immersed herself into in order to degrade herself enough to hook, it took nothing short of a military de-conditioning like in the Special Forces.

Watching the last person known to have seen Lynx on the Florida Coast walk away from me, resigned to let the whole situation drop, I knew what I had to do. Call Carson. Something I'd been avoiding, but the problem was too big for me. I needed his help, and quick. Women didn't just up and disappear without a trace.

I walked back with a full-blown knot in my stomach and slipped into my white BMW, flicking my finger into my green dice on the rearview, watching them rock back and forth in limbo, like my life, before I sped out. I brought those dice all the way from Sin City with me. Funny, my life had been hanging by a thread since I left there three years ago.

Palm trees fluttered in the breeze along Collins Avenue as I cruised along, hoping for a glimpse of long and lush almond-colored limbs, and not really seeing anything else. I tried to catch some of the beauty surrounding me, but I couldn't because the most beautiful gem I'd ever known was gone.

Gone.

two

Mike

SCRUBBING MY hand over my face, I rolled over and picked up my phone to look at the time. It was early. Seven o'clock in the morning on a Monday, my day off.

Lying back down, I dragged the small figure still snuggled tight next to me, even closer, feeling my dick rub against her ass as I ran my hand along her side and moved her hair out of the way so I could kiss her neck.

She moaned softly, a small, yet eager sound floating from her lips all the way back to me. It drifted along all my senses, brightening my day as my whole body popped awake at the promise she was making without a word.

And the girl made good on it throughout the day, following through with her unspoken promises of the morning. After all, it was my "day of relaxation."

Then she went to work, and I spent the night with a bottle of my good friend, JD.

SLIGHTLY HUNGOVER from my pity party for one, I brushed one hand over my buzz cut with one hand and threw open the side door to the Cove with the other, allowing the bright Miami sunlight to sift inside the cool, purple haze of the club. It was Tuesday, and the girls were having a planning meeting backstage with Petal, now back to her birth name, Staci. She was the latest in a long line of Asher's rescue projects.

Although originally taken in by Lila when she was the Tunnel's main headliner, and brought into the Tunnel fold as her protégé, Petal had become Asher's responsibility when Lila moved to Cali.

So now I was tasked with making Staci into a legitimate businesswoman, if that was what one called a woman with nothing more than a GED who had started out lap dancing at Sin City's finest adult establishment, and was currently settling in to take over the Cove, Miami's steamiest night spot.

It wasn't exactly what one would label as success, until you took into account where the girl came from and where she was going now. If not for the fucking Tunnel, Staci might be whoring herself out to some fat, sweaty fuck with a small dick—like Lynx did—so it was a big fucking whopper of a success.

And just like that, my mind was no longer focused on my business day, but tied in knots over the girl I couldn't forget or let go of. *Motherfucker.*

"Hey, Big Mikey," Marta called out to me with a smile, drawing me out of my fog and dragging me unwillingly back to the present.

"Hey, babe," I said while giving her a chin lift. She'd left my bed less than twenty hours ago. I owed her a decent hello—at the very least.

The beautiful specimen in front of me was the first girl I discovered in Florida. I met her at the pool when I was back scouting locations for the Cove, and decided to bring her in to dance when she solicited me to hire her as an escort.

Asher warned me not to sleep with her, but I couldn't fucking listen to my friend, mentor, former boss, and current partner. As if he really knew shit about relationships. The dude had messed up the first decade of his own kid's life while hitting up every easy lay in Vegas, stringing along a woman who loved him.

But this girl Marta was incredibly hot, all curvy and exotic with dark tanned skin, more like black coffee than café au lait, contrasting with light blue eyes and long, flowing highlighted hair. And she was soft and caring in a way I wasn't used to. None of the women in my life so far had treated me that way. Not my pill-popping mom; my bitch of an ex, Rochelle, who slept with my dad; or *her*, the one who left me high and dry, holding my dick in her hands and stomping my heart on the floor.

There was no way I could resist Marta's charms. I was so hard up, constantly worked up, and she was so easygoing about the whole thing. The girl took what I gave her—a dinner here, a sleepover there, a day spent in bed once every week—and never asked for a damn thing more.

It was fun, sexy, easy, and absolutely nothing more. Zero emotions involved. *After a lifetime as Mr. Relationship, I'm that guy. Mr. Cold and Removed.*

The outer club was mostly quiet as I headed a little deeper toward the back. A slow R&B vibe serenaded the main floor as I tossed a gaze over the whole sparkly, scantily clad group gathered for the meeting. "Hello, ladies. Y'all good?"

Yes, I'd adopted a little bit of a Southern twang in the four years since ditching the desert.

Staci spoke for the whole gang of iridescent beauties. "All good, Mike. We have seventeen bachelor parties prebooked for this week, all of them complete with limo, booze service, and VIP treatment. I'm giving the ladies their assignments and working the dance rotations, so everything is fully covered and leaving space in the schedules for walk-ins and other groups."

"Good. You got this, honey," I said before I slipped back to my office. It wasn't upstairs like Asher's at the Tunnel, but it was just as tricked out. Private bath and shower, wet bar, leather couches, and a full video feed to the club were just a few of the features I installed. I spent a lot of time there, mostly because I ran a tight fucking ship when it came to the club, and there was nothing I didn't have my two eyes on.

Or at least one eye, while the other scanned the window facing the streets of South Beach...